*I Live in*
*the Slums*

# *I Live in the Slums*

## STORIES

**CAN XUE**

**TRANSLATED FROM THE CHINESE BY**

**KAREN GERNANT AND CHEN ZEPING**

YALE UNIVERSITY PRESS ■ NEW HAVEN & LONDON

A MARGELLOS
WORLD REPUBLIC OF LETTERS BOOK

## CONTENTS

*I Live in*
*the Slums*

## Part One

I live in the slums. I didn't settle firmly on one place to live. I could stay anywhere as long as it had a stove. This area produces coal: all the homes used coal to keep fires burning at night. I just lay in a corner of the kitchen stove to keep warm. I was afraid of the cold at night.

At the bottom of the steps was a large expanse of lowlands. The slums were in this low-lying land. It was torture for people to live here. Even children were disturbed at night—so much that they couldn't sleep. They would cry out in fear, spring out of bed, and run out the door barefoot. They would run and run in these confined alleys, because if they stopped, they'd be frozen stiff. Their parents had to wait until daylight to go out and bring them back. These parents were all skinny and very dark. One could see only the two whites of the eyes swiveling in their faces. I observed that they seldom slept at night; they just lay in bed and dozed. And even though they were only dozing, they dreamed a lot. Not only did husband and wife converse in dreams, neighbors also conversed through the flimsy walls woven of thin bamboo strips. From what I overheard, I was sure they were dreaming. Sometimes they argued in dreams, or fought, but they didn't come into physical contact with each other. They brandished their fists in the air.

I forgot to comment on the houses. The houses were row-houses, attached to one another. Was it out of fear that these people built their houses this way? As I saw it, one could live in any of these homes and actually be living with everyone. Each home had a main entrance, but there weren't many windows in the rooms inside, and the windows were small and dark. In the winter, I couldn't quite remember which homes had stoves and which didn't. If I made a mistake and entered a home without a stove, the children in that home would pull on my feet and refuse to let me leave. I would struggle so hard to break loose that the skin on my feet would be scraped. The families without stoves probably ate their food raw, and that's why they were so wild.

I got acquainted with the house mice during the daytime. During the day, the houses were much lighter than at night. Hearing something gnawing bones, I thought it was the cat. I jumped down from the hearth and ran over to have a look. Ah, it wasn't the cat; it was a house mouse—twice as large as ordinary house mice. Damn, it was chewing the old man's heel! I saw the white bones, but no blood. The house mouse was excited, chewing loudly—*kakaka*—as if nibbling the world's most delicious bones. I knew this old man well. He was raising two pigs behind the house. The pigs were squealing with hunger in their pen. Could he have died? I circled around to take a look at him in bed. He hadn't died. He was fiddling with his glasses. He generally sat in the doorway wearing these glasses and looking at the design on a piece of paper that he held up to his face. He looked at it for a very long time. If his heels had been gnawed off, how could he go out and feed the pigs? At last the house mouse ate its fill and turned around. He gave me a slight nod of his head, and at the same time his protruding tummy hit the floor with a thump. I was very curious, wondering how he could still burrow into a hole. This room didn't have such a big hole, and the house mouse didn't burrow into any hole. Instead, it lazily circled the room once, as though in pain from overeating. When I thought of what he ate, I wanted to throw up. After circling the room, he felt sleepy from his meal and dozed along the wall. He paid no attention to me.

The old man sat up in bed, about to bandage his heel with a rag. He had prepared the rags earlier for this purpose. He made a lot of noise tearing up cloth. He seemed to be strong. He kept wrapping his foot until it was encased in one large package. The pigs squealed more and more insistently. They were on the verge of leaping out of the pen. He got out of bed and stepped on the floor without putting a shoe on his injured foot. He went outside to feed the pigs. What was this all about? Why did he let the house mouse bite his heel? Was there a tumor in there and he was letting the house mouse perform surgery? What admirable willpower!

When I looked at the house mouse again, I noticed he was even more swollen. Even his legs had thickened. Was this because he had eaten something toxic? He was asleep. I felt oppressed. With a heavy heart, I walked out the door for some air. Winter had passed, and the children playing outside didn't want to go home. Some slept next to the road. Their parents weren't worried about them, either, and let them sleep outside as much as they wanted. The children didn't have to do anything, anyhow. Aside from running around, all they did was sleep. Some probably couldn't even distinguish between day and night. And they didn't care. They cared about only one thing: the arrival of the wheelbarrows. Wheels creaking, the wheelbarrows carrying food passed through from small alleys. The children ran up, each one leaping onto a wheelbarrow—sitting with high and mighty expressions on top of the flour. The wheelbarrow operators from other provinces smiled a little and didn't shoo the children away. People said they came from the icy, snowy plains. When they unloaded the flour, the children ran off. The frowning adults opened their doors and feigned lack of interest in the food. "What's the weather like in the north?" they asked the men pushing the wheelbarrows. "There'll be one more cold snap."

Generally speaking, I didn't live very long in any one home, lest they consider me a member of the family. Still, as soon as I appeared, they took note of me. They placed leftover food on the hearth, and I ate it in the still of the night. In great contrast to the house mice, I always felt ashamed of eating. I ate quietly, doing my utmost to make no sound. In fact, I still ate greedily, even licking the dishes clean. All the families treated me fairly: whatever they ate, they would leave some for me. Of course it was always leftovers. What kind of thing did they think I was? I rarely heard them talk about me. They merely spoke briefly, indicating their awareness of me: "Here yet?" "Yes." "Eaten?" "Everything." They were very aware of me, but they didn't want to say so. To me, their brief conversations in the dark were as loud as thunder. It took a lot of strength for me to jump from the floor to the hearth. Noticing that, they placed a short stool next to the stove. They were so considerate of me that it weighed on my mind. I mustn't get too close to them, and I especially didn't want to be drawn into their family disputes. What I mean is the children's roughhousing at around midnight. What kinds of demons were frightening the children? Did they think demons were hidden inside their home? And so they felt safe when they stayed outside? At such times, the mother would stand at the open door and say repeatedly, "Come back, my dear. Where can you flee to?" The mothers' legs were all shaking. Were they awake?

■

I had climbed the steps many times in the past, intending to get away from this confusing place. The sun was so radiant that it would crack the tender skin of my back. I actually had no shadow on the highway. Oh! My mouth and tongue dry, I walked and walked on the blacktop road. All I could think of was finding a dark place where I could rest and drink some water. But where was there any dark place in this city? The outer walls of buildings were made of glass, and the roofs were metal. When the sun shone on them, it was like fire. People moved soundlessly in the rooms. Although they wore something like clothing, I could see their innards and their bones. I pushed a glass door open and went in—and immediately felt as if I had walked into a large furnace. The surging waves of heat would dry out all the fluids in my body. I hurriedly turned and ran toward the door. Just then, I ran into him—that house mouse. The house mouse was holding the door watchfully, as though ready for battle. His hair was glossy and his eyes shining. He apparently had been born especially for this glass house. I recalled how he had gnawed the old man's heel, and I didn't dare cross swords with him. Pretending nothing was wrong, I walked away. But how could I feel that nothing was wrong? All of my skin was going to fall off. Many echoes resounded in this hallway. I was dizzy from the vibrations. I mustered my last bit of courage to look up. Ah—I saw . . . I saw that dream—the dream that was behind all other dreams at night. I began crying. But my two little eyes were dry. I had no tears. Would I die soon? People walked back and forth constantly in the hall: they were transparent. Sometimes, they brushed past me, and I smelled their dry, clear fragrance and sensed that these people's bodies contained no fluids. And so they didn't have to worry about drying out. I was very smelly. Though I was going to die soon, the stench from my body kept assailing my nose. Just then, I heard the door: it was the house mouse opening it. I stumbled out as fast as I could. The house mouse looked scornful. How had such a short, tiny mouse managed to open the door?

It was much better outside. Although I was being sun-dried, the temperature was much lower. A midget gave me a popsicle. I finished it in a few bites. Along the blacktop and cement roads, there were only glass houses like furnaces. I had no place to hide. Passersby wearing black clothing walked past in a hurry. They looked composed, and no one was perspiring. You could almost say that a chill passed through their gazes. I also remembered those people in the glass houses. Were they a different species or did they become transparent when they entered these houses? An old saying came to mind: "Rich and poor live in different worlds." I had to go down the steps. I had no way to stay up here.

Walking with my head down, I ran into a passerby. That person stumbled over me and slowly fell. Rolling his eyes toward the sun, he said, "It's cold, so cold." He didn't want to get up. What was he thinking about? I couldn't keep watching him, for I had to hurry along. Otherwise, I'd fall as he had. Behind me, that person shouted, "You're so ugly!" Was I ugly? I didn't know. It was a novel thought.

Ah, I was home! Good. First I went to the old man's slop basin and dunked myself, moistening my skin. It was really comfortable and relaxing! But why were the two pigs howling incessantly? Had something urgent occurred again? I walked into the old man's room; he was bandaging his foot. His grandson was sitting next to him making a fuss, asking to see the old man's wound. That thin little boy was furtive, and I had never had a good impression of him. As soon as the old man started bandaging his foot, the boy ripped the bandage off and rolled around on the floor. He said if he wasn't allowed to look at it, he'd kill himself. Finally, the old man finished bandaging the wound and stood up. He went to feed the pigs. The boy sat in a dark spot, his eyes wide open. What was he looking at? Hey, he crawled under the bed. Was he hiding? I heard the old man pouring feed into the trough and heard wheelbarrow operators passing in front of the house. Today this home was making me feel insecure. I needed to find a different place to rest. With that, I left quietly and slipped into the home across the street.

This family didn't raise pigs, but it did have an emaciated black goat tied up behind the house. It was gnawing a radish. What did they usually feed him? The black goat sized me up and stopped nibbling on the radish. Although his feet were tied and he couldn't walk even a few steps, he didn't feel at all inferior. His bright gaze was such that I began feeling inferior. I thought of the food that people ordinarily prepared for me—all set out nicely in dishes, but they gave him only a small radish that was no longer fresh. Was it this that he was proud of?

The man of the house filed keys by the light of a lamp. A small vise was on the table. He filed very quickly, and the bright lamplight shone on his savage face. He was like a ghost. The keys he had filed were packed into a wooden box. There may have been several hundred keys. What locks did these copper keys open? I hadn't seen these locks. Perhaps there weren't any. The room smelled of sulfur, and I began sneezing—one sneeze after another. Mucus dripped into my mouth. Finally, I grew used to it. I didn't go up to the stove. I just squatted on a stool and rested. Just then, I heard the man talking with his wife. She was sitting in a dark spot trimming vegetables to cook. Her voice was faint. At first, I didn't see her.

"I bent down and picked it up. Who cares what it was? I just brought it back." Her voice was a little exultant.

"You did the right thing," the man said, in a low muffled voice.

"I used to walk very far, as if a ghost were pulling on my feet."

"That ghost was me, wasn't it?"

"The rooms are full of these things."

"It's good to go back and forth among them."

"The thing! Very, very scary! One year, after I brought one back from Long County . . ."

All of a sudden, they stopped talking. And the man stopped filing. Something puzzled me: Were these two people talking in their dreams? Not long before, I had heard them talking about this in their dreams. What were they doing? They were listening closely to that goat. The goat apparently was ramming the wall outside— time after time. Had the rope snapped? This couple was evil. After ramming the wall for a while, the goat stopped. Perhaps it was injured. The man resumed filing keys. The file made a rasping sound against the copper. It gave me a headache. I was going crazy. Holding my head, I dashed outside.

The hemp rope on the black goat's foot had broken, but he hadn't run off. He craned his neck in the direction of the dark house. The goat was a slave by nature; no matter what, he couldn't leave his owner. Just then, the woman of the house came out with a new rope coiled on her arm. The goat wanted to run, but the woman clamped down on him with hands like iron tongs. As he cried sorrowfully, his leg was tied up again. The rope was tied on top of the old injury; I couldn't bear to look at it. The woman returned to the house, and the black goat seemed to lose all his energy. He lay torpidly on the ground without moving. I couldn't bear this scene. I squatted down facing him. I wanted to bite the rope and break it for him. The rope was new hemp and very strong. Still, my teeth weren't bad, either. I squatted there, biting and daydreaming. I imagined I was guiding the black goat to escape to the east end of the slums where there was an empty pigpen. People had once raised a spotted pig there, and then it died of poisoning. He and I could take refuge there and depend on each other. Wherever I went, I would take him along and not let him sink into slavery. As I was thinking this, I was hit hard on the head and nearly fainted. He had kicked me with his free leg. I hurt so much I couldn't even describe it. I rolled around in the mud for a long time. When the pain subsided a little and I held my head and moaned weakly, I noticed the black goat standing there as if nothing had happened. This guy was extremely wicked. How could this kind of animal be raised in the slums? Hard to say. Weren't there also the house mice? If one had no contact with them, one wouldn't know how ruthless they were. Really, he was standing there basking in the sun as if nothing had happened. Now and then, he also took a few bites of that small smelly radish. He was as complicated as the couple inside the house: there was no way to tell what was in his mind.

Something poked me from behind. It was the midget. Didn't the midget belong to the world above? How had he gotten down here? "I took the elevator down," he said. "It's great because it allows me to be above and below at the same time. Hey, your skin is too white." Was my skin white? My skin was khaki colored. Why did he speak such nonsense? Let me think. That's right, he was color blind. Maybe people living in glass houses were all color blind. The midget and the black goat glanced at each other. I thought they were communicating. Maybe I was too jittery. "My parents were living down here," he said. I was surprised to hear this. If he was from here, how come I had never seen him around? "Because I'm in the elevator. Ha-ha!"

The midget called me "Rat." I wasn't at all happy with this form of address. How could I be considered a rat? I was much larger than a rat. He let me go inside with him. The man and his wife had disappeared, and the house was quiet. I started sneezing again. The midget said, "The master always sprays disinfectant because he's so afraid of dying." Then the midget suddenly made a weird sound and fell face upward on the floor. I bent down to look at him and discovered that his ankles were padlocked to the feet of the table. Who had done this? Under the table was the wooden box containing the several hundred keys that the man had made. I shifted the box to a spot in front of the midget. He sat up and tried to unlock the padlock with the keys. This room was making me very jittery. If it weren't for the black goat outside bleating twice, I would almost have thought that he was the one playing tricks. The midget stepped up his pace, growing more and more impatient. He had already thrown dozens of keys on the floor. I became vaguely aware of something. I had to get out of here right away.

I ran outside, and bumped into the old man. The old man was just the same—one foot bandaged with dirty rags and a cane in his hand. The difference was that quite a lot of blood was spattered on the pant leg of his good leg. He pointed at the house and told me to go inside and take a look. I pushed the door open carefully. I had barely looked inside when I became so frightened that I shot out. What was I afraid of? Nothing was inside—only an empty room. Even the furniture had been moved out. The old man came over and said, "The key. It's here." What key? I didn't get it. He went on, "The key you're looking for. Ayuan has it." I peered in again. I didn't see his grandson. Leaning on his cane, he crossed the street. Was he going to see the midget?

I walked on—walked a long way. In the slums, the sun always came out suddenly and withdrew suddenly. Everything was dreary here—I mean outside the houses. The houses were generally dark inside. That was okay when one got used to the darkness. A child was lying sound asleep beside the road. He was a little like Ayuan, but he wasn't Ayuan. Then who was he? I especially noticed his bare ankles where he was scarred from having been scraped by something. Wasn't it a rope? I pushed his head, and he spat out a string of names of flowers. Then he laughed. A piglet ran up—the spotted pig that the old man was raising. The piglet smelled the boy and ran off. The boy laughed even louder. Was it a laugh? *Gagagaga*—it didn't sound much like a laugh. Did he belong to the nearby home? The door to this home was open. I went in.

All of a sudden, I felt sleepy and climbed up on the stove to sleep. Before long, the man came in and lit the fire. He was a butcher with a long beard. He pulled fiery red tongs out from the fire and waved them in front of me. The tongs brushed against the hair on my chest, and I smelled the charred odor. Just as I was wondering whether he would burn me to death, he tossed aside the tongs and sat down on the floor. In the room in front, his children were singing. A children's chorus suddenly rose from that room. It was as if doomsday were coming. I looked at the butcher again; his beard was quivering. What scary memory had taken hold of him? I jumped down from the hearth. He didn't move. It was as though he hadn't seen me. When I slipped over to the room in front, the children had already left. I saw only a girl's back. I thought, Did the butcher's daughter dream every night of hot blood spurting from the sheep's neck? Was that why she sang children's songs? Who was poking me in the back? Hey, it was the midget again. He had finally unlocked the padlock. He said, "Look, he's here, too." The child who looked like Ayuan slid in. And then—bang!— the butcher bolted the door! The three of us were locked into the room. The little boy's weeping was muffled. The midget covered the boy's mouth with his palm and tried to calm him down. I wanted to cry, too, because I remembered the fiery red tongs. What was the butcher doing in the kitchen? Finally, the little boy stopped crying, and the midget said, "I'm really happy." Maybe he was happy to see that we were done for, whereas he would soon be saved by the elevator. Now he was holding the boy and sitting on a chair. The child whimpered a little, his shoulders heaving. All of a sudden, I remembered: he was the one who gave me a popsicle when I was in the furnace-like area above. He was really a nice person.

The butcher never did show up. The little boy (the midget called him Drum) was being held by the midget and talking in his sleep. He said he was the elevator, and all the people here had to rely on him. Without him, they couldn't live. He was bragging in his dreams, and the midget chimed in. The midget said, "That's true, that's true, you cute little boy." All of a sudden, Drum broke free of the midget and scratched the midget's face with something. The midget fell over. Drum held up the thing, which kept flashing light. I was finally able to see it: it was a copper key. The midget moaned on the floor and kept saying softly, "Oh, Drum. Oh, Drum." How could a key have so much harmful power? I thought of the man who filed keys. He was a taciturn man with a lined face. His hands were like an old tree's roots. I had seen him break quite a large file! Holding up the key, Drum walked toward me. I considered hiding, but didn't. I wanted to see exactly how much harmful power this little thing had. But what happened next surprised me. Drum handed me the key and motioned to me, indicating that he wanted me to stab him with the key. The key was large, much like a small knife. I stood there at a loss. We heard the butcher roaring in the kitchen, as though enraged. Was he pressuring us?

When I was on the verge of stabbing Drum in the neck with the key, he took hold of it and thrust the key into his neck himself. Blood spurted out, and he collapsed weakly on the floor next to the midget. Nauseated, I turned and vomited. Just then, the butcher opened the kitchen door and entered. He was holding the fiery red tongs. He raised the tongs in front of me, and I hastily dodged away. And so I once more smelled my scorched hair. "Oh, Rat. Rat, this is a rare opportunity," he said. This was so annoying. He was also calling me rat. He opened the main door, carried the midget out, and threw him out next to the street, and then returned for Drum. He carried him out, too. Then he bolted the door again. I thought he intended to come and deal with me, too, but he didn't. After a while, those two guys rammed against the door, desperately wanting to enter. How had they recovered from their injuries so quickly? They were so strong that they were about to ram the door open. Taking advantage of my being distracted for a moment, the butcher jabbed me in the chest several times with the fiery tongs. At first I shook all over, and then I fainted. In my confusion, I saw myself on a burning mountain. The fire was burning my whole body, but I didn't feel any pain. And I actually thought that I'd be fine after the fire burned out. There was a mountain across from me. It was on fire, too. Children were singing in the fire. Why did the voices sound familiar? That's right! They were the butcher's daughters—who else could they be? Their singing was so beautiful! I looked at myself: ah, my legs had been burned off! I couldn't move now. Wasn't this what he had whispered to me? "Oh, Rat. Rat, this is a rare opportunity." He had pushed me, too, not letting me fall completely asleep. But I was afraid. I closed my eyes and fell asleep regardless.

When I woke up, I saw a large gray eye gazing at me. That was the butcher's daughter. Her eyes were asymmetrical: one was large, one small. I considered this large eye indescribably beautiful, so I never thought of her eyes being asymmetrical. She looked desolate: Was this little girl worried about me? When I moved, intending to touch her, she moved away a little. I was disappointed. "You—what are you?" she asked, her tone so desolate that I almost shed tears. I came to her home frequently: Why did she ask such a question? Was it my manner that made her feel desolate? Not until then did I take stock of myself. I was fine. Nothing had changed. Ah, one of my feet had a burn mark, but that wasn't remarkable. I had just lost a little hair there, that's all. What was I? Was this a decent question? I came to their home year after year. I stayed on the stove, and the butcher always treated me to delicious animal innards. After eating, I dozed on the stove. I was always drowsy when I stayed with this family and so I'd never gotten a good look at these girls. When they worked quietly in the kitchen, I thought they had never paid any attention to me. Now it seemed I was wrong: they had not only noticed me: they had also talked about me. Otherwise, why would she have asked that question just now? It seemed she still expected something of me. I asked myself again, What was I? But I didn't know. How could I dispel this pretty little girl's inner desolation? I didn't dare make eye contact with her, for if I did I would start crying. "I'm the third child, the youngest," she said suddenly. "Dad's in the back nailing together a wooden cage."

Before I grasped what she had said and became aware of what was happening, a black net covered me from the head down, entwining me. Someone was pulling me to the back of the house. At one side, the girl said excitedly to that person, "Are you going to throw him into the well?" I had no way to struggle. I simply could not move.

But the place where they threw me was definitely not the well. It was simply the small alley behind their home. Wrapped up in that fishnet-like thing, I couldn't move, and the small alley ordinarily was deserted. They evidently meant for me to die here. What could I do? It would soon be dark, and night in the slums was always cold. I curled up. I heard the butcher's daughters singing once again. I could tell that the one singing most resoundingly was the girl who'd been with me just now. It was so cold, so cold. My burned foot was numb. I uttered a shrill scream. Perhaps the people inside heard me, for the singing stopped and then resumed. Listening closely again, I could hear the dreariness of the songs. Captivated by the singing, I temporarily forgot the cold. As my mind wandered a little, the cold slashed my skin again like little knives. Perhaps all of my skin had swollen. I hoped my skin would soon be numb. What else could I hope for? I thought of the midget and Drum. Were they still in that room? Or had they been thrown out just like me? What kind of lives did the butcher and his three daughters live?

I could see a ball of light through the net: it was people passing by with lanterns. "Why do they always throw their prey out on the street?" the one holding a lantern grumbled to his companion. They stopped when I squealed. Above me, they talked in low voices, hesitating about something. The first one to speak raised his voice suddenly: "How long has it been since we've passed through here?" The other one replied, "Fifteen years. Back then, it always rained at night, and icicles more than a foot long hung from the rafters. Now it's a lot warmer. Why does he still make noise?" As they talked, they squatted down and freed me from the net. I lay on the ground, because I was numb all over and couldn't move. What was going on? I realized that two people were helping me, but I didn't see them. There was just that lantern all alone on the ground. It shone on the netting. Now I could see that the netting that had entwined me so strongly was actually thin and small, made from something that was a little like the membrane on some animals. I squealed again. I was thinking I would regain consciousness by squealing. Just then, the butcher's little girl opened the door. I heard her greet the two people. She was wearing a cape. She looked very valiant and heroic in bearing. But I couldn't see the two people. They went in and took the lamp with them. All around, it turned dark once more.

I tried to roll over. With a scream that took all of my energy, I was finally able to move. I rolled to the corner of the wall of the butcher's small house. It wasn't as cold here as in the other place just now. I slowly recovered a little feeling. I could hear the conversation in the house very clearly. I heard the three girls fighting over who could kiss the two men whom I couldn't see. They were swearing and making an uproar. Then the little girl probably hurt her two older sisters with some kind of sharp object. The two older girls let out frightening wails. But soon it was quiet inside again. Had the little girl achieved her goal? With a creak, the door opened a little and the lamp emerged. Looking malicious, the little girl stood at the entrance. Sparks of electricity flashed from her large eye. The lamp floated in midair and gradually moved far away. Finally it disappeared in a corner in the west. All of a sudden, the girl bent toward me and said, "Did you see it all? You little thing, you did see it all! Hey, I suffer too much hardship in my life, don't I?" She covered her face with her hands and began crying. After crying for several seconds, she suddenly stopped and said fiercely, "Did I cry? No! I never cry. Just now, I was laughing! I laughed so hard!" She picked me up with both hands, lifted me to her shoulder, and carried me into the house. Throwing me onto the stove, she walked away. I saw the butcher sitting indifferently on a wooden stool and smoking a cigarette.

■

I live in the slums. I was born here, and I grew up here. At night, I lodge with a family that has a stove. In the daytime, I poke around everywhere into people's privacy. I know all kinds of secrets here, but I don't understand the mysteries of these secrets. On the outside, these secrets look beautiful but terrifying. Is this why I'm always eager to poke around?

## Part Two

I live in the tunnel under the slums in the lowlands west of the city. When you come to the wall around the chemical plant, you see a long, long staircase. At the foot of the stairs is our slum—a large area of simply constructed houses squeezed together in rows. I used to lodge in other people's homes. Actually, I had stayed with all the families who had stoves in their homes. And then, on a gloomy day, I stumbled into the tunnel. That day, the owner had laced my food with poisonous mushrooms. Having spotted this, I fled in a hurry—like a refugee. It was midnight, and everyone's house was locked. I didn't dare knock on anyone's door. As I continued walking in the cold, I bumped into a mutt. This cur wanted to kick me away. Frightened, I ran off, but the dog chased me. I ran as fast as my feet could carry me, paying no attention to directions, and then fell, confused, into the tunnel.

When I first fell in, I couldn't adapt because it was too dark to see anything. It was just like being blind. Everything was quiet at first, and then I finally noticed that this was a delusion: many little critters were grubbing around, chiseling endlessly. Strange to say, three people were sitting among them, doing absolutely nothing; they just said a few words now and then. I approached and listened closely: I heard a few vacuous empty words, such as "After a house is built, one doesn't have to live there. It's better to live in the wilderness." Or "People, uh . . . People need to know themselves." They took turns repeating these two sentences. It wasn't a good idea to move around. I had to avoid bumping into any of these guys whose bodies seemed iron-hard. I had to sit motionless on the ground. Somewhere above, that cur still barked nonstop. Despite being far away, it was menacing. I looked up and saw a hazy light. That's where I had fallen from.

I squatted in the dark place, recalling what had transpired between the master and me. In the afternoon, as I napped on the stove, he had passed by. He patted me lightly on the back in a rather sentimental way. "Rat, ah Rat, what are you thinking?" he said hoarsely. I hated his calling me rat, and I despised his sentimental manner. I didn't think this man was one bit masculine. He often sat in the open doorway and washed his pale feet. He was a narcissistic guy. I generally didn't have my defenses up around people, but this time I must have had a faint foreboding. Who would have imagined that this person could be so sinister and ruthless? When he fried the poisonous mushrooms, I was sitting on the pile of firewood next to him. His hands shook, and his dejected, long face looked more wrinkled than usual. At the time, I still thought he was going to poison the rat with the mushrooms. It never crossed my mind that in fact I had become the "rat" that he spoke of. The three poisonous mushrooms were buried in the bottom of the rice. I saw them when I poked around in the rice. What in the world was he thinking?! Did he think I would meekly eat them? I already knew this man was mean—he had killed all the cockroaches in his home—but in general he had been quite good to me. He was a widower. When I stayed with him, instead of giving me the leftovers as the others did, he cooked for both himself and me. I couldn't figure out what had happened to cause him to change. Maybe nothing at all. Maybe he was simply showing me how ruthless he was. An asthmatic old man who stayed at home—how ruthless could he be? Poison was a coward's way. I knew, however, that just one of these mushrooms could kill a person. So he was determined to kill me, and I fled. This had happened in the afternoon. Now I sat in this hell awaiting fate's verdict. In my mind, a voice kept asking, What in the world happened? I didn't know. Really didn't know. Everything was baffling. A person passed by. Although I couldn't see him, I could sense his weight as he stepped in the mud. He stopped next to me and said, "After a house is built, one doesn't have to live there." This man was annoying, and I got up without a sound and moved away from him. It never occurred to me that the moment I moved, he would push down on my back. He was strong. All I could do was lie quietly on the ground. Words flashed through my mind: People, uh. People need to know themselves. But I wasn't a person. I couldn't speak.

He pushed me against the ground, but then his attention wandered and he let go. Naturally, I slipped away at once. This place seemed to be a flat area packed with little animals that were excavating. I kept bumping into them in the dark. I knew they were small, but I had no idea what kind of animals they were. One of them was stuck halfway down in the hole he was digging. He screamed shrilly. I bent over and gripped one of his legs and mustered all my strength to drag him out. It didn't occur to me that he would attack me insanely. Still, since I was several times larger than he was, I quickly overwhelmed him. I pounded his head against the ground more than a dozen times. I kept this up and then finally left him for dead. I was afraid of running into those people again, so I wanted to hide or join the ranks of the excavators. When I tried approaching the little animals, they were hostile, as if telling me this was no place for me. They pushed me hard and berated me mercilessly. I had nowhere to go. Every time I thought of squatting and resting for a while, some guy would come over, lay claim to my spot, and push me away. Why did they overreact to me? Frightened, I looked up at that spot where the light came in. Listening closely, I could still hear the cur's barking. Maybe I should climb up and go back there. He hadn't bitten me, so how could I have imagined that he would bite me to death? Now I regretted having acted so precipitately. Before giving it any thought, I had simply fallen into a place where I didn't belong. I had spent so many peaceful nights on people's stoves, and sure, maybe I was a little nosy, but this couldn't have been why I was kicked out. And probably the poisonous mushrooms were meant only to scare me: he knew I was cautious and wouldn't just blindly eat whatever was placed before me. Alas, there was no point in saying all this now.

Eventually I was surrounded. These little things that were as rigid as iron collided with me time and again. They rammed my stomach, my face, and my feet. I kept screaming hysterically. The more I screamed, the harder they hit me. I nearly fainted from the pain. Then that person arrived, and the little animals hid. He kicked my stomach and said, "He isn't fit to live in this wilderness." Why did the man call this place a "wilderness"? Plainly, it was a tunnel under the slums. If it were really a wilderness, why couldn't one see the sky? Whatever. Why should I care? I could tell from his voice that he was the person who pushed me into the ground. I was too sore to move. I didn't *dare* move, either. If I did, he would push down on my back again with his iron hands. "You can't see," he said. "This is an advantage for us. You can't see us. Why do you need eyes in this sort of wilderness? Here you go—Enjoy your dinner"— a round thing rolled down my neck. I grabbed it and took a bite. It was so peppery that tears streamed down my face. It seemed like an onion, but not exactly like one. The person told me that this was what the man of the house where I had lived had sent to me. That bastard actually remembered me. Deep down, I hoped he would talk more about the man, but he became distracted again. Whistling, he stood up and left. I tried moving. All of a sudden, my pain vanished. Could it be because of this onion? I shed tears as I nibbled the onion. I felt completely satisfied. Oh, I had to do something: I would excavate! I dug quickly with my front legs, and before long I had dug out a hole. I kept digging until I was covered in mud. I hallucinated that I would dig something out. Each time I dug down, I felt that thing bounce under my claws. What was it? Come on, come out! Let me see what you are!

Digging and digging—each time, I sensed that something wanted to emerge, but only mud came out. I had dug one hole, and the thing below still lured me on. If I could, I would wedge myself into the earth to bring it out. Just then, I remembered the little guy who was stuck in the hole he had made himself. I had misinterpreted his scream. Actually, he had screamed from pleasure, but I had thought he was distressed. What kind of precious magical land was it that could attract so many animals to dig here! Did digging eventually yield the thing they yearned for? And what were those people doing here? Hadn't one of them handed me the food my old master sent? Perhaps a secret path led to the ground above. Oh, shit! One of those animals was digging next to me. Uh-oh, he had broken through my hole. He had come into my hole! This was a quiet guy. I touched him all over. I actually touched stiff wings on his back. I had never seen such a strange creature before. I pushed hard. I wanted to push him out, but he started snoring. He actually fell asleep in my hole. Since my hole and his were now connected, I took the opportunity to move over into his hole to take a look. Ah, this thing had dug a tunnel—a tunnel within the tunnel. Were all these guys doing the same thing? I didn't dare go far. I sensed danger because I heard suspicious sounds in the tunnel. Maybe the noise was made by other little creatures digging somewhere nearby; maybe some things were lurking there. Who knew? I felt my way back to my hole and stayed there with this guy. I felt a little safer. Since falling down here, I had never felt safe. Although digging had lured me, I really didn't want to go any deeper. I wasn't an underground animal.

It wasn't bad at all to squat in this hole with this thing that was sound asleep. It was much better than staying out there being pushed and bumped back and forth. I looked up and saw the light again. That place seemed to have a door. The door opened, then closed. The hazy beam of light changed subtly. Deep down, I felt homesick. Lying on the clean stoves had been so comfortable, and never-ending adventure had filled the nights . . . Had the slums thrown me out? But wasn't this also part of the slums? Those people just now—weren't they in direct contact with the ones above? Just then a terrible odor interrupted me: the thing was farting! This was no ordinary odor—the fumes gave me a splitting headache. Utterly unnerved, I jumped out of the hole. I wished I could kill this thing for giving off such a toxic odor.

He woke up. Fluttering his bizarre wings, he flew about two meters into the air. The fumes dissipated. I wanted to get away, but I either stepped on someone's foot or was prodded hard by another one: they wouldn't let me leave. That thing stopped for a while in midair and then fell into the hole with a thump. Anyhow, he had finished farting and seemed to have resumed sleeping. "Someone is really restless and can take wing in his sleep," one person said at the side. This person fanned himself—and washed his feet in the wooden basin, just as my old master usually did in the past. "This is a flying squirrel. Sometimes it digs underground. Sometimes it flies. But it doesn't fly more than three meters high, that's all," the person said while swooshing the foot-washing water. This man's actions made me suspicious: What kind of place was this, anyway? Were there houses nearby? Pushed and squeezed by the little animals, I'd better jump back into my earthen hole. I felt a little drowsy and lay prone to rest on the flying squirrel's back. Touching those thin but rigid wings, I wondered whether I would dream with him in midair if he flew again. I fell asleep. Before long, I heard my old master call me, "Rat! Hey, Rat! Fly up here fast! Do you see me?" I looked up and saw him in the light far away. I had no wings. How could he ask me to fly? I wasn't yet wide awake when the flying squirrel beside me carried me up to midair. I lay prone on his back, feeling I had ascended to the edge of paradise. He was really strong! But we soon descended into the hole again. The flying squirrel had never awakened: he'd been snoring the whole time. What a lucky little thing. "Underneath the hole is another hole. Do you dare go down?" The speaker was the man washing his feet in the wooden basin. "Ha-ha. The world above is the world below." His piercing voice made me very uncomfortable.

All of a sudden, I remembered something from my childhood. Back then, I was close friends with a little girl in the family I stayed with. She took me swimming in the pond. Before going into the water, she would say very seriously, "You mustn't go to the center because you might slide into a vortex." I didn't understand what she was saying. We would linger at the side of the pond, grabbing willow roots and smacking the water. The girl's name was Lan. She'd say, "If you want to escape, I can help you." I really disliked that kind of talk. Where would I escape to? I was quite comfortable on the stove in her home. And I was so afraid of the cold. I would freeze to death in the winter wilderness. Lan read my mind. She said, "You wouldn't have to escape to another place. We can do it right here." I thought this was nonsense. Remembering this, I sensed that she had known all along of the underground secrets of the slums. Maybe all the children in the slums were as precocious as she was. Those children had purposely fled from the houses to be frozen stiff outside, hadn't they? What bizarre ideas entered their minds at midnight? Later on, the girl married someone from far away and left the slums. I didn't know if that was considered "fleeing." At home, she was a prim little child who was fearful all day long lest disaster befall her. Her dad often joked that she "had been born in the wrong place." Now as I recalled her and her flight, I wondered if I was thought to have fled. Was this the place she hoped I would reach? It was warm here, and with no distinction between day and night you could sleep whenever you chose. You didn't need to climb up on someone's stove. You just needed to dig a hole and squat inside it so that others wouldn't push you. And it was okay without light when your eyes adjusted to the dark.

Damn, that man had poured his foot-washing water into my hole. I jumped out in time, but the flying squirrel was asleep in the slop. He didn't care; he was still snoring. "He lives in his dreams," the man said. I didn't like to get muddy, especially with his foot-washing water. It was disgusting. How could the flying squirrel have been unaware of this? This foot-washing person must have been a sadist. I felt I'd better move a little way away from him. But when I started to leave, he chased me, shouting, "Where are you going? Where? Do you want to get yourself killed?" He spoke so fiercely that—once again—I didn't dare move. I stood next to a large rock. The little animals joined forces to push me, causing me to bump into the rock again and again. Later all my bones were about to splinter, and I lay motionless on the ground. That was when they stopped pushing me. I heard the flying squirrel fly again into the air above. The person said, "Look at him. He's so calm. Is gracefulness learned? No, it's innate." The light—even farther away now—had blurred. The flying squirrel flew past in the dark. Maybe he was flying to another place. It must be great to have wings! I had touched him. His body was much like mine. The wings must have been a product of evolution. He slept and woke up whenever he wished, and he stayed or flew away whenever he wished. What a natural and unrestrained lifestyle this was! Now I understood what it meant to "live in one's dream." How had he become so privileged? Even if I evolved more, I probably couldn't grow wings on my back. He was a different species. Then what was I? People called me "Rat," but I wasn't an ordinary rat. I was much larger. I was a maverick, a loner. I had only faint memories of my parents and wasn't interested in the opposite sex, and so I wouldn't have descendants. I was a thing that looked like a rat but wasn't a rat. I was a pilgarlic who had sponged off others on stoves in the slums and had carelessly fallen into the tunnel under the slums.

I resumed digging the hole. The moment I started, all my paws tingled with excitement. Keep at it, keep at it—something really wanted to come out. Someone next to me was also digging. He dug and dug and all of a sudden shouted "*Oh, oh.*" He must have dug far enough for the thing to emerge. I wanted to do that, too. I couldn't stop. I turned toward the left and detoured away from the rock. My God—so many ants: I had struck an ants' nest! Oh!! I jumped out of the hole and scratched and hit myself all over. I wished I could pull my ears off. Those little things had bored into my body by biting through my skin. This was much worse than death. As I was feeling desperate, I heard the person say coldly, "You really need to take a bath." The water in his wooden foot-washing basin gurgled as he moved it. Despite my nausea, I jumped into the basin headfirst. He pushed me down with both hands and ordered me to swallow his foot-washing water. In a daze, I drank quite a lot of it. Then he poured me out along with the water, and shouted, "Go back to your digging!" He left. How could I still dig? I kept bumping into the ground with my head. I thought to myself, "It would be better to die! Better to die . . ." I rolled and rolled around on the ground. After a while, a sudden thought came to me, and gritting my teeth, I started digging again. This time, when I dug into the mud with my claws, I distinctly sensed the little things passing through my claws to return to the ground. I hadn't been digging for very long when I began to relax. How could this be? How? I felt afraid of this land.

I sat in my newly dug out hole, surrounded by the little animals that were rushing about. I buried my head deep in the ground. I was afraid they would bump into me. I didn't dare dig again, for fear of getting mixed up with the death-ants again. As I squatted down there, I heard a rumbling sound coming from an even deeper spot. If I could concentrate, the sound was clear, but if I relaxed a little, it was inaudible. While listening, I remembered something that happened when I was sleeping in the blacksmith's home. The little boy there was called "Neighbor Boy." Neighbor Boy got up every day before daybreak. Without putting on a coat, he pushed open the gate and went out to stand on the street. The blacksmith and his wife shouted from their bed, "Boy, boy!" The hubbub made it seem as if he had committed suicide. But why didn't they get out of bed? I walked to the door and saw Neighbor Boy standing there talking with someone. "Do you hear me? Do you hear?" he asked worriedly as he looked down, as if the other one were underground. He stamped his feet. Over here, his parents also stamped their feet in bed, "Boy, boy!" They were nearly crazy with worry. I didn't know why I was thinking of Neighbor Boy. I was emotional, feeling that I wouldn't see this family again. "You can't hear me, but I can hear you," a little girl (it seemed to be Lan) said. Where was she? Why did she seem to be underground? She had moved far away when she married, hadn't she? "You can't hear me, but I can hear you," she repeated. Ah, she was indeed underground! I lay down and pressed my ear against the ground. I heard, not a rumbling sound, but Lan talking in the silver-bell voice of a child. Was Lan still a child? Hadn't she married in a faraway village? The day she left as a bride, I'd seen her carrying her favorite little stool. Although the voice was like a silver bell, I couldn't understand what she was saying because it wasn't the local tongue. Bored with her jabber, I sat up and stopped listening. A wheelbarrow passed by, its wheel sounding like a child weeping. How odd that a wheelbarrow was underground. Had it always been there or had it fallen in from the hole? The wheelbarrow stopped beside me, and the person squatted down and handed me two biscuits almost as smelly as the flying squirrel's farts. But once I had food, my stomach began rumbling with hunger. I hadn't eaten for a long time. I wolfed the food down. The person began laughing and continued with his food deliveries. This place seemed to be a relatively orderly society. Then what was it like at the greater depth where Lan was?

Finally, I calmed down and listened to the little girl Lan talk. When I lay down in the bottom of the hole and planted my ear against the ground, I could hear her voice. Now I heard her clearly. It wasn't a rumbling sound, nor was it a child's bell-like voice. Rather, it was the voice of a fourteen- or fifteen-year-old girl. It was the Lan I knew so well, the girl who had taken me to play in the pond. Yet I still couldn't say I understood her. I didn't. I seemed to understand every word of that dialect, but when I put them together, I had no idea what she was saying. But now for some reason, I wanted to listen to her. Maybe I'd gained patience because of eating the smelly biscuits from the wheelbarrow, or maybe the voice brought back memories of the good times we'd enjoyed together. In any case, I lay on the ground absorbed in listening to her. How had she arrived where she was now? Although it was dark, if I looked up I could see a shaft of light from the opening to the hole. She must be in a world of total darkness. Damn. What had she been thinking of when she went to that place to get married? From her intonation, I guessed she was telling a story. Maybe it was about the pond. As I listened, I recalled our friendship again. I felt I had fallen in love with her. I—a "rat"—had loved a *girl?!* I was stunned and hurriedly dismissed this idea. I called out twice toward the deeper underground. My voice was thin, like a child's voice. I was unable, though, to speak as they did. When I shouted, I merely intended to tell Lan that I had heard her and that I missed her. No sooner had I stopped calling her than everything below turned chaotic: many voices struggled to speak. It seemed they were all Lan's voice, and yet it seemed they weren't—rather, it sounded more like a bunch of women with foreign accents quarreling with each other. I took a deep breath and raised my voice. I shouted again. Below, it immediately grew quiet. After a few moments of silence, even more voices rose, louder and louder.

"Rat has a future in his work," the person went on. "After he learns our ways, he'll be able to shoulder certain responsibilities. He's come here to learn."

He walked around next to me. I felt that he was talking to himself. Why? What was he saying? I understood his dialect, but not what he meant. I shifted my attention to him. Had he fallen down here? Or had he always been here?

"From the shout he made, I knew I could place my hopes on him. Since he had gotten in touch with those down there, I was sure he would shout like this a few times every day. The air and meals here are good for him."

He said I had gotten in touch with "those" down there. Then should I continue digging down? Was someone using me, and if so why? It was even noisier below; even the mud under my feet was vibrating a little. For some reason, I didn't want to dig the earth separating me from those women. I was a little afraid. In my mind, I said, Lan, oh Lan, we're together again. Thinking this, I felt comforted. Each time the noisy struggle stopped, I heard Lan say, "You can't hear me, but I can hear you." This was all I could understand, but why did Lan want to say this? She didn't seem to be talking to me. Maybe she was talking with someone underground. The flying squirrel flew over. I heard his wings flapping—Oh! He was so free. Lan was imprisoned below. Yet when I heard her talking, I didn't think she was a bit upset. Instead, she seemed proud. I recalled again that she had talked with me in the past about escaping.

Maybe there were two kinds of escape—one was to escape to the city center or run off to another province and disappear in a boundless distant place. The other kind was like Lan's method—to escape below. Had she slid down from the vortex in the pond? Back then, her dad had laughed at her for "being born in the wrong place." Maybe he had told her to come down. Lan was probably talking with her dad. A person had arrived at such a deep underground, and yet could still hear everything her family members were doing above. What was that like? The women below grew quiet. *Coo-coo-coo*, like doves. Maybe they were going to sleep. All of a sudden, Lan said sternly, "You can't go there!" Her loud voice startled me. And then it was quiet. I sat up. I heard busy sounds all around, and that person's chiding. That person—he was chiding as he washed his feet. He was forever resentful of little animals for being too lazy.

I kept thinking of what Lan had said. Where did she say one couldn't go? Certainly, this dark place hid frightening things. I'd have to be very cautious. The incident with the ants was a good lesson. To avoid disaster, I'd better just sit and not move. This newly excavated hole was my home. Just when I was thinking of this, the person carried the wooden basin of foot-washing water over here. He yelled, "Watch out!" as he threw the water into my hole. Once again, flustered and exasperated, I jumped out. All the hair on one side of my body was wet. He kept picking on me. Was he in charge of all the little animals down here? In this hole, I could hear Lan talking, but now he had made it impossible to stay in my hole. If I went elsewhere, it was hard to say if I'd still be able to hear Lan. If I couldn't, I'd be very lonely. The flying squirrel flew over again, rubbed my nose, and flew away. He let out a really stinky fart. I wanted to break away from this person, because he never let me rest. I felt he was intentionally malicious. Maybe he even hoped I would die: his actions implied it. Couldn't I try to escape?

I had to escape. I couldn't be sure where I could go and where I shouldn't. I just moved ahead and let nature take its course. Oh, there was a fence here. Oh, could there be a vegetable garden inside the fence? I could hear even more little animals inside it. Sniffing as I walked along the fence, I soon discovered a break in it. I went through the hole and came to an even more exciting place. But it was an even worse place to stay. Every passerby shoved me, a sign that I was unwelcome. After a short while, I discovered the difference: none of the little animals here was digging holes. Sometimes they moved; sometimes they were still. When they were still, a whistle sounded in the distance. On hearing the whistle, they all rushed in that direction. When they were running, the whistling stopped and so they began hesitating and finally stopped again. Then they listened attentively once more. Before long, the whistling resumed from a different direction, and so they once again rushed in that direction. Before long, they stopped again. I was among them and felt keyed up. It was both chaotic and orderly here. Everything was decided by that bizarre sound coming from an unknown place. No, I couldn't adapt. They ran so fast, and while they were running they shoved me down on the ground and stepped on me as they went past. So the next time they were waiting for the whistle to sound, I fumbled my way back to the break in the fence where I had come in. I wanted to get out. I had just leaned out from the fence when that person punched me in the nose and roared, "Are you looking for death?" This was a really strong blow, and I nearly fainted from it. I sat on the ground and heard him say, "Try to escape! Just keep trying. I'd like to find out if your skull is made of iron. Huh!" Naturally, I didn't dare try again. Now all I could do was act as wild as these other guys inside, because I couldn't just sit here without moving. If I did, they would stampede me to death. Hey, they were starting to run again. Even though my nose still hurt, I ran along with them. But they stopped after just a few steps. I didn't react in time and kept running. So I stumbled against one of them. He was a big one with long sharp protruding teeth. He sniffed at my belly with his long snout for a long time. I closed my eyes, waiting for death. Luckily, just then, the whistling started again. He threw me down and ran. I lay on my stomach on the ground, while lots of them stepped on my back to move ahead. I was afraid they would make mincemeat of me, but after a while they stopped stepping on me and detoured around me instead. Somehow, I unintentionally touched the fence once again. There was another break in it. Should I sneak out through it? Was that person standing guard outside? No, he wasn't here. I emerged. It was quiet all around. Was this the wilderness? I saw a house with a kerosene lamp in front of the window! How could this exist underground?

As I walked toward the house, I thought of the words that man had just spoken, "looking for death." Was this what I was doing now? What would be in the house? Ha! A child was brushing his teeth in the doorway. He spat water all over my face! "Let him in if that's what he wants," someone inside said. This was the very master who had fed me poisonous mushrooms, wasn't it? I went in. Hey, this really was his home! Great. This was great, I had returned to the slums. Just now on the road, I had noticed some indistinct houses, but hadn't dared believe my eyes. When I climbed up to the stove, I sensed gratefully that I was home again. The master took out a bowl, filled it with food, and placed it in front of me. I saw at once that it was poisonous mushrooms—three of them in the rice. Although my belly was rumbling with hunger, I hesitated. Did I really want to die? No, I didn't! I didn't want to die! The master was staring at me. "Are you going to eat? If not, I'll take it away." He seemed to be chuckling. I immediately buried my head in the food and began eating. Without even tasting it, I ate it all. My mind went blank. I heard the person clap twice and say, "Great! Great!" What was so "great"? It must be night, but he said, "I'm going to repair the road." He went out with a hoe. It was so dark, and yet he was going to repair the road! I jumped down from the stove and inspected the house. It was the same as before, and so was the furniture. The child was sitting under the table playing with a top. The spinning top was buzzing loudly. This made me uptight. So it couldn't be night, because everyone was going about regular daily activities. But it was dark, and the lamp had been lit. How could they see? The child stopped the metal top with one hand and said to me, "Rat—oh, Rat, why have you come to my home? Dad has gone out to the back to dig a grave. He'll be back soon. Let's spin the top together. As long as the top doesn't stop, Dad won't kill you." With all his strength he started the top spinning again, and it spun at lightning speed. The buzzing gave me a splitting headache. That person came in, set the hoe down, and looked in both directions. He was probably looking for me. I heard him take my empty bowl from the stove and wash it. He was cursing something. Next to me, the child said, "Dad is very afraid of tops." He let the top stop and asked me to try it. I had barely gotten the hang of it when it began spinning—it even left the floor. The child said, "You're really good at this."

But I still couldn't stand the sound made by the spinning top.

I even tried to run away several times, but after running two steps I went back under the table, because the child shouted at me, "Do you want to die!!" It was weird: his voice sounded the same as the voice of the man washing his feet in the wooden basin of water. Then the child put the top in his pocket and said, "I have to make things harder for Dad." He asked me to sleep under the table with him. The master came in and stood in the middle of the room nervously stamping his feet. He shouted, "Tusheng! Tusheng!" He was calling his son. Couldn't he see that we were under the table? "Tusheng!!" he began snarling, and all of a sudden he bumped into the wall. The dry cow pies pasted onto the bamboo wall fell to the floor. Tusheng hugged me tightly because he was snickering and his whole body was shaking. I was shaking, too, but it was because I was afraid of Tusheng. If this kid could handle his father like this, wouldn't it have been an easy matter for him to kill me if he wanted to? The master's face was bleeding. He climbed up from the floor and dejectedly went back to the stove and continued tidying up the dishes. He was really afraid of his son.

Tusheng wanted me to sleep under the table with him after this. "We can play with the top whenever we want to." He took the top out of his pocket and told me to polish it with my face. Each time I did that, I heard a roar in my head and saw stars. Although this was hard on me, I was in a much better mood. "Okay, okay now," Tusheng said. "From now on, our domain is under this table. Don't go back to the stove." When he said this, I thought of his dad. His dad was a nice person, quite kind to me. I actually doubted that he wanted to poison me. I wanted to express my remorse to the master. I heard him crying. Maybe he thought his son was lost. Tusheng didn't let me take a step. He said that when his dad cried, one shouldn't bother him. I heard a noise at the door, and someone came in. Tusheng made a face, pulled out the top, and set it spinning. The person screamed and ran off. As for me, I was getting sort of used to the top. It no longer bothered me so much. Could this little thing be making Tusheng and me invisible? Why couldn't his dad see us? A magical top! Magical! How could there be such a rarity?

"Tusheng! Tusheng! I can't see you. I know you can see me. Answer me."

This sounded familiar. Who had I heard say this? He sadly picked up his basket and went out to buy groceries. I felt as if my heart had been pressed down by a rock.

Tusheng told me to sleep holding the top. He said something good would happen. In my dreams, I was sleeping on a huge top disk. I could see everything: the flowers and grass, trees, rocks, little animals, and other things. They were all levitating. The sun, by contrast, was descending and rolling back and forth in front of me. It was as though I could touch it with my claws. Someone anxiously shouted under the disk, "Can you see me? Hey? Can you see me?"

■

I settled down in this home. The slums were my home. I was born here and grew up here. I don't remember how old I am, but I do remember things that happened a long time ago. Back then, the houses in the lowlands had just been built and weren't really like houses. They were more like temporary work sheds. After the houses had been built, the sun withdrew. It could shine only on the fence. The children fell to the ground and slept. In the early morning frost, their faces were frozen purple. I remember all of this.

## Part Three

My tangled relationship with people was probably the main reason I continued staying in the slums. When I was little and had only a thin layer of hair, I was placed on a family's stove. Did Mama give birth to me there, or did this family mercifully take me in? I stayed inside a pottery bowl with fragments of cloth in the bottom of it. If the fire was too hot, the bowl would be scalding, and if I wasn't careful, it would burn me. My body was blotched with scars for a long time. As for food, the family served me a spicy brown porridge in a small dish. Maybe that porridge was a soporific, too, for I would sleep all day after eating it. It relieved the pain from being scalded. But because I was asleep, I rolled around inside the bowl and was left with even more extensive burns. Most of my body was affected, and I was in constant pain. I considered escaping from this bowl, but the blisters on my feet had broken and ulcerated. How could I jump out? Sometimes I heard the man and woman of the house talking about me, "Will the little thing die?" "No way. It's a born survivor." Were they hurting me on purpose or didn't they know what I was going through?

Despite all of my injuries, I gradually grew up. One day, their child overturned the pottery bowl, and I fell out. I saw the bowl suspended on the edge of the stovetop. On an impulse, I bumped the bowl with my head, and it fell down and broke into several pieces. I looked at the room again and saw all those strange things that I hadn't seen before. I didn't know what they were. Not until later did I figure them out. There was one thing I never understood until I finally grew up. This was a framed portrait of an old man with a white beard hanging on the wall. I thought it was a real person because the husband and wife talked to the old man. When they went out, they said, "Dad, I'm leaving." And when they returned, they said, "Dad, I'm back." If they had done something out there, they would ask, "Dad, did I handle this right?" When they spoke, the frame rocked and made a *ding-dong* sound as if answering them.

I recovered from my injuries soon, and before long I could jump down from the stove. I jumped to the top of the table, stood on my hind legs, leaned on the wall with my front legs, and tried hard to get close to that white-bearded old man. All of a sudden, I was whacked on the back of my head, and I lost consciousness.

I awakened at the side of the road, and so I knew there were streets outside the house. It was such a large slum. I gradually recovered my memories of the slums and the city up there. Before the day ended, I became familiar with the entire slum, for I realized that each of its nooks and crannies had always been stored in my memory. At night, I returned to the family's stove to sleep. They seemed to welcome me, even preparing food for me. The boy said, "He was out all day and now he's back." But I wasn't out for the day by choice. Someone had placed me out there next to the road. Who? I glanced involuntarily at the old man on the wall. Ah, in the lamplight his face was invisible. I saw only the two flames shooting from his eyes. In my fear, I had shrieked and dashed to the door. The master and his wife came out, caught me singlehandedly, and patted me on the back. They said repeatedly, "Rat, oh Rat, calm down! Come back!" I stopped struggling. I was shivering on the stove. I had concluded that it was the old man on the wall who had clubbed me and caused me to faint, and then had thrown me outside. Later the master had blocked the door and windows so that I couldn't open them. Now they went to sleep. So did I, but I felt a burning gaze fixed on me. No matter what, I couldn't fall asleep.

Flames filled my mind. I forced my gaze away from that wall and looked instead at a dark corner. I remembered the city. It was so big, but it was uninhabited. The glass houses were empty, and the people lived in the slums down there. How sad. I remembered the glass houses next to each other. I decided that one day I would go up there and look around. The master had said there were people up there. Some hid in wooden casks, garbage cans, and dumpsters. When the sun set behind the mountain, they emerged and raced out to the deserted streets and made a commotion.

I let my imagination run wild and like a thief hid myself here and there in the house. Then I realized that no matter where I hid, I couldn't escape that gaze. I couldn't figure it out: Why didn't this old guy walk out of the frame? Had he hidden himself behind the glass or had his family done this to him? In the inky darkness late at night, the master and his wife embraced tightly in bed. Now and then, they cried out softly, "Ghost!" Steeped in nightmares, they couldn't intervene in what I was doing. I could sleep in the rice barrel or in the big cupboard. They had no idea. Naturally, if I shed hair in the rice, they grumbled about it when they ate. They didn't blame me; they were terrible at making logical connections. Once I even slept in their big, wide bed. Hiding in a corner against the wall, I listened to their conversation up close. One said, "You think Dad can't see us, don't you?" The other said, "I can at least hide in my dreams, can't I?" It was odd. When they spoke, I looked at the wall again. The fiery gaze had vanished. I was surprised and thought to myself, Have I entered these two people's dreams? But just then the woman shrieked, "Ghost!" And then the fiery gaze shot across again. The man said, "Dad, oh Dad. Dad, oh Dad." The husband and wife burrowed under the quilt, which then stuck up like a hill.

I was afraid and slipped out of bed. I screwed up my courage and looked outside. Under the dim streetlight, someone was squatting and slaughtering a white cat. The noise made me retreat a few steps, and I quickly closed the door with my head. Oh! Compared with the terror outside, the house was a refuge. The moonlight shone in. The hill of the quilt was hazy. I remembered the pasture where my ancestors lived. It was big: you couldn't see across it. Back then, our clan members rushed back and forth there. They were hiding from something, too, much like the two people in this house. They often scuttled over to the pool in the center of the pasture. They couldn't swim, and the next day their corpses floated in the pool. I was lost in memories, trying to figure out what my ancestors were hiding from.

One day the couple went out, and their son Woody got into big trouble—he shattered the glass in the frame with his slingshot, and the shards of glass ruined the old man's face. Woody ran outside to hide. By nighttime, he still hadn't returned. The couple were silent about this. They threw the ruined frame, along with the old man, into an old trunk and then paid no more attention to it. Every day, I was troubled by a question: Was the old man still alive? I'd learned my lesson earlier, so I didn't dare open the trunk. The old man was no longer a threat, but the atmosphere in the house remained tense. It was even scarier in the silence. Had Woody's disappearance made his parents numb? I wanted to go out and look for Woody—help them out a little. But out of self-respect, I didn't want to go out in the daytime. My appearance wasn't very elegant—it was sort of like either a rat or a rabbit, but not quite. (I remembered what these two animals looked like.) I would surely attract attention. I didn't want to be surrounded and stared at by people. I opened the door twice during the night. Each time, I saw the same person squatting under the streetlight killing cats. Once, it was a black cat, once a calico one. The cats' screeching almost made me faint. The husband and wife were no longer hiding under the quilt. They didn't even undress but just dozed on the edge of the bed against the wall. I slowly came out from under their bed. I heard a series of sighs from the trunk. The old man must have been badly hurt. This couple had been absolutely obedient to him in the past, so I couldn't understand why they didn't show even minimal filial piety. They just ignored him after stuffing him into the old trunk. They were still clothed as they sat on the bed: Were they waiting for something to happen? They didn't seem to notice the sighs in the room, because they were snoring lightly. I quietly slipped over to the trunk and placed my ear on it. I heard glass exploding inside. I was really scared. Suddenly, the man spoke up: "Where's the new frame? Don't forget to hang it tomorrow." His wife giggled abruptly.

I missed Woody. It was lonely without a child at home. He had no bed in the house but just slept anywhere. I used to think this was strange, but later I got used to it and felt he didn't need a bed. He didn't sleep much. He was always rushing about. He went out five or six times a night. I had no idea what he busied himself with. I only knew that the couple were very proud of this naughty boy. They frequently lay in bed and talked about their son's future; they seemed to think he could save them from poverty. But they also feared this change. They said they'd leave if things changed. Woody frequently took items from the house and sold them. Once I saw him carrying on a transaction at the front door. When his mother was cooking and couldn't find the scoop, Woody said that I had carried it off and lost it. "He just cares about having fun," he told his mother. She stared at me, as if intending to hit me. But she didn't. For the time being, she substituted a wooden club for the scoop. Although Woody had been mean to me, he was an interesting boy. I was crazy about him. Probably his parents felt much the same as I. This kid was adorable. I liked him. One moment, he'd be sitting at home, and the next moment he'd be on the neighbor's roof. God knows how he got there.

Could the old man with the white beard have died? I wasn't sure. All I knew was that the master and mistress no longer cared about him. I didn't know why, but I was saddened as I imagined the old man shut up in the trunk, as well as his face that had been cut by glass. When I remembered the earlier incident, I thought maybe he wasn't the one who had made me faint and thrown me out on the street. Then who was it? Woody? Didn't he want me to be close to the old man? Two days later, they really did hang a new frame on the wall. The frame, however, no longer held the old man, but a yellow chrysanthemum. This yellow chrysanthemum fell far short of the ones I remembered: it was a little washed-out and a little withered and its background was an overcast sky. After hanging the yellow chrysanthemum, the couple no longer conversed with the frame. They stood and gazed at the flower, but I didn't know what they were thinking. I wondered if the flower was substituting for their father. I was displeased with them because at night when I planted my ear on the trunk, I still heard feeble moans. Now they paid no attention to their "dad." They paid attention only to that flower. Finally, I realized that people's feelings were changeable. People were so fickle! I thought, We probably aren't the same. I—an orphan left to roast in a pottery bowl on the stove—I still remembered my parents and ancestors. And I remembered my hometown—that pasture and even the pool in the middle of the pasture.

I remembered all of this really well and could call everything to mind without the slightest effort. But these two people: yesterday they had called out "Dad" as if they couldn't leave him for even a second, and today they had completely forgotten him and were showing feeling only for the little flower. As for their father, they had put him into a shabby trunk from which he could never escape. I was too young back then and usually confused the real person with his portrait, so I was displeased and angry with the man and his wife. I made up my mind to leave their home.

I saw them pushing a pedicab out. I knew they were going to sell rice; that was what they did for a living. Generally they didn't come back until evening. After they left, I went up to the stove and ate a huge meal, then jumped down and went outside. Their house was at the end of the row. I slid along the wall for a long time without running into anyone. The doors to the houses stood open. Where had everyone gone? All of a sudden, a child dashed out of one home. Shrill curses followed him. Sure enough, it was Woody. He went across the street and disappeared behind a strange house. I followed him and reached the front of that house. It *did* look like a house. It had eaves covered with grass. Looking more closely, though, I noticed it had no doors or windows. It didn't even have walls. It was a solid thing, with two caves leading to the inside. I stood there, not daring to enter the caves. After a while, Woody walked out of one of them. He was a little bent over, to avoid hitting his head on the ceiling of the cave. He saw me and walked over. He took me in his hands and lifted me up in the air three times. Then he patted me on the head and set me down, saying, "Rat! Rat! Rat! I've missed you!" His clothes were filthy and full of holes. He stank. What kind of life was this little kid leading now? When he saw me staring at the dark cave, he began laughing. "This is a prison." As he said *prison*, I remembered my ancestors' cages—rows of them on the grasslands, each with a front door. If someone entered, the door automatically closed and locked. At first the buddies were excited when they went in. They collided and bumped around inside irritably, making the iron cages rock back and forth. At night, they calmed down. You can't imagine the power of the clear, cold night air of the grasslands! But they had to stay there a long time before they would die: they knew this. When their parents walked past the cages, the children inside had already fallen into meditation. As I was thinking of this, Woody pushed me playfully and asked, "Do you want to go in? Do you?" I felt I hadn't thought it through and so I kept retreating. Woody guffawed and told me this was a phony cave: you went in from the front and exited from the rear. "Look at me. Aren't I all right?" Since I didn't want to go in, he said we might as well forget it and just move around outside. We circled to the back of the house. I looked and looked again—I didn't see any exits, that's for sure. Woody told me, "You can't see that kind of exit with your eyes."

After running into Woody, I forgot why I had come out here; I was hell-bent on following him. I didn't know why I had no willpower. Thinking of my ancestors, not one of them minded parting from mankind, as I did. My ancestors were warriors who dared to come and go on their own. Not one was afraid of dying. Woody walked and walked, and then stopped again and petted me. What did he mean by this? I grew nervous as I recalled that he had shattered the old man's frame with a slingshot. He was actually really violent. I noticed some people standing on the roadside looking at us. Even after we walked far away, they were still watching. What was Woody plotting? We walked past row after row of houses. I never knew the slum was so big. I had only stood in the door-way of Woody's home and had only seen places that were just a little farther away. Sometimes I saw a woman come out. When she caught a glimpse of me, it was as if she'd seen a ghost: she immedi-ately ran back into the house to hide. So then I knew that the slum was large, but just how large I didn't know. In my memory, the grass-lands were the largest thing under the sky.

I didn't know how long we had walked when I realized that I had once more reached the front of that solid house. Woody said, "Hey, Rat, we're here." It was dark, and the two caves looked at me threateningly. Saying he needed to rest, Woody entered the cave on the right. I stood there terrified, not knowing what to do. Under the streetlight ahead of me, that person appeared again. He squatted there and slaughtered a black cat. When the black cat screeched the first time, I thought I was going to lose my mind. And that's when I entered the cave on the left side. After I entered the cave, I heard that startling screech again. I'd better hurry ahead. After five or six steps, I saw an exit and came out. I turned around and, sure enough, saw the back of that house. I wanted to return to the cave because I could still hear the cat's screeching. Where was the cave? I recalled what Woody had told me and felt my way for a while along the wall, but to no avail. I couldn't find the entrance. All I could do was rest for a while under the eaves. If I walked around aimlessly, there might be an accident. The cat was still screeching. It would probably die soon. I curled up and squatted in order to get warm. Two stars trembled above the wall in front of me. The night air grew colder, and the stars trembled more violently, as if they would fall. I remembered the stars in the sky above the grasslands:

they were linked, motionless, in the night sky. They were stars of eternity. What in the world were these two stars? I was concerned about them. Sure enough, just as the cat screeched one last time and stopped breathing, one of the stars fell. It even skipped a couple of times in the sky and drew a "W" in white. "Hey, Rat, you mustn't get lost in that kind of thing," Woody said to me from the cave. He must be hiding in a warm place, and had left me out here in the cold. He didn't approve of my stargazing. Okay then, I wouldn't look. I'd close my eyes. But I opened them again right away. It was so scary: I saw—no, I couldn't speak of the things I saw. Never. I didn't dare shut my eyes again. My heart couldn't stop thumping. I was still fearful. I'd better just look down. What was going on with Woody? He didn't go home, and yet he didn't go far away, either. He just wandered around the slum. What a strange child! Had he seen the stars in the grasslands? Probably not. If he had, he would have left here a long time ago. The city's glass houses were nothing compared with the sky of the grasslands. One was like an elephant, the other like a centipede in the corner of a furnace. Hey! What was I thinking of just now? Was I looking down on the centipede in the corner of the furnace? Those glum things were awful. You couldn't figure out what they were thinking. They also loved getting together, and when lots of them assembled, the scene was absolutely disgusting. Oh, the wind that I feared so much was rising again—gnawing my bones. Woody, Woody, you're heartless. You should at least allow me shelter from the wind. I opened my mouth to scream, but I had lost my voice. Even though I tried very hard, I was the only one who could hear myself. I looked up. In the darkness above the wall, the stars had disappeared without a trace. My eyes were liberated; I could see whatever I wanted. I saw the man straddling the wall and holding the dead cat in his arms. The streetlight reflected his pale face. Every now and then, he put his nose close to the cat's body as if sniffing it. There were some kinky people in this world. You thought he was killing cats for fun, but he looked desperately grief stricken.

It was probably almost midnight when Woody emerged from the cave. When I saw him, he was bending over in front of me. He stroked my nose, and I recoiled, for his hand was as cold as an ice cube. He said he had squatted in the icy cave most of the night. "I was frozen in there like a fish and unable to move. I have to go in there to freeze from time to time. I'd stink if I stayed outside too long." That's right. I recalled that Woody had never bathed at home. It hadn't crossed my mind that it was so cold inside the cave that I would have found it utterly unbearable. Just now, I'd complained that he hadn't let me enter. Woody said, "Nothing on your body can rot. You don't need to freeze." He asked me to go with him. We passed a few houses in the dark and came to a small thatched hut. Inside, an oil lamp was burning. On the floor a small copper basin was half-filled with water. Woody took a packet of powder out of his pocket and dumped it into the basin. It had a pungent aroma. After a while, a group of house mice showed up. There must have been at least ten or twenty of them. They climbed up the basin and slipped into it, and then flipped over on their ash-colored stomachs and floated up. They were in a hurry to get it over with. It didn't take them long. I was secretly worried and kept saying to myself, "Damn, damn!" Woody bent down, dredged up the corpses, and put them in a cardboard box. Just then, the strong aroma grew so heavy that

I became dizzy and nearly threw up. Woody's voice seemed to float in the air: "Rat, oh Rat, hurry up and get in!" Something seemed to push me from behind, and I jumped and fell in. As I sank, my mind went black. I had only one thought: I'm done for.

I didn't awaken until the next day. Maybe Woody had placed me on this rock so I could dry out in the sun. I was in unbearable pain. I opened my eyes and saw gashes all over my skin. I could see the blood inside. And Woody? Woody wasn't there. Next to me, wheelbarrows passed one after the other. Sometimes it seemed they would crush me. I figured I'd certainly die if I continued lying there. I tried hard to roll to the side—and almost fainted from the pain. I rolled over to someone's threshold. Outside the gate were puddles of urine. I was soaked in urine, and when it seeped into my wounds, it cut like a knife. Inside the house, a man and woman were talking. To my surprise, it was my master and his wife. The master said, "Do we have any of that spice left—the kind that Woody swiped?" His wife said, "There's one packet left. He made off with two packets." An aged voice spoke up in the house: "What you're thinking of is suicidal!" Then all was quiet. I could hear the man and wife speaking softly and sighing. They must have seen me: Were they discussing what to do with me? I wished they would pick me up and carry me into the house. I longed for the days that I had spent in their home. After all, there was no place like home. There was nothing good about being covered with cuts and bruises and left at the roadside. But the master and his wife didn't intend to take care of me. They were talking about Woody. I said to myself over and over, Woody, Woody, you little brat, what are you plotting with your parents? Just then, I heard the aged voice again, and the man and his wife ran out in a panic. They didn't even see me. I was sure of that. "You're the rat in their home," that old man said from above. I exerted myself to turn and look up. I saw the old frame hanging over the door. It was vibrating slightly, and bits of glass were falling from it. This was the old man, but I couldn't see his face. I could only see bits of glass stuck in that frame. Suddenly, a loud sound came from within, and the frame flew out and landed next to the road in front of the house. Then a wheelbarrow rolled over it. I tried several times to struggle up, but I failed. Two children ran out of this house. They bent down and took stock of me curiously for a long time. They called me Ricky. I had no idea why they gave me a person's name. I was used to that family calling me Rat. "Ricky is going to live with us for a while. We should hide him just in case." The taller one held me. I saw that he was one-eyed. No, he had two eyes, but they had grown together. His eyes didn't see what was across from him, but looked at each other. How bizarre. How could two eyes look at each other? But this fact was right in front of me. Before I had time to get used to this, they shut me up in an inky-black place that had a lot of feathers. As soon as I lay down, the feathers leapt up. Although it was hard to breathe, I wasn't in as much pain. I heard the two boys fighting, and then they said loudly in unison, "Let Great-grandfather decide! Let Great-grandfather decide!" Next I heard glass shattering. Don't tell me there was another frame in this house.

When they opened the box where I was staying, I looked closely at the brothers: each one's eyes had grown together. Neither looked out; each of them looked only at the other. They gave me a plate of red sauce. Its spiciness set my throat and tummy on fire. But I felt great: my pain had vanished.

I was going to stay in this home for a while. The slums were my home. It didn't matter which house it was; I could live in any of them. How would the two children with eyes grown together treat me? Now my name was Ricky. I'd better get used to this name—Ricky. See: he has come in. Although he didn't look at me, as soon as I saw his eyes looking at each other, I was uneasy. I wanted to hide in the pile of firewood there.

### Part Four

One late autumn day, I climbed up to the thatched roof on this house. It was so relaxing there. Below, the two people were still fighting violently. They had smashed all the pottery bowls and pots to smithereens. For two months, I'd been living in fear and trepidation. Especially that older brother: whenever I saw his vicious brown eyes squeezed together in one spot, I thought I was going to die. Although these eyes threatened only each other and not me, I still felt that they concerned me. Day and night, I could hear knives being sharpened in some corner of the house. How could there be so many knives? I squatted on the rooftop, fearful that they'd find me. If I were down below, as soon as they finished fighting each other, they would vent themselves on me. Once the older brother almost cut off my ears. I surreptitiously considered whether I should leave. I'd been leading a miserable life with these brothers for several months. I often stayed hidden in a cardboard box under the bed. With nothing to do, I spent my time worrying about depressing things. Mainly I was concerned about the slums, and of those worries, I worried most about floods. I thought that if the city were inundated, the slums would become a vast body of water. I remembered there'd been a flood more than a hundred years ago. Back then all the people in the slums escaped, leaving only the house mice. Later, in just one night, all the house mice were killed. Why hadn't they escaped? They should have been the most alert to this kind of natural disaster. I really didn't want the slums to turn into a vast body of water. After all, this was my home. Once I settled down in a certain home, I generally didn't go out again, but I did take journeys around this region in my mind. I rearranged the houses here as I liked, then mixed them up, then rearranged them . . . Sometimes this was how I got through the endless, long lonely nights. In my mind, I cut the rowhouses apart into freestanding ones, each with its own cellar. A stonecutter from the city was chiseling in each cellar. I thought this kind of scene was lovely. Like the ancestor I remembered, I was an aesthetician. Because of talking with the sun, that ancestor had been burned alive by the toxic sun on the grasslands. Back then, his story was passed down throughout the pasture.

I mustn't make any noise, because they knew I had disappeared. "Ricky! Ricky!" they shouted for me. Exasperated, they searched the entire house. Then they probably thought I had run away, and so they went out looking for me. With the house now empty, I slid down from the hole. I was exhausted and wanted to sleep. Shards of pottery were everywhere, and a lot of water had been splashed on the two beds. They had even dampened the cardboard box I slept in. Not caring whether it was wet or not, I burrowed in to sleep. Just as I was about to fall asleep, the brothers returned. The younger one screamed like a pig being slaughtered. I craned my neck and saw that his right foot had been punctured by a bamboo stick. His older brother was looking on, his two blood-red eyes staring at each other, his fists clenched. Damn, there was no way to go on sleeping. This younger brother whose face was frighteningly pale looked as if he would faint from the pain. But he was still shouting, "Ricky! Ricky! I can't die like this!" Why was he shouting for me? Did I have something to do with his injury? Did I make him walk barefoot all the time? I slipped out of the cardboard box and over to the middle of the room. The younger brother was brandishing his hands like crazy, as if fighting with someone invisible. His wide-open eyes—like a dead fish—weren't looking at anything. Could he be about to die? His older brother hung his head. From behind, he seemed a little sorrowful. I edged closer to him. Without looking, he kicked me—kicked me back under the bed. Huh? Didn't either of them welcome me? But why did the younger brother shout my name? He shouted again, "Ricky, I'm going to take you along with me!" With that, he extended his hand as if to pull out the bamboo stick. Did he think I was the bamboo stick? Was he out of his mind? Oh, he really did pull it out! The bamboo stick was dripping with blood! He fell from the chair onto the floor, with his head pointed backward and his arms crossed in front of his chest. I didn't know if he was dead or not. I quietly climbed out from under the bed and sniffed the bamboo stick on the floor. Oh, what was this? Under my very nose, the bamboo stick jumped twice and turned into a soft, succulent thing. The long sticky thing had a small eye in it. That was a shameless round eye, definitely from my race. No wonder the younger brother had called that thing "Ricky" just now. I looked again at his foot. The wound had disappeared. "You—eat that thing," the older brother said to me. I looked at him—his eyes had turned into one! That oval eye was in the center of the space between his eyebrows. But it still had two pupils. My image was reflected in both pupils.

I was really scared. I placed my head on the floor right away and waited to be hit. But the older brother didn't attack me. He just put the thing in front of my nose and coaxed me, "Ricky, eat this. Nothing will happen if you do." I tried to bite the thing from the end where the eye was, but that eyeball popped right out and slid down my throat. And so in my confusion, I did eat it. I didn't have time to chew it. I sensed that it stopped in my stomach, and I tasted something salty. Was it the younger brother's blood? I felt squeamish and just squatted in the corner gasping. I wanted to throw up. The older brother said, "Ricky, it'll be okay after a while. Don't worry." Was it the eye that had given off the salty flavor? My God. In the pasture, if you looked closely you could see that kind of eye hidden under stalks of grass. That was an eye just like the ones my parents had. They were everywhere, everywhere—I was a little dizzy. I shut my eyes, wanting to fall asleep.

The brothers lowered their voices. They weren't fighting, but seemed to be settling accounts. I was feeling awful. Was I the one who was going to die after all? My mouth and throat began swelling. My tongue changed into a large immovable stone. "Three times five is fifteen," the younger brother said. "Yes, subtract fifteen," the older brother answered. He went on, "How many days do you think he has lived in our home?" The younger brother mumbled as he calculated. Were they calculating my age or when I would die? All of a sudden, I realized that I couldn't roll my eyes. My gaze was fixed on the wall in front of me. A red scorpion on that wall crawled slowly toward me. Was he an assassin? I had no idea, because my vision was blurring. The scorpion grew bigger and bigger, and more and more frightening. Next, something stung my nose, and I blacked out.

After I came to, the first thing I heard them say was: "Ricky has thirty days left." My heart sank, and everything went black before my eyes, but I relaxed again right away. I felt comfortable from head to foot, and the swelling had subsided. I looked again. The one who had died wasn't I, but the red scorpion—it had flattened out and was stuck to the ground. Life had faded from its body. The older brother picked it up with tongs and threw it into the garbage.

They went out. The house was quiet, and I squatted there remembering the eye and the long thing that I had just swallowed down. All of a sudden, without turning my head, I saw a house mouse behind me. How strange this was: I was seeing with my back. There was an eye in my back! Was it that eye? It must be! On alert, the house mouse had emerged from the hole. After making sure no people were at home, he climbed up to the stove and ate all my food. The house mouse simply ignored me and swaggered back to the hole. Luckily, I didn't feel hungry. I still felt quite nauseous. They had said I still had "thirty days." What did that mean? I had heard the saying that one day was equal to a year. So did thirty days mean thirty years? I had no idea. I was frantic: Was a fatal event about to occur? I looked into the garbage can and was stunned! The scorpion not only hadn't died, its body was inflating: it was four or five times as big as it used to be. It stood up and clawed its way up the edge of the can. It was going to come out! I immediately dashed across, opened the door, and ran outside. I certainly didn't intend to be stung by him a second time!

I had hardly turned into the street when I ran into the two brothers. The older one grabbed me by the ear and said, "Ricky has come out, and so he has one fewer day." They ordered me to go home. I walked in front. Behind me, they were slapping each other. When I reached the door, I turned around and saw them clutching each other by the chest and squatting on the ground without moving as if they had congealed. With their four eyes so close together, I wondered if each brother would now see the other's eyes. But when I burrowed between them, I saw that each brother's eyes were still seeing only his own eyes, and they were acting as if no one else were present. I didn't get it. The large scorpion had walked out and was near the door frame. All of a sudden, the two brothers let go of each other and stood up. The scorpion swaggered out the door as if drunk and turned right. I didn't know where it was going. The younger brother said in a low voice, "Ricky went to call on someone." Huh? Were they calling the scorpion "Ricky"? Was it because the scorpion had eaten things inside me and thus had changed into something much like me?

Finally, I went back inside. Well, after all, there was no place like home. I climbed up to the stove to take a nap, for I was exhausted. Just as I was closing my eyes, I saw a terrifying scene: outside the window that furtive black cat was eating the red scorpion! This was so scary, so sickening! The scorpion's back leg was still struggling outside his mouth. The cat twisted his neck a few times and swallowed the whole scorpion. This scene was so ugly that I was now fully awake. All at once, I sensed that my entire body had become eyes, for not only could I see ahead, but I could also see behind myself, and not only could I see the exterior, but I could also see the interior. For example, I saw the scorpion continuing to struggle in the cat's belly. And looking at myself, in my abdominal cavity an eye was wrapped in membrane—the very eye that I had swallowed. So the scorpion hadn't died, and before long it would make its way out of the cat's stomach. I didn't dare watch any longer. I closed my eyes. But this was even worse, for I saw so many people and events inside myself. There was the pasture, and on the turf were countless holes. From each and every one of the holes, others of my species were sticking out their heads and watching. An eagle flew past—an eagle so large it covered the sun. An animal—it appeared to be something between a rat and a crow—was flying and running on the grasslands. He didn't fly high: he seemed to stick close to the underbrush and skate there. I didn't want to watch, but these scenes wouldn't go away. I wondered how that poor little thing had escaped the eagle's evil clutches. Before long, the eagle swept downward, and all the scenery disappeared. But the immense blank space did not disappear: it was a dazzling white. I could faintly hear an infant wailing. The younger brother said, "Look at how soundly Ricky is sleeping. He must not be dreaming at all. I'd bet on that." The older brother asked, "What do you want to bet?" "Your wheelbarrow. Come on over and you'll see."

I wasn't asleep. Or maybe I was. Anyhow, I kept looking at my insides. I wasn't tired. Although everything disappeared later, with only dazzling whiteness in front of me, I smelled the wind on the grasslands and a hint of animal skins. When that house mouse woke me up, I was throwing myself into the embrace of what I thought was Grandpa's shadow. The house mouse bit me in the butt, almost drawing blood. His eyes shone: his objective was clear. His eyes differed from those of our clan. Why had he come here? To eat my food, that's why. When he saw no food on the stove, he bit me. This house mouse was unusual. He actually thought I was his food and that he could take a bite whenever he wanted to. I glared at him, and he glared at me. He wasn't one bit afraid of me. When he saw that I was awake, he knew he couldn't eat me, and so— enraged—he jumped down to the floor. Though he patrolled once

more around the house, he still found nothing to eat. Then he retreated unwillingly into his hole. I started thinking about this house
mouse. He had been living in this house from the very beginning.
Was he a mutation of my species? Of course he was. I could tell that
just by looking at the shape of his eyes, though his expression was
different. Probably he had shrunk to such a small size because of the
changed circumstances. My clan and my ancestors had never eaten
our compatriots, yet he didn't observe this taboo. He considered me
his food. Sure, I guess he didn't consider me his compatriot, but I
*was* several times bigger than he was. Why wasn't he even a little
afraid of me? See? He was popping his head out of that hole again.
I was alarmed at the way he looked, because he clearly thought of
me as lunch. I'd have to be more careful from now on when I slept.
I still didn't understand one thing: In all these years, why hadn't he
ever attacked me? Was this change related to the present attack on
the red scorpion? Was he acting unscrupulously because the master
had said I had only thirty days left?

In order to evade the house mouse's gaze, I came down from
the stove and went outside. Why was it so quiet outside? Had all
the people left? I looked back: the house mouse had followed me
out. Why did he have to follow me? Where had the two brothers
gone? I mustn't doze off, because this guy was right behind me. I
went to the home across the street, pressed my ear against the door,
and listened. I heard someone's ragged breathing inside. The door
wasn't locked. I pushed it open and saw a fat woman with asthma
on the bed. Since I had opened the door, the house mouse scurried
in, too. He climbed up on the big, carved bed and crawled over to
the woman. He bit an artery on her neck and sucked the blood.
The woman gradually began breathing more easily, and, looking

comfortable, she closed her eyes. The house mouse's stomach was swelling, and when he slid down from the bed, he could hardly walk. He swaggered slowly over to the wall, where there was a hole much smaller than he was. He struggled hard to squeeze in and finally succeeded. He shrieked because he was being pressed from both sides. This was good for me—finally, I broke away from him. I turned around and went back to my home, intending to get a good nap. But the door was latched from the inside. Who had done that? I had to squat outside and wait. The brothers soon returned. When they realized the door was latched, they climbed up to the window, but something attacked them from inside. Covering their eyes, the two fell to the ground. Before long, the door opened, and an old white-haired woman came out carrying a paper bag. She unwrapped it in the doorway, and I saw inside it. It was arsenic. I recognized it, because when I was young, people in that family often added a small amount of arsenic to my bowl. She left to go to another house.

When I entered the home, I noticed the house mouse lying, bloodstained, on the floor, its head separated from its body, and a kitchen knife next to it. Had the old woman done this? How could the house mouse have died here? Hadn't he just now gone across the street? Oh, right, it was the tunnel. He had dug out a very long tunnel. He had come through the tunnel and died here. His stomach—filled with the blood he had drunk—was still distended. What had happened in this room? Let's imagine: 1) The old woman had set down a certain kind of bait, and the house mouse had been lured out of the hole. The old woman had caught him and cut his head off. 2) Or the house mouse, acting on his natural instincts, had bitten the old woman in the leg, and she had chopped off his head.

3) Or, after eating the bait the old woman had put down, he had decided to commit suicide, and the old woman had held out the knife for him to bump into, he had collided forcefully with the knife blade, and his head had been separated from his body. We don't have to go on imagining: there are many possibilities, but for now it's impossible to know exactly how it happened. Why was there such a bizarre stench in the house? I found the source of the odor, and it was indeed that house mouse. How could he have rotted so soon after dying? But it was true. Yellow pus oozed from his stomach. Tiny gray insects squirmed in the wound on his neck. Maybe even before he died, his body had been rotten, yet I hadn't noticed. I picked him up with tongs, intending to throw him out, but the moment the tongs made contact with him, his flesh fell off and his bones shattered. So scary! I was scared out of my wits! He turned into a pool of slush; only his gray hair hadn't vaporized. I freaked out, threw the tongs down, and hid on the stove. I was frantic. I glanced subconsciously at the window: ah, both the brothers' faces were there, and each face had only one eye—that kind of eye with two pupils! The two pupils were still watching nothing but each other. Suddenly, I realized that these weren't the two brothers. Who were they then? Had they come to catch me? I slid down the stove and hid in the firewood. I supposed they couldn't see me now, and I fell asleep peacefully.

Indeed, they were not the two brothers, but they bore a slight resemblance to them. These two one-eyed young people now lived in this home in place of the two brothers. I remembered once when I'd seen the older brother change into one eye. Were these two people variants of the first two? Probably not. I was sleeping in a cardboard box under the bed, when, at midnight, the two on the bed shouted in unison, "A flood's on the way! Flood!" Then they ran out, barefoot. As soon as they left, I climbed via the stove to the thatched roof. Gazing into the distance, I saw black clouds rolling in overhead. Lights went on in all the houses in the slums. Yet no one emerged. Were they waiting? I waited, too, but nothing happened. Finally I felt bored and was about to go down. Even if there was a flood, where could I escape to? I couldn't go into the city: I could lose my life in a day in the inescapable city heat. I couldn't go far away, either, for I could die of terror on the way. Never mind, I would just go back to the cardboard box and sleep. Oh! What was that? The two one-eyed people! They carried two corpses out of a house. They were taking advantage of the chaos to rob and kill! But no one saw them. Was it possible that they were making no noise? No! Ha, here was another one! Had those people died for some other reason, and they were simply dealing with the corpses? It wasn't raining, yet black clouds descended. Now I couldn't see anything well. Even the lights in the houses had dimmed. Was a flood really on the way? Then I'd better sleep on the roof. If disaster struck, I might get lucky and survive. I had heard people talk about floods. When a house was totally sealed up by surging floodwaters, no one inside could survive. I heard that in such circumstances, it didn't matter how quick-witted you were or how strong, you would never locate the doors and windows. Everyone in the slums knew this, and so why didn't they do as I did and climb up to the roof? Just now, the two people were running all over the streets shouting "Flood!" Everyone must have heard them. They had heard, they must have heard!

The water rose higher and higher. It didn't block the doors immediately. I heard the flooding water rush down from the stairs over there. I guessed—a depth of fifteen centimeters, half a meter, a meter . . . and still I heard no one fleeing. If anyone was fleeing, their wading would be audible. It was alarmingly quiet all around. How high had the water risen? I couldn't see. Something tickled my feet. Snails. They wanted to climb up my body. I dangled my rear feet below the roof to probe. Sure enough, my feet touched water. No doubt the entire slum was inundated. But the water didn't seem to be rising continually. And the people? Where were the people? Had water blocked all the doors? Were the people all dead? I started crying soundlessly. Above me, the sky had brightened. I listened again: the sound of running water had stopped. Someone was calling me—"Ricky, Ricky." Wasn't it the two brothers? No one else called me by this name. I glanced out: the mist had broken up. Even though the houses were submerged, the lights were still on. I could see people's shadows wavering on the windows. What kind of flood was this? Someone came outside and brushed his teeth in front of the house. The swaying ripples distorted his shadow. "Ricky! Ricky!" The sound came from underwater. Soon it would be light. What time was it?

"Ricky, come down! Come down! Now!" The voice underwater grew impatient. I leaned over and slid down, landing at the neighbors' doorway. How strange: I had gotten a good look at it just now and I'd felt the water, yet now it turned out to be a huge transparent membrane covering the entire slum. It was light now, and the sun was out. But the sunlight couldn't penetrate the membrane. The neighbors' door was open, and I ran inside. Lying on the floor were the old man and his wife, rolling their eyes and spitting up water. Had it really flooded? Where had the water gone? The old couple used to raise large, gray edible pigeons out in back.

The pigeons were very ugly, but their voices were dreamlike. When dozens of them cooed at once, even pedestrians became drowsy. When the old couple walked by the door, they seemed to be dreaming. Generally the old man held his wife's hand and walked a little in front of her. He felt his way along blindly with the other hand. Dragged ahead by him, the old woman grumbled, "Can't you walk a little slower? Can't you?" The floor of the house was dry, with no trace of a flood. I just sensed a kind of fine gossamer floating in front of me. I accidentally inhaled it and sneezed a lot. I approached the old woman and nuzzled her cheek with my nose. She woke up and shouted, "Honey! We aren't dead! We didn't die!" At first she sat up, and then—tottering—she stood and walked over to open the wardrobe and shut herself inside. I heard her crying inside. The old man also sat up and shouted loudly, "Why didn't we die? Why? Were you talking nonsense? Huh?" When he couldn't find his wife in the room, he went out. Shading his eyes with his hand, he looked into the distance. He kept watching, as if waiting for something to happen. I slid over to the door, too, and looked out: I saw the transparent gossamer that I'd noticed earlier. In the distance, it turned into waves. Was this a flood? No. I didn't sense that I was in water. Then why had these old people blacked out on the ground? They had also been spitting up water just now, as though their stomachs were full of water.

Carpenter Wen passed by, a steelyard in his hand. He said to the old man, "I'm weighing this. I have to weigh it." He pretended to grab something from the air with his left hand, and then placed that "thing" in the tray of his steelyard. It was strange: the steelyard was like a seesaw, rising high on one side. What could be so heavy? The gossamer? But the tray of the steelyard held nothing.

The old man looked closely as he finished weighing it, and said, "Oh, this has to be weighed." Frowning, Carpenter Wen said, "I've been weighing things ever since the flood started last night. I'm exhausted." Just then, I saw the two brothers standing across the street. They seemed to be staring at Carpenter Wen, but I knew their eyes could look only at each other. "What's this?" the old man asked Carpenter Wen as he pointed to the gossamer in the sky. "It's the thing I weighed," Wen said, his eyes shining. He raised the steelyard, grabbed something from the air, and placed it in the steelyard's tray. When he finished, he turned it over and weighed a new one. He was gasping for breath. The old man watched anxiously, his head following the movements. He prattled on, "Then we don't have to be afraid of floods anymore, do we?" As he spoke, he drooled and his hands shook. He seemed to have one foot in the grave. Nearsighted, he moved closer and closer, trying to get a good look at the steelyard. He was getting in the way of Wen's work. Wen shoved him indignantly, and he fell to the ground.

Just then, the old woman who had hidden in the wardrobe came out. She sat at the entrance, smiling—revealing her toothless mouth. She'd been crying just now. What had made her so happy? "I, I, I . . . ," she said with her sunken mouth. Carpenter Wen dropped the steelyard with a thud; his forehead was covered with sweat. As if waking from a dream, the old man asked him, "What's wrong? What's wrong?" "Even weighing this four or five times in a row, it weighed nothing at all. Could this mean . . ." He held his head dejectedly as if it would explode. "This happens often. Often." The old man did his best to console him. But he snarled and ran off holding his head. He didn't even take his steelyard. The old man picked it up. He wanted to imitate Wen and weigh mirages plucked from the air. The old woman was exhilarated. But whatever they did, they couldn't catch any weight. Time after time, the steelyard swung down. They worked hard for a long time but had nothing to show for it. They had to give up. While this was going on, the two brothers kept watching.

The old couple stood watching the sky: the gossamer was thickening, and soon it congealed into large drops of water dripping down. I retreated to the house to escape the rain. Why weren't these two old people afraid of the rain? Across the street, the brothers shouted, "Flood! Flood . . ." Their voices gradually faded into the distance. The old woman looked up, as though swallowing the falling rain. What the old man did was even more straightforward: he simply lay down on the ground, letting the rainwater splash silt on his face. He closed his eyes and slept. I looked around a little in their home, hoping to find a bite to eat. This home was strange: it didn't have even a stick of furniture. Had it been dashed away by the flood? Or had there never been any? If so, did they sleep on the floor? There was a jar on the stove. I climbed up and took a look. What I saw scared me so much I nearly fell. My heart pounded for a long time. That large jar was full of the red scorpions that I'd seen before. When I recalled the one that wouldn't die, I had goose bumps all over. Ah, they'd been raising these things at home. I saw two of them climb up the edge of the jar trying to get out. On another side of the stove was a willow basket: inside was the bacon that was so delicious. But now I didn't dare go over and eat it. The old woman came in. "Rat, did you find some food?" she asked. How'd she know? Then she waved her hand and "hissed" twice, and the two scorpions went down. She took meat out of the basket, cut it, and put it in a dish. She sat down and chewed the bacon slowly in her toothless mouth. She'd forgotten I was hungry. I pulled her trouser leg with my mouth, but she remained indifferent—absorbed in her meditation. Desperate, I bit her leg and swallowed down a mouthful of her flesh. Oh! I'd become a house mouse! I was so ashamed. She moved and leaned against the wall, muttering, "I—I'm in so much pain . . ." I had bitten very deep—close to the bone, but I'd drawn no blood. Her flesh was a little sour; it tasted pretty good. In a daze, I looked at the wound; I wanted to take another bite. But the old man came in. He grabbed a wooden stick and hit me. I thought my spine was broken. I lay on my stomach in the middle of the room, unable to move. "Leave him here to die!" the old woman screamed. Then, supporting each other, the two exited. They locked the door from the outside.

Except for my eyeballs, which could still turn, my whole body was paralyzed. Was I going to die? She'd left me there to die. Did this mean that I still had to wait a while before I actually died? I lay on my stomach on the floor and thought and thought. I thought of that pasture, where an eagle circled overhead every day. I'd been accustomed to that scene. But one day, she flew so high that even though I had great eyesight, I could only look on helplessly as she disappeared into the blue sky. At that time, the whole pastureland was ebullient: all of my species emerged from their hiding places. They ran wildly all over the pastureland: everything was chaotic. The eagle never appeared again. Just then, I saw the house mouse. Hadn't he died? I'd seen with my own eyes that his head was separated from his body. Maybe he was a brother of the dead one. God, even his expression was the same! I grew quite emotional, though I didn't know exactly why. He approached me and smelled my butt. How strange: it was like a bird pecking at my butt, and the tickling revived me. Then I saw the bloody mess in his mouth. Ah, he was eating me. I grew so excited that my paralysis vanished. I turned and looked at my butt: he had bitten a hole in it. Although I was in pain, the tickling that had revived me was a lot better than the paralysis I had just experienced. I approached him, hoping he would take another bite out of me. But he'd eaten his fill and was weary of eating. He didn't even smell me, but withdrew and stayed there watching me. The more I saw of him, the more I felt he was like the already dead mouse. Could he be his twin brother? That one also had a white spot on his left leg . . . How could this be merely co-incidental? I remembered again that the old woman had just said I would die. Was I still going to die now? How would I die? I was facing this mouse. Before long, his swollen stomach flattened. He had a really good digestive system. When he looked at me again with starvation in his eyes, an idea came to me. I showed him my meaty chest, hoping he would take another bite. He looked me up and down, but didn't bite. Once, I thought he was going to, but he just licked my hair, as if vacillating. In the end, he abandoned the idea again. After another cunning glance at me, he squeezed into the hole at the foot of the wall. I was disappointed! A kind of odd disappointment. What on earth did I want? Did I want to become him? He had a clear-cut objective in life, as well as his own home (that hole). He had never been like me—wandering around and choosing homes at random. Mouse—oh mouse, why didn't you eat me? I, I didn't know what I should do with my body. To me, this body was now superfluous.

In the corner of the room, I licked the hole he'd bitten in my butt. The hole wasn't bleeding nor did it hurt. Could the mouse's saliva be a narcotic? I did my best to recall how I felt the moment he bit me, and I could only vaguely remember that it felt like being pecked by a bird. Maybe even this feeling wasn't real. Maybe I wasn't aware at all when he gnawed at my butt. Look, the mouse had come out again. He stared greedily at me with his shiny eyes, but he stood at the opening to the hole with no intention of coming over. When I walked a bit closer to him, he retreated a little into the hole. I was crestfallen. I gradually realized my real status in the slums.

■

The slums were my home, and also the hardest place for me to understand. Generally speaking, I didn't make a deliberate effort to understand it. Destiny drove me from one place to another. I'd been underground, I'd been to the city, and I'd lived in all kinds of homes in the slums. There were often crises in my life: the threat of death was ongoing, but I was still alive. Could this be because my ancestors were living in the depths of my memory and protecting me? Oh—that boundless pasture, that eagle disappearing into the vast *qi*, those kin who lay on their stomachs in the underbrush! Thinking of them, I felt I knew everything and was capable of anything. But this was in my memory. The reality was absolutely different. In reality, I knew almost nothing, though I had experienced so much . . .

### Part Five

I climbed this simply constructed blockhouse: as far as the eye could see, the rows of thatched slum houses were quietly bending their heads in the mist. I knew their humility was feigned. All these houses harbored sinister intentions. But I had to live in them.

I was a son of this mystical land. Sure, it was gloomy here, but I was used to it. I had grown up here. Now in the midst of dreariness, I meditated constantly. I couldn't get a good look at the inside of the thatched huts. They were too dark inside. Their design had totally ignored the way eyes function. Once when I moved into a house, I thought only two people lived there. Later, I found out there were twelve! I cowered in a corner of the stove: the fire came close to lapping at my skin and hair. They never stopped cooking because they had twelve stomachs to feed. With only one room, they slept anywhere. Two of them even slept under the bed. At midnight, I couldn't locate any of them. They had disappeared. I stood on the stove and ran my eyes over the empty home. I wondered why I couldn't keep up with these people's train of thought.

Once, I had moved into a house where I thought the family was small and simple. I was happy because I'd be able to get a good night's sleep. But at midnight, an earthquake almost jolted me from the stove to the floor! By grabbing the iron hook from which bacon hung on the wall, I managed — just barely — to keep my footing. I looked back: seven or eight people were breakdancing wildly. They seemed drunk. They were being flung from one wall to another. They resembled each other, so they must be from this family. Then where were they in the daytime? Some rooms were actually deserted; they just pretended to be inhabited — a garbage can and a broom at the entrance, and the door closed but not locked. I pushed against the door, entered, jumped up to the stove, and slept in the corner. I awakened at midnight and still saw no one. I jumped down and looked for something to eat, but found nothing. The house smelled of mold. Evidently it had been unoccupied for ages. I slunk around in the darkness, a little fearful. Just then, I heard a sigh. The sound came from the ceiling. The woman who had sighed didn't seem to be in pain. Probably she was simply tired. But the sound was incessant, and I couldn't stand it. My chest was about to explode, and so I dashed out and wandered all night in the cold. Sure, most of the time I blended into the landlords' lives. I hated them, because they always closed in on me, and yet, and yet, I was curious about their lives—those lives that I usually found incomprehensible. In the end, my relations with them deteriorated each time, and I left in search of another home to live in. It upset me to think of this. When was this blockhouse built? My impression was that although conspiracies riddled the slums, no major disturbance had occurred. So what was the point of building this blockhouse? To resist outside enemies? City people certainly wouldn't come to these lowlands. People here and in the city had nothing to do with each other. I couldn't imagine where any enemies would come from.

It was getting dark. I ran down from the blockhouse that had gradually turned ice-cold. Another one of my species was running in front of me. He had a somewhat longer body than mine, and a bigger skull, too. A spot of white hair was growing on his left hind leg, somewhat resembling the two house mice I knew so well. But he wasn't a house mouse! He ran to the small pond and jumped in. My God! I certainly wouldn't jump into the icy water! At first he was still visible. He swam and swam, then disappeared. Clearly, he had dived deep. I stared blankly for a while at the edge of the pond. I thought of what had happened early this morning: the woman of the house had thrown me out. She disliked my dirtying the stove in her home. That wasn't true, though. I ate and slept on the stove every day and so I couldn't avoid leaving a little trace of my presence, could I? But she couldn't put up with it! She was obsessed with hygiene. When she had nothing to do, she swept and dusted. This made absolutely no sense. I had never known any other slum dweller who did that. Such a simple, crude house. Even if it was spotless, it looked no different from any other houses here. But this woman (I knew the others called her Auntie Shrimp) never gave me a break. If I tracked in a little dirt, she brandished a broom and swore at me for a long time. At mealtime, she wouldn't tolerate my dropping a single grain of rice or a sliver of vegetable onto the stove. She scrubbed my fur viciously with a brush every day, not stopping until I screamed. As for her, she spent a lot of time taking baths in the wooden basin. Whenever she had time, she heated water and bathed and washed her hair, as if she wanted to scrub away a layer of skin. Auntie Shrimp loved to talk at midnight. Maybe she was talking in her sleep. She always called me "the little mouse." She tossed and turned in that wide bed and talked incessantly: "The little mouse doesn't care about hygiene. This is dangerous. There's pestilence all around. If you don't want to get sick, you have to be strict about hygiene. My parents told me this secret. The year they went north and left me behind, they urged me to clean up every day. I was a sensible girl . . ."

Early one morning, she stood up in bed and shouted, "Mouse, did you take a bath today? Something smells rotten!" She got out of bed and scrubbed me with the brush. It hurt so much that I screamed. I had always slept on the stove, but one day all of a sudden that displeased her. She said I had turned the stove into something unlike a stove. She said if this continued, she and I would both come down with the plague. With this, she threw out the jar that I slept in. Broken-hearted, I was going to jump down from the stove, and then I glimpsed the murderous intent on her face. Oh—

was she going to kill me? Her face was flushed; she held a kitchen knife in her hand. I thought that the moment I jumped down from the stove, she would chop me into pieces. And so I hesitated and retreated to a corner of the stove, making room for her to clean the stove. But she didn't do that. She kept saying, "Aren't you coming down? You aren't coming down?" As she spoke, she brandished the knife and pressed the back of the knife against me. I had to risk my life and jump down. She twirled the knife and chopped. Luckily, I dodged out of the way in time, and she chopped the muddy floor. The door was open, so I rushed out. Behind me, she shouted abuse, saying that if she saw any trace of me, she would kill me. How had my relationship with her evolved to this point? At first, when I drifted to her home, she had been so genial! She not only fed me well, she also arranged for me to sleep in a jar, saying this would keep the flames from lapping at my hair. But before long I experienced her mysophobia. At the time, I didn't think it was a serious problem. One day, she suggested cutting off my claws (because they were filthy). That's when I began to be on guard. What kind of woman was she? I started avoiding her. Luckily, it was all talk and no action. And so I kept my claws.

She cleaned the house so thoroughly that it created endless trouble for her. For example, she had to brush the soles of her shoes whenever she entered the house. She covered the windows and doors with heavy cloth. The inside of the house became as dark as a basement. She used much more water than other people did to clean vegetables, wash dishes, and take baths. She was forever going to the well to fetch water. She was always busy. I didn't know how she made a living. Perhaps her parents had left her some money. She wasn't much interested in men. She merely stood in the doorway, idiotically watching a particular man's silhouette, but she never brought a man home. She was probably afraid outsiders would make her house dirty. But then how had she taken a liking to me in the first place, and even let me in? I was even dirtier than those men, wasn't I? And I rarely bathed with water. When I first arrived, she combed my hair with an old comb. After combing my messy hair, she threw the comb into the garbage. With some satisfaction, she pronounced me "very clean." Now, remembering this, I thought she was sort of deceiving herself. But she persisted in thinking that she could do anything. She was a conceited woman. From that day on, she brushed me every day. It hurt a lot. But at least I was much cleaner than before. I used to get along well with her, even though I despised her constant cleaning. Still, as long as I stayed inside the jar on top of the stove, there was no big problem. Who could have guessed that her mysophobia would worsen?

One day, she actually found a metal brush to brush my fur. I was bruised all over from her brushing, and I screamed the way pigs do when being butchered. When she let go, I ran off and cowered under the eaves of another home. I was still bleeding from my back. After the sun set, I couldn't stand the cold, and I was afraid I wouldn't be able to endure the night and would die outside. A young girl with a pointed face noticed me. She squatted and looked me over under the dim streetlight. Dressed in a short-sleeved shirt, she was also shivering from the cold. "King Rat," she said, "you mustn't stay here. If you do, you'll die because it'll freeze tonight. Are you imitating those children? They've been doing this for years. As soon as they learned to walk, they went outside to sleep. That's the way they've lived for a long time. Go on home, King Rat. If you don't, you'll die." And so I walked back slowly. Finally I was limping with almost every step. I was cold and in pain, almost losing consciousness. When I got home, it was probably close to midnight. The light was still on, though Auntie Shrimp was in bed snoring. I climbed on top of the pile of firewood next to the stove and squatted down to rest. Then, probably because of my loud groans, Auntie Shrimp woke up. She got out of bed and looked at me by the light of the kerosene lamp. Before long, she set the lamp down, turned, took a jar of balm from the cupboard, and smeared it gently on my wounds. "Mouse, why didn't you tell me I was hurting you when I combed your hair?" she rebuked me. This confused me greatly. What was illusion? What was reality? Did I know this woman at all? Anyhow, the balm helped. I could finally breathe, and then I fell asleep on the woodpile.

The very next morning, the incident that I described above happened. Even now, I have no idea what Auntie Shrimp's real idea was. Yet, when I ran out of Auntie Shrimp's home, I realized that it was indeed filthy outside! These were the slums, after all—what could you expect? I seemed to be stepping on human waste with each step I took. The side of the street was filled with human waste, dog shit, and puddles of urine, heaps of decomposed vegetable leaves, the guts of animals, and so forth. Swarms of mosquitoes and flies were fluttering around and entering your nostrils. I couldn't put up with it anymore, and I climbed up that blockhouse. I sat on top of the blockhouse for a long time without recovering my equilibrium. I didn't understand: How had the outside environment worsened so much in the few months that I had lived in Auntie Shrimp's home? People said that the slums had never been clean, but I had been almost oblivious to that. Now the filth had completely polluted the air—so much that I wanted to throw up. Even though I was on top of the blockhouse, I still felt that everything below was a huge garbage dump. The stench rode the wind. The people on the street looked down at their feet, covered their noses, and hurried on. I seldom went out during the few months that I stayed with Auntie Shrimp. And even when I did, I went no farther than the neighbors' eaves. Otherwise, Auntie Shrimp would have constantly told me to wash my feet and she would have scolded me mercilessly. And so, was it simply by comparison that I finally realized how filthy the slums were? Had Auntie Shrimp been training my senses over the last few months? Maybe I had never before noticed that passersby covered their noses as they walked past. Maybe the sides of the streets in the slums had always been heaped with dirt, and I had simply never noticed. Thinking back on the past few months of Auntie Shrimp's slavelike life, putting myself in her shoes, and then thinking about myself, I couldn't help but shudder. However, I still had to thank Auntie Shrimp—for in the past, I was covered with pus-filled pimples, I was toxic from head to foot, and I had eaten filthy food. But after spending a few months in her home, I had no pus-filled pimples and I understood the importance of hygiene. People of the slums were too apathetic. How could they have grown so lazy that they let the doorways become dumps for waste and dirt? Not only was filth overflowing into the air here, but it also seeped underground. The asphalt roads and the cobblestone sidewalks were stained by a thick layer of something black and greasy. Even the mud was dirty, filled with ash and oil. Why hadn't I ever noticed this before? This blockhouse, though, was clean, as if no one had ever come up here and heaven's wind and rain had cleaned it naturally. This granite structure must be very old. Plumbing the depths of my memory, I found no trace of it. Was it because no one had ever come here that it was so clean? Why hadn't others come up here?

I stood at the side of the pond, thinking of all kinds of things. I would soon freeze to death. My top priority was to save my life by finding a home to move into. I noticed a house with a door that wasn't shut tight and thought I'd go in and deal with any consequences later.

"Who's there?" An old voice spoke in the dark. I curled up quietly against the foot of the wall, afraid the man would see me, but he got up unexpectedly, shone a kerosene lamp on me, and said, "Ah, it's a snake." How the hell had I changed into a snake? He poked me with a club and I took the opportunity to roll into the house. How bizarre this was: a heatwave rolled through the house, and I immediately warmed up. The stove wasn't on, so where had the hot air come from? I saw that familiar mouse stick his head out of the hole. Three scrawny roosters stood under the bed. The man of the house was short and little. I couldn't see him very well because his head was wrapped in a white towel. He drove the roosters out with the club, and they jumped up. One flew to the windowsill, scattering the smell of feathers all over. When the little red-tailed rooster passed by me, I was actually scalded! Its body was as hot as red-hot coals. Just then, the man squatted down and looked me up and down. His face was triangular, and his cruel eyes were hidden under bushy eyebrows. He swept my legs with the club, and I jumped away. "This snake is really odd . . . ," he muttered. He still considered me a snake. Was this because I didn't emit heat? What were these roosters all about?

He suddenly gave a weird laugh and said, "Auntie Shrimp . . ." The sound seemed to come from a tomb. I looked around: sure enough, Auntie Shrimp's face appeared at the door. She was laughing in embarrassment, but she didn't enter. He waved his hand, and I still thought he was going to hit me, but his hand merely slipped past once and a heatwave dashed against my face. I blinked: Auntie Shrimp had disappeared. The little rooster jumped from the windowsill to his shoulder. The man stood up, and dragging the club, circled once around the room. When the two roosters on the floor dashed past me, scalding my nose, a blister appeared immediately on my nose. What the hell? This old man seemed to want to find the two roosters, but the roosters ran right past him and he didn't even see them. He just struck the air with his club. The little guy on his shoulder gurgled, keeping time with his swaying. Its claws cut into his clothes. I scurried under the bed because I was afraid he would hit me. I had barely squeezed under the bed when something struck me in the head. I almost fainted from the pain. When I pulled myself together, I noticed a lot of little animals that were similar to me. They formed a circle around me. Their thermal radiation almost prevented me from opening my eyes. Were they my kin? How had they become so heat-resistant? In my hometown in the past, our pasture was icebound most of the year. We hid in dugouts. We never knew what "high temperatures" meant. What was going on now? They turned into balls of fire, and yet they could endure this! Were they surrounding me in order to destroy my physical being? If so, why weren't they taking action? At the door, Auntie Shrimp was saying to the man, "Have you destroyed that virus? Where did he go? He goes all over the place and might spread disease." She actually said I was a virus! The old man answered, "Don't worry. This place is for high-temperature disinfecting. We'll take care of his problem." "Then please do that." Auntie Shrimp seemed to really be leaving.

I was being roasted. I couldn't open my eyes. Could they be treating my virus? Those who were like my kin were glaring at me. My eyes stung, and I shed tears. I couldn't see. The old man swept under the bed again with his club, and my kin ran out. He pressed me against the wall with his club. "Go ahead — just try to run!" the old man said. I heard myself cry out twice from the pain. My voice sounded like that of a house mouse. How could I sound like a house mouse? I struggled, but the club didn't budge. Soon I would suffocate. Everything went black before my eyes. Was I going to die? It was so hot. But suddenly the man loosened his grip on the club and said, "A snake can't warm up." I touched the blister on my nose. Indeed, my claws were ice-cold. No wonder he said I was a snake!

Had I been disinfected? I had no idea. I slowly came out from under the bed and once more heard Auntie Shrimp's voice: "I've never seen such a clean mouse before! But he'll be dirty again tomorrow and he'll have to be roasted again. Huh! If he were like the others, I'd take him back." By "the others," I knew she meant the ones who were supposedly my kin. They had become burning pieces of coal, so of course they couldn't have viruses. But how had they gotten like this? Auntie Shrimp didn't seem to be planning for me to go back. She stared at me coldly from the window. Did they really intend to roast me like this every day? Even if they did, how could a snake turn into a red-hot coal? My kin who had been swept out from under the bed lined up along the foot of the wall. The old man swept across with the club. Routed again, they scurried under the bed. Tired out from hitting them, he stood with arms akimbo in the middle of the room and said, "You sluggards! Watch out — my club means business!" I looked under the bed: those little things were trembling! The little rooster flew from his shoulder to midair, then dropped down and set off a heatwave in the room. When this wave struck me, I fell back a few paces and leaned against the wall. I noticed that the landlord wasn't emitting heat, and yet he wasn't afraid of it, either. How come? He set down his club and took something to eat out of the kitchen cupboard. He seemed to be eating little black balls. Judging from his table manners, the food was hard. A cracking sound came from between his teeth: Was he eating something metal? What strong teeth he had! Just then, a ray of sunlight flashed in from the open door, and all at once I got a good look at his face. A huge tumor on the left side of his face pulled his mouth and nose to one side. The tumor was so red that it was almost purple. To my surprise, a brass ring was pierced through the top of it, and pus ran out from that ring. Damn, his body was so toxic, and yet he devoted himself to disinfecting animals! People, huh? Oh, people. No way could I understand them! He chewed and swallowed down all those little balls. His teeth were like steel. "Yi Tinglai! Yi Tinglai!" Auntie Shrimp was standing at the door. Why was his name Yi Tinglai—"First Responder"? How weird! Auntie Shrimp said, "I won't feel better until he's as clean as you. He always gets dirty!" The old man gave a devilish laugh. I couldn't see even one tooth in the dark cavity that was his mouth. How had he bitten those little balls? "Are you leaving now? You aren't taking him with you?" the old man asked Auntie Shrimp. "I have to go. The road will be blocked soon. As for the little mouse, I'll leave him with you. I'm sorry to give you so much trouble." "Has the plague arrived yet?" "Yesterday. Two died. I was afraid the little mouse would get sick, he's so dirty." I was alarmed by this talk.

Once more, the man took a large plate of black balls out of

the kitchen cupboard and put it on the floor. This kind of ball was much smaller—only a little larger than a house mouse's poop. My kin crowded around and ate in a hurry, making creaking sounds. I wanted to eat, too, but I was afraid they would scald me. The man said, "You little snake-mouse, it isn't time for you to eat yet. They're eating pieces of coal. Can you swallow that?" Naturally, I wasn't interested in letting coal burn my stomach. I didn't think I needed to be disinfected that way. Just then, he carried out a bowl of black liquid, saying I should "wash my innards" with it. Noticing the bubbles on the dirty black water, I hesitated. He bellowed, "Hurry up, or you'll die!" And so I started drinking. After drinking it, I felt dizzy and my heart swelled with longing for my hometown. That pasture, that sky. Snowflakes swirled in the sky, and my kin hid in the caves. Would they all die soon? No, they were fine. They had diarrhea: they would get rid of all the dirty things they'd eaten in the summer! Their insides would be clean! Ha. I was the one with diarrhea. I'd gotten rid of a huge amount. The man focused all his attention on me. "Are your insides clean?" he asked. I twitched my tail to indicate I was finished. The man spread around some ashes and swept my poop under the stove. He seemed to think poop wasn't dirty. So why was it necessary to wash my intestines? It was impossible to guess their thoughts. "Auntie Shrimp left you to me to deal with," the old man went on. "Stand up. Let me look at you." I went weak in the knees; I couldn't stand up. I lay on my stomach on the ground and couldn't move. I thought I was going to die. "Can't you stand up? Forget it then. You're all like this. Your grandfather came calling one year and ate every last bit of my roasted pork. But when I told him to jump up to the stove, he couldn't do it!" The old man chattered on and on and lay down on the bed. Then my kin who had eaten their fill left the plate one by one, lined up against the wall, and fell asleep.

It was getting hot in the house again, and meanwhile, strength was returning to my legs. I tried a few times and finally stood up. It was so hot! Really hot! The coal briquettes must be burning in the man's and my kin's stomachs. They were all sleeping, as if the high temperature had left them very content. All of a sudden, the three roosters started fighting in the middle of the room. The two big ones attacked the little one, ripping his crest apart. The little rooster's face was a mass of blood. He squatted on the floor and tried hard to hide his head amid the feathers on his chest. The other two still didn't let go of him: they continued attacking and pecked him all over until his feathers fell off. Blood gushed out where they had pecked. It looked as if he would die at the hands of his buddies. Just at this horrible moment, he flew swiftly upward. Spreading his wings, he flew like a bird and then dropped down heavily. He set off a heatwave in the house, and I was about to suffer a heatstroke. He struggled a few times on the floor, then lay motionless. The other two crowded around and pecked at his feathers, stripping him of one bunch after another. They worked brutally and rapidly, and soon the little rooster was absolutely bald. While the roosters were creating an uproar, my kin were sleeping, but one house mouse emerged. He was exactly like one that I'd seen in another home in the past—also with a white spot on his left hind leg. He exerted himself to bite the little rooster on the back and ripped off a piece of flesh. He ate it right away. After eating one piece, he went back to tear off another piece, turning the little rooster's back into a large cavity. By the light shooting in from the door, I could see the guts in the cavity. The house mouse came over to me with the flesh in his mouth, and — showing off — he chewed it. I smelled a strong rotten stench. Was it the odor of this flesh? Hadn't the little rooster just died? His flesh should have still been fresh, shouldn't it? Oh! The little featherless rooster actually stood up shakily! The hole in his back was very conspicuous. He walked shakily over to me! The house mouse — still with the flesh in his mouth — scurried into the hole. The little rooster's naked body was pale, and the blood on the crest congealed. He stared at me with round eyes. I sensed that if he came a bit closer, I would be burned by his thermal radiation. He jumped a few times, and some little marblelike balls bounced out of the cavity in his back and dropped to the floor, igniting flames. They soon burned up, leaving no trace. He jumped some more, and a few more balls flew out. I watched idiotically. He jumped and jumped, not stopping until his body was empty. Then he fell onto the floor. His thermal radiation vanished. I walked over and poked him. God, all that was left was one layer of skin! Even his bones were gone. As I considered looking more closely at this little pile of dirt, the man on the bed spoke.

"He came here deliberately to exact revenge, and he died in my house. I can't stand dead things. I hate the sight of death. I was afraid of nightmares for quite a while, and so I worked even harder at disinfecting the place." With that, he got out of bed and squatted next to the little rooster's remains. Shifting it with tongs, he muttered, "It's the plague, isn't it? The plague." I thought to myself, He's been burned out. All that's left is a little empty skin. How can it hold the plague? Since this was the plague, why didn't he throw it out immediately instead of moving it with the tongs? Suddenly he turned to me, stared vengefully with his triangular eyes, and scolded, "You! What are you looking at? This is nothing for you —

a snake—to see!" I was afraid he would stab me with the tongs, and so I scurried under the bed. From there, I saw him drop the rooster skin into a bowl and place the bowl in the kitchen cupboard. I was shocked! This person didn't do what he said, but just the opposite! The other two roosters came out, too. They circled the man and yelled. They flew up and pecked him. Were they protesting? And if so, what were they protesting? They had all (including the mouse) dismembered the little rooster, and now when the man had put his remains into the cupboard, were they unhappy with that? Why was this room so hot? The man stuck his head under the bed and asked, "Snake, do you want to eat? I won't give you charcoal briquettes because if you eat them, you'll be burned so much you won't even leave any ashes behind. I'll give you this, okay?" He threw a big bunch of grass under the bed. I was no herbivore. When I left the grass in disgust and went over to the wall to sleep, the fragrance emitted by the grass drew me back. What was this scent? I tried a few bites. This succulent thing left green juice at the corners of my mouth. I was so excited! I was about to jump up. I wanted so much to jump to some other place, though I couldn't say where. It seemed connected with shadows. And so I scurried to the shadows behind the big cupboard. Oh! The scent of the grass grew stronger. My longing for home tortured me. Why was I still staying in these slums that were like garbage cans? I mustn't hesitate: I must rush back to my hometown. My brain was about to explode with memories of her. But my legs were so thin and weak: it took a lot of effort to go to the city just once. I didn't know the way to the grasslands— it was thousands of miles away, so remote. I might die on the way. I shouldn't think about these things. Covered all over with the virus, I could only stay in this garbage can, cleaning up and being disinfected all day long. Why did he feed me grass from my homeland? Did he intend to shatter my longing to go back home? Was it all about what he was doing? Did he think this would be good for me? Oh, my home, my hometown — In this life, I could never return. I had never imagined that I would be able to eat grass from my home — sure, this grass was from there. I remembered so clearly: this was what my ancestors ate every day long, long ago before I was born. Had this landlord been there? Or was an envoy traveling between the two places? While pondering this, I fell asleep. Someone was talking in my dream. It was Auntie Shrimp. Auntie Shrimp said I could walk to the grasslands. "You just need to try, and your legs will get stronger." What did she mean? I'd better get up fast and try this. I opened my eyes with an effort and saw the landlord look under the bed. His staring triangular eyes freaked me out. He said, "Over there on the corner, two snakes were burned to death. The entire region is being disinfected. How could they escape? Huh." He told me to come out.

I walked out shakily and saw that he had once more placed the dish of the little rooster's remains on the floor. He told me to eat that little thing. I didn't want to. He struck me in the head repeatedly with the wooden club. I passed out and then came to. After a while, I really couldn't stand this. I decided I'd better suppress my nausea and swallow this little thing. After doing that, I felt ill. I rolled my eyes. I wanted to throw up, but I couldn't stand up. I lay on my stomach on the floor. The house mouse stuck his head out of the hole in front of me and looked at me with a weird expression. What? Was he waiting to eat me? Just look at his expression! I was nauseated again, and everything blurred before my eyes. Oh, he was nipping at my face! I was losing my mind and stood up. He kept biting me and wouldn't let go, as if stuck to my face. I thought he must have bitten through my face. I couldn't move. If I moved, a piece of skin with hair would be ripped from my face. From above, the landlord said, "Snake, oh snake. This is testing your endurance." I smelled sewage on the house mouse's body. He was so filthy, and yet the old man let him live in his home and run about as he pleased. All of a sudden, he let go of my face. I rubbed my face with my front claws. It wasn't too bad—he had probably just chewed a few tooth cavities. The odd thing was that this fiendish thing immediately fell over in front of me, his belly swollen and black blood running out of his mouth. He'd been poisoned! My body was hypertoxic! How come the old man's disinfectant hadn't worked? Had he really wanted to rid me of poison, or had he wanted to turn me into a hypertoxic substance and use me to poison the mouse?

He was sitting with his back to me. The view of his back resembled something I was familiar with. I gave it a lot of thought, and at last I figured out what he reminded me of: he was like the person-shaped rock in my hometown! It had come to the surface out of the mud and stood straight up in the center of the pasture. It was like a person, but it wasn't one. Many of my kin loved to run around it. "You mustn't stare at me all the time. I came from the pasture," he said without turning around. Lined up against the wall, my kin listened attentively. Now I saw that all of us had come from the pasture! I remembered the harsh climate, the crystal-clear blue sky, the summer which passed so quickly that it seemed unreal, the countless secrets concealed in the underbrush, the eagles circling in the sky all day without tiring . . . These recollections were killing me. I wished I could abandon my physical body and blend into that place . . . I had no idea how I could remember things that happened in the era of my great-grandfather's generation and even his father's. Those things could appear in my mind at any time and be compared with the shape my life had taken now. I knew that, even if it were possible to go back, I would be unable to adapt to that climate. More than half my kin died there every year just as early winter descended. If I were there, I'd surely be the first to die. There was no plague in the grasslands. You just felt bone-penetrating cold, and then your heart stopped beating. And so my kin didn't say someone had "died," but said someone had "chilled." Although I wasn't there, I remembered that black-tailed guy. He lay there facing up, watching the gray clouds massed above him, opening his mouth slightly, and not moving. He was as cold as ice—rigid. I remembered, too, that year after year, even though new kin were born, our numbers were decreasing. I didn't remember whether we had fled later. We must have. Otherwise, how could these kin here in the slums, including me, have arrived here? "Let me take the little mouse home, let me take the little mouse home, let me . . ." Auntie Shrimp kept saying this outside the door, but she didn't come in. Maybe she was afraid of the heat.

■

The slums were my home. This home wasn't exactly what I wanted: everything was difficult, and perils lurked at every turn. But this was the only home I had. My only option was to stay here. I used to have a homeland, but I couldn't go back to my homeland. It was useless to yearn for her. I stayed in these slums of mine: my eyes were turbid, my legs thin and weak, my innards poisoned over and over again. I endured, I endured. That gigantic eagle in the sky over my native place appeared in my mind—and brought me strength.

## OUR HUMAN NEIGHBORS

I'm a middle-aged male magpie who lives in the suburbs. Some tall poplars stand next to the primary school, and my home is set up in one of them. Originally my parents, brothers, and sisters, as well as my grandparents, lived here, but now they've all disappeared.

Let me tell you about my nest. Sturdy, beautiful, and symmetrical, my nest is something to be proud of. It's practical and stable, with an ingenious opening. It's particularly cozy inside. The outer layer is made of mud and grass, and the inner layer is made of fur and feathers. This dark, soft home gives us great happiness. Back then, my wife and I pulled together and worked hard to build this unusual nest. I fancied a certain attractive willow twig. It would serve as the best possible roof beam. Sure, it was heavy, but I was young, and I picked it up all at once in my beak. But just before I could fly to the sky with it, an urchin ran up and pounced on me with an iron-tipped bamboo pole. He hit me hard in the back. My beak relaxed its grip, and the twig fell to the ground. Even now, I can't figure out why he wanted it. And after he picked it up, he broke it in half and fiercely stuck the two parts into the mud. I was injured and had to stop working on the nest for the next ten days. During that time, my wife kept nagging me: "Don't irritate those people, don't irritate those people . . ." I was so ashamed. After that,

I didn't dare look for stuff near the primary school. I went over to a hill and carried wood materials back. It was a long way away, and sometimes this took a whole day. I would carry a load for a while and then rest a while. I admired my wife: she could always find suitable materials in our neighborhood. She was much more efficient than I. The main thing was that she had never provoked those people; I don't know how she had managed this.

In the end, we did finish the nest before winter. At that time, twenty-one magpie nests were built in these poplars, like babies born to the trees. I had compared all of them to ours. I felt that the nest my wife and I had built was the most impressive and its design the most ingenious. It was also much cozier than the others. Maybe we were congenitally different from the others and had a kind of innate skill? But my wife never thought of it in this way. For some reason, although our nest was well fortified, I felt uneasy, worried that people would shoot us. When I crouched there at night, I was afraid that some schoolboy would quietly climb the tree and smash our nest with a tool. I couldn't help feeling anxious; this was a consequence of my injury. Still, it turned out okay; our lives were tranquil and meaningful.

■

Now let me tell you about the small garden. Behind the school was a little garden that no one took care of. Wildflowers grew there — rhododendron, balsam, canna, gardenias. So many varieties! The soil was fertile, and an abandoned pool was filled with dried leaves. The little garden was where we foraged for food; it supported us. We often went there for meetings — we would have discussions as we hunted for food. We made an awful lot of noise. The sound of magpies is hard to take, but the monotonous language is full of warmth—and you can understand it if you only try.

A skinny woman often sat on a stone bench next to the pool staring at it blankly. I observed her for a long time: How were she and the pool connected? Had her children drowned in it? Or was she thinking of committing suicide by throwing herself into the pool? I thought her gaze was eerie. But my wife didn't think so. She said this woman was intellectual and sentimental. My wife's perception was always accurate. One time, I was searching for insects under the rhododendron. When I looked up, I saw that the woman had passed out and fallen off the stone bench. At the moment, no one else was there—not my wife and not our neighbors, either. I was extremely worried. I hopped onto the woman and screeched loudly, over and over. Later, she slowly regained consciousness. The first thing she did after she came to was to grab me. God, I'd never been captured before. I didn't move. My heart was beating like waves in a big river. She stood up slowly, took two steps, and knelt down next to the pool. The pool was full of water. What was she doing? She pushed me down in the water. I don't know how long it was before she threw me into the wildflowers and walked away. I recall that when I was in the water, I actually felt sort of lucky. I was drenched. When the wind blew, I shook from the cold. It was then that I finally realized that I hadn't died. I was still alive. And the several insects I had found were still beside me. I had to carry them back to the nest; my wife was sitting on her eggs at the time. I hastily mustered my energy, spread my wings, and let the wind blow the water away and dry my wings. I shouted to myself, "This is wonderful!"

My wife listened quietly to my story, her eyes shining with emotion. Later, baffled, she asked me, "It's impossible to understand what's going on in people's minds, isn't it?" I absolutely agreed with her. I certainly couldn't understand what I had just experienced. Afterward, I ran into this woman one more time. I couldn't help approaching her, but she didn't pay any attention to me.

■

I'd also like to tell you how my magpie relatives gradually faded away. It was really lively back then! First thing in the morning, our singing could be heard everywhere. Human beings thought that our language was too monotonous, too ear piercing, too intrusive. Wherever we gathered in large numbers, people glared. We were too self-absorbed. It was understandable that people reacted this way. To tell the truth, I didn't like it when we made too much noise, either, but as soon as we got together we couldn't control ourselves: everyone made a screeching sound. It was really unpleasant. How had we come up with this kind of language? I thought about this frequently, but I couldn't understand, no matter how hard I tried. When I was a child, I asked my father about it. He glared at me and told me to shut up. He said indignantly, "How dare you doubt your own species?" After that, I didn't dare ask anyone.

Our silhouettes were everywhere—in the little garden, on top of the nearby classrooms, and in the playground. Temperamentally, we were carefree birds. Why wouldn't we speak out loud? The weather was so good, there were insects to eat, more family members were constantly being hatched, there was entertainment everywhere, we had new games to play every day—we had millions of reasons to yell and make noise. The kids who chased us with bamboo brooms unexpectedly turned into our playthings, too. We teased them, and they held up their brooms and hit at us repeatedly. Their faces flushed as they struck out at us. They were annoyed. That was truly our golden age, the age of sunshine!

The school gardener was a woman more than fifty years old. She had small eyes and a sallow face, and often wore an artificial smile. She loved watching the children chase us. She raised her long arms and slapped them on her thighs, unable to contain her mirth. This disgusted me. She spent much of her time watching us, as if she had nothing better to do. I thought this was quite fishy. But she treated us well. She dug out the earth next to the shrubs with a hoe, exposing the insects to attract us.

Later, I noticed that it was because of this school gardener that some of us began disappearing. No one knew how they vanished; no one ever saw a magpie being hunted and killed. The plot was carried out quietly. Everyone except my wife and me thought highly of the school gardener. That assessment reminded me of what my wife thought of the skinny woman next to the pool. Could it be that people who were near magpies were all fond of killing? My father said that this woman "clearly understood the profound mysteries of the natural world." In Father's eyes, she was almost an irresistible spirit. And so Father sacrificed himself early.

It was a pleasant morning when Father and I went to the playground together. The ground was damp from an earlier shower, and from a distance we saw the school gardener digging there. I was touched, thinking that she was really considerate of us. We flew over and saw the school gardener remove her red-orange work hat and raise it to the sky when she stretched. She looked at us out of the corners of her eyes with a jeering expression. But that lasted only for a split second; then she put on a poker face. On the alert, I put some distance between her and me. As I looked for insects, I kept stealing glances at her. She was so hot that her body was radiating heat. I wanted to run over and peck at her butt! But Father wasn't the least bit alarmed by her. He followed close behind her, as if he were her pet. On the other side of the playground, children were shouting; they were apparently fighting. Several children fell to the ground, while another group continued fighting. I didn't like seeing bloody scenes, so I turned my back.

Later on, I ate too much and got sleepy. I lay down under a bush and dozed for a short time. When I woke up, Father was no longer there. The school gardener was gone, too. The red-orange hat had been placed on the bush. I thought Father had gone home, and so I flew back. But Father wasn't there.

The strange thing was that Mama knew Father had disappeared from the school gardener's side, yet she kept complaining that Father had "gone off to live a comfortable life alone." She was rather angry but not at all sad. I didn't understand why. I unintentionally mentioned the red-orange work hat to Mama. I didn't expect that Mama would grow excited:

"Oh, that's it! That hat! Oh, that's it! That hat! Oh . . ."

She screeched on and on—repeatedly making the same irrelevant point. All I could do was leave.

Later, when I told my wife about this, her reply was also irrelevant. This was the first time I had felt alone.

My wife, however, said something that made me uneasy. She said, "You need to take better care of your mama."

I felt she was implying more than she said, and so I had to be more careful just in case.

The next day, I went to the school again. The school gardener was still weeding and acting as if nothing had happened. I put a lot of distance between us. In the entire morning, only a few neighbors came by. My ma didn't show up at all.

When I went home near evening, my wife told me that my ma had disappeared.

"But I was watching the school gardener the whole time!"

"You're really set in your ways," my wife reproached me.

My wife didn't tell me what she had guessed, but I thought she knew what was going on. Sure enough, three days later, as we were at the door to our nest watching the sun set, she said, "There are all kinds of ways to play the game. You have a one-track mind."

I didn't utter a word. She was right: in fact, I wasn't good at considering all angles. I couldn't imagine where my mother might have gone. I had perched here for ages. Crossing over to the other side of the school enclosure would be out of our domain. If we saw a confused guy fly to the west side of the department store, we would be almost frightened to death. Of course, no one would try such foolish things except for one crazy bird. Sure enough, he had never returned. But Mama hadn't gone crazy; she was always clear-headed. Still, my wife was quite good at predictions, but she wouldn't repeat them to anyone.

A few days later, one of our neighbors in the next tree went missing. That was a stretch of scary days: after three months, only ten birds in our clan were left—and that included our two children. That's when my eyesight began blurring. Time after time, I saw overlapping images everywhere. Even when I looked at my children, I didn't see two of them but six of them. Only when I looked at my wife did I see just one image. As for the neighbors, they became a large flock of countless things. And so I still felt surrounded by an enormous clan. My wife was happy that I felt this way; she didn't want me to feel downcast because of loneliness.

But one noon, they all disappeared, leaving only my wife and me. I stood on a branch of the poplar and saw a lot of children and some adults running around, all grasping long bamboo poles and shouting. Even I—a magpie who was not very nimble—could sense disaster coming. My wife laughed grimly. Not seeming to mind in the least, she was pecking at a hole on the branch, as though investigating whether something was escaping from the inside. Suddenly, I began to suspect that I was seeing a hallucination produced by my double vision. When I asked my wife about this, she calmly answered, "That's it. It's a hallucination. However, an urchin is climbing the tree; he's destroying our neighbor's home. He's efficient with his tools."

The whole tree was swaying, and I didn't dare go over to watch. I said to my wife, "Let's fly away."

"No." She said resolutely, "We'll go home."

"Why go home now? He probably intends to smash our home, too. We have no way to defend ourselves from humans."

But my wife was going home, and I'd better stay close to her and get into the nest.

Snuggling up to each other, we shivered at the door of our home. I heard her heart thumping. How strange this was: her heart was in her chest, and yet I could hear it; my heart was in my chest, and yet I couldn't hear it at all! At this moment, my vision was very clear; I saw no overlapping images. I saw that red-orange work hat. It wasn't an urchin just now. It was the school gardener. She climbed up until she came face to face with us.

My wife inclined her head, as though flames were shooting

from that person's eyes. She said to me, "This is truly surprising: I saw your mother in her eyes."

Nothing happened. She clumsily and slowly descended, and our gaze followed her into the distance. Why did she have to destroy our neighbors' nest? It had been abandoned long ago. Was she threatening us?

That night, my wife and I felt terribly lonely: we buried our heads in each other's wings, and we each sensed a deep cavity in the other's body. But after just a day passed, both of us felt stronger. We even went so far as to fly to the playground and wait for her to appear, but the school gardener didn't show up again.

■

Okay, let me talk some more about those people. There were more and more people, and they built houses along the little roads in front of and behind the school. Originally, there had been only two thatched cottages here, which seemed to belong to two school janitors. Now there were at least fifty houses with tile roofs. The residents were people whose identities were unclear. They didn't like to talk, and their faces were expressionless. In the morning, each of them went out carrying a bag; men and women dressed the same. I had stopped over on their eaves and heard the din they made inside. They often came to blows inside the house, sometimes even breaking the windows and frightening me. But as soon as they went out, they turned taciturn and melancholy. I wondered what kind of work they did. Were they under a lot of pressure?

My intuition told me that these people were hostile to us, and I said to my wife, "You were right to tell me not to provoke those people."

It didn't occur to me that my wife would say, "These people aren't the same as the people from before. We should get in touch with them."

I had always respected my wife; many of the things she said to me were predictions which were realized later. Then how was I to understand what she was saying now?

I perched on the tile roofs and watched them and eaves-dropped on their conversations, and when they flung the bags they were carrying onto the tables at outdoor bars, I went so far as to fly over right away and rummage in their bags. But my cleverness in such trivial matters didn't do any good: I didn't discover anything, and I had no idea what I should do to "get in touch with them."

I noticed that the way my wife treated these people was neither servile nor overbearing. She often went to the ditches near their homes to grab insects to eat. Sometimes she perched on their doors and watched cockfights.

"Their passion for life went up a notch today," she reported excitedly to me.

But as I saw it, they didn't have any passion for life. They merely had a kind of unusual pastime: to shut the door and fight (maybe it was a quarrel; I couldn't get a good look at what was going on inside). What did my wife mean by their passion?

"You're really getting old. Didn't you notice that they're consuming more and more kerosene in their oil lamps?"

"What oil lamps?"

"The ones that light their homes at night."

Measuring the level of passion for life by the consumption of oil in the lamps? All at once, I got it. My wife was remarkable! Just think: these glum people were exhausted from working all day in the city. After eating and cleaning up, they lay down and went to sleep: that certainly didn't count as feeling passionate about life. But now, they lit the oil lamps at home and engaged in all kinds of activities (I don't know exactly what activities). Sure enough, this was a huge change!

To verify this, my wife and I furtively flew over to the rooftops and squatted there. We heard explosive sounds ringing out of every house. Sometimes, bullets even flew out of their windows and whizzed in the air. Hearing all this, my wife and I were both frightened and excited. We wanted to fly away, and yet we also wanted to stay here longer . . . oh, what exciting nights those were! Wine bottles dropping and breaking! Oh, the odd cries unlike human sounds!

After we returned home, my wife said, "We're really lucky." I remember that when she said this, we were distinctly aware that a huge monster had climbed our tree, and our nest was shaking violently. This had never happened before. My wife and I were thinking the same thing: this was revenge for our having eavesdropped on their indoor activities. In that moment, we could have flown away, but for some reason we didn't move. We trembled in the nest, hoping that the thing would descend quickly.

Later, something happened. We passed out, but we didn't die. We were shaken out of the nest and fell to the ground. What kind of fierce beast was this?

"It's the school gardener," my wife said.

"Impossible!" I shouted. "The school gardener is just an old woman. How could she be so heavy? That thing is like an elephant. Look! The old poplar tree has been crushed and three branches were broken!"

My wife said nothing. She was deep in thought, her expression absentminded.

Maybe it really was the school gardener. Her hat had fallen under the tree. Maybe she was a shapeshifter.

I flew several times toward the playground, but didn't see her. Probably she had really retired.

Our nest sustained a little damage, but we repaired it. The people living in the tile houses were quiet in the daytime: they went into the city quietly and returned quietly. On weekends, the women washed clothes, and the men dug some holes behind the houses, but we didn't see them sow any seeds. My wife eventually joined them. Strutting, she landed on their table and on their stove. I shivered for her.

These people still acted viciously toward me. When I tried to get close to them, they looked as if they were saying there was no need for me to exist in this world. I despaired.

I began to miss the skinny woman from the pool in the small garden. Where had she gone? How could she have disappeared without a trace? She evidently wasn't a teacher in the school, and she wasn't part of this group of people. Could it be that she lived in the city?

In the middle of the night, the houses caught fire, perhaps because someone had made too much of a disturbance and knocked over an oil lamp, igniting something flammable. This seemed the most likely to me. It was a magnificent sight: my wife and I perched on a poplar twig and took it all in. The conflagration turned half the sky red; even the school classrooms were illuminated. How could the fire be so big? It was as if people had dumped a large quantity of kerosene into the fire. Even harder to understand was that no one escaped. We didn't see even one person on the road. My wife and I smelled scorched flesh. We were shaking. For some reason, we had an urge to fly into the fire, but we restrained ourselves.

An hour passed, and then another hour. The fire was still roaring. What was happening? The fire kept changing. At first, it was golden yellow, then red, and at last—three or four hours later—an eerie greenish-blue. I don't know where the flames came from, soaring so high. I suddenly had an idea: I was so scared that I fell down under the tree, because my whole body was paralyzed.

"I know what you're thinking," my wife said softly beside me. "I'm thinking the same thing. It must be corpses that are burning. What else could it be?"

I was speechless. I saw the raging flames and unexpectedly felt like crying. Was I really sympathizing with those people? Of course not: they didn't need sympathy from me. I was nothing but a magpie. I moved alone slowly toward the nest. And so we endured a terrifying night—I staying in the nest, my wife staying outside.

Not until the sun was high in the sky did my wife and I leave our nest. We flew over to the houses that lay in ruins. The fire had gone out earlier, yet traces of smoke were still visible. We jumped into the houses whose windows and doors had been incinerated, but they were vacant inside: there was no furniture, nor were there any people. My wife let out a loud sigh: "These people were so refreshing!"

In fact, that's what I thought, too, but I had never been able to express it as precisely as she did.

People wouldn't live here again for a long time. I was depressed.

When my wife and I flew over to the public toilet, we saw a familiar figure. That's right: it was the school gardener. She was scooping out the holes the men had dug; these holes covered the entire area of residences on this street. She focused on loosening the mud in the holes with a rake. We furtively flew behind her to have a look. What we saw was inconceivable: inserted into each hole were several white bones—some big, some small. They stood like mushrooms.

I was stunned. I couldn't help but screech. The old woman had turned toward me. As soon as she saw me, I calmed down. She looked both startled and admiring. Evidently, my reaction wasn't as bad as it could have been; she seemed to understand me. And, surprisingly, my wife's expression was exactly the same as hers!

Ha-ha—Is the story I've told today long enough? I'll stop here and continue tomorrow.

## THE OLD CICADA

A heatwave rolled into the city, and reports of elderly heat-stroke victims streamed in continually. Sirens wailed, and pet dogs lay panting in the shade.

It was much better in the suburbs, where tall poplars and willows provided shade. All day long, cicadas sang in the trees. After it rained, toads chimed in with their bass voices. The numerous sparrows and magpies leapt lightheartedly among the branches and in the thickets. All of them affectionately shared their food, with only occasional brief clashes. Magpie couples were living on the crowns of a few old sky-skimming poplars. A little lower was the cicadas' paradise. Not far away were picturesque multistory buildings. The cicadas sang continuously, never interrupted by the glum people going in and out of these buildings. Their loud singing was proud, intense, and aggressive, filled with the high spirits prompted by the summer heat. It's true that some people were deeply annoyed by these singers. They glared with hatred at the old poplar tree above the bicycle shed. But what could they do? Year after year, the cicadas had a symbiotic relationship with the poplars and willows. The cicadas could be destroyed only if you cut down all the large trees. And if you did that, the temperature of the residential district would rise many degrees. The cicadas didn't know this. They sang from an excess of enthusiasm — because of love, because of the urge to procreate. They drank their fill of the sap generously provided by the large trees and found the blazing heat wonderful. Especially when the humidity rose, the thickening layers of clouds hinted at a certain ancient memory, and they burst into song. Their leader was generally the elderly cicada squatting on the highest branch. The other cicadas admired him greatly, and even the magpie couples listened attentively to his song. Before long, the chorus rose like surging waves and occupied the sky above.

The old cicada, whose body was both dark and bright, had sturdy wings, but seldom used them. He always stayed in the same place — the strong branch a little below the magpies' nest. He was a loner, immersed in memories. He had stayed underground for a long time — precisely eight years, according to the magpie couple. Everyone knew he was very old. Still, his energy hadn't diminished. But why was he so solitary? Was he still living in his memories, sensing neither the fellows all around nor the vast blue sky? Cicadas seldom live underground for eight years. That time had completely shaped his character.

He was an old bachelor who'd never had a love life. After eight years, he had emerged from under the ground, climbed up the tree, and assumed his present form. Everyone felt that he was extraordinary.

It was an extremely hot and humid day. Even in the suburbs, people were sweltering. Air conditioners buzzed, and people were light-headed. Going outside was like plunging into a huge oven. The corner of the bicycle shed on one side was cooler, but because of the intense sunlight and the still air, the large trees still seemed tense, and the old bachelor just stayed where he was. His thoughts entered a place beyond his colony. He felt a little sentimental and a little distracted. He quietly lifted his right leg, and suddenly heard a jumble of singing all around. The racket surprised him a little, because he had never paid attention to this singing. He lowered his head and thought. And then, faltering and stumbling, he began to sing. He thought that his song was a little different this time. Everyone else stopped singing. His voice seemed strange even to him, yet he went on with even less restraint. As soon as he stopped singing, the chorus between heaven and earth rose. The old bachelor almost fainted. Of course he didn't feel ill. Quite the opposite: he was extremely moved and joyful.

This was how he became the cantor. And although he was the cantor, he was still a loner. He didn't talk with anyone and closed himself off.

He knew that some of the residents here wanted to get rid of him. Some people lingered at the foot of the tree for a long time, eyeing his branch. And a young kid always aimed a precisely calibrated slingshot at him. The pellets had whizzed by him many times — and each time the old bachelor felt empty inside. He didn't know how to avoid humans' hostility, for he had never avoided anything. He was still calm as he led the chorus. It was only when a pellet flew by that he suddenly stopped for a second. Then, once more, he continued. There were so many of his kind, and all of them listened respectfully to him and followed him. How could he slack off? When he thought of the colony, his golden legs and belly emitted dazzling white light, and he would grow very excited. At such times, people would mistake him for a meteor.

There were so many cicadas in the courtyard in this apartment complex, and people didn't welcome their singing. But they felt entitled to sing under the beautiful sky. They wouldn't change for humans. Trees—both large and small—were immersed in their passionate singing. The trees voluntarily provided the cicadas with food; they loved these little living things. Although the old bachelor didn't interact with his fellows, he felt anxious about their future. From his perch, the highest, he scanned the area and saw their silhouettes in the massed green leaves. He felt that they trusted this secular existence and were content with it. Yet this was precisely his greatest worry, though he had no way to transmit it to the others. Singing was the only way he could communicate with them. From the beginning, he had been strict and cautious, never talking with anyone. He was stately, admired by the younger ones. His branch was his alone. From the time he began leading the chorus, everyone had loved him, but none dared approach him, much less discuss anything with him.

From that branch, he could see in all directions. He had been aware of the spider for a long time, and this discovery certainly didn't make him happy. In the corner of the bicycle shed, the spider had spun a large web between the eaves and an old wall. On the other side of the wall was a storage room heaped with blurry indeterminate gray things. Most of the time, the old spider hid behind the storage room's wooden window frame. When his quarry was caught in the web, he would pounce like lightning and do away with the victim in fewer than thirty seconds. Insect remains were scattered under the gloomy gray web. Inside the victim were flies, ladybugs, grasshoppers, and other insects. Occasionally, there were cicadas, too. The old bachelor had already seen one of his fellows murdered. He would remember that as long as he lived. He was depressed for two days. He even flew to the willow tree next to the shed and looked carefully at the remains on the ground. While he was doing that, he thudded to the ground. Then he stood up and slowly circled the pile of things. It was like mourning, and it was like a search. When he flew away, the air he fanned like a small whirlybird echoed heavily. The spider behind the wooden window frame inclined its head, thinking about this mystery, and reached no conclusion.

The old toad finally died at the hands of the kid with the sling-shot. It was raining a little that day. Beneath its large stone, the toad poured out its memories of love. This disturbed the entire apartment complex for most of the night. At sunrise, the toad was still filled with so much ardor that it actually jumped to the foot of the tree. Three pellets in a row hit and killed it. The youngster cheered and took away its carcass. The cicadas could not comprehend why, though they had heard of people eating toads. Even so, the old bachelor didn't think the toad's fate was a sad one. Someone who had been so passionate all night long must have experienced genuine blessings. The cicada's song became clearer and lighter. The other cicadas were a little surprised, and then they cheered up. After the rain, the chorus was irresistible.

The spider's huge web caught two more cicadas, inexperienced young explorers. The old bachelor watched the spider deal with them like lightning. But the victims couldn't have suffered too much, since the spider's poison was very strong.

The old bachelor made strange, broken sounds in the direction of his fellow cicadas. But he remained aloof. His fellows could understand only his singing, so no one responded. A young female cicada fell into the web; the old bachelor heard her brief, distinct moans, and fell into a trance for days: What did her moans really mean? Sometimes, he thought it was suffering; sometimes, he thought it was not only suffering but also a certain kind of extreme excitement. Could the female cicada have sought her own destruction? He felt numb all over. He saw the leering youth approach. He dodged, and the pellet whizzed past him. When he'd encountered this in the past, he'd been calm. But this time he agonized.

Why was he drawn to the slingshot? Had he felt this temptation in the past or had it come upon him just now? He tried to call out. Once, twice, three times—his voice was stiff and dry. Not one person noticed this. Even the youth with the slingshot was only briefly distracted, and then he walked away indifferently. The old bachelor was ashamed. In order to understand the temptation, he stopped singing for three days and let himself drift. He slept and awakened, awakened and slept, and he always heard the call of the toad that the youth had killed. Its calls were shockingly loud. Each time he opened his eyes, he saw dazzling light flashing between heaven and earth. It made him dizzy, and he had to close his eyes. Ah. How could the toad be so strong? When he closed his eyes, he even saw the old toad approach him, as if it wanted to pass on to him a mysterious affection. Its protruding eyes seemed extremely eager. When he opened his eyes, the toad had vanished.

It was raining. Still dazed, the bachelor didn't hear the thunder, nor was he aware of the heavy rain falling on him. He didn't know how much time had passed when the southeast wind carried the indistinct sounds of the old toad and his fellow cicadas' singing. It was strange, he thought, that the two different songs could harmonize. It was even stranger when he considered that it hadn't stopped raining, so where were they singing? As he listened more attentively, he thought the singing was coming from between deep layers of clouds. When he looked through the curtain of rain, he saw that the old spider on the wooden window frame was also absorbed in looking at the rain. He seemed to see himself in the old spider's manner.

◾

The remains under the spiderweb attracted the residents of the complex. The old bachelor's remains were quite unusual. Although they had already broken into four pieces, if you reassembled the pieces, it was still a complete cicada—and his body was twice the size of ordinary cicadas. But his head had vanished. What sort of fierce fight had taken place?

The spider had vanished, too. The youth had seen the spider, and he looked for it behind the wooden window frame, but found no trace of it. He thought to himself, Could they have died together? Where had the cicada's head gone?

The cicadas' chorus rose again. The young cantor's voice was jerky and faltering. He sang hesitantly for a short while and then stopped, and the whole chorus slumped into silence. Then this unusually prolonged silence was broken abruptly by an enthusiastic chorus like the surf. It had never been silent before. Was this silence an awakening? All the cicadas turned their gaze toward that high branch. A grotesque old cicada stood in that familiar place. Everyone saw the gigantic head and the disproportionately small body. It was he: he had struggled to come back. He had grown another body and was concentrating on developing that body. His fellow cicadas knew that if he put his mind to it, he would succeed.

Then what was the significance of his body breaking apart? Maybe in those split seconds, he was demonstrating this to his opponent, and letting the sense of ultimate emptiness deflate its arrogance? Or the opposite: Was he regarding the spider as his witness, and would he reveal to it the secret of rebirth? Some young cicadas inspected below the spiderweb. They were thinking to themselves that no matter what kind of fight it was, it veiled a frightening suicidal instinct. They thought it was heroic and moving, and they also found it quite stimulating.

The old cicada didn't have time to complete growing his new body before the season changed. He squatted unmoving on the branch all day long. He dreamed of tender leaves, of flower petals, of the tadpoles in the ditches and the water lilies in the mountain ponds. Since he had lost his amplifier, he had no way to communicate his ardor to the other cicadas, but in the last days before the chill of autumn, he sensed an unusual happiness every day. He could see whatever he wanted to see. Without even turning his head, he saw the newly arrived pair of magpies cavorting in the small garden. Sometimes, he would also think of the spider, and when he did, his new little legs would exude some poisonous juices, and he would weakly call out. He was murmuring, "Who is the spider? Isn't it simply me . . . ?"

He became cemented to that branch.

The autumn wind destroyed the spiderweb and blew away the old cicada's remains. At last the sweltering heat subsided. The lonely poplar leaves took on a nostalgic yellow color. Now only the magpies and sparrows were still singing. They sang brokenly, off and on, artlessly, forgettably. What those old poplars remembered was the majestic, splendid chorus. Sometimes when the chilly wind blew in, they couldn't help humming a little, but—startled by their own voices—they returned to their silence and their daydreaming. The youth with the slingshot passed by under the poplars, his expression complicated by his bizarre thoughts.

## THE SWAMP

There actually was a swamp right in this big concrete forest of a city. Older people could still remember it. Ayuan wasn't old, but he knew of the swamp from hearing Uncle Sang talk about it occasionally.

One night after drinking too much, Uncle Sang was about to fall asleep as he sprawled over a big square table. Ayuan was chatting excitedly with the waiter about going into a small business together, when Uncle Sang sat up straight and started shaking Ayuan's arm. He yelled, "You have to be broad-minded in order to see the bigger picture! Everything I told you before was true! We mustn't let superficial things blur our vision . . . You, Liuma: you're a waiter here, but you're a schemer; you're too ambitious, and you aren't broad-minded. Why are you tugging at me? I have to get it all out; there won't be another chance!" He flung Ayuan's hand off.

In the blink of an eye, Liuma vanished. Waving an arm, Uncle Sang shouted, "He's gone into hiding! This schemer—he's gone off to hide in a place you would never think of!"

It took all of Ayuan's strength to drag Uncle Sang out of the bar. They turned into a long alley; Uncle Sang's home was at the end of the alley.

That evening, all the lights in the alley were out. Ayuan groped his way ahead in the dark. Uncle Sang stopped walking and grabbed hold of a streetlight.

"Damn you. Where are you taking me?"

"Your home. It's just ahead."

"I want to go to the swamp. That's where Liuma is hiding. You're panicky, aren't you? You've never heard of that place, have you? I'm telling you: the swamp is ahead on the right, under the Grand Theater! Take a look at those two stars: they've risen from the swamp."

Ayuan looked up: two stars really were stuck to the wall of that high structure. They weren't neon lights; they were real stars, glittering brightly. How could stars be on the wall? Two tall figures approached—Uncle Sang's two moody sons. They dragged him home, one supporting him on each side. Their footsteps sounded as if they were trampling through concrete.

Ayuan counted the days. Twenty-four days had passed since that night. He'd been exploring clues to the swamp all along. One night, he and an old trash collector were squatting in a small shed in a shantytown that would soon be demolished. The shed didn't even have a chair, much less a kerosene lamp.

"Listen, they're coming in!" the old guy said.

"What?"

"Piglets. They're a bunch of spiritual creatures, going from door to door."

Ayuan heard the pigs' breath and stretched out a hand to touch them—and felt their drenched and warm bodies. There were five or six of them. Slimy and sour-smelling, they were presumably very dirty. Coming into physical contact with them made Ayuan happy.

"They're from the swamp. They're the only ones who can go

back and forth frequently. If an ordinary person goes there just once, he'll end up half-dead from exhaustion, but they go back and forth . . ."

"Can you tell me how to get there? I don't mind exerting myself."

"No one can tell you. Something like this can't be taught."

"Is it under the theater?"

"Yes. And also under the playgrounds and each and every building. In ancient times, this city of ours was a swamp. Now it's only these piglets that can locate the road that runs through there. But tonight they've come back, so you'd better wait for another opportunity."

The old guy had stood up and gone outside. The piglets huddled around Ayuan for warmth. As Ayuan petted them, he felt a deep sense of brotherly affection. Leaning against the wall, he sat on a board and let the piglets wriggle around his legs. He planned to keep his eyes on these piglets and follow them to the place where he longed to go. After a while, he fell asleep. Halfway through the night, the piglets made a ruckus when two people entered the room. But the people, who seemed to be beggars, left soon, and the piglets clustered around Ayuan again.

When he awakened at dawn, the piglets were gone, leaving no trace of their ever having been in the room. Ayuan recalled what the old trash collector had said: "They're a bunch of spiritual creatures, going from door to door."

Another night, when Ayuan was in a brothel, the prostitute named Fragrance whispered to him, "Ayuan, if you die so young, what will people think?"

"I never said I was planning to die," Ayuan retorted.

"Maybe not, but you're acting like someone who will die tomorrow."

"You're mistaken, Fragrance. I still haven't gone to the swamp. Why would I want to die?"

As soon as he mentioned the swamp, Fragrance looked blank. She stole quietly out of the bed and sat to one side.

She told Ayuan to pay up.

Handing her some money, Ayuan left her room without a word and walked out of the brothel.

Much to his surprise, when he looked back, the brothel had retreated into the distance and was separated from him by a vast wasteland. In the wasteland, several birds were making bloodcurdling calls. Was this the swamp? No, it wasn't. He heard cars starting up, and a car was driving over from the wasteland. And then another car drove past. Ayuan thought, The brothel is in the suburbs. He had never noticed there was such a large wasteland.

A car stopped beside him, and Uncle Sang's tall younger son got out.

"Get in. I'll give you a lift," he said.

The car sped to the city center. It was after midnight. Looking out the window, Ayuan saw that the entire city was dark; even the streetlights were off. He didn't dare ask where they were going, but inwardly he was secretly hoping.

"We're here," the younger son said softly.

Ayuan got out, and the car took off at once.

At the side of the road, he gazed around for a while: he could see the supermarket and the movie theater. As if emerging from the underground, a scalper appeared in front of him. Ayuan was so startled that he shivered.

"Want a ticket?"

He paid and walked unsteadily into the movie theater.

A crocodile took up all the space on the screen. You couldn't see the background or hear any sound. You could see only close-ups of every part of its body projected over and over again. It was boring. Ayuan sensed that the place was full. An old woman sitting next to him whispered, "Do you want to see *Night in the Swamp*? I can take you to see it."

Crouching, they made their way out, Ayuan following close behind the old woman.

Before they had walked very far, the old woman sat down on a wall outside the theater. She said, "I'm out of breath. I can't stand being even a little keyed up. Why are you standing? Sit down. You're blocking my view."

Ayuan sat down and took hold of the bony hand she extended.

Just then, they heard noise from the theater: a battle seemed to be starting on the screen. Someone shouted hysterically.

"When we parted beside the hot springs, both of us knew it was forever," she said abruptly.

"Who?"

"My lover and I. Actually, how could anyone think it was a hot spring? It was merely the swamp, that's all. The sun shone all day, and the sunbaked water was hot. I was actually afraid of leeches— wasn't that ridiculous? I learned a lot at that place. I think it's located at—"

"Located where?"

"Nowhere. No one place is right." She forced a smile. "But that's where I was from. See, I'm missing two fingers on this hand because they were damaged by leeches. When you sat down just now in the theater, I knew what you were looking for. You found the right person."

"So can you take me there?"

"Where? That place no longer exists. It disappeared. It's gone, just as my fingers are. Only two empty spots remain."

"Tell me about 'the night in the swamp' that you and your lover experienced."

"We did have a night like that, but I can't remember it. It's only some specks in my memory."

Ayuan stroked her hand, the one missing two fingers; he wanted to ask her some more questions, and yet he would rather let her talk of these things on her own.

"At this hour of the night, I can see far into the distance. If no one blocks me, I can see as far as the borderland. Although I have those specks in my memory, I don't care at all. Look, that crocodile is looking up."

"Please continue."

The old woman's head drooped to her chest, and she made no sound. Ayuan shook her twice, but she still didn't move. Ayuan stood up and looked ahead, but nothing lay in that direction. Only the dark night. In the theater, a beast roared, probably a tiger.

Ayuan left the entrance to the theater and walked aimlessly ahead. He was a little uneasy. He thought that just now, when he was with the old woman at the entrance to the theater, he must have gone to the swamp. He simply couldn't see it. Tomorrow night, he would go somewhere else and try again to find it.

.

He went to the bar again, but didn't see Liuma there. Liuma was on vacation. A young woman with big eyes was taking his place. She looked agonized.

She sat down and asked Ayuan to buy her a drink. Her mind was somewhere else while she stared at the wineglass.

"They put too much pressure on him," she said.

"Do you mean Liuma?" Ayuan asked nervously.

"No, I mean myself. I always refer to myself as 'he.' Although this is a little frightening to 'him,' it also has an advantage, for 'he' can go all out in struggles. Back in my home village, this isn't unusual. If a person goes all out in struggling with a crocodile, the person is likely to win."

"What time is it now?"

"Two o'clock in the afternoon."

"It was night when I arrived. Why am I still here?"

"You're the one who's been hanging around. These empty bottles are all yours."

"Who are those folks?" he asked, pointing at two sneaky people wearing white straw hats.

"Lower your voice a little. They're outsiders who raise turtles. They arrived in the morning and they've been waiting for you ever since."

Ayuan stood up, excited, and walked over to them.

Flustered, one of them stuffed something into his bag.

"Hello! I'm ready to go with you now," Ayuan said.

The two of them exchanged glances and smiled. One after the other, they walked out of the bar. Ayuan noticed that they were dark and emaciated. They looked like mountain people. Did they raise turtles on the mountain?

The young woman accompanied him to the door and whispered, "What they raise isn't turtles, it's a kind of scorpion that lives in water."

The three of them walked in the old part of the city—in and out of small winding alleys. They walked a long way, and Ayuan became fidgety. He wondered if they were trying to confuse him. Ayuan used to be familiar with the old part of town. But he hadn't been there for a long time, and the flagstone paths and two-story wooden buildings made him feel like a stranger. At last, they stopped in front of a three-story red brick building with a sign saying, "Wedding Photos." Ayuan was certain he'd never been here before.

After entering the photography studio, the mountain people said they had to go to the toilet. They left Ayuan behind.

The photographer had a mouthful of black teeth, and his gaze was sharp as a knife. Under the light, a girl heavily made up with white powder and wearing a flashy red satin gown sat motionless as she posed.

"Could you please carry on a conversation with this bride? She doesn't look animated enough," the photographer said to Ayuan.

Just as Ayuan was about to ask the bride something, to his surprise she spoke first.

"How did you happen to find this place? It's a secret spot, and if no one brought you here, no way you'd have gotten in! You're in luck. Maybe you can even see the great escape! Who brought you here?"

"Two people who raise turtles," Ayuan said.

"Oh, I see. The two scumbags!" the new bride said through her teeth.

The photographer pressed the shutter and shouted, "Perfect!"

The door creaked, and the two mountain people entered. The bride's face was instantly devoid of expression. She sat there unmoving, like a puppet.

Ayuan kept staring at her face. The more he gazed at her, the more familiar she looked. Who was she? She was here alone having her wedding photo taken. Where was the bridegroom? The mountain person with the droopy eyes spoke up.

"You think she looks familiar, don't you? All the people who live here seem to look familiar. At first, I wasn't used to this. I come here often. This young woman lives next to the White Sands Well— in the house with a copper bell on the door."

Frowning and waving his hand, the photographer said, "All of you get out of here. Leave, will you? The bride isn't in a good mood. I can't photograph her now!"

The mountain people stuck their tongues out and glided away. Ayuan stood there blankly, still thinking to himself, Who is she? The bride continued sitting like a puppet.

"Huh? What are you waiting for? If you don't leave soon, you won't find the exit!" the photographer urged him.

As if wandering in a dream, Ayuan walked out of the photography studio. The corridor was so long that he couldn't see the end of it. For a while, he walked ahead without thinking. Then he turned to the right, hoping to see the exit. He bumped into someone; that wasn't the exit, but the corner of the staircase. The person he had bumped into was the bride—still in the red satin gown. The ice-cold satin looked inauspicious and frightened Ayuan.

"Ayuan, don't go," she said. Her voice had become thin and feeble.

"How did you know my name?"

"Those two people told me. Now you can't go out. They brought you in and never intended to let you leave. This is a large place; you mustn't wander around aimlessly. Let's sit on the stairs and wait for nightfall."

"Is it dangerous here?"

"Yes. Hurry up and sit down."

Ayuan smelled the powder on her face.

"Are you going to be married soon?" he asked.

"Married?" She began laughing. "No way. I'll never get married."

Ayuan heard footsteps on the stairs and twisted his head to look, but it was like a black hole above.

"Is there a photography studio upstairs, too?" Ayuan asked. He spoke louder than usual to boost his courage.

Without answering, the bride looked reproachfully at him.

The footsteps continued down. Ayuan had to take another look. He saw a black bear paw. The bear paw stopped where it was and didn't move.

Cold sweat ran down Ayuan's back. He didn't dare breathe.

The bride looked contemptuous and sneered. She wasn't the least bit afraid. Ayuan felt really ashamed. To cover up his cowardice, he asked her again, "What's upstairs?"

"The swamp," she said.

"Oh! Can we go up there?"

"When it's dark. But in any case, you can't leave now, so just be patient."

Before long, it was dark, and Ayuan could see nothing. Then he realized that the bride was no longer beside him. He had no idea whether she had gone upstairs or slipped out of the corridor. But the bear was now going up and down the stairs, making a ghastly noise.

Leaving the stairs, Ayuan reached the gloomy corridor. A faint light shone at the far end of the corridor, but from where he stood he could see only a glimmer of light. He wanted to move toward it, and he also wanted to go upstairs to see the swamp. He couldn't make up his mind.

Someone in a certain room asked, "Who is it? Who's there?"

"Me. Ayuan."

"Are you the dealer who buys kraits?"

"No. I'm a mason."

"Get out of here. The great escape is about to start. Don't block the road!"

Ayuan stood pressed against the wall, hoping that his corporeal self would disappear.

The bride returned. As the two of them stood in the dark against the wall, the bride softly recounted her story.

Originally, she was to have married after another week, but one day the bridegroom had insisted on taking her to a park in the suburbs.

At the artificial lake, a large fish was hanging around in the shallow water next to the shore. It began raining, and the two of them slid down the bank. Only after they were in the lake did they find out that it wasn't shallow but instead was very deep, and the water was filled with aquatic plants. The bridegroom dragged her down. Entangled in the aquatic plants, she couldn't move; she could only sink farther. But she kicked off the plants, broke away from her bridegroom, and clambered up to the bank.

"It was spooky. You can't imagine such temptation."

"It doesn't matter. What happened, happened," Ayuan comforted her.

"What?"

"What I mean is that you're still alive. In the future—"

"Didn't you understand my story? What you mean is certainly not what I mean! God, why have I kept talking with you all along? How could you ever understand me? Impossible!"

Ayuan felt apologetic and embarrassed. She was right: he didn't understand anything about her. This was partly because he hadn't yet been in love, but also because his experiences were only shallow. He tried his best, but he couldn't share the emotions this girl beside him felt.

They fell silent for a while, and then the bride couldn't help herself: she began talking again.

"The more you struggle to get untangled from those weeds, the more tightly they wind around you. While I was underwater, I even heard him laughing! *Coo coo, coo coo*—a really bizarre laugh. And his face . . ."

"Yet you did struggle free." Ayuan's voice deepened.

"I did, but how could I kick him away? I'll never forget the scene down there. I'll go upstairs first. You wait here and don't move. I'll call you."

Her blurry figure left him. Ayuan remembered the black bear and thought, It must be a circus bear.

Now, except for one sound, everything was quiet. The gurgling sound of bubbles rose from the pool. From the beginning, Ayuan had noticed this sound, but there was no pool outside the building, and so the sound was absurd. Could the sound be coming down from upstairs? the sound of bubbles in the swamp? It wasn't at all like that. The sound definitely came from outside the building.

Ayuan waited a long time, his legs aching from standing, but the bride didn't call him. The photographer did come, however. His feet thumping, he flew down the stairs and arrived quickly at Ayuan's side. His breath smelled bad as he approached Ayuan and started talking. He touched Ayuan's head with one hand.

"I thought so, it's you. You're still here. Generally, we don't let people spend the night here. You played a little trick in order to stay here, didn't you? Do you want to learn the secrets of our trade? You're too ambitious!"

"Right now, I just want to go home," Ayuan said in disgust.

"You're free to go. No one's stopping you!"

"I can't get out. Where's the door?"

"It's right behind you. Give the door a push. Harder! That's it!"

The photographer pushed Ayuan out from the wall.

He stood in a small alley in the old part of the city. The houses on both sides of the alley were shut. Once more, he heard bubbles gurgling and rising from the pool—this time, more frequently than before. He started running, thinking that he had to run out of this alley before he would reach a familiar road.

"Ayuan—Ayuan!!"

Ayuan turned around and looked: the bright red satin gown was gleaming under the streetlight. The face of that ghostlike woman was whiter than plaster. He felt that the end of the world was upon him and began running for his life. At last he exited the alley. He turned once, and then again, and looked back: no one was following him. Only then did he slow his steps.

The two mountain folk stood at the junction of the old and new parts of the city waiting for him.

"We waited here to say good-bye to you. It'll be light soon," the two said in unison, as if they had memorized their lines.

"Good-bye, good-bye," Ayuan waved at them.

■

Ayuan was sleeping in a work shed. Today was his day off. At dawn, a male voice whispered in his ear, "This place was excavated in 1963. A large group of prisoners bubbled up from the darkness underground."

Ayuan sat up abruptly and shouted, "Is it the swamp? Is it the swamp?"

Strong light forced him to close his eyes. No one replied.

After getting dressed, he went outside, dragging his feet. He walked out of the work site and reached a small street, where he bought two sesame biscuits. Then he returned to the shed to wash his face and brush his teeth.

He had no sooner eaten the biscuits than he saw the two little mountain people peering into the work shed.

"Can you take me to the place that was excavated?" Ayuan asked.

"Are you talking of what happened in 1963? That place is now the largest hotel in this city," the older one said.

"The Milky Way Hotel? I would never have imagined that. Does it have a basement?"

"Yes, but it was locked up long ago. In the past, something awful occurred there. Come along with us, will you? Don't keep pestering us with questions; that's useless. Do you really think we'd lie to you?"

And so Ayuan went with them again. He was reluctant to give up his innermost wish.

"I want to go somewhere I've never been. Not a place like the Milky Way Hotel. Too many people are there. I want to go to a remote place that has no people, such as an abandoned factory. Can we find such a place in the city? Actually, I used to be quite familiar with the old section of the city, but now I don't recognize some of the places . . ."

Ayuan rattled on and on. The other two paid no attention to him.

After a while, Ayuan realized that the three of them had been circling around the same two lanes, one of which led to the shantytown where he had stayed earlier. Looking into the distance, he saw that half the sheds had been demolished. He thought, Perhaps it's my fate to be related to this place. Walking absentmindedly, he tripped on something and nearly fell. Oh, it was the piglets! They were scurrying fast in all directions. The younger mountain person said, "All kinds of animals live in swamps, except for water buffaloes."

"Look—the piglets are going into the Grand Theater!" Ayuan shouted in excitement.

In the blink of an eye, the two mountain folk disappeared.

Ayuan went over to the Grand Theater. A poster outside the theater pictured the piglets. They were actors! A male voice came from the theater's loudspeaker, "This is 1963. Mushrooms grow underground here. This is a girl's bowknot. Ladies and gentlemen, give me your attention . . ."

Ayuan lost no time in buying a ticket and rushing into the theater.

Lights were on, but no one was there. He made his way down a long aisle between the seats and climbed up to the stage. Just then, he tripped again. Oh, the piglets! Before he could get a good look at them, they disappeared behind the curtain, and the stage light went out. Feeling his way, he walked across and grabbed the curtain.

It was wet. God! It had so many layers that it was almost a forest of curtains. Panting, he squatted down. Wrapped in the damp velvet curtains, he heard the piglets moving—many of them. What on earth did the poster signify? Below the stage, a woman shouted, "Ayuan, Ayuan! Did you see the big-headed fish?"

Smothered by the curtain, Ayuan couldn't talk. His voice sounded like a whisper, "I—I . . . piglets."

At last, a piglet made its way to his feet. The piglet was smelly, but it showed warmth toward Ayuan. At once, he found it easier to breathe. The woman below the stage was still calling him, but Ayuan didn't want to answer. Holding the piglet, he trembled with excitement. The curtains groaned and wriggled gently. The thick curtains turned into living things; no light could penetrate from outside. Ayuan eventually figured out that the woman below the stage was the bride from the photography studio. He thought, What kind of life is this bride leading?

In this forest of curtains, Ayuan's mind was filled with many events of the past. He felt it was bizarre that although many of these things hadn't actually happened, nonetheless in his memory they had become his own experiences. For example, it was the bride who had had an accident in the artificial lake, but now this had become an event from his past. His palm was still scarred from being scratched by a shard at the bottom of the lake. When he thought of this, he licked his palm.

The loudspeaker blared again.

"In the spring of 1963, hundreds of bodies were floating in the artificial lake . . ."

It was always like this: the first sentence was clear, but the rest of it was indistinct.

He sensed that throngs of people had arrived at the theater. All the curtains suddenly rose. When the dazzling stage lights shone on his face, he nearly fainted.

"Look! It's the swamp!"

"Oh, yes, it really is!"

"This is the way it really was in 1963!"

When Ayuan heard the audience members remarking about this, he tried hard to remember what his life was like in 1963. He couldn't open his eyes, and so—in order not to fall—he had to sit motionless on the floor. His mouth began moving, but he couldn't be sure of what he said. It seemed to be related to 1963. The audience fell silent.

From the loudspeaker came the gurgling of bubbles, as if accompanying his words.

When he talked of bleeding, he tasted blood in his mouth.

"Piglets! My piglets—" Ayuan covered his eyes with his hands and shouted.

The stage lights went out, and Ayuan opened his eyes. The auditorium contained only empty seats. A dim light shone on the right side of the wall. Ayuan thought to himself, It's over. The show is over for today. He slowly left the stage from one side and walked toward the back door. It was as if he were stepping in soft mud. From somewhere within him came a shout that shattered his heart, "Piglets, piglets!"

When he reached the entrance, the two mountain people reappeared.

"Ayuan, have you said everything you had to say?" the older one asked.

"Pretty much. I did my best."

"Good. I was afraid you hadn't and that you'd regret it later."

Ayuan was grateful to them, but he also wished they were somewhere else, far away.

"Is this the place that was excavated?" Ayuan asked.

"When you were on the stage, didn't you use your feet to check each place you stood on?" the younger one asked.

"No. I didn't have time. It happened too quickly."

"Oh, I see. You couldn't stay calm."

With a wave of their hands, the mountain people parted from Ayuan, and then disappeared in the crowds on the main road.

Ayuan headed absentmindedly toward his workplace. When he had almost arrived, he suddenly started thinking more clearly. He shouted, "That was the swamp!"

He finally understood: the swamp is anywhere you want it to be. But wasn't this too scary? If his life had come to this, was this what he had been hoping for earlier?

Ayuan ate some noodles at the noodle shop in front of his workplace. He was a little uneasy. After eating, he went into the empty shed for a nap. No one else was in the shed. As Ayuan lay in bed, he recalled Uncle Sang and the red-garbed bride. Were they frequent visitors in the swamp? He thought that the swamp where they (including the mountain people) had been must really be an extraordinary place—much different from what he had just experienced. He had no way to go to the genuine swamp. All he could do was go through nooks and crannies in the city to acquire a sense of it. He wasn't sure, however, that anyone had actually been to the extraordinary place in his imagination. Ayuan fell asleep while thinking of these illusions.

When it turned dark, he was awakened by the noise of the other workers. Seeing that he was up, they approached him and asked, "Didn't you notice the two thieves? They dug a deep hole next to the shed. They jumped in and disappeared. That's when we discovered that they had stolen some of our things."

"Were the thieves short?" Ayuan asked.

"They were small and dark."

Ayuan walked outside the shed and saw the deep hole. He stood there for a while, knowing that he lacked the courage to jump in. Even if this pit had been dug for him, he wouldn't dare jump. He had exhausted his courage in the daytime. Feeling cold, he left at once.

•

Uncle Sang, who had been missing for a long time, reappeared. He caught up with Ayuan on the main road and shouted, "Ayuan, you failed to meet their expectations!"

"Who?" Ayuan asked.

"Your guides! Without them, you could've gone nowhere."

Uncle Sang looked sad, and then all at once he looked as if he'd lost his bearings.

Ayuan thought to himself, I lost my best opportunity. Every day, he saw the deep hole next to the shed, avoiding drawing too close to it. One day, when he went back to the shed after work, he saw that the hole had been filled in. No trace of it remained on the ground. Grass was even growing on that piece of land. Was this magic?

Pointing at a car in the stream of traffic, Uncle Sang said, "See those two guides? They're guiding others. I'm telling you that they could have taken you to the real swamp. They're my old drinking buddies. I entrusted you to them. Ayuan, isn't this precisely the only significant thing about living in this dry city?"

"Uncle Sang, what's up with the photography studio and the theater?" Ayuan asked, perplexed.

"I told you long ago. That's the swamp. Why weren't you patient enough to inspect them closely? You're too impatient."

Uncle Sang's son drove up to meet him, and Uncle Sang said hastily, "I have to go. Now I can't leave there for a moment. I have some land there where I grow lotus roots. Of course leeches are abundant there. Good-bye!"

The car drove away and soon disappeared. Ayuan thought, Since Uncle Sang blamed me for being impatient, why not go back to the photography studio in the old part of the city? I should be able to find that place. Uncle Sang was right: for people like Uncle Sang and me, the only thing worth pursuing in this dry city is the real swamp.

He boarded a bus, and half an hour later reached the old section of the city. He had no idea whether he would succeed in his exploration.

In his two-week absence, the old part of town had changed

greatly. But now and then one could still see the old two-story wooden buildings and even an old-fashioned public toilet. Remembering that he used to go in and out of these intestine-shaped alleys like a loach, Ayuan couldn't help but smile.

How strange it was that now he had no trouble finding the photography studio where he had stopped last time. It was still the same three-story brick building, but the sign saying "Wedding Photos" was missing, as was the main entrance. The building seemed to have been reoriented: the entrance no longer faced the small street.

Ayuan was leaning against the red-brick wall, his ears pricked up. But he heard nothing.

A girl eleven or twelve years old walked up.

"Hi there, what are you doing?" she asked.

"Do you know how I can get in?" Ayuan asked in embarrassment.

"Go in? You can't. This building has no door."

"Is anyone inside?"

"Of course."

"What I mean is, Don't the people inside ever come out? How can they never come out?"

"Why not? I've never seen them come out. Not even once. You're a fool if you go on waiting."

The girl glanced contemptuously at Ayuan and looked at him doubtfully for quite a while before leaving.

Ayuan circled to the back of the building. Sure enough, there was also a brick wall behind the building. Although there were some windows, they were on the second and third floors. He looked down and saw the sign he'd seen before—the words "Wedding Photos" were blood red. Ayuan recalled the long red satin gown that the bride had worn. How come the sign had fallen down? This time, he'd better do as Uncle Sang had said and patiently investigate this building. He decided to keep watch.

The morning sunlight fell on the sign. The words that were painted blood red actually lit up in the fire, and a funny smell filled the air. Ayuan heard someone stick his head out a window and shout, "Fire! Fire!"

Ayuan thought, What does this little fire have to do with the people inside the building? But the entire building rapidly filled with noise. People seemed to be dashing around. They poured basin after basin of water down from the windows. The water didn't actually hit the fire, and yet the fire began shrinking, as if intimidated by the people's actions.

A garbage collector came over and stopped his cart. He bent and picked up the charred remnants of the sign, looked at it, and threw it into the cart. Just then, someone in the building dumped a basin of water on him. He grimaced at Ayuan and said, "It's really dry today, don't you think?"

His hands on his hips, he stood below the window, as though he didn't intend to leave anytime soon.

Ayuan heard bubbles gurgling in the garbage cart. When he took a look, it was empty except for the sign in the bottom of the cart. Ayuan wanted to move closer to get a better look, but the garbageman pushed him away. He was so strong that Ayuan nearly fell.

"What do you think you're doing?" he asked Ayuan furiously.

"I just wanted to see if there was a swamp in your cart." Ayuan was aggrieved.

"What makes you think it's okay to spy on things? Get out of here!"

Pedaling his cart, he took off. Ayuan heard the merry sound of a series of bubbles rising from the depths of the water to the surface.

The people in the building continued pouring water down. Ayuan wished they would pour it on him, but they didn't. After a while, the place where Ayuan was standing turned into mud, so he circled around to the front of the building. The wall with no door was just the same, but someone was standing there. It was Uncle Sang.

Uncle Sang walked over to him. Patting him on the shoulder, he said, "Ayuan, I can't help but worry about you! You're a nice kid, but you're wasting your time. You haven't done your job right."

"Uncle Sang, can you tell me how to do it?"

"Me? No, no, no. This can't be taught. I came to see you because I was worried about you. Now that you've heard my warning, you should be okay."

Like the garbageman, he unhappily flung Ayuan aside and walked off.

Ayuan walked over to the small clearing and sat on a tree stump. He thought he should wait here until something occurred. Hadn't Uncle Sang said he'd missed his opportunity?

He waited and waited, but nothing happened. The building was quiet, and no one passed by. He was surrounded by a deathly stillness. Just then, it suddenly turned overcast and then quickly grew dark. It was morning: how could the sky be dark? Ayuan was hungry, so he decided to go to a small restaurant for a meal.

The restaurant was deserted. He ordered a large bowl of pork soup and downed it quickly.

Something bit his ankle, and he yelled, "Ouch!" Looking down, he saw the familiar piglets! Ayuan wondered if they had come because he had just now eaten their relatives for supper. After the piglets had made a circuit of the room, they ran out.

When Ayuan stood up to pay the tab, the waiter asked, "Do you want to stay here? It's fifty yuan for a bed."

"What kinds of guests usually stay here?" Ayuan asked, frowning.

"What do you think? They're poor people who've come here to try their luck. This is the only part of the city that still has some opportunity. The other places are closed up."

"What opportunities are available here?"

"You ask too many questions. Do you want to stay or not?"

"Yes."

Ayuan followed him to a room behind the lobby. Two of the three beds in the room were occupied. The room had no electric lights, but a kerosene lamp was lit. The clerk pointed to the empty bed. Ayuan had no sooner sat down than the clerk blew out the kerosene lamp and left.

Groping in the dark, Ayuan found the pillow and quilt. He unfolded the quilt and lay down.

"You'd better not sleep too soundly," a person said from the bed across from him.

"Do opportunities come at night?"

"Don't ask. You shouldn't ask about this."

Ayuan stopped talking. He was uneasy and sleepy. He didn't sleep well. Every five minutes he awakened in alarm. Each time, he heard the people in the other two beds planning something in low voices. He heard them mention "iron cage," "dungeon," "torture instrument," and so forth—dark and ruthless things. As he was on the verge of figuring out what they meant, he dozed off again. And so he never figured out exactly what they were talking about.

At midnight, Ayuan sensed that his feet and neck had been tied to the posts at either end of the iron bed. Probably the other two men had left. When he tried to move a little, the coarse rope tightened. He realized he had to lie still in order to alleviate the pain. Just then he heard the sound of bubbles that he hadn't heard for quite a while, and he calmed down at once. A hand at the door was holding a wavering candle, but then quickly retreated. A woman's voice said, "What an adorable guy."

The sound of bubbles was rising from underneath the bed; it was as if his entire person were submerged in water, gurgling and gurgling. He had waited a long time: wasn't it this that he'd been waiting for? In this city that was so dry that cracks opened up everywhere, what a lucky man he was! His insteps tickled, but he forced himself not to move, for he didn't want to interrupt this great moment of feeling so lucky. The woman spoke again, "Now he can die without regrets."

Ayuan recognized her voice: she was a former neighbor. She was an assistant at a vegetable stand, where she didn't talk and never even made eye contact with customers when she sold vegetables. What had made her so talkative now? Every time Ayuan was about to fall asleep, he was awakened again by her.

"Is this the swamp or is it a dungeon?" Ayuan asked angrily.

The woman didn't respond. Maybe she had slipped away.

But the sound of bubbles had also stopped, and Ayuan's feet and neck were now free. He got out of bed, walked to the window, and looked out at the dim backyard of the hotel. Two old-style waterwheels had been set up in the middle of the yard. Two dark figures were bent over, operating the waterwheels. Their actions made no sound.

Ayuan shouted, "I'm coming to help you!" Then he jumped down from the window. He didn't land in the backyard, but in a hole. Although he wasn't injured, the fall was painful. Someone said, "He hasn't paid for his room yet. This kind of jerk is shameless. And his body is so dry that even the crocodiles would show no interest in him. Isn't there better stuff than this in the city?"

This frightened Ayuan. As he climbed out of the hole, he said, "I came to help with the waterwheels . . ."

"There's no water here!" the man rebuffed him. "More than a hundred years ago, there was, but now there are only alligators and snakes. Alligators lie in the dirt hole; all the armor on their bodies has disappeared, and they've become slippery all over. Do you really want to operate the waterwheels? Okay, I'll help you!"

He shoved Ayuan, and Ayuan stumbled ahead several steps. When he came to a stop, he rubbed his eyes and saw that he was standing next to the main road. He was in the city's new district. A car stopped beside him, and the door opened. His face wreathed in smiles, Uncle Sang got out.

"This is great!" He patted Ayuan on the shoulder as he said, "Look—the leeches didn't suck all my blood, and the alligators didn't eat you. From now on, you can go there any time! Just take the roads you're familiar with, and you'll have no trouble. Don't you think I'm right? Hang on a second. Look!"

Ayuan saw the two mountain people in a black jeep flashing by.

"Is today Monday? Ayuan, you have a job. You've got to go to work now. However, our swamp welcomes people from all occupations. Next time, you just need to take the roads you know. You can go whenever you like. It's so dry in the city, you can't stay here all the time."

The two of them parted at the intersection.

Ayuan returned to work, where he noticed that the deep hole next to the shed had reappeared. A crowd of people stood around it. As Ayuan approached, a worker asked him, "Ayuan, I saw someone jump down into the hole at dawn. Was it you?"

Everyone stared at Ayuan, showing their admiration.

"It was . . . I jumped down from the window, but . . . ," Ayuan said hesitantly.

"That's terrific! Absolutely terrific!" Everyone cheered.

Ayuan noticed little animals climbing up from the side of the hole. It was two of the piglets! The piglets were sticky and filthy, giving off a smell that Ayuan knew very well. Ayuan squatted down and petted them, and in awe, the workers made a path for them, and the two little animals ran away.

"God! They came from over there!" Young Hu was the first to shout.

"Who could have guessed that? Who would ever have thought of that?" Several people sighed in dismay.

The workers looked anguished. Someone suggested quietly, "We'd better go have a drink."

And so they left together.

Ayuan went back to the shed by himself. He lay on the bed, thinking that he didn't have the guts to jump into the deep hole. This could only happen by mistake. The bride from the photography studio had wanted to slide into the deep, bottomless lake—another thing he could never do. Uncle Sang must have seen what sort of person he, Ayuan, was. He was always waiting—waiting until dangers befell him by mistake.

A whistle blew outside. Ayuan changed into his work clothes and put on his hard hat. He followed the foreman to the work site. When he recalled that Uncle Sang had praised him for having "a job," he cheered up.

"You didn't go out drinking. I'm glad to hear that. You're a tough guy! The others are worthless cowards," the foreman said, as he walked along without turning his head.

When Ayuan stood on the scaffolding and looked out at the city, he heard bubbles echoing incessantly in the currents of air. Moisture-laden air blew over his face, and he couldn't help shouting, "Uncle Sang, I'm here now!!"

He saw the gray sky pushing against him, as if it would crush him.

## SIN

I had a wooden box in my loft. Everyone in the family knew about it, but no one had ever opened it. The year I was born, Father gave me this box he'd prepared. Mother was in charge of storing it. Father was a very crafty guy who always came up with long-term plans that often stretched to the unforeseeable future. And then he simply forgot his plan. For example, this wooden box. When he gave it to Mother, he said very seriously that the contents of the box were confidential. He meant to open it himself when I was grown up, for it contained something important having to do with my future. But after I grew up, he forgot. Mother didn't remind him, either; perhaps she didn't believe that Father had anything so terribly wonderful stored in the box. After living with him for many years, she knew him like the back of her hand, so she didn't even mention it to him.

The box was made of ordinary fir, with a layer of lacquer slapped over it. It had a little lock—a common enough lock, which had rusted over the years. Maybe it was habit or maybe Mother's attitude had affected me; in any case, I never considered unlocking it. After Father and Mother died, I threw the box into the loft one day and never gave it another thought. I didn't have the curiosity one should have about some things. And yet I was endlessly interested in things that shouldn't have concerned anyone. I was born this way; I couldn't help it.

In August, my cousin, whom the family dubbed "Killer," came to stay for a while. She was in her early thirties, yet her forehead was covered with wrinkles, surprising for one her age. When she walked, she held her head high. I didn't like to be around her because she spoke unkindly; sometimes her words could even be murderous (Father was one of her victims when he was alive), so in the family we all spitefully called her "Killer" behind her back.

"Rumei," she sat down and began talking, "that fashionable colleague of yours started spreading rumors about you yesterday among people I know well. But I've seen you walking arm in arm with her on the streets. What's this all about?"

"Mind your own business. If you have to butt into other people's business, then you'd better not stay with us," I said in disgust.

"But it wasn't because of this that I came here," she said pensively. "I came because of—that box!"

"Box? What box?" I knew at once what she meant, but I deliberately feigned ignorance.

"Don't think that just because your father died a long time ago you can ignore this. That's childish. You're just like your sneaky father—a sinner. You can't cover this up."

She stood legs apart, hands stuffed into her pants pockets. She looked like the old maid she was. I recalled that several years ago, even though I knew it was not very promising, I had introduced her to several men. None had worked out. It was only because I hated her that I'd made these introductions, but she hadn't hated me for doing it. Quite the opposite. She had thanked me for my help, thus making me really uneasy. Not until later did I understand that nothing I did could hurt her.

I asked her why she thought so badly of my father. She gave me a probing look and sneered. She said I must have been all too aware. Otherwise, why would I have hidden the box in the loft? This was a sin.

"I didn't hide it. I just happened to put it there, okay? You surely don't know what's in the box, so why do you conclude that I'm guilty?" I didn't think I could bear this.

"The contents don't matter at all. A person has to take responsibility for what she does. You'd better not say 'I just happened' very much. Who knows if you 'just happened' to do this? Huh!" She swung her flat rear end emphatically.

I didn't want to pay any more attention to my cousin. If she wanted to stay here, okay, but I didn't have to keep her company. With my briefcase under my arm, I left for work.

But I was uneasy, worried that something would go wrong at home. And I remembered that I'd forgotten to lock the drawer which was filled with personal correspondence.

In the afternoon, I left work early and rushed home. When I got there, I set my bicycle down and dashed into the house. Sure enough, she was sitting at the desk reading my letters. On hearing my footsteps, she replaced the letters in the drawer. She looked embarrassed.

"How dare you read my letters?" I paled.

"I'm just a little curious, that's all." She voiced her objection as she stood up. "Why are you taking this so seriously?"

"If you want to stay here, you mustn't be so curious!" I shouted.

"Do you think I came here out of curiosity about you? You shouldn't have such a high opinion of yourself!" She shouted, too. Standing with arms akimbo, she looked scary.

Hearing us arguing, my husband ran in to break it up. As soon as he tried, my cousin made even more of a fuss. She said she had come here in order to prevent a sin; this sin had been planned for decades, and so forth and so on. My husband was baffled. It was odd that she didn't bring up the issue of the box in front of him. She just kept arguing, saying she had to stay here until the whole thing was cleared up.

I thought this was a little fishy. I had placed the box in the loft. You could see it if you stood in the middle of the room. Yet my cousin hadn't mentioned looking for it in the house, nor had she asked me where it was: this wasn't where her attention was focused. Everything was obscure. Maybe the box was nothing but a pretext for staying in my home to satisfy her old maid's curiosity or to take revenge on me for something. She was too complicated. Since I couldn't get a feel for her temperament, I decided not to argue with her anymore. I acted as if nothing was happening. At dinner, I talked with her as usual. She ignored my overtures and kept a straight face. Then she turned to my son and spoke with him of the subtle relationships between parents and children and took the opportunity to develop this idea for a while.

"Sometimes it takes several generations for a sin to be completed," she announced complacently as she raised her head. My son listened to her piously without blinking an eye. He adored this young auntie.

Not many people were as freewheeling as my cousin. She didn't even have a formal job but merely had a stall on the street where she sold cheap silk stockings. The income from that kind of work was not very steady. She had fallen out long ago with her parents—to the point where they no longer saw anything of each other. So when business was slow and she lacked spending money, she came here. Although I inwardly hated her, at the same time I also admired her nimble and straightforward way of thinking, and I was subconsciously affected by this. So I wasn't against her staying, but I didn't expect her to aim the lance at me this time. It was as if she were determined to pin down a certain private thing about me.

I was thoroughly annoyed. I didn't know what kind of trouble my cousin wanted to stir up. She didn't care at all about my family. She claimed she had to perform "surgery" on my family. When she said this, her face was absolutely expressionless.

Today my boss had criticized me again because I was agitated and had made mistakes in filling out reports. His tone was terribly harsh. I wanted to spit in his face. I thought of the problem at home and felt it was time to drop a hint to my cousin that it wasn't right to interfere in other people's lives. I kept thinking about this, and on the way home I seemed to reach a decision.

As soon as I went inside, I heard laughter from her and my son. I had to acknowledge that although she had never married, she was a genius at enjoying children—much better than I. Was this why I was jealous of her? But it wasn't pure jealousy; other factors were mixed in with it.

My cousin and my son had installed a new light switch. They'd been laughing just now because they'd succeeded. Of course this was much more convenient, but I had forbidden my son to handle electrical wires. He was too young and didn't understand the basic guidelines. When I looked inside the room, I was startled: they had taken the wooden box down from the loft and placed it on the chair so they could stand on it to work on the light switch. In stepping on the box, they'd left several footprints on it. I rushed over and took the box down, and staring at my cousin I spat out the words slowly through clenched teeth:

"This — is — the — exact — same — wooden — box — you've — talked — about — so — often. It's been up there all along." I pointed to the loft.

"Really?" my cousin laughed. "Then how about opening it?"

"I don't have the key. Father forgot to give it to me," I said, disheartened.

"And you forgot to tell him you needed it, didn't you?" Her tone softened. With the tip of her toe, she moved the wooden box; as she did so, its contents made a suspicious sound. Mimicking her, my son also pushed it with his foot. The two of them pushed it back and forth. Their actions were so disgusting that I was sorry I couldn't slap them.

I bent down and picked up the box, took it back to the loft, and wrapped it in cloth. As I was doing this, neither my cousin nor my son looked at me. They had begun a game of chess. I was superfluous.

"Didn't you say you came here because of the box?" I reminded my cousin. "Didn't you say there's a sin hidden in the box?"

With her eyes fixed on the chessboard, she said, "Did I? Maybe I did."

"It's been up there all along. I see that you haven't bothered to glance at it."

"I don't need to. I've known it was there all along, and I've known that you didn't have the key. Hey, did your father have a particular reason for not giving you the key?"

"No. I'm sure he simply forgot."

I don't know why, but even though I had wrapped the box in cloth, from then on all of us—my husband, my son, my cousin, and I—kept unconsciously casting our eyes at it. This situation made me uncomfortable. Often, when we were talking with one another, we suddenly fell silent as we looked simultaneously at that cloth package. My cousin was always the first to avert her eyes, and then she would titter. And I would blush from indignation.

In order to prove my cousin's thoughts groundless, I started searching for the key Father had left. It had to be somewhere; it couldn't have been cremated with him and placed in his urn. First, I opened a large bundle of his things. I turned them all over, from the large ones to the small ones, and looked through them carefully to see if the key might be with them. I spent three days doing this secretly in the bedroom—after work and out of my cousin's and husband's sight. But I didn't find anything. Never mind the key to the box, there was no key at all among his effects. I finally recalled that when Father went out, he had never taken the house key with him, thus often inconveniencing himself. My thoughts turned to Father's friends and relatives. Would any of them know? I knew he'd been close to his younger sister. There was nothing they didn't discuss. I decided to call on this elderly aunt.

Although winter had already passed, my aunt was still all wrapped up in a heavy scarf and shivering constantly. Sucking in air, she kept muttering, "Killer weather. So cold. Why would you venture out in this cold weather?"

I explained why I had come. My aunt stopped shivering, shot a glance at me, and said, "No. He never mentioned that key. Your father was the fox in the family. He never told the truth. Whenever he came over here, he wanted to borrow money. So many years have passed. Why are you still concerned about it? It's tough to figure out what your father was up to."

"But the box is still here. He left it to me. Can I smash it open and look inside?"

"This isn't my business. You can see I'm old. After a while, it will be difficult for me to talk. Why would I bother about his things? I sit here and often dream of skiing with your father in the courtyard. Back then I was six and he was eight. Even at that age, he was already a trickster. If you don't want to let this matter drop, you can go and see his old friend Qin Yi." Her toothless mouth was shriveled; she seemed to want to say more. Suddenly, she dropped her head, closed her eyes, and fell asleep.

I figured it would be impossible to get any useful clues from my aunt. I might as well go home first. I decided to visit Qin Yi the next day. I hadn't seen him since Father died almost seven years ago.

Qin Yi lived on a small winding lane. It had just rained, and there were puddles everywhere. After I walked along this lane, my pants and feet were all spattered. Ahead of me was a little old man being chased by an old woman with a large wooden stick. She kept stumbling and falling, and she was crazy with rage. For his part, the old man was as nimble as a goat as he leapt over one puddle after another. Later, the old woman tired and sat beside the road cursing him. The old man went into the house and hid. He was Qin Yi, who had been Father's young friend and student.

When I went inside he was jittery. He didn't ask me to take a seat, either. He was only too anxious for me to leave. But after hearing my question, he seemed interested and invited me to sit down and have some tea.

"Although he was my teacher, I have to tell you he was a big fraud. I've said this all along. He was always hiding boxes and saying there were huge secrets inside that he would explain later. But he never did. I have a box of his, too. I opened it a long time ago, and it was empty. He was still alive then, and I asked him about it. He said he was joking, and that he hadn't imagined I would smash it open. By saying this, I don't mean to encourage you to smash your box. Just leave it alone. Maybe there's a little something inside."

"Yes, of course there's something inside. I heard it. It's also heavy. After all, he was my father." I felt a little resentful of Qin Yi. I didn't know why my father had trusted this kind of person.

"Maybe, maybe. He was your father. So you believe there is something in it. But I know nothing about the key."

Later on, I also visited a cousin, one of my father's former colleagues, and one of my mother's confidants, and still didn't learn anything.

As the story about my box made the rounds among my acquaintances, some people found excuses to call on me. They would sit down and glance at the loft. Whenever I looked at them, they would turn their eyes away and look down and exchange small talk. Each time, my cousin would stick her hands in her pants pockets and stride back and forth.

One day, my cousin's parents—a very boring couple—were among the visitors. After they sat down, their eyes slid to and fro like a thief's and they made impertinent remarks belittling today's youth. Then my cousin came over and cursed them. She said they hadn't been invited. She wanted them to take off.

"Don't think I don't know everything about you," her mother said as she left. "Some people look all right, but actually they are thoroughly rotten. Just listen to what people say about you."

When the visitors were gone, my cousin was still furious and gasping for breath. All of a sudden, she grabbed my collar and shook it hard. She said, "Was it you who started talking about the box?"

"I talked with some people—with my father's relatives and good friends. So what? This isn't some terrible secret! Outsiders must have known of it long ago."

"You fool!" Utterly exasperated, she let go of me. "What makes you think outsiders knew about this? With your parents dead, I'm the only one who knew. Now everyone is interested in your box. Do you think your father can still rest in peace in the ground? You're doomed. You sinner!"

I could see I'd made a mistake. Avoiding her eyes, I spoke haltingly, "I'm . . . just . . . not . . . convinced . . ."

Because so many people were coming over, all I could do was hide the box away, hoping to dispel their curiosity.

But visitors still showed up, sat at the table, looked down, and didn't look at the loft again. They didn't say anything, either. They thought their manner would signal that they knew all there was to know. I realized that as soon as they left they would talk about me maliciously. Qin Yi was one of the visitors, confirming for me that it was he who had spread the rumors. This evil was gnawing at Father's corpse all the time.

One day when I came home from work, my son complained

to me that even the kids at school had started talking about us. He couldn't stand the looks he was getting from others. His face filled with rage, he wanted me to open the box and get it over with. "Isn't it just a wooden box? Why did you hide it?" He said I had hidden the box, yet he was the one who ran into trouble everywhere he went.

"They're also gossiping about murder. It stresses me out," my son said indignantly.

I thought about the mistakes I'd made. But the root of all of these mistakes stemmed from Father's having given me a locked wooden box without a key. Why on earth had he hated me so much?

My husband wearied of neighbors and relatives shuttling in and out of the house. I often felt that he was surreptitiously observing me to see if I would give in. One day, after hesitating for a long time, he finally said, "Rumei, let's give it up."

"What's this 'us'? You're talking about me. I'm telling you I don't care what you think about this matter. That's right. You! And all the rest of you, too!" I glared at my cousin. She was looking at the ceiling.

"Why are you so obstinate? We can break the box open and look inside. Isn't that the way to get to the bottom of this? What on earth are you afraid of?"

"No!" I shouted, and then dashed into the bedroom and shut the door.

I dragged the box out from under the bed and shook it next to my ear. The contents seemed to be withered leaves, straw, or letters. When I shook it a few more times, I thought it was none of these, but merely some broken bones or small pebbles or wood chips. What was inside the box was really hard to determine. Could

Father have simply been playing a prank? What kind of person did he think I was? The same as Qin Yi? Actually, what was the essential difference between Qin Yi and me? The only difference was that up to now I hadn't smashed open the box. There must be someone who understood, and that person was probably my cousin. Otherwise, why would she have said that it was because of this that she had come to stay here? In the seven years since I put the box in the loft, it hadn't attracted any interest. That's right: my cousin created this disturbance. Maybe Father had dropped her a hint and she'd picked up on it. She was very bright.

When I thought of how Father had regarded me, I felt thoroughly disappointed. I threw the box down, and a vague plan arose in my mind. Yes, I was going to retaliate against the dead—Father and also Mother—and consign them to hell. My husband entered quietly and noticed the box on the floor. He mistakenly thought I had yielded. As he stood under the lamp, his lanky body appeared to be floating. I heard him sigh. He seemed to be talking to himself: "It shouldn't have grown so serious in the first place. Who cares about things that belonged to the dead? It would have been okay if everyone had continued being in the dark, wouldn't it? The past few days, those people have really been driving me nuts."

Early in the morning, my cousin packed her things. She stood up right after breakfast and announced she was leaving. My son immediately shouted in protest, saying she shouldn't leave so soon. They hadn't finished yesterday's chess game.

"What's your rush?" I looked her straight in the eye.

"You no longer need me here," she smiled. "Evils will continue, but there won't be any serious problem. I'm relieved. And I can't stay here forever. It's already been long enough."

I held back my rising anger. "Didn't you say you would curb the evils?"

"I was just exaggerating. We all like to boast, because it makes us feel important. I have to deal with my own problems. As you saw, the two old folks came here making trouble. They were extremely malicious. They wanted to kill someone!" Then she hefted her backpack, waved her hand, and left.

"I never thought she could have put up with this situation," my husband whispered.

"Could you? What's your 'situation'? Do you know? Don't play innocent! We're a little too old for that." This startled him. He sneered and went outside.

My son also left the table, glared at me, and walked away.

Outside, people were talking. The neighbors. They were crowding around my husband asking him something. I felt a roaring in my head. Everything was like an arrow in a bow.

My husband seemed to be saying something, and they all suddenly understood. They marveled and slowly dispersed.

I couldn't take it anymore. I grabbed the tape recorder and smashed it on the floor. No one paid any attention to me. They had all gone. I returned to the bedroom and took out that wooden box and shook it a few times next to my ear. I heard the sound of withered leaves, or perhaps they were letters or photographs. It was possible, too, that they were bones or wood chips. At this moment, my curiosity kept mounting. My anger was mounting along with it. I put the box in a bag and hurried outside.

When I returned, my husband was waiting at the door. His face was somber. My son was with him. As soon as my son caught sight of me, he ran off.

"Did you throw that thing into the river?" my husband asked, his hands starting to twitch.

"So what if I did? It's mine. I can do whatever I want with it."

"Sure. You have the right." His gaze was wandering, and his hands stopped spasming. "Rumei, tell me the truth. Aren't you afraid? Especially when you wake up in the middle of the night?"

"Why should I be afraid? Can being afraid solve the problem? Who can avoid it? Your plight isn't any better, either."

"Oh, yes! Now I get it. What a fool I've been! Thanks to your awakening, I now understand everything. We don't have to be such sticklers for form, do we? You and I want the same thing. We just deal with it differently. Your father was really an old fox. He was always disguised well. I wasn't at all suspicious of him. Don't worry. Those people won't be back. They all have their own troubles. You could just as well have opened it and taken a look before throwing it away, you know?"

"No!" I said with finality.

After that, my husband and son drew away from me, though we were still talking and laughing together. They acted as if nothing had happened, but I could see it all written on their faces. They often glanced absentmindedly at the loft, as if to remind me of the sin. This went on for days.

Actually, I was often startled awake in the middle of the night. At times like that, I seriously thought of making an identical box for my son, and putting withered leaves or several newspapers or a few wood chips or a few slices of something else inside it. I even discussed it with my husband. My husband concluded that I wanted to shift the responsibility.

When I had nearly forgotten her, my cousin reappeared. Her

face was tanned and her hair was scorched brown. She still looked very much the way an old maid looks, with her hands stuffed into her pants pocket.

"Are you here to investigate the case?" I ridiculed her, while doing my best to look relaxed.

"Who has time for that? I've been traveling on business all along. When I was in the Gobi Desert, I considered staying there. Then I thought, Isn't everywhere the same? The same evil, the same deception, so I decided I might as well come back here. How are all of you? Did time heal the wound?" Looking up, she swept her eyes toward the loft, and a fleeting smile skimmed over her face.

"There's still something I don't understand. You were so serious about this matter. And then you just forgot it all? Do you treat your own issues like this?"

"Of course," she laughed, "I act just the same. Everything is but an assumption, and we need to be flexible in dealing with each of our problems. Your father was a very flexible guy. He was never left with no way out."

"So you just faked the serious manner to remind me. Is that it?"

"I can't say I was faking. At the time, what I said was all true. Later, with the problem on the table, I believed you understood it all, and so I left your home. What kind of outcome do you want? Nothing can be completed. This is the conclusion. I remember there was a wooden box, right? Your father loved these childish games, and he purposely concocted mysteries. In the past, you were really numb. If I hadn't reminded you, you wouldn't have noticed anything, would you? In fact, there were also some special characteristics to your father's methods. A box!" She burst out laughing, and then turned serious again. "There's no point in being so earnest about this. Why would it matter if you had opened it and looked inside? You're still too stressed out. You aren't flexible."

Just as suddenly as she had appeared, my cousin vanished. One night, I encountered her mother on the street. The old woman was standing alone looking in all directions. I knew who she was looking for.

"She couldn't have gone far, Auntie. She told me she'd be around. She's probably somewhere nearby."

"I'll make her pay for what she's done." She squeezed these words out from between her teeth. In the cold wind, her face was frozen purple.

Before long, my uncle—my cousin's father—died. She didn't show up, but I knew she was still here. She was a ghost, a person like Father. Perhaps someday, she'll walk into our house again and announce that she has to investigate another of my sins.

When I was a kid, we lived in a place where all the neighbors shared a kitchen. It was large, holding more than ten coal stoves. It also had a tap; everyone took turns getting water to wash vegetables. Cooking was easy in those days, for in general each family had two dishes every day — greens and tofu, or greens and strips of meat fried with pickles. The kitchen was liveliest when people were cooking. We all chatted in loud voices, mingled with the *ding-dang* noise of metal scoops striking the woks.

If we all stopped making noise at the same time, we could hear a strange buzzing sound coming constantly from the other side of the kitchen wall. People said that a workshop on the other side of the wall made tin gardening pots. But it had been closed for several months, probably because there wasn't enough business. Ordinarily, when we walked through that narrow passage to reach the street we saw a big lock hanging from the workshop door. What was making the buzzing sound? Adults paid no attention to things like this; they acted as if there was no sound.

We loved playing hide-and-seek in the kitchen at night. By then, most of the stoves would be cool and the lights turned off. The two or three stoves that kept the fires burning inside looked like monsters, each with a single fiery red eye.

Xiaoyi and I climbed from a stove to the top of the partition and stood in a dark spot under the ceiling.

"There's a ladder here," Xiaoyi whispered.

I went down the ladder with him to the other side of the partition. So dark! But you could hear noise in the kitchen: probably some hapless guy had been caught there. Xiaoyi didn't want me to stir. I grabbed his hand and moved slowly ahead with him. I was shaking.

"Are you here?" someone asked in a rather weary voice.

"Yes, yes!" Xiaoyi said enthusiastically, as if trying to please that person.

It was hot all around, and a faint aroma reached us. Was someone stir-frying soybeans? Xiaoyi wanted me to sit down, so I sat on a pitted stone bench. This wasn't a bit comfortable. I sensed many people around me, and the atmosphere was tense. They seemed to be observing my attitude about something, but I had no idea what it was.

"Take a stand," Xiaoyi said, as he poked me.

"About what?" I asked.

"Whatever. Who cares? Hurry up!"

Someone walked over and stepped on my instep with his heavy boot. My foot seemed to be broken. I screamed in pain.

"Good," said Xiaoyi. "This is also a declaration." He relaxed.

But the girl next to us wasn't happy. Girls are girls, not like us boys. They're always unhappy with others, always grumbling. Whatever you do, they're never satisfied.

I stood up with tears in my eyes. I was groaning. There was no way I could continue sitting on that stone bench.

The girl put something in my palm. She said they were soy-beans—as a reward to me. Hadn't she been unhappy with me a moment ago? So why was she rewarding me?

Soybeans were being lightly stir-fried in the iron wok, but I couldn't see the wok, nor could I see the stove. This was truly odd. Could it be a smoldering fire that was burning with no flames? It was so hot. I put the two soybeans in my mouth and chewed. They tasted quite good. My instep still hurt a lot. I propped it up on the stone bench, and stood there bent over. The boy on my left said something to me, but I couldn't hear him well. He was angry and shouted, "Why don't you leave?"

But I didn't intend to go. Maybe I was waiting to eat soybeans, or maybe I was curious about this place.

"I'll wait a while," I said in a faint voice.

But that boy heard me right away! He shouted to everyone all around us, "He wants to wait a while! He wants to watch us! But we won't let him do what he wants."

Everyone in the room roared. What they all said was: "He's too ambitious!"

Then they laughed their heads off. I was super scared. I thought they might attack me. But they didn't. I heard the spatula as the soy-beans were frying, and I smelled the aroma. That girl rewarded me with a few more beans. This was exciting! But Xiaoyi came over, grabbed my arm, and ordered me to leave with him.

We went up the stairs, climbed the partition, and returned to the large kitchen. No one was there. It was already midnight. Only the few stoves with fires still burning were visible.

I took the soybeans out of my pocket and looked at them from time to time. They were ordinary fried soybeans. When I put them in front of my nose, I could smell their aroma. What kinds of people were engaged in secret activity at midnight on the other side of the partition? I heard their voices, but didn't see them. In the daytime, without letting Xiaoyi know, I sneaked to the workshop gate. I planted my ear against the locked door: it was silent inside. I listened for a long time, until I wearied of it.

"I miss the tin workshop. Can you take me there again at night?" I asked Xiaoyi.

"No way." His answer was straightforward. "Last time we went there by accident. If we make our plans in advance, a leopard will be guarding the entrance, and you'll have no way to get in."

"But how do they—and even that girl—get in?" I asked.

"They live there. There were some buildings in this town that you thought were empty, but in fact they were inhabited. I've heard my grandpa speak of this. But I've been to only one of them—the tin workshop."

Afraid that I would ask him more questions, Xiaoyi took off in a hurry.

I was bored. I had no interest in the big lively kitchen; only the mysterious air of the tin workshop could stir me up. Dad was yelling at me hoarsely, urging me to hurry up and get on with the cooking.

I reluctantly washed radishes, chopped them, and placed them in a large pot of water. Then I stood there, dazed. I noticed a brick in the wall had loosened, and filled with expectations I watched it, but time passed and nothing happened. When I turned the radishes with my spatula, I heard a sigh from over there: "It's so lonely here!"

It was a girl's voice, but not the girl who had given me soybeans.

My sister came over with a big smile. She grabbed the spatula from me and deftly scooped the radishes and spatula into a bowl.

"Hey—this boy is daydreaming!" she announced to everyone.

Everyone in the kitchen burst out laughing. I hated her.

When I looked again at the partition, I saw nothing going on at all.

A group of people standing around a large wok fried soybeans in the dark: I was greatly attracted to this kind of thing, for you never knew what might happen next. I felt great esteem for Xiaoyi.

Xiaoyi was hiding from me. The more he did this, the more my hopes soared. I thought, My friends are on the other side of the partition. Over there, things I'm interested in are happening. I forgot the pain I had suffered that night. What I remembered were the faint aroma of the soybeans and the vague excitement in the dark. I decided to go all out for it.

◾

To be safe, I waited until late to slip out of my home—it was probably midnight.

I felt my way into the kitchen and saw those three monsters' red eyes again. I climbed up from one of the cold stoves—climbed to the top of the wall. It was very quiet on the other side of the partition. I crouched on top of the wall and explored below with one leg. But it was useless: the ladder was gone. Damn that Xiaoyi. I was tired and afraid and filled with regret. But I didn't want to go back to the kitchen, either. Then I heard a voice rise in midair: "You may just walk down. It's okay."

This alluring voice belonged to the girl who had given me the soybeans. I couldn't help it: my center of gravity lurched. God! With one step, I touched solid ground. I steadied myself.

The room was still hot, still suffused with the faint aroma of soybeans, still dark. I couldn't see anyone. For some reason, tears filled my eyes. Luckily, no one saw this. I knew that people were all around, but they didn't make any noise. No sound came from the soybeans, or the iron wok either. Now there was a sound. It came from the kitchen. It seemed that my neighbors were frying vegetables in the kitchen. They were talking in loud voices, and their voices had turned pleasant. Was it already daytime over there?

A hand pulled me down, and I sat once more on the rough stone bench. My butt hurt a lot.

"We've been waiting for you," a voice close to me said, "in order to learn what things are like over there."

"Are you interested in what goes on in the kitchen over there?" I asked. I was surprised.

"You mean you aren't?" that person asked in return.

And then no one said anything. With no one speaking, I couldn't tell how many people were in the room. Maybe four or five, maybe twenty or thirty. What was certain was that they were listening attentively to the sound—the variable rolling clamor that came from the kitchen on the other side of the partition. Someone over there was laughing out loud: it seemed to be my sister. And then the others laughed, too. I should have been in the kitchen as well, but I was sitting here in the dark because it made me feel vaguely excited. These people who didn't show their faces were just like conspirators, and I kept feeling that something big was about to happen. Just think about this: I had descended from midair. This kind of thing had actually happened! I loved this kind of gathering so much. But why were these mysterious people interested in the vulgar things going on in the kitchen that I knew so well?

Later, when I ran into Xiaoyi, I told him my thoughts. He listened without saying a word. Then he sighed and said that this kind of question was rather abstruse, and he wasn't the right person to ask.

His little-adult expression made me laugh, and my interest in the partition over there increased. Tomorrow night, I would climb over there again. Without using a ladder, I still could descend to the ground. This was my secret.

## SHADOW PEOPLE

I was one of the Shadow People in this torrid city. In the daytime, when the city was blazing hot, people moved their activities to dark places — to rooms with windows covered with thick drapes. It was said that in the past many people were on the streets, but before long they began to go into hiding, partly out of shame and partly out of cowardice. Who dared confront the sun? Naturally, this change didn't take place overnight. At first, because of inner extrusion, people gradually became thin, and then even thinner, until they turned into shapes like flagpoles. Although there were no flags, a little something did seem to be fluttering at the top — neither quite like people's hair nor quite like hats. Later, even these flagpoles retreated shamefacedly indoors. But if an outsider ventured to walk into a house (most houses weren't locked), after rubbing his eyes to adjust to the dark he would find no one at all in the darkened room.

Where had the people gone? We hadn't gone underground, nor were we hiding inside the hollow walls. We were simply in the room. If you carefully investigated the foot of the bed, the back of the bookcase, the corners of the room, the backs of the doors, and other similar places, you would discover pale shadows flexing and twisting. That's us, the cowards. Worms hide in the earth. We hide indoors. It seems an odd way to live.

I had been traipsing around for a very long time before I reached Fire City. I still remember the longing I felt on the way. I thought I was going to the Crystal Palace—the most beautiful place found in legends. It was night when I arrived. I remember that someone dragged me into an old room smelling of broth, and then I heard someone say, "He can never leave."

I lay on a huge wooden bed. It wasn't just I; several other people were lying there, too. Thick drapes blocked the rays of light. It remained dark inside, even though dawn had come a long time ago. I wanted to sit up. I wanted to get out of bed and go outside. The old codger next to me held me down with his powerful hand and said, "You'd be looking for trouble if you went outside naked, wouldn't you? One time, someone here did go out rashly, and then he died of shame."

Why had he asserted that I wasn't wearing clothes? How unreasonable! How arbitrary! I wanted to argue with him, but I couldn't say a word. My brain was empty. It was really absurd. I had wanted to go to the Crystal Palace, but I had fallen into this dark place, into a city run by power politics. But the broth wasn't bad. There was a cook in this room, though I couldn't see him. I couldn't see anyone. I just heard their voices. Then, all of a sudden, I started drinking some broth. After finishing it, I threw the bowl up in the air. I wanted to see if someone would come to retrieve it. No one did. The bowl didn't fall to the floor, either; I don't know where it flew.

Now, with no one blocking me, I got out of bed and groped my way to the door. I opened it a crack. All of a sudden, light streaming past knocked me onto the floor. And the door closed automatically. The blow just now was so powerful that I felt I'd been struck by lightning. There was a little light in the room now, and I could distinguish about five shadows on the bed. I held my hand out toward them, but touched only air. This was so scary! I fell to the floor and sat there feeling anguished. I heard the old codger: "Lei Xiaonan (my name), if you're thinking about going out, you'd better not tell anyone."

He actually knew my name. What did he mean by what he said? I couldn't touch this old codger, and yet he could push me down and restrict my movements.

This house was large. At one end of it, someone was cooking soup. I sat on the floor, unable to think of any countermeasures. I had arrived at night. Now it was probably morning.

"Someone who was treated to a good meal was not a bit grateful."

The voice came from the other side of the room; perhaps it was the cook talking. Everyone on the big bed laughed out loud. "So you've been after appreciation all along," they said in unison.

Just then, I smelled meat burning. The whole room was permeated with this nauseating smell.

I burrowed under the high bed and lay there. It was even darker here and should be safer. However, someone whispered in my ear, "I'm going to go on strike today." It was the cook. This was where he always slept.

"Are you a local?" I asked after a pause.

"Of course. In the past, during wartime, we fought in the streets until we were covered with blood."

"And later?"

"Later, the sun became more and more toxic, and we had to move to these shady places."

"When the sun sets, can you go out?"

"The setting sun is a thing of the past. Now the sun no longer sets."

"That's not true. I know it was night when I arrived here."

"I'll tell you what happens. The sun does set briefly every day, but only for a few seconds—or at the most, two minutes. It was at that moment that you arrived."

I wanted to ask him some more, but he started snoring. I couldn't touch him, either. Perhaps I was the only one in this room with a physical body. My left hand was here, and my right hand was here. I could touch my face.

The sound of snoring filled the entire room. How odd. Why didn't I feel even a little drowsy? I was too excited. My thoughts began roaming around in the midst of the snoring sounds. Over there in the stove, which was as big as one in a farmhouse, the bright coal fire was belching blue flames. Two shadows crouched at the sides of the stove. They kept talking in whispers. A *sss-woooo, sss-woooooo* came from them as they grew longer and shorter. Their conversation, however, didn't stop for even a moment. People enjoyed many advantages when they were transformed into these wispy things.

At my feet, behind the large cupboard, there were also a few shadows. Sometimes they snored and sometimes they didn't. They were worried. Whenever they stopped snoring, they muttered some short phrases: "Inhaling!" "Attention!" "Hold up." "Fling it out." "Throw it in." It seemed they had trouble sleeping. Maybe, whether asleep or awake, they always lived like this.

All of a sudden, a wind chime rang near the window, *ting-ling, ting-ling,* startling me. All the sounds in the room ceased. Everyone was listening intently. I couldn't stop myself from clambering

out from under the bed. This drew curses from all directions, probably because the noise I made interfered with their listening. What
significance was this bizarre wind chime transmitting? Arching my
back, I glided over to the side of the window. It was still sounding,
but no wind was blowing. I lifted the curtains gently, my eyes nar-
rowing in the glaring white light. I saw it suspended on the window.
It was shaking by itself, as though it were alive. I couldn't look at it
very long, so I had to let go of the curtains. A deathly stillness filled
the room. It took about two minutes for the wind chime to stop
shaking. At first, the several persons on the bed sighed, "Finally."
"Man's extremity is God's opportunity." "All's well that ends well."
The cook also came out. He was on the bed when he said to me,
"Your wandering back and forth in this room is making me light-
headed. I really shouldn't have fed you soup. Just look at how much
space you're occupying in this room."

"I certainly didn't intend to occupy your space," I said, cha-
grined.

"But you did, anyhow."

"Then what should I do?"

"You should leave, instead of taking our space. Whoever
dragged you in here in the first place was an idiot."

His words made me disgusted with myself. I dashed over to the
door. At the worst, I might die, but—regardless—I was going out. I
took a deep breath, opened the door hurriedly, and pounced on the
air outside. Behind me, I heard several wind chimes.

My memories are confused. Things that happened when I first
arrived here seem to have occurred yesterday. After I left the large
house, I was almost blinded by the dazzling white blaze. In particular, the glass windows of the large mansions were launching one

flame after another into the air. This city was going to be scorched. I hurriedly sought shelter in a small box at the side of the road. It was an abandoned newspaper kiosk, its windows blocked with cardboard. By all appearances, someone before me had used it for a shelter. No, wait a minute, someone was inside right now.

"You've been evicted," he said. "Were you evicted because of your frivolous behavior?"

A deep sense of shame that I'd never felt before took hold of me. I really wanted to burrow under the ground and never come out. I couldn't remember exactly how old I was, but anyhow I was no longer young. How come I was still behaving like a frisky colt? I had never realized this when I was still at home, but when I arrived here my true nature was revealed.

The person talking with me—a talking shadow—was glued to the tin wall. This person seemed overcome with worries. I asked if I was invading his space. He thought about this for a long time before answering: "Space isn't an issue in a place like this. I'm here only temporarily to take a rest. This is a public newspaper kiosk. Who would be able to stay here long?"

I was relieved, yet my sense of shame didn't vanish. My hands, my feet, my chin, my messy beard, my vulgar voice: all these made me really ashamed. Not to mention having been evicted from the large house: I couldn't even think about that, for if I did I'd go out of my mind. I closed my eyes: I no longer wanted to see anything. On the wall, he sneered a couple of times. I didn't know if he was laughing at me or not.

"Who are you laughing at?"

"Nobody. People like us enjoy sneering a couple of times when we have nothing else to do."

His words weren't very friendly. I certainly didn't want to stick around here, but where could I go? This person was hanging on the wall, and a faint smell emanated from him. He made me feel really uncomfortable. Maybe I smelled even worse and I simply wasn't aware of it. In despair, I raised one hand to my eyes. My hand had withered. It was like two layers of skin wrapped around bones. And that wasn't all: the bones in my hand had become thin and pliable.

"Brother, I see that you're extruding yourself. You'll soon become as thin as a sheet of paper."

After saying this, he floated away from the door with a *puh*. The form of a person was hanging where he had been. Involuntarily, I pressed myself against the vacancy, and then heard another *puh* sound. Had I also been transformed into a shadow, glued up here? I could still see and touch my hands, my chin, my shoulders, and my vulgar face. It's just that these parts had somehow become thinner.

I could still move. I strode toward the door and looked out from a crack in the door. The rays of light were no longer so dazzling, and a dark green color had appeared everywhere. I saw three shadows against the trashcan; their voices reached my ears. They were scrambling for a box of fast food that someone had thrown away. At first, they argued loudly, and then they compromised and took turns grabbing things and eating. I remembered the cook and the broth in the house. Why didn't these shadows go into the house? Had they also been evicted? It appeared that those who were inside the house were powerful. No wonder their talk betrayed a superiority complex. When I first arrived, had they thought I was important and discovered only later that I wasn't?

The sky's deep green color grew darker and darker. A sentimental watery hue unfolded in the air. All of a sudden, I remembered why I had come to this place: someone had stolen my family heirloom, a valuable ink stone. I had sued him and been crushingly defeated. I'd almost forgotten this, but now at last I began to remember. I skipped trippingly along the road like a swallow. Why did I feel so humiliated just then? I looked at the people who had been picking up food to eat from the trashcan; now the three of them were wrapped around the top of the concrete lamppost. They were on top of the world as they rested. Their heads took on their original triangular shapes as they slept. Even in slumber, these heads didn't behave well: they bumped into each other like naughty children.

A lot of old houses stood on both sides of the road. Taking stock of them, I thought that, although they were old and damaged, the gray walls and black doors appeared forbiddingly haughty. Probably the shadows in the houses had undertaken a significant project. I looked straight across and saw a long, black shadow extrude itself from the eaves and then hang from the wall. Next to it another shadow did the same. They shook in the watery air, looking hopeless. This old house was the very one I had just stayed at. What was going on inside?

"Now he's much more composed than before, but he still has a frivolous tail."

I looked up: it was one of the people twisted around on the lamppost who had said this. All three of them were awake now, and their heads had become thick dark shadows again — stretching out and drawing back as they looked at me.

"Perhaps he will never lose that tail. He can't transform himself into one of us."

I skipped a few times on the sidewalk. My body really was as light as a swallow's. Could I fly, too?

I walked in front of the two shadows hanging on the wall and heard the sound of weeping. It was a man and a woman. The woman's shadow was a little thicker. The outline of the man's shadow was difficult to distinguish if you didn't look carefully. Perhaps this was because the woman had exerted herself more in life. Why were they so woeful?

"The sun will come out again. Sooner or later, we'll have nowhere to hide," the woman said through tears.

"You chose to get out of there. No one forced us," the man said.

"I can't help but belittle myself in there. I'd rather take the risk of leaving."

"Sweetheart, I love you so much."

The two shadows embraced briefly and separated quickly.

My skin felt prickly. All around, the dark green color was gradually lightening: the sun was coming out. The two shadows both looked dejected: they were elongated and thin on the old wall, as if wanting to blend in. Would they die from being exposed to the sun?

It was hard to tolerate the sun. I had to slip back into the old house.

"I've come to occupy the space again," I said to the Shadow People in the house.

The room was silent. I smelled the broth. Had they slipped out like the two on the wall? I groped my way to the large bed. It was empty. I wanted to lie down and rest a while, but a sense of inferiority seeped out from the bottom of my heart. This wasn't my bed: how could I lie on it?

Then it would be all right if I lay down under the bed. I felt around under the bed. There were cobwebs all around. I grabbed a large bunch of them. This gave me goose bumps. I flicked my hands repeatedly and brushed them off repeatedly, too. And still I was uncomfortable. The backs of my hands itched and prickled. Had I been bitten by a poisonous insect? Little by little, I could see the furniture in the room. I walked toward that enormous stove.

"Ha-ha." Someone on the front of the stove laughed.

This was the person I had run into outside.

"You can't drink that broth."

"Why not?"

"Because you still have a tail. Wherever you go, you occupy space. This broth isn't for people like you. The old man thought that as soon as you entered this room you'd be able to transform into one of us, but you still have a tail."

This person apparently wanted to make things difficult for me.

"May I at least rest on the bed?"

"No."

"Are you the manager here?"

"We manage ourselves. But you're a different matter."

As we spoke, he twisted around, and two gusts of evil wind blew toward me. It seemed that everyone here was my superior. I had a tail which I couldn't cast off.

"Try swaying as I'm doing," he said.

Imitating these shadows, I twisted a few times. God! I was almost done for. I fell apart. The sky was no longer the sky, and the earth no longer the earth. My body seemed to be turning into a worn-out fishing net suspended in the air. I felt like throwing up, which was even worse; I was going to make a complete mess of myself.

"Sway a few more times." I heard his voice again.

But I couldn't. This was harder to take than dying. I collapsed, my face on the floor. The broth on the stove was bubbling. I heard him stoking the fire with an iron hook. Evidently when a person was transformed into a shadow, he could still do his work. It was clear that I wasn't made of the same stuff. I will always have a tail, but lamentably I'll never be able to touch it. At this moment, I so much wanted to be transformed into one of the Shadow People. I really admired these guys who swayed to and fro. Even their sadness was sublime. If I died some day and became a nut-brown strip hanging on the wall and thus didn't occupy any space, how wonderful that would be! I remembered that in my childhood, when the southern snowflakes floated to the adobe wall of our home, the wall's color deepened and the snowflakes disappeared. The fire which heated the house of course also warmed the adobe walls.

He slowly floated to the large bed over there, swayed elegantly a few times, and then calmly dropped down onto the bed. A small green star twinkled briefly in the dark and just as quickly disappeared.

"Did you see that just now? It was really bright!" I burst out with this, despite my stomachache.

"It's something inside us. Some folk say that we became Shadow People precisely in order to see it."

"When you saw it just now, were you happy?"

"Uh-huh. But it's meaningless to answer questions like that."

I was depressed. I felt it would be tough for me to go on staying here, but I couldn't go back either. It was out of the question for a shadow with a tail to live among people at home. In my hometown, physical labor was the only work available, and I would have to work every day there; I wouldn't be able to live the idle life as I was doing now. I had yearned for an idle life since I was a young man. Finally

it was being realized, but why was I still wavering between consider-
ations of gain and loss? People are never content.

It was noisy outside: people were coming back. They probably
saw me, for they fell silent. Just then I was squatting, sticking tightly
to the side of the stove. I figured they hadn't yet made up their
minds whether they wanted to drive me out again. I was prepared
to leave at once if they drove me out.

"I never imagined that he could be transformed this way." The
cook was the first to speak. "He just has a tail left on the outside."

"Now we probably shouldn't drive him out," said the old man
who had slept beside me.

They all entered, leaving the door wide open. At this moment,
the light outside was very strong; it shone snow white on the area
next to the entrance. I figured they had left the door open for me. I
thought they wanted me to decide on my own to leave. The stillness
in the house had told me this much. Gnashing my teeth, I rushed
out. I rushed out with my feet, certainly not with my tail. It was only
they who could see my tail.

I heard people inside the room applauding. They appreciated
what I had done.

The burning sun stabbed my skin, and I ran around crazily. I
wanted to find a shady spot for shelter. All unaware, I fell into an
underground carport. I could finally relax. The gasoline odor was
hard to take. I looked up. Several shadows were hanging on the
damp wall. They kept whispering.

"Is this up or down?"

"I think it's up."

"I think it's down. Isn't there something dusky here?"

"Take another look. It definitely isn't something dusky."

"No, it isn't. There is layer upon layer inside. Then it must be up."

"I don't think it's up, either. If it were up, then how could people trample on that thing?"

A big truck drove up, dark and blurry. But it was a strange truck—it made no noise. That was terrifying. It was being driven slowly, and it approached gradually. The guys on the wall were silent. The truck scraped against the wall as it drove up. Was it going to crush me to death? Clinging to the wall, I stood on tiptoe. How I wished I could hang effortlessly on the wall as these people were doing.

"Help!" I heard myself shout.

But it drove past, and I was still alive. I had just let out a sigh of relief when it came back.

"This time, it'll turn him into meat pie," someone above me said.

I held my breath, feeling absolute despair. It was my destiny, since I couldn't transform myself into a shadow. When it pounded past, my ribs hurt a little, because I was terrified of death. Yet they didn't hurt too much.

I hadn't died yet. I felt my ribs: they were fine. But hadn't I seen the iron front of the truck crushing me? Now none of those shadows on the wall above made a sound.

The truck kept going back and forth for a long time, and I became rather used to it. Nonetheless, it was unquestionably a truck—I even touched it with my hand. Then I must be the issue. Was I still a human being? If I was, how could I have been repeatedly crushed and yet still be okay? If I had already turned into a shadow, why did my ribs hurt?

The truck drove ahead into the dark tunnel. I stood stuck to the wall, not knowing what to do. The other vehicles in this carport looked like junk, abandoned years ago. But it was hard to say whether the truck that struck me was also a piece of junk. Someone was driving it. I had made eye contact, and he looked like a robot. But he had a real hand, a man's hairy hand. He had even reached out and touched my face as he passed. The hand was icy cold. I shivered.

"I want to leave." I couldn't stop myself from saying this to the people above me.

It was a long time before someone asked, "How is that possible?"

Following the wall, I made my way toward the exit. I heard them talking about me behind my back, but I couldn't hear their exact words. Each time I moved, the air made a *puh* sound, as though I'd broken a layer of membrane. I would soon reach the exit. The sunshine dazzled me, and I hadn't yet decided what to do. Should I actually go out? Just now, hadn't someone said it was impossible? As I wavered, the large truck drove up again. This time, it bumped into me and sent me flying. Slowly, I landed in a dark spot—perhaps the innermost part of the carport. I fell onto the ground, but I was unhurt. Maybe that's because I had already transformed into a shadow. The cement floor was a little damp from humidity. The odor of gasoline was less pungent now; perhaps I had grown accustomed to it. The large truck had disappeared. It was as though it had driven up especially to bump into me.

"There's no broth here. How do you live?" I asked loudly.

No one answered. They must have thought I was very vulgar. I had really begun longing for the broth in that old house. You could never forget the food once you had tasted it. At that moment, the large stove and the cook were magnified in my imagination. I thought that life in the old house was the life of my ideals. Like that other person, I could stick to the wall of the stove and go to the stove whenever I wanted to drink the broth.

I wasn't a bit hungry, so why did I keep thinking about the broth?

Against the wall, I unconsciously shifted toward the outside once more.

"He is really stubborn," groaned someone above.

I came rushing out. I figured out where the old house was and closed my eyes as I rushed over there. The sun was burning this deserted city—it was quiet everywhere. I was accustomed now to hurrying along with my eyes closed, and in any case no vehicles were on the road so nothing could run into me. I could open my eyes a crack every thirty seconds and see a little of the surroundings. And so, after a short time I reached the old house.

"I'm back again," I said as I entered.

"But no one here welcomes you." I heard the cook's voice. "There's only one use for someone like you: to be added to the stew in this large pot. You still have a tail, don't you?"

He asked me to approach him so he could look at my tail. I did, but he changed his mind and said, "I don't have to look at it. It's too hard; it hasn't ripened yet." Then he told me, "You'd better lie on your stomach on the floor and not move. Then no one can see you. If they can't see you, they won't be annoyed."

Complying with his instructions, I lay down. It was incredibly different this time. I heard all manner of noises coming up nonstop from cracks in the floor, from the walls, and from the ceiling: a lot of people were telling stories from those places. Their voices were bewitching—wonderful in both tone and expression. I was carried along by those fantastic snippets of sound. The mysterious voices narrating these stories filled this old house—waves upon waves, like a big river surging. Although I couldn't hear the end of any story, I was so excited my body shook as though I had malaria. I—this shadow with a tail—began twisting around crazily. I was hurting so much I groaned loudly, but I couldn't keep my body from moving. I was going to die! I was going to die!

All of a sudden, a bell rang, and the voices fell silent. Ah, the wind chime! I was still twisting, immersed in a beautiful story: even if I died, I wouldn't regret this. The ringing stopped, then started again. This time it sounded like a warning; perhaps I was the one who needed a warning. I involuntarily stopped twisting. I hadn't fainted even though it had been unbearable. How odd! The wind chime didn't ring again after warning me. I looked up and gazed around the room. All the shadows had disappeared. Where had they gone?

I stood up and walked around. I couldn't hear my footsteps. I jumped, and then jumped some more, and still I heard no sound. The only sound in the entire house was the *puh*, *puh*, *puh* coming from the broth in the big pot on the stove. I walked over, scooped soup into a bowl, and drank it. The broth smelled good but I couldn't detect any flavor. Maybe the flavor was too complex, and I just couldn't describe it. After finishing a bowl of soup, I felt strong all over.

I lay down on the floor again and listened intently. I didn't hear those sweet voices. I heard only the depressing north wind blowing hard outside, one gust after another. Tired of listening, I twisted my head around and looked back. Ah, there was my tail. My tail was as large as a dinosaur's. In the dim light, I could sometimes see it and sometimes not. It was real and illusory at the same time. It had grown on my back and was a support for my whole body. Now I understood what the cook had said. He had spoken that way because he envied me.

I—a shadow with a tail: I belonged to the Shadow People, and yet I was different from the others.

## CROW MOUNTAIN

I'd been waiting for a long time for Qinglian, who lived on the fifth floor, to take me to a place called Crow Mountain. It was a vacant five-story building on the brink of collapse. It used to be the municipal office. I had passed by it only once, the year I was four. I remembered Mama pointing at the large, tightly closed windows and saying to me, "This is Crow Mountain!" All kinds of questions occurred to me right away. "What do you mean, it's a mountain?" I asked. "It's obviously a building. Where are the crows? Are these windows shut so tightly because they're afraid the crows inside will fly away?" Dad was standing beside me. I wanted to ask still more questions, but he cut me off: "Come on, let's go!"

Later we moved to another part of the city. It was Qinglian who told me more about that building. Qinglian was only fourteen but already a beauty, and I envied her. She always frowned as she said to me, "Juhua, Juhua, how can you be so ugly? I'm embarrassed to be seen with you." I knew she was kidding, so I didn't get mad. We had been talking about Crow Mountain for a long time. Everything I knew about it came from Qinglian. Though I could still vaguely remember that large building outside the city, I hadn't been back a single time. The city was too big. But Qinglian went every year because her uncle was a gatekeeper there.

"They're always saying it's going to collapse, but actually it isn't. It'll be fine for decades. It's so much fun inside!" she said.

Year after year, I pleaded with her to take me there, and finally she agreed to take me one Saturday. It was a Monday morning when she made this promise. Those five days dragged on forever, because I was afraid she would change her mind. I needn't have worried, though, for we finally set out for the building as scheduled.

On the bus, Qinglian frowned sternly and didn't say a word. Whenever I asked a question, she just shook her head.

After we got off the bus and walked along the dirt road, I began to relive all my memories. Not far from the office building was a well. Back then, its water had overflowed into the nearby fields. My dad had filled a bottle with the well water and given it to me to drink. Now the well had gone dry, and the nearby paddy fields had also disappeared and turned into wasteland.

"When we reach Crow Mountain, you can't just keep asking questions."

I thought Qinglian was making it sound like a big deal just to impress me.

Her uncle lived in the basement. Qinglian knocked several times, but he didn't come to the door. Qinglian said, "He's always like this." She said we could go inside first and look around. As soon as she touched the door, it opened. She dragged me in. The door closed with a creak. We could see nothing inside.

"Qinglian, Qinglian, where are you?"

I sounded like a mosquito; my voice was distorted.

"Juhua, I'm in the mountain valley . . . Take it easy. Just lift your feet high and walk . . ."

Her answer came from somewhere far away, and I thought she

must be somewhere above me. Was she hanging out with the crows on the fifth floor? I did exactly as she said, and started lifting my feet and walking. But it seemed as though my feet were being held in place by a powerful suction on the floor. I was sweating all over. When I lost heart and stopped trying, Qinglian's voice rose again.

"Juhua, there are red cherries here!"

She was still above me. I started trying hard again, and this seemed a little more effective. The floorboards sounded as though they were cracking, which frightened me. When we were "horse vaulting" at home, Qinglian was the "horse" and I vaulted over her. Every time I jumped over her, it felt as though I were chopping her head off with my legs. The very thought made me tremble. Now, stamping on the cracked floor was giving me the same feeling. I realized I had managed to take several steps. My arms flailed in the dark, and I wanted to hold on to something.

I stepped on a small animal that squealed weakly. Could it be the crow? It didn't sound like one. Maybe it was a rat.

"Juhua, you're on the second floor now. That's great. The floor tilts to your right. Can you tell?" Qinglian seemed a little closer as she shouted to me.

"Sort of . . . I guess."

This time, my voice was back to normal. But I had taken only four or five steps. How could I have reached the second floor so quickly? And since it was the second floor of a building, how could there be a slope? She kept telling me to try harder, and threatened me by saying if I didn't do so, there would be an "accident." So I began lifting my legs high and setting them down, just like a robot, lifting them up and setting them down. But I wasn't getting anywhere. I was back where I had started.

The floor was tilted at an angle, and I slipped and fell. And kept falling. Where was I? Was that what Qinglian meant when she said there would be an accident? Oh my God, I must be about to enter hell. I eventually slid to a halt. When I stood up, I was free to walk around. But I didn't dare just walk wherever I wanted, because I was afraid.

"Have you come here to play games, child?" It was an old man's voice.

It was probably Qinglian's uncle. And since her uncle was here, this couldn't be hell.

"No, I've come, I've come . . ." I didn't know how to answer.

"There's something here that's even more fun. Can you see me?"

"No."

"Try harder."

"Oh, I think I can see a shadow. Are you on my right?"

"No, I'm on your left."

"Then I was mistaken. I can't see you, Grandpa. Are you her uncle?"

He didn't answer, and he didn't say anything else. Perhaps he had gone.

He had asked me if I'd come here to play games, so maybe all the people who came here did so in order to play games? Once I thought carefully about it, I broke into a cold sweat. What a terrifying game this was. I sat down on the floor and thought back on my years of friendship with Qinglian.

She lived with her widowed mother on the fifth floor. Our family lived on the first floor. She was like a tulip—not a rose or a narcissus. A tulip. And I? I was just a plain old daisy. Qinglian wouldn't have admitted that we were close friends. She liked being a loner. Sometimes she called me "Little Daisy" to show that she looked down on me. But I still liked it when she called me that, even though she was only a year older than I, because I thought it made us sound close.

She didn't play with me very often. When the two of us were together, we just played simple card games. When I asked her what she played at home, she replied listlessly, "I have to work. There's no time to play." She had never invited me to her home. I had heard that she and her mother did embroidery. One day, I ran into her on the street and tore the linen cover off the bamboo basket she was carrying. I was stunned when I saw her work. She took it out so that I could look at it more closely. It was a piece of double-sided embroidery. One side was a scene of the ocean; the other was a waterfall. I was speechless. I gripped her hand—the one holding the embroidery. She angrily dropped it back into the basket and pulled her hand away.

She wouldn't let me ask any questions about the embroidery. She looked glum. She said I wouldn't understand, and of course I didn't. I couldn't imagine what it must be like when she and her mother embroidered together. I had no idea. Qinglian's mother looked like an old monkey. She always crept when she went up and down stairs. She smiled at me when we met but never said a word. I had no way of approaching the remote world inhabited by Qinglian and her mother. Was this why I adored her?

Now Qinglian was taking me to this place, but wasn't the distance between us just the same as it had always been, like the distance between heaven and earth? I had wanted to see the inside of Crow Mountain for years. I had even imagined an exceedingly tall tree in the middle of this building. Now that I had muddle-headedly tumbled into this dungeon, was it really what I'd hoped for?

Dismayed, I heard Qinglian call out again. She sounded far away, as if calling down from the sky.

"Juhua, after you go up the slope, don't stop to pick the cherries. Once you start, you won't be able to stop. You have to be resolute."

"Qinglian, Qinglian! I'm done for! I can't get to the place you're talking about."

I heard my voice rebounding like an ear-shattering explosion. How had things come to this? I made an effort to stand up, and held out my arms to feel my way as I walked. I touched a pillar! I hugged it tightly. I was overcome by emotion.

"Why are you hugging my leg, kid? You have to do this by yourself."

The old man's voice came down from above. The smooth pillar turned out to be his leg! I blushed. I hated myself for not being better at this. So this person was a giant. Who was he?

"I'm Qinglian's uncle, the gatekeeper here."

He was talking from somewhere above me. He could see through to my thoughts. Qinglian's uncle was a giant. She'd never told me this. I felt somewhat reassured; this place wasn't a dungeon; it was merely the basement where Qinglian's uncle lived. I wondered whether he'd been testing us by not opening the door when we'd knocked for such a long time. How strange he was.

"Hello, Uncle! Qinglian and I came to see you. Can you tell me where I am? And where Qinglian is? My name is Juhua."

"I've heard her speak of you, Juhua. Of course, you're in my home. Where else could you be? Generally, I don't let anyone in. Anyone I let in can get whatever he or she wants. Juhua, think carefully: what do you want?"

"Me? I want to go wherever Qinglian is," I said loudly.

Then I saw a little light across from me, as if someone were carrying a candle, or as if a candle were floating along of its own accord. When I moved toward the light, I sensed someone holding me back.

"Uncle, is that you?"

No one answered. After spending so much time in the dark, I couldn't tear my eyes away from the light. I was afraid it would vanish. All of a sudden, the pinprick of light became a gigantic pillar of light as wide as a bowl, which kept stretching upward. I realized that this wasn't a five-story building—it was a huge vacant room. The column of light penetrated the roof and shot toward the sky, and I finally managed to approach it. I tried putting my hand into the column itself, and immediately the tragic caw of crows reverberated. Frightened, I drew my hand back. After resting a while, I had to try again. This time I couldn't put my hand in because a strong electrical current threw me to the floor. The crows, the crows! I thought my head would explode.

I lost consciousness. It was a very long time before I came to and heard Qinglian's feeble voice coming intermittently from far away.

"Juhua, there are so many . . . Are you coming? Oh . . ."

Her voice was drowned out by the caws of the crows. I stepped away from the pillar of light and hid in the dark. The floor was shifting under my feet, and in relation to the column of light, I sensed that I was ascending. Perhaps I had reached the third floor! The crows' caws changed to whispers. I had never heard crows make sounds like this. Perhaps they weren't really crows?

"Qinglian!" I heard myself cry.

I couldn't find the wall. Why not? Wasn't I in a large building? Even if the building had no floors, it must have an outer wall. I walked and walked, and still couldn't find the wall. The crows had all flown down below me. I was excited to think that I was in a vacant building where I could walk up and down freely. I could tell I was walking fast. But where was Qinglian? I had no destination, and I was disoriented. No, I still had some sense of direction. My aim was to avoid the pillar of light. So was I going in circles? No. Look, I was ascending again, perhaps as high as four stories, I thought, since there were no floors.

"Qinglian!"

"Don't shout . . . I'm almost there . . ."

She would be there soon. Maybe she was approaching the peak of Crow Mountain along a path that had red cherries and maybe chestnuts along the way. I had nothing here. We were on the same mountain, but I was also in a vacant building. How bizarre. Ah, I saw the giant's feet cross the pillar of light. He made no noise as he passed by.

"Uncle!" I shouted.

"Don't shout. Be quiet!" he said.

The sound echoed all over the room, as if Uncle's voice were booming from a loudspeaker. Qinglian's uncle must be a powerful man. She'd never told me what she did here, even though she came to see him every year. She was good at keeping secrets. How would it feel to have a giant for an uncle? I simply couldn't imagine. I suddenly recalled her embroidery of the waterfall and the ocean. Ah, now I dimly understood her. She belonged to a different world. As for me, I was only a shallow young girl. No wonder I admired her. Not one of our neighbors knew that Qinglian's uncle was a giant. Was it something she wanted to hide? I thought it was quite the opposite—something to show off. Qinglian and I saw things completely differently. She was different from all the rest of us.

I kept walking. How far had I gone? I had been calling out to Qinglian, but she didn't answer. Had she reached the mountaintop? Was she unable to hear sounds from below? The floor under my feet rose much higher again, but judging by the height of the pillar of light, I was still quite far from the roof. Maybe I wouldn't ever get there; maybe that place belonged only to Qinglian. The path she'd taken had everything—flowers, birds, cherries, chestnuts. I, on the other hand, was surrounded by darkness. When I was a child, Dad had dragged me past this building, because he had known that I wasn't made for places like this. I never guessed that after so many years I would be able to revisit this place—and even see the giant uncle. When I considered this, my excitement rose again.

Look, he was crossing the pillar of light again! When he wasn't talking, there was no sound to be heard. His feet stood on the level where I was; his head was probably on the mountaintop.

"Uncle!"

He didn't answer.

I continued wandering in the dark. Snowflakes were falling inside the column of light! Or rather, not snowflakes but extremely tiny birds falling toward the ground. I heard the gentle thumps as they thudded to the floor, and then they scattered. Although I couldn't see them, I could sense the vitality inside this deserted building. They didn't call out, but I kept hearing their voices. All of a sudden, the shrill caw of the crows rose, and then the column of light disappeared, and the room fell deathly still again. Perhaps this was a gigantic crow. It called out three times, and then the silence grew even more frightening. My blood curdled. What was going to happen?

I grabbed something out of the air. It seemed to be a lizard. It was odd: I felt particularly tender toward the tiny critter I was holding. I even stuck it on my face. The thought of its being alive was comforting. Something alive was here with me, but it bit me on the face and my face swelled. The wound smarted, but I didn't want to just throw it away. I kept clutching it. Maybe it wasn't a lizard after all. It had rough skin.

There was a buzzing sound, and the air seemed to be vibrating. It was probably Uncle talking, but I couldn't hear a word he was saying.

"Juhua, I'm really happy . . . You've managed to get hold of . . ."

Qinglian's voice came from a faraway place above me. I thought wherever she was, she wasn't in the building. Maybe she was in outer space. What had I gotten hold of? Did she mean this little creature I was holding? This was a cold-blooded creature. I was holding it in my hand. It had no wings, yet it could actually drift in the air. I decided to take it home and raise it.

I was excited about going home. Qinglian, you gave me such a bizarre experience. Now I really wanted to go home, but I also really wanted to try some new things. What I wanted most right now was to meet up with Qinglian. Did she still care about me? She certainly wasn't avoiding me. This was the first secret the two of us had shared. I decided not to tell my parents about Crow Mountain. Then again, Qinglian and I probably wouldn't meet here. This seemed to be one of her principles: she had to be in her place, and I had to be in my place. My face was numb where it had been bitten. Would I die? The little thing bit me again on my palm. It hurt a little, but it was much more exciting. If I brought this little wingless thing that could still drift in the air home with me, it could drift back and forth in the air all day long. How jealous the neighbors would be when they saw it!

But where was the door? I couldn't find it, and so I had no way of leaving. I sat on the floor, the little thing in my hand. I listened closely. It was the roar of a faraway waterfall, and I imagined what it must look like—the mist of the waterfall against the sky.

"Uncle," I said to the air.

"Have you gone where she is?" I immediately heard Uncle's voice and then the echoes in the vacant building. I felt a tremor, like a small earthquake.

"No, Uncle! Qinglian is far away from me!"

"You're such a silly child," Uncle laughed.

The floor where I was seated shook with the sound of his laughter. I was terrified.

He finally stopped laughing. Once again, I saw the candle drifting in the air. A door appeared where the candle was. I got up at once, walked over there, and pushed the door open. Next to the door was a small basement room. A weak beam of light on the floor passed through the window. The room was neat, and there was even a mosquito net over the bed.

When my eyes grew accustomed to the light, I noticed many small bookcases lining the wall of the room. There was an ancient book on the table, and next to it was a pair of small spectacles. There were also some ancient books on the bed stand. Wasn't Uncle a giant after all? Was this his room? Why did I think it must be his room?

The door creaked open, and a humpbacked old man with glasses and a goatee came in. Who was following him? Oh my God, it was Qinglian!

"I came into this building from another entrance," she said. "When I turned around, you weren't there. After playing for a while, I came down here. What do you think of my uncle's place?"

"Don't ask questions like that, dear." Uncle put his hand on her shoulder. "They bring bad luck."

I noticed that Uncle had a pointed red nose. He looked quite wretched.

■

Qinglian and I took the bus again. I felt a surge of emotion. Qinglian's expression was indifferent. All of a sudden, I thought of the little thing. Where had I left it? I gazed at my palm; there was no wound there. Then I felt my face; there was no wound there, either. I was filled with regret and sadness.

When we were almost home, Qinglian suddenly said to me: "You're welcome to go back there with me anytime you like."

I cheered up as soon as she said that. I had a secret! This was our secret—Qinglian's and mine.

Catfish Pit was a neighborhood in the downtown area packed with old two-story wooden dwellings. Woman Wang lived in a room on the left side in one of those buildings. She was old and single, with no child. Not many acquaintances ever looked in on her. This place would soon be demolished, and all the residents would have to move to tall apartment buildings. Everyone was apprehensive, asking one another, "What's it like to live in a skyscraper?" Woman Wang was the only one who didn't care. When the demolition notice was delivered, Woman Wang was cleaning her huge kimchi vat. Looking up, she said to the worker, "Just put it on the tea table."

Then she picked up a long bright-red hot pepper and placed it carefully in the bottom of the crock. She added two pieces of fresh yellow ginger.

"What do you think of the proposed compensation?" the young man asked.

"Fine. Whatever. Please leave."

The man stole away like a cat. Bending her head, Woman Wang continued working. She added greengage plums, beans, gherkins, Sichuan pickles, and other things to the kimchi crock. Every time she added something, she closed her eyes and imagined what it would taste like. Of course, she wasn't making the kimchi just for herself—she would never be able to eat everything in such a large crock. See, weren't those two kids sneaking a look? They were the Pao brothers from the neighborhood—two gluttons.

Woman Wang dragged out another, smaller crock from underneath the bed. She took the lid off and quickly picked out a sword bean. The two kids ran over at once. Woman Wang broke the sword bean into two parts.

"I want this part!"

"Give it to me!" They both wanted the larger part.

"Close your eyes!" Woman Wang said strictly. "All right. Off with you."

The two brothers ran like the wind.

After a while, another person showed up—a little girl named Little Ping. She walked slowly over to Woman Wang, her eyes sliding around.

"Granny Wang, I'd love a red pepper. One with the sour flavor of greengage plums. That kind."

"Tell me first how much money you've collected."

"Two cents."

Woman Wang had taught Little Ping to keep watch in front of the candy shop counter. If a customer dropped some small change, she had to step on it right away and pick it up after the customer left. Little Ping never tired of this game; she'd been playing it for several months.

"Here's a red pepper."

"Thank you, Grandma Wang."

Little Ping took the red pepper, but didn't eat it right away. Nor did she intend to leave. Grown-ups had said there was a ghost in

Woman Wang's home. She wanted to see that ghost; the more she feared it, the more she wanted to see it.

Woman Wang shoved the pickle crock underneath the bed, stood up, and turned into the kitchen in the back. She washed her hands, intending to rest in bed for a while. All of a sudden, she noticed Little Ping standing behind the mosquito net hanging on her bed. Her mouth kept moving—nibbling the hot pepper a little at a time. Woman Wang couldn't help but laugh: this little girl was good at enjoying herself.

Woman Wang lay down on the bed. Eyes half-closed, she asked Little Ping, "What do you want to be when you grow up?"

Little Ping didn't answer. Woman Wang felt the wooden bed swaying in the shadows. No, that wasn't right: it was the floor swaying. She sat up in a hurry and got out of bed, put on her shoes, and ran outside. She stopped at the door, turned around, and shouted, "Little Ping! Little Ping!!"

But Little Ping wasn't in her home. Woman Wang thought and thought, and then went back to bed.

Woman Wang looked at the window. On the top left side, it had turned a rose color. This was Woman Wang's secret: each time she looked at the window, the same pane of glass turned rose. Woman Wang thought that Catfish Pit had a peculiar climate. This didn't necessarily affect other people, but she was constantly aware of it, mostly because of her kimchi crock. At midnight, she clearly heard the *glub-glub* sound of the water coming out of the rim of the crock's cover. She smelled the faint aroma of the kimchi. She imagined the delicious little gherkins walking and walking on Mother Earth, walking until they came to the sun setting over the horizon and then finally stopping, fading gradually into a very long dark shadow. At times like this, she would murmur to herself, "Ah, Catfish Pit—my home."

But Catfish Pit would soon vanish. Woman Wang thought, If Catfish Pit disappeared, Woman Wang of Catfish Pit would no longer exist; she would become Woman Wang in those tall apartment buildings. This was a big deal. Was it because of this that Little Ping had hidden just now behind the mosquito net? This little girl knew almost everything. She understood everything.

Another child showed up. First he knocked politely on the door, and then quietly pushed the door open. His name was Little Yao. He was always wary, like a little adult.

"Granny Wang, I miss your gherkins. The ginger- and pepper-flavored kind."

Woman Wang looked at him sleepily, and then bent down and opened a green crock and took out a gherkin for him.

As he ate it, he smacked his lips and looked all around with his big eyes.

"What are you looking for, Little Yao?"

"I saw Little Ping come in, but I didn't see her go. Is she still here?"

"Good question," Woman Wang said.

Woman Wang urged Little Yao to leave. The boy hadn't yet left when a bell echoed somewhere inside Woman Wang's head. She looked up: the rose color on the window had disappeared, and everything in the room had returned to its usual gray color. The ringing sound came and went. It was far away.

"Granny Wang, is Little Ping calling you?" Little Yao asked, staring at her.

"Maybe. Have I forgotten something?" Woman Wang was a little nervous.

"Did you cover the kimchi crock?" Little Yao asked earnestly.

"You're really watchful. But this time it was another kind of thing."

"I'm leaving. Good-bye, Granny Wang."

He hurried out, as though afraid that Woman Wang would ask him something else.

Woman Wang lay down again. The boy's reminder had sharpened her hearing. She had a good idea of what was happening in her home. In the daytime, when she went out to buy groceries, she had seen the bulldozer. The demolition wouldn't start for another three months. Why had the bulldozer shown up so soon? Little children probably liked this kind of thing a lot. When the tall apartment buildings were constructed, the unfinished rooms would be a great place for them to play.

Woman Wang closed her eyes. She felt that her thoughts could penetrate five hundred meters underground, where there was a layer of quartz. There were cavities in the quartz, and some harmless gases had accumulated in those cavities. She said, "What a wonderful place—right here in Catfish Pit!" She felt another earthquake. This time, she knew what it was. The children in this place were so smart—she hadn't been that smart at their age. She was no longer alarmed; she didn't even open her eyes. She just enjoyed the pleasant sensation of the wooden bed swaying. The swaying wasn't very strong, and it stopped quite soon.

A rose-colored light skimmed over the window, and then once more it became an ordinary window. She heard the old woman Yun, who lived upstairs on the right side, coming downstairs. She was always like this—taking two steps down, then stopping; taking another two steps, then stopping. From the staircase, she looked at the scenery on the back streets. Woman Wang thought, The inhabitants of Catfish Pit are all expert observers. Even the children. At this moment, she was hoping for another earthquake. She wanted to see—what did she want to see? Was she just hallucinating? She was also waiting expectantly. Some things take time to become clear.

■

Woman Wang ate dinner later than usual because there was something on her mind that she couldn't let go of.

She finished eating and was nearly finished with cleaning up when a sound came from under her bed. Excited, Woman Wang grabbed a flashlight to take a look. From behind the kimchi crock, Little Ping was gazing at her.

"Little Ping, did you pick up some money?" Woman Wang's voice quivered a little.

"No—I mean yes, I got two pennies. Look!"

She held up two pennies. In the dark, they glinted silver white.

"Are many people out on the street?" Woman Wang asked.

"Just me. Actually, I didn't go anywhere. I've been hiding under here. I explored with my hands and found these two coins."

She crawled out slowly, stood up, and said she had to go home.

"I'll come back and find some more coins. There's as much money under your bed as there is outside the candy shop. I'm patient. I can feel around in the cracks . . ."

"Did you find the quartz?" Woman Wang asked her.

Stunned, Little Ping immediately fell quiet and nodded her

head firmly. She said, "Yes. Yes! Quartz, and also granite—mostly bits of gritty damp earth. Why is it so wet under there?"

Without waiting for Woman Wang to reply, she hurried away.

After Little Ping left, Woman Wang shone the flashlight under the bed again. There seemed to be a hole at a spot to the right. Looking more carefully, she decided there wasn't a hole. All the floorboards were in place. Woman Wang washed her hands and face and went back to bed. How strange—Little Ping had left, and yet the wooden bed was vibrating a little. She'd been startled by the girl's words. How the hell had she seen through her secret? Woman Wang counted the years: she figured the girl should be eleven. She'd been coming here for years and begging for kimchi. Didn't this make her a conspirator? She liked money, and so Woman Wang had suggested that she pick up money in front of the candy counter. Who knew that the child would play the same trick under her very own bed? When was that? It seemed it was the year her father died. She was then a student in the girls school. She had arranged ahead of time to run up the mountain with her desk mate after school and make her way into that grotto. While they were playing with flashlights and shining them on the cliff path, the girl told her earnestly of her aspirations. This had startled the young Miss Wang greatly: she wanted to be a pilot. Miss Wang thought she was bragging because actually she was so cowardly that she even screamed when a bug fell onto her clothing. How could somebody like this dare to fly? But the girl's actions proved that she was bold. She suddenly started running and disappeared deep into the grotto. Miss Wang waited and waited, but she didn't reappear. Now *she* was the cowardly one. Retreating from the grotto, she went home in a daze. The next day in school, they didn't greet each other. She didn't even meet the girl's eyes. Thus, Woman Wang had realized early on that she herself wasn't a brave person.

She made up her mind that she would be one who waited. And so she waited. She waited until she was old. Over the years, some things that she waited for did happen to her. She moved into this wooden building when she was forty years old, intending to stay here forever. But now all of a sudden it was going to be demolished. At first she had been indifferent. Gradually, she had started paying attention, because there were some procedures to deal with. That girl hadn't been able to realize her dream of flying; instead, she married a biscuit-shop owner and ran a barber shop herself. Apparently, she expected more out of life than Miss Wang did.

It was Little Ping's suspicious behavior that had led Woman Wang to think of her former desk mate. The little girl was even more enthusiastic. None of the boys her age could be compared with her. Woman Wang had seen her potential a long time ago. Who could have imagined there was small change under her bed, yet Little Ping had been searching under there for a very long time, crawling around back and forth. Sooner or later, her "dream would come true."

Woman Wang didn't fall asleep until late that night. Before she did, the kimchi crock made noises four or five times, but nothing happened. Later she walked over to the side of the pit. Aware of the risk of falling in, she still hesitated to retreat right away. She heard someone down there saying, "Just close your eyes and jump and you'll be free!"

Then she fell asleep. But she woke up before long. She turned on the light and saw some smog in the room. Had something caught fire? She got dressed, put on her shoes, and walked out to the street. Then she turned and looked at the wooden building. No, there was no fire. But there was firelight in Woman Yun's apartment. Maybe she was burning some documents before she had to move. Woman Wang knew that some people wanted to burn certain old things in their homes so as to leave no trace behind. Woman Yun must be that kind of person.

Woman Wang had no destination in mind. The lights of the nearby snack bar were on. A man was sitting alone at an outdoor table, absorbed in drinking from a bowl. When he looked up, Woman Wang saw that it was the neighborhood mason. It was late at night, and the bar was closed. Nobody was inside. How could he have been served?

"Woman Wang, our good days are almost over. I was too troubled to sleep and came to sit here for a while. Then someone just handed me a bowl of sweet rice wine. I didn't notice who it was. It couldn't have been a ghost, could it? Anyhow, at a time like this, drinking sweet wine and sweating all over, you feel all right again!"

He took a matchstick out of his pocket and picked his teeth. He was staring at the door.

"What do you mean by 'good days'? You must really like living in Catfish, don't you?" Woman Wang asked. The middle-aged man was at a loss.

"Do I like living here? I've never thought about it that way. I'm just scared. I'm used to living here, and now I have to move. It's normal to be afraid, isn't it?"

"But aside from being afraid, do you really not want to move?"

"Me? I don't know. In my dreams, I'm always moving—moving over here, moving over there—back and forth. This made me sweat all over in my dreams. Now, finally, I'm going to move for real, but I have cold feet."

They laughed together. Woman Wang felt that the laughter was particularly strident in the darkness.

The mason kept staring at the door. Maybe he thought someone would come out and give him something to eat. He was the kind of person who always wanted more. All around, it was dark. This was the only place with a light on. Walking past him, Woman Wang merged into the darkness.

There were a lot of little noises in the darkness, sometimes loud, sometimes soft. The mason rose from the table. He was lurching, as though he would bump into the door. Was he drunk? The door creaked. From where she was standing, Woman Wang couldn't tell if the door was open or not. After a few seconds, the mason rushed inside. The light at the entrance went out. Woman Wang thought, Probably it was only when the mason saw her walking over that he had made a point of coming out of the diner and sitting at that table. Under the dark cloud of the impending move, all kinds of schemes were faintly discernible.

Circling the alleys, she headed home. Someone approached her hurriedly. Under the dim streetlights, Woman Wang saw a stranger's face.

"Do you think there are a lot of opportunities inside? Could it be the opposite?" he asked.

"Are you a mason, too?" Woman Wang asked.

"Sort of. I always want to leave a way out, but I can't. The neighborhood is too old. Bugle calls are everywhere. Everyone has to forge ahead."

"You're right." Woman Wang stopped, looked at this person,

and nodded her head. "After moving, what will you do? Will you open a tile shop or something like that?"

"No, I won't do that. All I'm good for is selling that kind of invisible thing."

Just then, Woman Wang realized that she was at the door of the diner again; the door was half-hidden, and it was very dark inside. When the stranger sat at a table, the light at the entrance came on again. The stranger seemed tired. He rested his head on his arms, and he looked at the door with wide-open eyes. Woman Wang thought he was struggling with himself over something.

She decided to go home. She walked fast without looking back.

When she finally got home, she turned on the light and sat at the table to rest for a while.

All of a sudden, she sensed that someone outside was trying to remove the latch of her door. Though it was only a slight noise, it was persistent. Woman Wang was annoyed because she had intended to go back to sleep.

She walked over and opened the door. Standing there was the second mason, looking quite awkward.

"I'd like to talk with you, but I don't know what to talk about."

As he spoke, he looked over Woman Wang's head. He was really arrogant.

"Talk about your business," Woman Wang answered quickly. "What do you actually sell?"

The young guy had no manners. She didn't invite him in.

"I sell some old things. I can't explain. Every few months, people come to talk with me about business. They pay me some money. My words are the only things they buy from me. Sometimes I wonder if I'm selling the Catfish."

He looked bewildered and stared blankly.

"That's what I wondered. Maybe you are selling the Catfish," Woman Wang said loudly.

The mason panicked. He turned around and ran off. Woman Wang covered her mouth and began laughing.

She bolted the door. It was as if a movie of the earth cracking were playing in her mind: small cubes of bright crystal quartz clanked as they rushed up from the cracks. Her scalp felt numb. She fell asleep.

She slept until dawn. After she awakened, she was still thinking about what the mason had said. Did he live here in the Catfish neighborhood? And if so, why had she never seen him? This wasn't a big place: it wasn't even one kilometer in circumference. The night before, she had smelled quartz on his body; it had made her hair stand on end. She believed he wasn't a real mason.

After she got up, she remembered that Woman Yun upstairs had burned documents. She walked outside and looked up and saw that all the doors were tightly closed.

■

When Woman Wang was selecting a carp in the market, out of the corner of her eye she noticed Little Ping's mother.

Little Ping's mother kept stirring the fish around with her pale hands. Suddenly she was stung by fish fins. She cried out in alarm as blood gushed from the back of her hand.

"Oh my!" shouted Woman Wang.

She took out a handkerchief and bound the wound for her. Then she looked up, and saw the woman's smiling eyes.

"Woman Wang, does Little Ping bother you too much? She's a problem child."

"Not at all. Little Ping is well-behaved. She's never bothered me."

"Really? I've wanted to see what she's like in your house, but she won't let me."

"You may come over whenever you wish."

The smile in the woman's eyes vanished. She looked dejected and glum. She was a conventionally pretty woman. Little Ping didn't resemble her mother at all. She looked the way she was supposed to look.

Woman Wang was about to leave when the woman asked, "Would you like to go and see Little Ping? She's out in back on the croquet ground playing a game she made up. I'm kind of confused because she plays it all the time."

They walked to the edge of the abandoned croquet ground, where they saw Little Ping crawling on the ground. Her eyes were covered with a large handkerchief. Woman Wang searched the field with her eyes, and before long discovered the coins. Three altogether. Each one was thrown into a different corner. Little Ping was fumbling around and crawling slowly in the field.

"See how patient my daughter is," the woman said, distressed.

"You're worried about her. Why?"

"No. I'm not worried. I just feel, I feel that the place she wants to go is so far away! Will she give up halfway there?"

Covering her face with her hand, she ran off. She didn't seem very happy. What was she concerned about? Without making a sound, Woman Wang was watching Little Ping. Little Ping had already picked up one coin. She knelt there and lifted it up. The coin sparkled in the sunlight; this was like some sort of ceremony.

"Little Ping! Little Ping!" Woman Wang shouted at her.

"*Shhh*. Don't say anything. I'm working!" Little Ping replied quietly.

Once more, she concentrated on crawling. Woman Wang left the croquet ground and went home.

She ran into Woman Yun at the door. Woman Yun said to her, "Those people from the management council came again. I have no idea why they keep coming here. We're all willing to be relocated — it's just a matter of living somewhere else. Don't you agree?"

"Yes, that's it. I don't care one way or the other about moving," Woman Wang said.

"You don't care?" Woman Yun raised her voice all at once.

She glared maliciously, as if she wanted to pierce Woman Wang with her gaze.

"I'm saying — It's okay with me to move. These days, even the dead sometimes have to be relocated. I actually . . ." Woman Wang couldn't go on.

Woman Yun walked past her haughtily.

Woman Wang remembered that she had burned documents during the night. Woman Yun had lived in this wooden building as long as Woman Wang could remember. Back then, she had been a young single girl who wore thick makeup. She lived upstairs, and no one had ever been seen visiting her. Yet surprisingly, she had so many documents to destroy. Could she just be bluffing because she felt bad about having nothing to leave behind?

Woman Wang gutted the fish, washed vegetables, and sat

down to rest for a while. Her hand brushed against her pocket: inside was something hard. To her surprise, it was a small packet of coins wrapped in plastic. She poured the coins out on the table, and found that the packet also contained some fragments of quartz. She leaned close to smell it. It smelled of sulfur. She thought back: she was certain that Little Ping's mother was the only one who had come in close contact with her at the market. What kind of information was she transmitting? At a loss, Woman Wang made out the vague outline of quartz. In her excitement, her hands began trembling. To her surprise, mother and daughter had been colluding all along. These coins were dull, not in the least shiny. Some were encrusted with mud. They wouldn't interest people. They were absolutely unlike the ones that Little Ping had picked up. But how to explain these bits of quartz? Maybe Little Ping's mother had made her way into Woman Wang's fantasy. Woman Wang remembered her pale arm and the blood flowing from her hand. She was also a woman of the Catfish neighborhood, mysterious and complicated, with a lot of stories.

A sudden impulse came over Woman Wang. She grabbed five coins, bent over, and tossed them under the bed. The vats of kimchi all made slurping sounds, as if they were surprised.

Woman Wang had eaten only half her meal when she heard firecrackers. It was the building whose foundation had been laid first. That building was going to transform the entire structure of Catfish Pit. She supposed that everyone here was probably paying careful attention to the noise, just as she was. But the move truly didn't make any difference to Woman Wang—she did not belong to Catfish, nor did Little Ping's mother. Catfish neighborhood was too narrow to hold their ambitious hearts. Watching the way Little Ping's mother grabbed the fish in the market, Woman Wang sensed that this woman's body contained an unusual vitality.

Someone knocked on the door. It was probably that mason again. Woman Wang didn't respond, and the person stopped knocking.

The mason was quite annoying. It was best to ignore him, but it was not easy to do so. He was one of the city residents who didn't sleep all night. Woman Wang could always sense their existence. If she hadn't gone out that night, she wouldn't have seen the mime performed at the outdoor snack bar. What an upside-down change was happening to this world! She had run into them by chance, yet they had been clinging to her ever since. Did this make any sense?

After tidying up the kitchen, she opened the door a crack and looked out. That youth was standing across the street, apparently at a loss. Some people walked past him. He approached them eagerly, wanting to talk with them, but they never responded. It seemed he was not a local mason, but he didn't seem to be a tramp, either. That night, hadn't the light at the restaurant's entrance been turned on for him? He wasn't an outsider with no connection with Catfish Pit.

Woman Wang bolted the door. She was going to take her noon nap.

She slept under the mosquito net, her train of thought rising and falling like waves. She thought of the mason who kept moving his home in dreams: What had he been doing with the people in the bar at midnight? Woman Wang seldom went out at night. Yet when she did, just once, Catfish had revealed itself completely to her. What an exciting and boisterous nightlife there was here in

Catfish: even when it was quiet, the quietness was no different from the noise. Woman Wang couldn't help but break into laughter.

■

"Little Ping, we're all going to move into those tall apartment buildings," Woman Wang said.

"I've gone to the city several times to look at those skyscrapers." Little Ping's mouth twitched. "Skyscrapers aren't interesting. But I picked up quite a lot of things in the firefighting lanes."

She pulled a live lizard out of her pocket and placed it on Woman Wang's table. Then she pulled out a young sparrow and placed it on the table, too. Neither animal moved. They seemed scared out of their wits.

"Did you pick them up in a skyscraper?"

"I walked up and down, and then up and down again—Oh! I've never gone down to the ground floor. Granny Wang, what do you think the ground floor is like?"

"I think it must have many sparrows and many lizards. Little Ping, why don't you go down there and look? Make up your mind and close your eyes, keep walking down—and then you're there. It doesn't take any effort. Then you can enter the basement. Many people live there."

"Granny Wang, I have to go now."

Little Ping put the little animals back into her pocket. She looked dejected. She didn't look at all satisfied with Woman Wang's answer. She knew too much for her age. No one could fool her. Woman Wang looked at her. She felt a little regretful: this little girl was hard to deal with.

Years ago, the first time the little girl showed up, she hadn't come over for anything special, but just to eat her kimchi. At this moment, Woman Wang felt that Little Ping was like a full-feathered bird flying up to the sky. She couldn't help but look out at her receding back — the little girl already looked like a sexy young woman.

Ms. Wen sat in a dark room pondering the structure of the universe. Then she stood and opened the window, whereupon all kinds of dark shadows wandered in. The room turned half-light, half-dim. *Poo, poo, poo* . . . came the noises from the shadows. Ms. Wen felt herself sinking; the ceiling and four walls were scattering in all directions. Ms. Wen wasn't suspended in the air, however. Rather, she stood firmly on Mother Earth, all kinds of things clustered tightly around her. She didn't feel as if she was tied up, though; instead, she felt pleasantly free.

"You're on the second floor facing southwest. It's the room with an apple on the windowsill. It's a medium-size room with simple furniture and a typewriter." The voice came from a tape recorder.

"Thank you for telling me where I am. But who are you?" Ms. Wen was puzzled.

"I'm your friend. You don't have to know my name, because we're in touch with each other only inside this building. This has nothing to do with the outside world."

These words must have been recorded in advance. How odd! Now she was going to do some deep breathing exercises. Each time she inhaled, the shadows also rapidly flew into her nostrils, and her body sank continuously and slowly. During this process, Ms. Wen always wanted to know where she was—Where was she in this "cosmic building"? Was she facing west? But the recorder wouldn't respond to her questions very often. So she was puzzled most of the time. It was okay to be puzzled, but she did long to be oriented. The answer would come from the recorder sooner or later. When it came, it always happened unexpectedly, and it made her feel fantastic. She loved what was going on inside the cosmic building. The walls and ceiling had scattered—Wasn't that true? The voice from the recorder made it clear that she was in a "medium-size room" located "on the second floor," "facing southwest." These descriptions couldn't indicate any place outdoors. But she also kept sinking; she couldn't remain inside a room. It was really hard to decide where she was. How wonderful to be in this delicate uncertain state! Maybe she was simultaneously in both the south and the north, but the announcement was always clear, making her feel that she could depend upon this reality.

Years earlier, Ms. Wen had looked forward to this kind of exercise. She had looked forward to being in a large building of uncertain design and groping her way into a strange room. But this had come about only in her old age. She had now done this many times. The more she exercised, the more the building expanded—that is, there were more and more strange rooms and floors. It was almost impossible to figure out which room or floor one was in, or where the corridor led, or where the entrance could be found. Once, she had groped her way to the end of a corridor. As she hesitated to take the next step for fear of stepping into emptiness and falling, the corridor turned again. And so she involuntarily entered a windowless room that was terribly small—only one square meter. The moment someone closed the door behind her, it became unbearably stuffy.

She wanted to leave, but the more she struggled, the smaller the room became. The four walls pressed in on her, and she dozed off in terror. She slept standing. Finally, at dawn, she heard the voice from the tape recorder say, "This room is in the southwest corner of the seventh floor. It's a storeroom." Just then, Ms. Wen discovered that she was standing in the corridor; on her right was the staircase going down.

There was no elevator in this building; Ms. Wen found it exciting to climb the stairs late at night. Once, she recalled, she had alternately climbed and rested until at last she had climbed twenty-five stories. The twenty-fifth was apparently the top floor; the corridor extended in all directions. It was like a gigantic tower. The faint light glimmering above seemed about to be extinguished. When she steeled herself to open the door to the roof garden so that she could go outside and look around, she found that there was no roof garden. Instead, there was a staircase continuing to go up. A little afraid, she closed the door and turned around, intending to go down the stairs. But she couldn't find the down staircase. No matter which direction she took, when she reached the end of the corridor, she came to the up staircase, as though being forced to continue to climb up. Ms. Wen sat down on the wooden bench in the corridor to nap for a while. A noise awakened her: someone was coming down the stairs with slow, heavy steps. It was an old man, wearing a tartan duckbill cap. He walked over to her, and looking into her eyes, he said, "It's always heartwarming to run into old friends in foreign countries." She knew she had answered him, but she didn't remember what she had said. They walked to the end of the corridor, and as they rounded a corner, they exited the building. Ms. Wen looked back. The only thing behind her was an average-size six-story concrete building. The roof was slanted and covered with ornamental tiles. The old man left in a taxi. Ms. Wen wanted to go back inside and look around, but someone had closed the main door and was locking it from the inside.

That building was on the same street as her home: it was a place for senior citizens' activities. But not many elderly people went there for recreation. After Ms. Wen retired, she had asked her neighbors about this. They had told her, "It's really stuffy inside, not suitable for elderly people." But after going there just once, Ms. Wen was captivated by this building—especially the room for chess and card playing. That spacious room had an unusually high ceiling. Usually only two or three people were playing chess. By afternoon, no one was there. And so Ms. Wen made a habit of going there in the evening. It was a few months later that the metamorphosis of the building occurred. A wall and ceiling disappeared. When Ms. Wen looked up, the stars were visible. There was a design in the starry sky. She heard a deceased cousin laughing beside her: "This pastime belongs to you alone." These words gave her goose bumps all over, but they also heightened her curiosity. From then on, she went to the senior citizens center every few days. Later this became stranger and stranger. The oddest thing was the time this six-story building turned into a bungalow shaped like an octopus. In the center was an immense hall, surrounded by numerous endless walkways. On either side of the walkways were rooms that looked like offices. Ms. Wen experimented: each walkway tempted her to take an infinitude of walks, but after walking for a while, Ms. Wen became afraid. Then she returned to the hall in the center. A transformed building was so dangerous and yet so alluring! The most interesting thing was that when she walked on the concrete walkway, she could hear a shadow play being staged somewhere. It was just like those she had seen as a child—striking the gongs, beating the drums, acting and singing. It was so exciting. Still, Ms. Wen didn't like to walk straight down without looking back. This was not only because she was afraid, but also because she thought doing so was beneficial.

A former colleague ran into Ms. Wen coming back in the evening and began talking with her.

"Ms. Wen, you enjoy exploring by yourself," she said.

"Um. What do you think of this structure?" Ms. Wen felt cold sweat running down her back.

"I can't evaluate it. That's too risky. You're really a brave explorer. I admire you! Wasn't this senior citizens recreation center constructed just for you?" The colleague's tone was enigmatic.

"But in the daytime, other people also go in," Ms. Wen argued.

"Others? They don't count. They just go in, chat for a while, and then withdraw."

After they parted, Ms. Wen was astonished to realize that this colleague really understood the situation. Maybe she was also paying attention to the same thing? If so, could one say that this senior citizens center had been built for this colleague, too? This ordinary, six-story gray structure attracted no attention on the street. Every morning, a janitor opened the main door and cleaned all the rooms, as well as the corridor and staircase. Because this building had only one staircase and twelve apartments, the janitor would wrap up her work by noon. The main door stood open. The female janitor, wearing a rat-gray uniform, always waited until late at night to lock up. The next day she reopened it at dawn. Ms. Wen wondered why she would rush over here late each night to lock up. Ever since her colleague had pointed out that this building had probably been constructed for her—Ms. Wen—Ms. Wen had grown more suspicious. Could the janitor be leaving the door unlocked for her? This thought horrified her.

In the past few years, Ms. Wen had become more and more composed. She thanked the sinking exercise for this. That was because as soon as her body sank downward, her thoughts rose—as free as a bird flying in the sky. At such times, her misgivings about the janitor also disappeared, even though she had met her once late at night and been subjected to her questioning. The more she performed the sinking exercise, the more adept she became—almost reaching the point where she could sink or rise just by thinking about it. At the beginning, she had done this by herself, and the exercise had also been restricted to the room she was in—usually the one for chess. Later, after all the walls and ceilings had scattered, when she came and went and whirled freely in midair, it seemed the whole building became transparent and was an extension of her body. She carried this intangible building everywhere she went. In other words, the very existence of this building depended upon her. When she wasn't thinking about it, the building disappeared; and when she gave it all her attention, the structure once again appeared clearly. This pastime was great fun. One time, she even ran into her son Feng in the corridor. Her son was wearing mountaineering clothes, as if he were going far away. "Feng, were you looking for me?" "Yes. They said that you were climbing up. I, too, want to enjoy the scenery up there, and so I came here. But how high is it? I can't see it." "Who can see it all of a sudden? You can experience it only while you're climbing. Let's turn to the right. There must be a roof garden in front of us. Oh, this side is the left, this side the right."

"In this kind of place, Mama is still hanging onto her senses. That's really impressive." Before she realized it, Ms. Wen had walked out the main door with her son. That's all Ms. Wen could remember. Later, her son admitted to her that he had been terrified by the height of the transformative building, and had wanted to give up. Then he took hold of Ms. Wen's arm as they went down. After this, Feng didn't bring up the incident again. Maybe he thought it better not to speak of it.

The senior citizens recreation center was Ms. Wen's secret, but it also seemed to her that everyone knew this secret. Besides her two sons, some retired colleagues—affecting a casual manner— also asked her about it. Ms. Wen thought, A certain kind of structure is closely related to everyone's life, and that structure always has to be embodied in some real objects—buildings, for example— otherwise, there would be no way to see it or visualize it. Had she discovered the structure of the senior citizens recreation center, or rather had the structure kept sending her messages, luring her to be part of it? Perhaps once this kind of thing happened to someone, he or she would naturally draw people's attention. And so Ms. Wen now sensed that she was enthusiastically surrounded by people. Everyone seemed to expect something of her. Even the vegetable vendors in the market were talking about her. "She transformed an ordinary building into a thing resembling fate." "People say that if a building went through infinite changes, this must have been caused by someone's physical force." Ms. Wen just happened to hear these comments. The two people were purposely talking loudly; obviously, they meant for her to overhear them. The vegetable vendors' feedback heartened Ms. Wen. New hopes kept surging from her heart. If the structure was revealed in everything in the world, she could speak from it at any time to anyone she wanted. Yes, she had to continue with this because it was connected with happiness. Ever since last month, as soon as she stepped into the starry sky, a roof would appear above her. She felt perfect. She wanted to transmit the profound mystery of euphoria to other people. That is, one could enter into different things and become the thing itself. Of course, this involved having some skills; she would be happy to pass these skills on to others. She would share her experiences: how to discern directions by touching the walls, the doorknobs, the staircases, and so forth. And how to determine the scope of her movements according to the height of the ceilings and the length of the corridors.

Going to the senior citizens center to meditate had become Ms. Wen's privilege. This began as a casual visit to the building after she retired. One day, after eating dinner and tidying up the kitchen, she went out for a walk. She remembered that she had run into a retired school principal. He had said that she "looked healthy." Then she had passed the senior citizens center and noticed that the door was open. The lights were still on in several rooms. Curious, she walked in. She went first to the Ping-Pong room; the two Ping-Pong tables stood quietly under the light. No one was likely to come here. And so she withdrew and walked into the chess room. On the chess table was a drawing of a person's head. The drawing was blurred; perhaps it wasn't a picture of a person but the contours of a granite cliff. Ms. Wen sat down and looked at it, and wondered which old person would paint like this. As she kept looking, she went into a sort of trance. In her trance, she felt faintly excited. She heard a tiny disturbance on the ceiling; it came in fits and starts—sometimes vehement, sometimes quieting down. What kind of animal was making this noise? Ms. Wen climbed up on the table, intending to find out what it was. She had no sooner stood on the table than someone opened the door. Zhong Zhidong, a retired electrician, stood at the door. Embarrassed, Ms. Wen got down from the table.

"I came to have a look because the lights were still on," Zhong Zhidong explained.

"Apparently I'm not the only one concerned about the senior citizens center," Ms. Wen said.

"Naturally. We're always concerned about this center," Zhong Zhidong said firmly.

Zhong Zhidong left soon. Ms. Wen sat down at the table again. The noise coming from the ceiling had stopped. Ms. Wen looked again at the drawing. This time, she saw that it was a drawing of a building. The method of drawing was quite distinctive: looked at from various angles, the structure of the building was quite different from the number of its stories. At first, she thought it was a drawing of the senior citizens center, and then she thought it was a drawing of the building where she had taught. Finally, she saw that the structure drawn on this piece of paper had thirty-three stories; it was much like an office building in the city center. Her interest aroused, Ms. Wen didn't want to leave anytime soon. Inside herself, she began feeling almost as energetic as she had when she was young. She wanted to engage in activities in this building. Of course, just then she had no idea exactly what activity she would engage in. For a while she went upstairs, and then came downstairs, then went up again, then down again. While she was walking up and down stairs, she found that the entire building was pressed to her heart, making it exquisitely private. It was as though someone were asking her amiably, "Turn left or right? How about going to the room on the south side of the eighth floor . . ." She certainly heard the voice of the person making the inquiry, and she responded casually. She felt comfortable both physically and mentally. Then came the metamorphosis. How many exciting scenes had she experienced? Ms. Wen asked this inner question out loud.

Late at night, Ms. Wen walked out of the senior citizens recreation center with great satisfaction. On a night like this, the transformation of the starry sky and the city depended upon her will and her passion. She stopped next to a newspaper kiosk, gazed at a dark shadow approaching slowly, and said distinctly, "Once more."

Lu-er was grinding glutinous rice with a small mill. This was simple, boring work; he had no choice about doing it. Mother kept urging him to hurry up because she needed rice flour to make dumplings for the Lantern Festival. He was almost finished when he heard the sound. At first, it was like a train in the distance, approaching bit by bit, louder and louder. The noise was nonstop. Squeezed within it now and then was the explosive sound. Suspecting a landslide, Lu-er kept asking himself, "Should I run? Do I have to run?" He made up his mind to flee for his life. Taking nothing, he ran.

Not one person was in the village. Lu-er ran through vegetable fields, ran across the little bridge, and ran to the open country. He ran until he could run no longer before stopping in his tracks and standing there gasping for breath. His face turned red. How odd: when he was running, the sound was present the whole time, as if a mudslide were chasing him. Now, the moment he stopped, the sound stopped, too. He looked around: people in the fields acted as if nothing had happened. On the path to his right, some people were carrying brooms to sell in the market. The mountain ahead of him was standing still as usual. Nothing had happened.

He dawdled on the way home. His mother cursed him loudly

because he had run out without finishing what he was told to do. She had had to do it by herself. Lu-er wondered silently, Just now, when he had fled, where had his mother gone? Hadn't he shouted several times to warn her? Lu-er didn't dare ask his mother; he wanted to make his way through the kitchen and stay out of her way. But she wouldn't let it go; she followed him into the kitchen.

"Why did you come back? Why didn't you just die out there?"

Angry, Lu-er flung the kitchen door open and went outside. Not until he had walked around aimlessly for a while did it occur to him to go up the mountain and investigate. Something must have happened on the mountain. Otherwise, what was that sound?

He encountered Xibao, who was carrying firewood down the mountain. He greeted him and asked if he had heard any weird sounds. Standoffishly, Xibao shot a glance at him and said, "Huh. Who cares? It isn't one bit interesting."

Finally, Lu-er climbed onto the cliff. Feeling resentful, he walked to the edge of the cliff, but he immediately retreated several steps and fell to the ground. Previously, two cliffs had faced each other here. They had been three or four meters apart, as if they had been cut apart. Several hundred meters below, a mountain spring roared. At this moment, the opposite cliff disappeared. Looking across, one saw only nothingness flashing past.

Lu-er sensed danger. His legs were trembling as they carried him quickly down the mountain. In his hurry, he tripped; the momentum sent him rolling a long way before he was stopped by a small fir tree. When he stood up, he saw that his clothes had been ripped in several places.

He wanted to tell someone what he had discovered. As his

mother scolded him, he chopped pig feed and waited for dark. Not until dark did he go looking for the little shepherd Ji.

"Ji, did you hear that?" he asked him impatiently.

"Oh, yes." Ji avoided his fierce gaze.

"Do you know where that sound came from? I went to check it out—"

"I don't care!" Ji suddenly roared, interrupting him.

He turned and went inside. Lu-er stood there, stunned.

Dad passed by from a small courtyard. Right now, the one Lu-er least wanted to see was his dad. He wanted to hide, but there wasn't time.

"Are you loafing again, Lu-er?" he shouted. "When we were kids, we worked all the time. We worked from morning to night! You are so irresponsible as a boy, what kind of man will you become? Just look: Ji is more mature than you are, isn't he?"

When they had almost reached the door, his dad suddenly said, "Don't let me down, Lu-er!"

Lu-er thought his dad knew what had happened and hadn't said anything because he was worried about him. What was his father so worried about?

Lu-er couldn't sleep. The scene on the cliff kept playing back in his mind. At the time, if he had walked ahead two more steps and found out what was going on down there, wouldn't that have been much the same as death? Everyone said that death meant going to another world. Naturally, Lu-er didn't want to go to another world, but lying in bed he couldn't keep from repeatedly imagining that he had fallen down the cliff. Just then, he heard his dad talking with someone in the courtyard. Sure enough, it was Ji. Ji must have had an important reason to come over so late. Lu-er got up immediately, put on his clothes, and walked out to the courtyard.

But Ji had left. His dad was standing there alone smoking a cigarette.

"Ji is really sensible," his father said. "I wish I had a son like him."

Lu-er stood there, head bowed, ashamed.

"Lu-er, look up and look ahead," his father spoke again all of a sudden.

Perplexed, Lu-er looked ahead. In front of him was the mountain. In the night sky, it had become a heavy dark shadow. All of a sudden, it expanded until it covered nearly half the sky. Soon, Lu-er could see nothing. Extending his hand, he couldn't see his five fingers. He groped around, intending to go back inside.

When he reached the stairs, he heard his father saying bitterly, "Lu-er, it would be great if you were Ji."

Lu-er went back to bed and started giving careful thought to what his father had said. Ji had been his friend all along—a child picked up along the street by Auntie Hua who lived in back of the tofu shop. He was a year older than Lu-er. Ji didn't talk much, but when he did, his words usually shocked people. Lu-er admired him. For example, one day, the two of them were playing outside; it was late before they went home. Lu-er was worried that he would be beaten when he got home. Ji consoled him, "Beatings will make your skin thicker, and then you won't feel any pain in the future." Another example: he taught Lu-er to sneak eggs into the pot where the pig swill was boiling, and when others in the family weren't looking, ladle them out and eat them. He summed up this method by saying, "If you eat a fresh egg every few days, in ten years you'll be a strong man." Lu-er's father didn't see Ji's dark side. He thought that Ji had better prospects than Lu-er. Dad said it would be great if he were Ji. Did he wish that Lu-er was an orphan? The more he thought about this, the greater his shock. He knew his dad was disappointed in him, but how could he now be reborn as an orphan?

Lu-er felt that the brightest spot in his life was his friendship with Ji. Ji was different from all the other village children, yet Lu-er liked hanging with him. But what was going on with him today? Had Lu-er exposed some inner secret of his and this had made him unhappy? Was the landslide Ji's secret? Or even worse: Was the landslide the inner secret of all of the villagers—and it could only be stored at the bottom of one's heart and never be spoken of? Thinking of these troubling matters, Lu-er tossed and turned in bed. Finally, when he was about to fall asleep, he thought of one person—Auntie Hua, a middle-aged woman who knew everything. He would sound her out on this tomorrow.

■

It was three days before Lu-er saw Auntie Hua. She always went to the market early in the morning to sell tofu and didn't return until dark. Lu-er's mother wouldn't let him go out after dark.

Consumed with worries, Lu-er was sitting under the eaves making straw sandals when Auntie Hua suddenly turned up in front of him.

"Were you looking for me?" she asked with a smile.

"Auntie, how did you know?" Lu-er blushed.

"You left footprints in front of my door. I knew you weren't looking for Ji. You were looking for me!" She pulled Lu-er up and looked him up and down.

"Auntie?"

"*Shhhh!*"

She motioned him to follow her. They came to the side of a well. Pointing to the mouth of the well, Auntie Hua asked Lu-er if he dared jump in. Lu-er said no, and Auntie Hua smiled.

"You're a good kid. I'll tell your father. I checked you out just now. You're free of any burden. Your father shouldn't worry about you. Go home, okay? Go home. There's something nice waiting for you!"

Puzzled, Lu-er went home. But nothing nice was waiting for him. Maybe it would appear at night? He continued making straw sandals. After a while, Ji showed up.

"Lu-er, I'm confused." He bowed his head and said despondently, "Has my mother been here?"

"Huh? What's wrong?"

"My mother has high hopes for me. Too high. The pressure's going to kill me."

"I don't get it. I thought your mother was fair and reasonable."

"She is, but people who are fair and reasonable also have their bad side. She makes you feel pressure. Our cattle were slaughtered a long time ago, and yet she sends me up the mountain. And then I saw something I shouldn't have seen. You know what that was. I don't want to talk of it. But my mama: I even think of leaving her. I think, Is it because I'm not her biological son that she tells me to go up the mountain and see that kind of thing? I think and think, and the more I think about this, the more I come up with hateful ideas."

"Your-ma-ma-is-very-kind," Lu-er said, one word at a time.

"Of course. Sure. And your dad and mama are, too. We shouldn't leave these grown-ups. Do you agree?"

Lu-er was uneasy when Ji looked him in the eye and asked him this. He answered reluctantly, "Yes." Lu-er thought, Actually Ji is talking about that matter. He went up the mountain often and knew the topography well. He had seen it. Why did he say "something I shouldn't have seen"?

"Ji, did you come to find me just now in order to speak ill of your mama?"

"At first, yes. But then I realized she's good to me. Lu-er, can you come out tonight?"

"My mother won't agree. But I can slip out the window. Just wait for me outside the courtyard."

Looking at Ji's back, Lu-er thought to himself, Is this what Auntie Hua meant by "something nice"? Even after Ji had been gone a long time, Lu-er was still really excited.

When he slipped out the window, Ji was waiting for him. Ji was wearing a straw hat decorated with many feathers. He was carrying a spear. In the bright moonlight, he looked like a savage. Lu-er was jealous of the way he dressed, and asked who had taught him to dress this way. Ji said he had learned it from a magazine that belonged to Auntie Hua's nephew.

"There are leopards out there. We can't go without a spear," he said.

He walked in front, and Lu-er thought he would head up the mountain. But he made a big detour and entered the rapeseed plot. When they walked in the vast rapeseed plot, Ji would stop every now and then and listen alertly to distinguish sounds. At those times, he raised his spear, as though to stab the sky with it, but then hesitated and didn't do it. Lu-er thought it was strange: Could they be in danger? Rapeseed was their village's main source of income, and so this plot was enlarged every year. Lu-er had no idea where the plot ended.

"Ji, where is the leopard?"

"It's wherever my spear reaches," Ji said arrogantly.

"But you haven't done anything with your spear."

Lu-er admired Ji greatly. He thought, Ji definitely can summon a leopard! This idea made his blood boil. All of a sudden, Lu-er saw the shadow of a gigantic person swaying in the sky. Each time the shadow flashed by, the earth seemed to vibrate along with it—but it was a light vibration. Ji raised the spear again. This time he was facing that human shadow in the sky. He flung his body out along with the spear, but he quickly tumbled to the ground.

Ji cursed through his moans. Lu-er asked if he was hurt. He answered, "I'd rather be dead." Ji's ambition was remarkable. The best Lu-er had ever done was jumping from a rock three meters high, yet Ji tried to leap into the sky! Lu-er looked up at the sky. It was the same sky; there was nothing unusual about it.

Ji sat up slowly. He asked Lu-er to find his spear. Lu-er found it quickly nearby. It had been broken into two pieces. Ji threw them into the rapeseed plot and said, "I don't want it anymore. I'm ashamed. When I was on the cliff—"

"What was happening when you were on the cliff?"

"Ah, I remember. It isn't worth talking about."

Lu-er was furious, but what could he do? Ji was very arrogant. No one could make him talk about something he didn't want to talk about.

"Now I have no spear. We might as well go home."

Each of them went back to his own home.

It was daylight when Lu-er's father awakened him.

"Lu-er, didn't you hear me call you yesterday in the rapeseed plot?"

"No."

"At the time, I was standing in another place, and Ji aimed his spear at me. I shouted your name. I wanted you to stop him. You—you just stood there idiotically watching him go down in defeat. Still, that was okay. Just great. You should learn from Ji."

"Dad, were you the giant?"

"What are you saying? You've heard too many stories of monsters."

Lu-er listlessly swept the chicken coop. Mama was drying beans in the sun. She was cursing him as she worked.

Inwardly, Lu-er kept saying, Should I run away? Should I run away . . .

By dinnertime, he still hadn't run away. He hated himself because of this.

■

Lu-er went to the cliff again. At first, he cut firewood around there. After bundling it with rattan, he felt he had to climb the cliff again. This time, he saw a strange thing. Plum, a girl from his village, was embroidering as she sat on the edge of the cliff. She was unattractive and plump, but grown-ups said she was by nature skilled in crafts, so Lu-er respected her quite a lot.

"Plum! Plum!" Lu-er's voice was shaking with fear.

Plum didn't answer. She sat there, cross-legged.

Lu-er's feet went out from under him and he sat on the ground. He crawled, doglike, over to her.

"Plum, tell me, what's down below?"

"Three lambs." She turned her head and spoke earnestly.

"Don't you get dizzy when you look across the way?"

"No. When I embroider at home, I do get dizzy, but here I'm fine."

"That's strange. I thought everyone was afraid."

"Of what?"

"Of the things across the way."

Plum laughed heartily. She placed her embroidery on the ground and stood up, facing the void next to the cliff, and somersaulted. Her soft little body gracefully unfolded in the air. Lu-er thought she was going to fall, but she came back as if ricocheting from an invisible wall, and stood steadily in front of him. Lu-er rubbed his eyes, as if he didn't believe the reality before him. Plum rushed again at the void and flipped over, and once more she rebounded. Lu-er even heard a *puff* from the air: Was it the sound of Plum knocking against the invisible soft wall?

"Oh, I have to go back and feed the pigs!"

Picking up her embroidery, she ran off.

Lu-er was trying to distinguish things in that vast expanse of white. What was inside? Nothing. When he stood up, his legs shook. Oh, he could do nothing. He climbed away from the cliff.

When he got home, his dad told him to help him clean out the pigpen.

As they stood in the manure pit, Lu-er heard his father talking to himself: "This is truly the best place to stay."

Father and son were busy for a long time. They stank.

After taking baths and washing their hair, Dad sat on a stool smoking a cigarette, and Lu-er sat there worrying.

"Hey, Lu-er, in a few more days, you'll be thirteen, but your mama and I are already old. I've been wondering recently: Are you unhappy about having been born to us? Sometimes, your mama and I wonder if you want to leave and go far away. That's a great idea, but what's wrong with staying in this village? If you stay, you'll appreciate it more and more."

"Dad, I haven't thought about going far away." Lu-er rolled his eyes in fear.

"You haven't thought of it yet, but sooner or later you will."

"I won't leave. If I did, I would die. I want to stay here my whole life and be with you! Ji feels the same," Lu-er said fervently. He blushed, a little ashamed of his ardor.

Dad looked him up and down, not at all pleased.

"Then do you think the village is a good place or not?"

Lu-er bent his head and said despondently, "I don't like to do housework, and I don't like to farm." All of a sudden, he raised his head. "Today I saw something strange! It was Plum giving a performance for me! I'd love to learn to do what she does. I wonder if I can."

"There's nothing that Lu-er can't learn." Dad's tone turned kindly.

"Then you've seen her performance?"

"Uh-huh."

So his parents had thought all along that he would leave the village sooner or later. This idea made Lu-er feel a little flustered — like the idea of the collapsing cliff. He couldn't bear to think about this in detail. Plum! Plum! Such an exciting girl! He wanted to stay in the village. His dad said there was nothing he couldn't learn. If he practiced every day, maybe he could learn to do what Plum did? God — the motion: even thinking of it made him dizzy.

Because Lu-er had worked hard in the pigpen that day, Mama was kinder to him. After dinner she let him go out to play. Mama said to Dad, "This child wants to go outside all the time."

Before he knew it, he was walking to Plum's home. Plum was leaning against the wall next to the main entrance of her home. She was doing handstands; she had probably been doing them for a long time. Lu-er stopped in his tracks and watched her. He watched for quite a while, and she was still leaning against the wall. Lu-er thought to himself, It must be really hard to learn a skill. Just then, the door opened, and Plum's uncle emerged.

"There's no point in learning this," her uncle said. "Plum is a girl. Sooner or later, she'll get married, so right now she can learn whatever she wants. You're a boy. Your father expects a lot of you. You have to work hard."

When the uncle walked away, Lu-er approached Plum. In the dusk, he could faintly make out the sweat on her forehead.

She ordered Lu-er, "Move aside. You're blocking my view."

Lu-er stood beside her; he couldn't keep from asking, "Plum, what are you looking at?"

Plum didn't answer. Lu-er circled around to the back of the house. Every once in a while, he glanced at Plum: he wanted to see just how long she could keep this up.

He waited until the sky was completely dark, and Plum was still clinging upside down to the wall. This girl was really a superwoman! Lu-er turned around: he felt discouraged. He walked out from behind the house and squatted next to her. He whispered, "How long can you keep this up?"

"I sleep this way every night," she said.

This made Lu-er sweat all over. A sound reverberated in Lu-er's head: he seemed to be hearing Plum berating him and telling him to leave. He stood up and left. He ran into Auntie Hua on the road. Auntie Hua droned on and on. He heard some of the words clearly: "Get going. Quickly. Something nice is waiting for you!"

Auntie Hua was always in good spirits, always saying that something nice was waiting for him. She had told him this the last time, too, and after that he had gone to the rapeseed plot with Ji. He had witnessed Ji stab the human shadow in the sky with a spear. Maybe that was the "something nice" that Auntie Hua had spoken of. What other nice thing would be waiting for him today?

Lu-er returned to his dark home and groped his way into bed. He had just closed his eyes and fallen asleep when a flash of snow-white lightning roused him. The lightning wasn't followed by thunder. Just then, he heard his dad talking in his sleep in the next room, "Lu-er! Lu-er! Why haven't you run away yet—I'm so disappointed in you! You're good for nothing!" Then he heard both his dad and his mama grinding their teeth in their sleep, as if chewing something hard.

He was scared. He coiled up into a ball, afraid to move, intending to go on sleeping, but his dad's voice grew louder and louder, almost as if he were hysterical and wanted to kill him. He ran outside. When he closed the door on his way out, it caused a huge, earthshaking sound, as if the house were collapsing.

He didn't stop until he had run straight to the Co-op. Lu-er sat at the simple table under the awning and caught his breath. He didn't know why his eyelids were stuck together. He bent over the table; he wanted to sleep, but he still didn't fall asleep. The Co-op door creaked. Two people walked out of the store talking. To his surprise, one was his father. His father and the shopkeeper were bargaining. Dad wanted to buy some cheap cigarettes; he wanted shopkeeper Gu to sell him two at a reduced price. The shopkeeper refused. He ridiculed Dad, saying that Dad was "a loach." Why did he say Dad was a loach? Lu-er couldn't figure that out. He was so sleepy, he'd better not think about anything anymore. Father and shopkeeper Gu walked off into the distance on the highway.

At last, Lu-er was awakened by a persistent, whiny little noise. He stood up and looked all around: the Co-op door was standing open; inside it was very dark. Where had Dad and shopkeeper Gu gone? Though Lu-er was afraid others would suspect him of stealing, he had to enter the shop. But the shop was by no means deserted. A saleswoman sat before a kerosene lamp counting banknotes.

"You're a thief, aren't you?" she asked, glancing at him.

On the wall to the right, a huge human shadow was swaying, just like the one Lu-er had seen that night in the rapeseed plot. Lu-er broke into a cold sweat.

"Get out of here. Now!" the woman reproached him.

Lu-er crouched down and made his way into an empty space in the display case. He snuggled up there without moving. He heard the saleswoman walking back and forth in front of him. She seemed to be moving goods. He even smelled her pungent, foul sweat. Suddenly, she approached him and squatted down with him. She held his hand and said in a small, shaky voice, "Kid, I'm so afraid. It's like this every night. He wants me to die."

"Who?"

"How could you not have seen him? You did see him!"

"The one on the wall—that one?"

"Yes. Thump my head a few times so I won't faint from fear."

Lu-er turned toward what he guessed was her head and slapped it. He felt his fist land on a ball of mushy mud. It made the back of his hand slippery. He shouted, "Aiya."

"Where are you?" he asked.

"Where else could I be? Next to you. You little rascal, did you come here to get killed?"

Her voice was low and constrained, filled with fury. She pounded on Lu-er's shoulder with something made of stone. Lu-er cried out in pain.

Lu-er crawled out the door. The door closed tightly. He had just struggled to stand up when the woman, who was carrying a basin of water, opened the door. She threw the water all over him until he was drenched. She kept howling, "Next time, I'll chop your head off."

When he got home, Dad was also there. He stopped him, held a cigarette lighter up to his face, and said, "I've changed my mind about you."

Lu-er tossed and turned in bed for a long time. He was thinking of the "nice thing" that Auntie Hua had spoken of. Then, dazed, he fell asleep. He dreamed of running away from the village and running toward the rapeseed plot. Above him, that huge dark shadow was about to press down on him . . .

■

Plum taught Lu-er how to do handstands, but Lu-er soon gave it up. When he was upside down against the wall, the atmosphere all around turned gloomy, like a gale brewing. The flying sand obscured his vision. The moment he left the wall, everything returned to normal. He tried this several times, always with the same result.

He rubbed his eyes until they were red. "You're really a loser," Plum said to him. Lu-er felt, too, that he was really good for nothing. The sparks of hope in his heart were extinguished bit by bit.

"What do you see when you're upside down?" he asked Plum.

"Me? I've never looked all around. Hunh." She answered self-confidently, "I'll be the best when I'm grown up, whether I'm married or not."

Plum's words startled Lu-er. He felt ashamed of himself. He despaired. Compared to Plum or Ji, he was no more than garbage. There was no place for him. Where could he run off to—a piece of garbage like him? Lu-er sighed.

"Lu-er, you don't want to do handstands. You don't concentrate well enough to learn this. Let's go to my uncle's home. There's something in his home that you want to see."

"Really? That's weird. How do you know what I want to see?"

"Of course I know."

Plum's uncle's home was east of the rapeseed plot. It was a one-story adobe house, half of it buried in the ground. You had to take a flight of stairs down to get inside.

After they came to a stop inside the large half-subterranean house, they saw no one there. But when Lu-er took a closer look, he realized the house wasn't empty: people were lying under three large beds and were now sticking their heads out and looking at the two of them. Just then, Lu-er heard a huge clap of thunder. When they had come down just now, it was a clear day; it had changed so fast! Plum whispered in Lu-er's ear, doing her best to keep her uncle's three sons from hearing.

"Lu-er, do you know why they don't sleep on the bed? They're afraid of being killed by thunder. The thunder in this rapeseed plot is awful: once it broke uncle and auntie's bed in half, and they were thrown to the two sides. Uncle is an experienced old sparrow, and so is Auntie. They aren't afraid of anything. But their sons are scared out of their wits—to the point where they can't even work. They lie under the bed every day and wait for that thing to come crashing down. I always wonder if it was on purpose that Uncle and Auntie built their house in the middle of the rapeseed plot. You know, no one builds a house in this kind of place."

"We're doing just fine! Don't you dare gossip about us!" one of the guys under the bed reproached her.

No sooner had he said this than a loud noise crushed and scattered everything on the ground—jars and vats, kerosene lamps, bowls and utensils. Lu-er felt that his own head had been crushed. Everything went black in front of him, and he fell to his knees. He heard Plum shout, "Look! Look! There's a large hole in the roof!"

As she shouted, Plum raced up the stairs and disappeared from there. Lu-er climbed up, thinking of fleeing, but someone pulled at his foot and he fell with a thump. It was Uncle's son.

"You coward!" he snapped. "Don't move!"

The ones under the bed emerged. They ordered Lu-er to close his eyes and stand motionless. Lu-er heard them climb the stairs one by one and go out. He opened his eyes and took a look: the stairs had disappeared. Maybe it was a movable staircase. Claps of thunder crashed down one after the other. Lu-er felt as if he were in hell. An inner voice kept saying, You're going to die! You're going to die . . . Involuntarily, he rolled under the bed. The roof tiles were continually being lifted off the house. Some of them fell to the ground. The room was getting lighter. Imagining Uncle's sons running in the rapeseed plot, he couldn't help but admire them. This was such a strong family! But why on earth had they wanted to live in such a place? All of a sudden, Lu-er felt exhausted: even his fear couldn't stave off an attack of sleepiness. He was dazed.

Several people picked him up. He wanted to break away from them, but he couldn't.

"Shall we throw him down there?"

"Yes!"

He was thrown onto a soft thing below.

"Lu-er, did you try to kill me?"

"Where are we, Dad?" he said feebly.

"Where else could we be? You scamp—you actually went so far as to jump from the cliff. I've never been happy with you, but I never imagined . . ."

His father's voice grew fainter and fainter, farther and farther away. A cool breeze blew against his face, and birds were chirping all around. This was so comfortable. He sat up. He didn't hurt at all. He looked up: the golden-yellow rapeseed plot was boundless, and bees busied themselves in the flowers. Where was Plum's uncle's home? He stood up and looked, but he didn't see it.

A path in front showed him the way home.

She hadn't wanted to give up her bungalow in the city. Twenty years ago, Zhou Yizhen had come down with a serious illness. The best thing to do was sell the house and move to an old apartment building in the distant suburbs—the living quarters for workers at a tire factory. She said to her husband, Xu Sheng, "Be patient for another year or two, and then you'll be free."

Xu Sheng glared and retorted, "Life and death are determined by destiny. We don't get to make these big decisions."

Living in the tire factory quarters was hard on Zhou Yizhen. She couldn't remember when she began to believe that she wouldn't die after all. She contacted a nearby woolen mill, and knitted scarves and caps for it at home. After cooking, she sat on the balcony every day and knitted, and she became steadily healthier. The air in the suburbs was better than in the city, and fresh vegetables were available. Zhou Yizhen regained her health, and the nightmare in her memory gradually dimmed.

Xu Sheng hadn't mentioned their former home for years because he didn't want to make her feel bad.

Although the city wasn't far away by bus, Zhou Yizhen had never gone back to see their old house. She wasn't very sentimental, but after all she *had* lived there half her life, had gone to primary and middle school there, and had worked in a factory, married, and given birth to her daughter. That bungalow figured in so many of her memories. Although she'd been away for twenty years, she often still lived there in her dreams. She rarely dreamed of the tire factory quarters.

Zhou Yizhen was planning to deliver her consignment to the mill Wednesday afternoon (she had knitted some baby shoes and would earn quite a lot for this) when the phone rang. It wasn't her daughter Jing. The woman on the other end of the line asked Zhou Yizhen when she would come to see her old home, as if they had an appointment. Zhou Yizhen remembered her the moment she heard her voice. It was the woman who had bought their bungalow all those years ago.

Her name was Zhu Mei, a single woman five or six years younger than she. Zhu Mei worked in a design institute. Zhou Yizhen remembered the evening she turned the house over to her. Zhu Mei kept standing in the shadows behind the half-open door, as though she didn't want others to get a good look at her expression. So many years had passed, and yet Zhu Mei was still thinking about her. Zhou Yizhen felt nervous, but she couldn't explain why. Zhou Yizhen said she hadn't thought about going back to see her old home, but she was grateful to Zhu Mei. It seemed she'd done the right thing in selling the place to her.

"Please come and visit. Will you?" the woman insisted.

"Okay. I'll come Saturday."

As soon as she hung up, Zhou Yizhen had misgivings. How could she have agreed? She wasn't superstitious, but she wasn't sure she could handle the memories of those days when she suffered from the terrible disease. Intravenous injections, handfuls of pills to swallow, and the frightening chemotherapy—she had nearly buried these dark memories. Was she now ready to revive them? And if Xu Sheng knew, he would surely not agree.

On the way back from the woolen mill, Zhou Yizhen began feeling better. She hadn't expected to receive so much—two hundred yuan! They could live on this for three months. Although she was fifty-five years old, she felt more energetic than ever. The world was green, and flowers were in bloom. Zhou Yizhen was sweating as she walked. She was also working out a new design for baby shoes. She nearly laughed out loud. When she was almost home, she decided that Saturday afternoon she would indeed go to her old place in the city and look around. She was proud of this decision.

After dinner, she told her husband about this.

"Zhu Mei isn't an ordinary woman," Xu Sheng said.

"Do you mean I shouldn't go?"

"No, no, this isn't what I mean. Why not go? Since you want to go, just go."

Xu Sheng's answer surprised Zhou Yizhen. She knew that it wasn't out of a lack of concern for her. How had he reasoned that she should go? Xu Sheng was a straightforward, fairly simple man. If he thought she could go, then she probably wouldn't have to worry about this trip. And she *was* curious about her old home.

The three days passed quickly. During this time, Zhou knitted an entirely new style of baby shoes; they were very pretty. Xu Sheng held the wool shoes up and looked at them from all angles. He was as happy as she was. "Remember to tell Zhu Mei how skilled you are at knitting." Zhou Yizhen asked why. He said, "I don't want her to look down on us."

Zhou Yizhen was startled. What an odd idea coming from her husband.

"I don't care what others think," she replied.

"That's good."

Zhou Yizhen was a little nervous on the bus. She was still sort of worried about going back. She kept saying to herself, If I continue thinking positively, there won't be a problem.

After getting off the bus, she headed for Jixiang Lane. Once there, she found a dilapidated lane where many bungalows had been demolished. It didn't look at all as it had in the past. The city was in the midst of rapid development: the changes in Jixiang Lane should not have been a surprise, but still she was shocked by the scene.

Eventually she reached her former home. Her little courtyard remained the same, but no one was there. Zhou Yizhen saw the faucet outside the door of the house: she had often washed clothes and mops here. She felt a little sick at heart, yet she quickly got hold of herself.

She knocked on the door several times, but no one answered. Curious, she pushed the door gently, and it opened.

It was really strange: the furnishings in the two rooms were exactly the same as the ones she had had in her home! Hadn't she moved all of them? What she and her husband had turned over to Zhu Mei was an empty house. With mixed feelings Zhou Yizhen sat at her old-fashioned dressing table. She didn't want to move, remembering the last time she had sat here. Back then, the bald woman reflected in the mirror had made her quiver.

She heard approaching footsteps. Probably the owner had returned.

Spotting Zhou Yizhen, Zhu Mei exclaimed, "Sister Zhou, how nice to see you! I'm so fortunate!"

"Fortunate?"

"Yes. You always inspire me."

"Hold on a moment. What are you talking about? And what about the arrangement of the furniture and the various decorative items?"

"Oh, you mustn't be confused. I designed it so it would look the way it did before you moved out. Back then, I came to your home several times. Have you forgotten? I was a designer. How should I put it? At that time, I had sunk to the lowest point of my life. I decided to cast off my old self and change into a new and different person. I happened to meet you in the hospital and learned that you wanted to sell your house. I followed you and your husband here."

"You made up your mind to change yourself into me?" Zhou Yizhen paled.

"That's right. Please don't be mad at me." As she answered, Zhu Mei looked Zhou Yizhen directly in the eye. "In fact, you saved me. See? I'm living a full and healthy life."

"Hold on, please give me a moment to think."

"Here—I brewed some tea for you. Have some. You don't look so good. Do you want to lie down and rest for a while? This is still your home."

Zhou Yizhen drank some tea and composed herself. Her gaze dulled and slowly shifted to those familiar furnishings.

"This is great," she said, insincerely. "I've truly returned to my former home. Is that my chopping knife? I cut lotus seeds with it in the processing plant. Zhu Mei, you must have gone to a lot of trouble with all of this. I can't believe my eyes!"

A neighbor stood at the door and looked in. He recognized Zhou Yizhen.

"Mei, you have company. I'm here to collect for the electricity. I can come back whenever it's convenient."

He didn't greet Zhou Yizhen. She felt awkward and dispirited. Did this neighbor think she had died? In the past, they'd seen each other every day.

"Yes, I have a guest. Don't you recognize her?" Zhu Mei said.

"She seems a little familiar. No, I don't know her."

He left, looking a bit terrified. Zhou Yizhen suddenly felt tired. She struggled to keep her eyes open. Zhu Mei's figure looked distorted.

"You're sleepy. Lie down. I'll help you take your shoes off. Yes, that's good. I'm going out to buy some groceries. We'll have dinner together tonight. What? You say there's a spider? Don't be afraid. There's one in this room, but it doesn't amount to anything . . ."

Before she fell asleep, Zhou Yizhen heard Zhu Mei close the door.

■

When Zhou Yizhen awakened, the sun had set. She had slept a long time. She felt that her behavior was strange: Why had she come to another person's home and fallen asleep on another person's bed? She had never done anything so out of character. She heard Zhu Mei busying herself in the kitchen, and so she made the bed and went to help right away.

Zhu Mei had cooked an appetizing meal. Zhou Yizhen thought she was very good at taking care of herself.

As they ate, Zhou Yizhen said, "Look, I'm so embarrassed that—"

Zhu Mei interrupted her at once. "Don't be. Please. This was your home in the first place. You can do whatever you wish here. Anyhow, I'm the one who invited you to come."

After dinner, they tidied up the kitchen together. Zhou Yizhen was going to go home. Zhu Mei said, "Didn't you notice a bed made up in each bedroom? This one is especially for you, even when you aren't here. I sleep in the inner bedroom."

Zhou Yizhen was surprised.

"I haven't discussed this with Xu. I don't think he would agree."

"Why not? I'm sure he would. Just phone him."

So Zhou Yizhen sat down and phoned.

"That's great," Xu Sheng said. "Since she really wants you to stay, you may take the opportunity to get better acquainted with each other."

Xu's attitude seemed odd to Zhou Yizhen, because he had never shown great interest in making friends, and he knew that Zhou Yizhen didn't enjoy it, either. Not without annoyance, Zhou Yizhen said to her husband, "Okay, then I'll stay overnight. Sure you won't mind?"

"No, of course I won't mind."

The moment she hung up, Zhu Mei clapped her hands.

"Your husband is so understanding!"

But Zhou Yizhen was unhappy. She was still annoyed with her husband.

Zhu Mei asked her to take a seat at the desk. She invited Zhou Yizhen to page through the large photo album she had placed under the desk lamp.

The pictures in the album were all taken in places that she couldn't have known better. She missed them very much: a stone lion in the lane; a cast-iron mailbox on the street nearest to her home; the shop that had sold sugar-coated dried fruit for more than twenty years; the date tree in the little courtyard; the clothes of all different colors drying beneath the tree under the sun. But the main person in the photos, Zhu Mei, didn't look familiar. And Zhou Yizhen noticed that her face was always out of focus, and her body wasn't much in focus, either. It was like a shadow. It was hard to believe that this was Zhu Mei. Looking more closely, Zhou Yizhen was startled because the main person in each photo actually looked like herself. Zhou Yizhen and Zhu Mei weren't at all alike: Zhu Mei had the features of an educated person; Zhou Yizhen didn't. What on earth were these photos about?

After Zhou Yizhen had paged through most of the album, she turned around. Zhu Mei had disappeared. So she got up and looked at all of the rooms. These furnishings and objects called to mind many sentimental memories. Under the present circumstances, she liked being sentimental for a moment. Sentiment was a beautiful thing. If she could cry, it would be even better. But she couldn't. It seemed that Zhu Mei had gone out. How could she leave her guest behind and go out by herself? But then, why couldn't she do this? She'd already said she wanted Zhou Yizhen to consider this home her own. It was quiet outside: there was only the deep sound of the wind shaking the date tree branches. Zhou Yizhen felt safe in this house. She regretted having stayed away for twenty years. She had misconstrued everything! If Zhu Mei hadn't invited her, would she have never returned? Could Zhu Mei have been calling her to come back throughout these twenty years in her peculiar way, and she hadn't heard? Zhou Yizhen kept thinking it over, sometimes sitting down, sometimes standing up and pacing. She sensed that the familiar objects in front of her were talking to her in low tones. Too bad she didn't understand.

At the corner of the wall was a little metal bucket with dried lotus seeds inside. Next to the bucket was a small bench. Zhou Yizhen's heart leapt happily! She sat down at once and started cracking open the lotus seeds. Though she hadn't done this for more than twenty years, she still knew how to do it! And she could do it almost without looking. It was as though she wasn't cracking lotus seeds, but picking mushrooms in the forest. She joyfully discovered one after another. As she did this, she didn't think back to her work in the plant when she was young. Quite the opposite: what she recalled were the good things that she usually didn't think of. For example . . . Ah, she was suffocating from happiness! She wouldn't die of happiness, would she?

"Zhou Yizhen, are you fishing?"

Zhu Mei's voice came from the door. Why didn't she enter? Was she playing hide-and-seek? Zhou Yizhen put the knife down and went to look.

No one was in the courtyard. Where was Zhu Mei hiding? Zhou Yizhen walked lightly under the date tree, intense emotions rising from within. This courtyard had five other homes; the lights were on in each one, but the doors were shut tight. Zhou Yizhen recalled that it was never like this in the past; back then, the neighbors felt close to each other, and doors always stood open. Did all these homes have new owners?

Without thinking, she walked out of the courtyard and came to the lane. So strange: at night, the lane didn't look at all dilapidated, as it did in the daytime. Instead, it was clean and tidy, and full of life. Although you couldn't see anyone, the street was giving off light, as though some liveliness were left over from the daytime. The entrances of all of the courtyard houses stood wide open, letting her thoughts run wild.

Zhou Yizhen caught a glimpse of a woman's silhouette entering a courtyard house in front of her. Ah, was it Zhu Mei? She shouted, "Zhu Mei!"

Zhu Mei dashed up to Zhou Yizhen.

"You've come out, too," she said with a smile. "Sure, why wouldn't you? At night, it's a Shangri-la here. Do you know who I was looking for inside? My lover. He's only twenty-eight—a guy who fears nothing!"

Zhou Yizhen heard the lewdness in Zhu Mei's tone. Ordinarily she wouldn't be able to stand it. But in this kind of moonlight, this kind of atmosphere, she felt that everything was reasonable. The fifty-year-old Zhu Mei should love a twenty-eight-year-old. If she, Zhou Yizhen, were a young man, she would want to fall in love with Zhu Mei: Zhu Mei was a rare treasure.

"Oh, so that's it. I've disturbed you. Don't pay any attention to me. I'm leaving," she said.

"No, don't go!" Zhu Mei raised her hand and said decisively, "Since you've come out, I want to enjoy this evening with you. Look, the twilight is so beautiful!"

"Yes. Yes," Zhou Yizhen murmured.

"We'll go to the plant where you worked before. Now it's been converted into shops selling a wide array of goods."

Zhou Yizhen wanted to decline, because for twenty years she'd been afraid of running into her former workmates. But Zhu Mei pulled her along in that direction; Zhou Yizhen thought that Zhu Mei was warmly enthusiastic. Why was she so exuberant? Zhu Mei told Zhou Yizhen: before the plant went out of business, she had been a temporary worker there for two years. After that, all she could do was return to her old trade as a design assistant. She had earned some money in design the past few years, but she still cherished her time in the plant. As she talked, Zhou Yizhen recalled the lotus seeds and felt intensely emotional. Without thinking, she said, "Those days working in the plant were splendid!"

"See!" Zhu Mei shouted. "I read your mind, didn't I? Even if a person goes only once to that sort of place, she never forgets it!"

When they reached the spot where the plant used to be, Zhou Yizhen saw that it had completely changed.

The workshops in the former plant were now small shops. There were colorful lamps everywhere, and people coming and going. Some of the shopkeepers looked familiar; they had worked at the plant. Some were unfamiliar. They welcomed Zhu Mei with open arms, but no one recognized Zhou Yizhen. The shops sold a variety of goods—kitchenware, appliances for lavatories, writing implements, metal fittings, children's shoes.

Zhou Yizhen was in a good mood when she saw her former workmates, even though they didn't recognize her. She was grateful to Zhu Mei for not introducing her to them; this was just as she wished. She walked behind Zhu Mei, feeling very relaxed. A joyful premonition arose within her.

Zhu Mei pulled Zhou Yizhen into a two-room shop selling chinaware. The shopkeeper was a middle-aged woman whom Zhou Yizhen didn't recognize. When she asked them to sit down, Zhou

Yizhen thought she seemed familiar. Zhou Yizhen had no sooner taken a seat than the woman dragged Zhu Mei off to the other room and left Zhou Yizhen to watch over the chinaware.

After a while, several customers showed up all at once. Flustered, Zhou Yizhen wished that Zhu Mei and the woman would come out soon, but they remained in the warehouse in back.

An old man picked up a teapot and asked the price. Zhou Yizhen replied that she wasn't the shopkeeper.

"If you aren't the shopkeeper, why are you standing here?" he reproached her. "You have to take the responsibility. Oh, I see the price. It's pasted on the bottom of the teapot. It's twenty-three yuan."

He counted out twenty-three yuan, placed it on the counter, and headed out. As he left, he said angrily, "You're the worst businessperson I've ever seen."

Then a young woman picked up a vase and sought out Zhou Yizhen. Zhou Yizhen told her the truth and asked her to wait a moment, because the shopkeeper was in the other room. She looked inside the warehouse, but no one was there. A door opened from this room onto a small street. The other two must have gone out for a stroll.

She returned and told the young woman that the shopkeeper was out.

"But you're here, aren't you?" the young woman said, staring.

Then the young woman said she had found the price; it was thirty-seven yuan. She placed forty yuan on the counter, took the vase, and left. Zhou Yizhen put the money away at once.

Every person who came in bought something. The last customer wanted to bargain with Zhou Yizhen. He was holding a large soup bowl and said fifteen yuan was too much. He asked Zhou Yizhen to sell it to him for ten yuan. Zhou Yizhen said the shopkeeper was out, and it wasn't up to her to lower the price.

"Why can't you? Didn't you sell several things just now?" he said in a fierce tone.

Zhou Yizhen was afraid. She shouted toward the back room, "Zhu Mei! Zhu Mei!"

The man immediately said, "Don't shout! Please! I'll just put it back, okay?"

When he swept past her, Zhou Yizhen saw that he was her former gang boss. Back then, they had sat in the same workshop opening lotus seeds. Why had he threatened her?

Zhou Yizhen was angry with Zhu Mei. She put the money in a drawer under the counter, closed the shop door, and ran out.

All at once, she relaxed. She thought, I came here just for fun. Why had Zhu Mei pressured me so much? Whatever happened in the chinaware shop was really a conspiracy. The surroundings had changed greatly, and there wasn't much lamplight. Zhou Yizhen had actually lost her way outside the plant where she used to work. Just then, she heard someone call her name. She turned around and saw her former workmate Bai E. Except for her voice, this woman had changed completely. Even in the dim lamplight, one could see that her face was dark and that she was very thin, yet she seemed in good spirits.

"Zhou Yizhen, come to my house!" she said eagerly. "I live alone now. You can live in my home!"

She gripped Zhou Yizhen's arm, and dragged her to a low house next to the road. It was dark inside. The two of them almost fell onto a bed with a big mattress. Zhou Yizhen struggled to get up because she hadn't taken off her shoes. Bai E was still holding her tightly. She said there was no point in following any rules in her home. It was best to simply fit in.

"It's dark outside. Where can you go?" Bai E's voice turned eerie.

Zhou Yizhen stopped struggling and calmed down. A minute later, her eyes closed heavily. She felt a quilt being put over her. She could faintly hear Bai E arguing with someone outside.

■

When Zhou Yizhen awakened, it was daylight. She saw her former workmate Bai E sitting beside the bed, quietly watching her; she looked fascinated. Zhou Yizhen blushed; she wasn't accustomed to people looking at her so closely.

"Yizhen, we've finally met," she said.

"Yes. Finally," Zhou Yizhen responded in kind.

"I thought I wouldn't be able to wait for this day."

"Everything depends on luck," Zhou Yizhen said.

"No! That's wrong!"

Bai E stood up angrily, and began pacing back and forth in the room. She was agitated.

Zhou Yizhen made the bed, whisking the dust from the quilt. She waited for Bai E to explode.

But Bai E didn't lose her temper. Her anger was suddenly replaced by happiness, and she whispered, "I know you came over from Zhu Mei's place. As soon as you arrived at her home yesterday, everyone from the plant knew. Everyone was eager to see you. I got to you before anyone else!"

"If that's the way all of you felt, then why did everyone pretend not to know me in the small shops? I saw several of my former work-mates," Zhou Yizhen said.

"Everyone was keeping an eye on everyone else. We had to pretend not to know you. We had to wait until night to take you by surprise and get hold of you. It's the way things are done here. I did it just like that, didn't I? All these years, we were curious. Everyone wanted to know how you had survived. You were everyone's hope."

After Zhou Yizhen washed her face and brushed her teeth, she sat down and ate breakfast with Bai E. Noticing that Bai E kept looking her up and down, she asked with a smile, "Is there some-thing nice-looking about me?" "I'm not looking at you, I'm look-ing at myself. When you left, you took my soul with you. I've been thinking all along, People say that Zhou Yizhen didn't die; she survived. What happened? I have to see her again. Last night, my dream came true."

Zhou Yizhen felt inspired by these words. She got up and made a few birdlike motions. And then she was a little embarrassed again and said to Bai E, "If someone as inconspicuous as I am can get a new lease on life, then the rest of you surely can! I want to tell you that everyone can experience a turn for the better. But now I have to leave you. Zhu Mei must be waiting for me. Thank you for your hospitality."

"Good luck, Yizhen. And thank you for keeping me company. The scenery last night was beautiful. The deer ran so fast."

Bai E's gaze fell. She stared, dazed, at an oil stain on the table-cloth. She forgot all about Zhou Yizhen.

Not until Zhou Yizhen left Bai E's home did she realize that Bai E's home was on a quiet street. It was two blocks from Jixiang Lane. She intended to go there and say good-bye to Zhu Mei before going home. She felt happy and a little puzzled. She thought that she wouldn't be able to put her thoughts in order until she got home. She had come to her old house and had encountered some novel things. The thing that surprised her most was that the people here all considered her one of them, as though she—Zhou Yizhen—had lived among them all this time. Even the customers in the chinaware shop didn't consider her any different from them. What on earth was the reason for this? Hadn't she vanished from here twenty years ago?

In the daytime, Jixiang Lane looked tumbledown again. The courtyard houses she had seen yesterday were once more invisible. Piles and piles of detritus and sand were everywhere, as if the path were going to be repaired. A large pile of coal was in the middle of the lane. She had to walk around it, and her shoes got dirty. Zhou Yizhen thought that Jixiang Lane was disgusting now. No one was in the courtyard of her old home. Probably everyone was at work. Zhu Mei and the woman shopkeeper from last night were sitting in the doorway, not at all surprised to see Zhou Yizhen. It seemed the two of them had spent the night in Zhu Mei's home.

"I put all the money for purchases in the drawer under the counter," Zhou Yizhen said. "I didn't dare do anything on my own in helping you with your business."

"It's all right! Never mind!" the woman interrupted Zhou Yizhen. "Your showing up was a pleasant surprise for us. Zhu Mei and I spent the whole night talking about you!"

"Talking about me?"

"Yes. You caused quite a stir in our circle. I'm leaving. Take good care of yourself! Bye!"

Zhu Mei and Zhou Yizhen watched her disappear into the courtyard.

"Zhu Mei, I've come to say good-bye. Visiting my old home has made me feel great, and it has enriched me, too. But—I don't know how to put it—it seems I experienced everything here through a layer of gauze. Nothing was very clear. Now I feel excited, but I don't know how to explain that. Can you understand what I'm feeling?"

Zhu Mei stared straight at Zhou Yizhen, then nodded and said, "I understand you, Zhou Yizhen. If I didn't, then who would? I invited you to come, and you came. This was telepathy, wasn't it? Twenty years ago, I thought I could live as you did. Now the facts prove that I wasn't wrong. Let me see you off."

When they walked out of the courtyard, Zhu Mei said, "Your shoes are dirty. You must have taken the main road over here. Actually, there's a side path you could have taken."

"Oh, I see! No wonder I didn't see the courtyard houses. How could I get lost in my former neighborhood?"

"Of course that can happen. Come this way!"

Zhu Mei pulled Zhou Yizhen over, and the two of them went to the forked road. The courtyard houses appeared, and the main entrances stood open as they had the night before. Zhou Yizhen saw again the scene in the lane from last night. This was really a quiet little lane! When had it been built? She hadn't seen these courtyard houses before, and yet they looked rather old. Where had they come from? Noticing Zhou Yizhen's puzzled expression, Zhu Mei began to laugh.

"Zhou Yizhen, you rescued me back then, and I've always

wanted to repay you. After you left, I waited year after year for you to return, and now you have. Tell me: What is your impression of your old home?"

"I feel that both the people and the view have totally changed. This place used to be rather depressing. But I'm not very sure about this impression. Maybe I'm the one that used to be depressing. Since I came back yesterday, I've been constantly excited. People here have been so warm to me. But I can't understand them, even though I was with them every day in the past. Zhu Mei, can you tell me how to understand my former workmates?"

"You don't need to fully understand us. All you need is to feel our love, that's enough."

Zhu Mei had no sooner said this than the bus arrived. They embraced and said good-bye.

When the bus started, Zhu Mei waved to Zhou Yizhen.

"Come back often!" she shouted.

Zhou Yizhen was dazed as she stood in the bus. Right up until the bus stopped at the street corner and she got off and bought some vegetables at a nearby vegetable plot on the way home, her train of thought was stuck in her old house. She resolved to gradually disengage from any curiosity about that old home.

## I AM A WILLOW TREE

1.

I'm withering by the day. My old leaves are drooping, and I'm not interested in growing new ones. My bark is dried up and cracking. The day before yesterday, five more of my leaves turned yellow. I can tell that even sparrows and magpies consider me a dead tree from the infrequency of their stopping on my branches. In the past, I was full of delicate new leaves that attracted worms, and so the birds loved to come and catch the worms. Jumping back and forth, they chattered and argued excitedly, as if they were in a meeting. Now they just regard me as nothing more than a rest stop. When they tire from flying, they nap for a while on my branches, and then fly away again. This is because I can't grow fresh leaves, and without fresh leaves the cute little worms have nothing to eat. I've become inessential.

Dusk is the most difficult time. The sun has not completely set behind the mountain. The garden is quiet. Outside the fence, the silhouette of an old farmer occasionally drifts by. The words "Rose Garden" flicker eerily on the garden gate. If I pay close attention, I can hear elegies. In the sky, on the mountains, in the little rivers, underground: singing is everywhere. These elegies are for me. I don't like listening to them, but the male voice in the distance is never willing to let go of me. He's really discourteous. Even if it's my fate, it's pointless for him to sing for me every day. Or perhaps he's actually singing for himself. He's still being rude in letting his songs travel so far, so widely. When the songs of sorrow begin, I have to be tolerant. I have to be patient until night falls and the person stops singing.

It's the actions of the gardener that created my current condition. Last spring, when I was a year-old sapling, he planted me in this grassy plot. As soon as I was put into the earth, I knew that the rose garden's soil was barren. It was mainly sand that could hold neither water nor fertilizer. The gardener simply spread a thin layer of rich soil on the surface and scattered some fertilizer. So though in the garden the flowers and plants looked luxuriant, this was a false impression that could vanish in the blink of an eye. The gardener also took care of me. He gave me some basic fertilizer, and watered me every other day. I adopted an attitude of muddling along. Back then, I still hadn't realized how painful it was to be a plant predestined to stay where you were planted. When he appeared at the garden gate carrying a bucket of water, I grew excited. My branches swayed, and I couldn't stand up straight. That was the water of life. The more I absorbed, the better I felt, and I grew more readily. It rains only two or three times a year here. When Mother Nature is not dependable, one can only depend on the gardener. We willow trees rely on the nutrition provided by water. I couldn't figure out why the gardener had to move me to this sandy land, and sometimes I imagined that this was a scheme of his.

The gardener's face was expressionless. None of us could figure out what was going on in his mind. The grass, flowers, and shrubs all had a high opinion of this man. I was the only one whose views about him wavered. For example, one day when he was near me he suddenly brandished a hoe and excavated. He dug deeper and deeper. With one blow, he chopped off part of my roots. I shook violently from the pain. Guess what he did next? He filled in the hole he had dug and evened it out, and then went elsewhere to dig. He often engaged in this puzzling excavation. Not only did he injure me, he also hurt other plants in the rose garden. The strange thing was that as far as I could tell, none of the other plants complained about him. Rather, they considered their injuries badges of glory. I heard all kinds of comments at night.

Taiwan grass: We generally don't know how our inner system operates. Although we're curious, we haven't received any information about this. It's the gardener who satisfies our curiosity. Even if we pay a high price for communicating with him, we're quite happy to do that.

Date tree: I greatly appreciate the way the gardener brandishes his hoe. In fact, he's much like one of my forefathers whom I haven't seen. Every day, I tried hard to imagine how he would look. Often at daybreak, I came close to succeeding, but in the end I didn't. The gardener has remarkable ability. As soon as he wields the hoe, I can see my forefather's fertile image against the backdrop of the boundless starlit sky. One time, he cut my taproot. That's when I was happiest. I greeted his hoe with my roots, as if it were my forefather.

Indian azalea: He's attractive when he carries water. He has aspirations. Otherwise, why would he choose the rose garden as our home?

Dandelion: This is an arid area. Every day I dream of pails of water. It's when I dream that my fine hair grows. The gardener is so kind. His two big water buckets lead me to dream constantly. Sometimes, I wish he would dig me up with his hoe and throw me into his empty bucket. I hear passersby on the road say that I have a lot of hair. They say I'm not like dandelions in the sand. They don't know that my luxuriant hair is related to the water buckets.

Wisteria: The gardener is brilliant! Although I don't love him, I think of him every day. Each time I start thinking of him, my pigment is enhanced, and I become quite beautiful. Some nice-looking people have also appeared here, but I've never seen anyone as perfect as the gardener. I'm always wondering how to attract his attention; I've never been successful, not even once. It doesn't matter how ugly I am, or how pretty, he pays no attention to me.

Sorrel: In general, we can't live in this kind of dry sandy land. But for some reason, ever since the gardener had us put down roots here, we felt that this was the most suitable home for us. The infertility of the soil is good for our species. Why? Because the feeling of being on the edge of death gives our internal being the power to grow again. We hear that those who live in humid areas don't have nearly as much vitality as we do. The profile of his steady back always gives us strength. He's our angel. I should say that he's the one who chose this garden for us. And so sometimes, when we hear rumors that a mysterious sect built our garden, we're furious!

There are also some faint humming, groaning sounds; I have no way to figure out where they're coming from. But those sounds are even more meaningful; they make me even more uneasy and curious. It's fair to say that these hidden inhabitants are the ones who maintain my interest in life. Even if the gardener hasn't watered me for a long time, and even if I'm dispirited in the state of being more dead than alive, I need only hear that humming and groaning and the shadows within me shrink and all kinds of desires are revived.

It's hard to say exactly what kind of voice this is. Mostly, it's a kind of narration without a specific audience, but someone can sense a provocative element in the strange tone. Anyhow, I did.

I couldn't see any logic to the gardener's cutting off my water. My roots were still shallow, merely inserted in the layer of sand. I had heard there was good-quality black soil beneath the sandy layer, but it was in a very deep place. Even after growing for ten years, our roots would not reach down that far. Of course the gardener had this much common sense. So did his actions indicate that he had abandoned me? If so, then why did he move me here in the first place? When I was in the nursery, I had no anxiety! Back then, we were ambitious and looked forward to realizing our aspirations after being moved here. In the misty starlight, I saw my destiny clearly many times. Back then, I didn't yet know it was my destiny; I thought it was merely a dark shadow. Then the gardener came, twice altogether. He was a remarkable person who didn't talk much. There was a black badge on his shirt, but I couldn't see the dark pattern very well. I felt strongly attracted to him: the moment he set eyes on me, I swayed wildly. You can imagine the result.

After being moved here and planted along with everyone else, I didn't change my soaring ambitions. I hoped that I would become the legendary towering tree, a big tree that could invite the stars to dream among my branches. In the nursery where I previously lived, there was an old willow tree like this. His branches and leaves fluttered in midair, covering the entire nursery. The workers in the nursery said they'd never seen such a large tree. They called it the "king of trees." Back then, whenever I looked up, I saw him. I modeled my future plans after him. I believed he was my future. The gardener smashed my hopes. At first, he placed me in the barren sandy ground, thus slowing my maturation. Luckily, he was still watering me. While he was doing this, I didn't grow terribly slowly. Probably it was my longing for growth that helped. After leaving the nursery, I concentrated more on the speed of my maturation. Later, he abruptly stopped watering me: there wasn't even a transition.

I still remember the first night of hardships. Because of the hopes I harbored, every moment and every second turned into torment. I thought he would remember this during the night and give me some water. A terrible thirst thrust me into a state between sleep and wakefulness. A person came and went. This person wore a long gown with huge pockets. Each of the two pockets held a bottle of water. When he moved, the bottled water gurgled. Was this the gardener? I could never be sure. The second night wasn't much better. The infinite quiet caused me to think even more about water. I almost went crazy. The moonlight made me jumpy, as if I had seen a ghost. The other plants in the garden were sound asleep. I was the only one who was awake. For some reason, I felt I wouldn't die, and the idea that I wouldn't die terrified me. When I was young, the king of trees told me a story about a tree that walked. I recalled this story, and so I tried to shift my root—the one on my left. I immediately fainted from the pain. When I awakened, it was light.

After those two pivotal nights, my restlessness gradually subsided, and I was kind of resigned to destiny. This didn't mean that I gave up trying hard to change my circumstances. It was to say, rather, that I did not again entrust my hopes for the future to the gardener's mercy. I believed that he would not treat me mercifully. He was impassive as he went past me, and his head drooped. His body language said that he felt it was no longer necessary to help me. I should support myself and rely on my own struggle to go on living. Was this possible? We plants could not live without water, and we couldn't obtain water from the air, either. We could only rely on irrigation. Of course I wanted to become the legendary tree that walked. I tried that three times, each time failing shamefully. How should I struggle? I became confused, as if a hammer were incessantly pounding on me. I saw the gardener carrying clean water from the little river and watering those who were grateful to him (they all worshipped him), while my leaves turned pale because of my terror. Without water, I had only death ahead of me. Of course I was scared.

While waiting for death, I fell unconscious. One morning, an old sparrow awakened me.

I was incredibly surprised that I was still alive. Hardly any water was left in my roots, and most of my leaves had dropped off. The leaves that hadn't fallen were yellowing in rapid succession. When dizziness surged up like waves, I felt that once I passed out I wouldn't wake up again. But I was wrong. Not only did I awaken, but I was particularly clear-headed. My perceptions were much sharper than before. On a fresh summer morning like this, a sparrow on my branch kept shouting to her lost child: What could be more moving? I don't know how she lost her child, but that monotonous sound of complaint that was unique to sparrows struck me as the world's most sorrowful dirge! What I thought was, Ah, I'm still alive! Only living things can experience this kind of emotion. As I was thinking this, I nearly turned into a sparrow. Each time she called out, my branch vibrated in concert with her, and I saw the image of a small sparrow in her mind.

The gardener noticed this drama between the sparrow and me. He strolled around in my vicinity for a while and then walked away.

Judging by his actions, he wasn't indifferent to me. So what was he waiting for? Was something going to happen to me? I felt an obscure hope arise, although I didn't yet know what it was. I secretly cheered the sparrow on, and the sparrow became aware of my existence. She kept shouting nonstop until she had poured out all her sorrow, and finally she realized that she needed to control herself. She jumped back and forth on my branches, and then suddenly spread her wings and flew to the sky.

She flew away, leaving emptiness with me. I saw the gardener sneer slyly.

A long crack ruptured my trunk. This crack penetrated to my very center. I would soon lose all my moisture, and death was not far away. Sometimes I awakened early in the morning and felt that I was floating lightly in the mist. "I" had already vanished, leaving behind only a small handful of leaves that were neither yellow nor green. Without the water that was essential to my thinking, all that was left were some inexplicable scraps and clues. Under the blazing sun, I was muddle-headedly reciting, "Go left, go right, go into the grotto." Whenever I recited this, I sensed that the gardener was hiding somewhere and gesturing to me, but I didn't know whether he was inciting me or impeding me.

In the years of suffering and the frightening depravity, the rose garden was no better than hell to me — because the gardener abandoned me.

2.

I fainted again. This time, it resembled real death: there was no suffering; in the blink of an eye, I lost consciousness. The last thing I saw was the gardener walking toward me with a saw in his hand.

But I wasn't cut down by the saw. After being soaked by a heavy rain, I discovered that I was still standing in the meadow. I began drinking water: after being parched and thirsty for so long, I felt that the flavor of water had changed! It was the spicy hot flavor that I loathed more than anything. What was happening? Oh, I couldn't bear it. I'd better not drink it. Still, I couldn't suppress my thirst. Without giving it another thought, I drank this spicy soup that had fallen from the sky. My withered roots began swelling quickly, and my leaves greened. My peers all around were cheering and skipping, they were so excited. But I was in unbearable pain as if my whole body was on fire. If I could move, I would definitely roll around on the ground, but I was destined to suffer in silence. At the extreme boundary of pain, I lost consciousness again and again. And again and again, I regained consciousness. I heard myself talking incoherently in the heat: "I'd rather die—"

Luckily, the rain ended quite soon. Still in pain, I saw the gardener stop next to me. He caressed the long crack on my body and began to laugh eerily. His malicious laughter infuriated me. I was so angry that I trembled violently, nearly losing consciousness once more. He left quickly and inspected his plants' growth after the rainfall. Everyone greeted him with cheers because rain was a gift from the gods, an unexpected gift. My response was the only contrary one. I was the only plant in the garden that wasn't irrigated. Now my swollen roots and my branches and leaves that had suddenly consumed so much water disgusted me. Indeed, I felt not only pain but disgust.

Before dark, the pain finally began to dull, or rather my roots, trunk, branches, and leaves became numb. Little by little, the sun withdrew into the hills, and the air was rain-freshened. Now and then, someone passed by the garden's gate. Each person was holding a small red flag. Beside me, I heard the Taiwan grass say that people were going to the hillside where there would be a party tonight to celebrate. "Because this is the first rainfall of the year," the Taiwan grass said in a gratified tone.

In the gradually descending darkness, I was coming to understand something: in this lifetime, I would never again be relaxed and joyful—qualities that everyone hoped for. I'd better learn to seize an alternative happiness in being parched, tense, and tormented. That sort of happiness was like the gardener's malicious laughter. If I learned to laugh as he did, perhaps a vast horizon would unfold before me.

The dryness of the next several days led me back to my previous state, but my feeling and my reasoning changed a little. I can describe myself as "composed." Previously, each time I saw the gardener water the others, I hated him, but now my feelings for the gardener changed all at once. I saw many layers of thought in the gardener's image: the way he carried the hoe on his back; the way he bent to dig the earth; the way he carried water buckets on his shoulder poles; the way he watered the plants; the way he fertilized; the way he spread manure . . . The more I observed him, the more interesting I felt he was. I believed this skinny guy possessed many different kinds of witchcraft that he would practice on me one after the other. All I had to do was wait, and it would eventually be effective.

This garden wasn't at all lush. Actually, it was rather bleak. The plants weren't arranged in any order; they were placed randomly. It was called a rose garden, but there were no roses; there were only some azaleas, chrysanthemums, and jasmine flowers. A few days ago, the gardener brought in two false acacias and planted them next to me. Then he left. He still hasn't watered them. Yellow leaves drooped from them, but they didn't complain about the gardener. I knew that all this was just the surface appearance. What differed from the nursery was that the plants here were confident they would survive. I had no idea where this confidence came from: Weren't they dependent on the gardener's watering them? What if the gardener got sick, or had an accident? I discussed this with them, but they ruled out my hypotheses; they didn't want to hear them. As for me, I, too, now felt I would survive. Since I had survived this long without being watered, I had no reason to think I couldn't go on this way. Oh, what a fantastic garden we were! It was hard to figure out whether this was because of the gardener's planning or whether it was because of our great effort that the garden was so extraordinary.

Look, the false acacias' leaves are dropping in profusion. Unexpectedly, the more parched they were, the more they perspired. I thought, When they have sweat out all their fluids, their bodies will be as dry as mine, and then we'll speak the same language. They were fantasizing now that they would become trees that could freely move around. From their bodies, I could see what the gardener had in mind. As for this rose garden, in fact who was the owner? You're sure to answer that it's the gardener. I used to think this, too, but recently I changed my mind. After my observations, I now saw that the gardener's actions were arbitrary. His line of thinking didn't come from premeditation; it was innate. Why didn't he water the false acacias? Because in his judgment, false acacias didn't need to be watered. Why did he water me at first and then stop? Because he thought I didn't need water and could still go on living (this was probably true). After being in the rose garden so long, I felt the future had become increasingly ambiguous. The shadows were thick behind the fence: in the dry transparent air, even more transparent monsters were roaming around. I didn't need to become a wandering tree; I only needed to stay here and wait for a certain change to occur. Change truly did begin.

At nightfall, a bunch of my roots awakened: I thought they had penetrated to a deep and unfamiliar region. That is, they had grown because of being watered by the spicy hot rain. Now there was still no water in this deep layer of soil where my roots were, but the solid earth unexpectedly imparted a sense of something similar to water. I felt itchy at the ends of my roots: this was an omen of growth. It was also an omen that something unexpected was about to occur. I estimated that my roots had penetrated more than one meter in just a few short days. This could be called "flying." It was a miracle. No rain had fallen for days, and yet they were still growing. Was I accessing another kind of nourishment to substitute for water? Was the "water of life" that was often spoken of no longer applicable to me?

Late at night, I heard the gardener's muffled voice. After his voice faded away, a tiny cracking disturbance echoed from within my body. The dusty old leaves on my head and face gave off some green fluorescence. This disturbance awakened the acacias next to me: they gasped in admiration. They nearly spoke in unison: "The gardener bestowed such a great favor on the willow tree!" They had no sooner said this than the entire garden erupted in excitement. Everyone was talking at once, but their words were indistinct. Only after listening attentively for a long time could I distinguish a word: *fireworks*. They were saying I was setting off fireworks. But all I had done was to emit a little light. Why were they making such a fuss?

The disturbance inside me quickly calmed down, and I felt hollow. In fact, I shouldn't have: Wasn't I growing, and even emitting light? Wasn't the gardener secretly supporting me? But I was still hollow. Perhaps I was looking forward to emitting light again the next time? Or because I didn't understand what was going on? Oh, gardener, gardener, be sure not to give me water. I racked my brains: I wanted to know what that invisible nutrition was. The gardener must know. They all envied me: I was the only plant that emitted light at night; I had gained the gardener's greatest support.

At daybreak, I was exceptionally hollow. At night, my leaves had nearly all withered. The trunk was even redder, the crack even deeper. I asked myself, Will I die today? Aside from thinking, I couldn't sense any living movement in myself. I couldn't even sense my roots. The fence was illuminated by the first rays of light, and the garden's silhouette gradually came into focus. In the air in front of me, a voice was repeatedly saying, "Who was that? Who was that? . . ." I wanted so much to see exactly who this voice was coming from. I thought that since "it" could utter sounds, it must be something real. But no. The voice came from gratuitous vibrations in the air: it was utterly terrifying!

Carrying water buckets, the gardener appeared at the garden gate. He stopped and glanced at me: after seeing me trembling, he laughed. It was that eerie laughter again! He turned to water plants, paying no further attention to me. The words in the air continued. I heard the Indian azalea say softly, "*Shhh*, that's a bear! A black bear . . ."

Could a black bear speak? Why couldn't I see it? Was I done for?

"A black bear. How amazing!" the Indian azalea said.

I thought that since she was seeing the amazing thing, and the gardener had also just confirmed that I was alive, I wouldn't die. Since I wouldn't die, what was I afraid of? So I also said something. "Oh—hey—hey!"

I had shouted three sounds in a row in midair! Ha! My voice came from this crack. It was surprisingly resonant, crowding out the sound "black bear"! Now there was no "black bear"; there was only my sound of "Oh—hey—hey!" vibrating repeatedly in midair. The plants in the rose garden listened in astonishment. I could still hear the Indian azalea mutter in amazement, "It's really a black bear. Who can imagine it?"

Only after a long time did the echo of my voice quiet down. I remembered the Indian azalea's words, and I felt renewed terror. Could it be that I myself was the black bear? In the past, when I was in the nursery, everyone had heard the terrible bloody tale about the black bears. Back then, the black bears had consumed all the animals on the opposite mountain, leaving only themselves. Then they massacred each other . . . The Indian azalea was the most truthful plant; she had never told a lie. Had she spoken the truth just now? As she saw it, in the beginning the voice in midair was mine, and the later one was mine, too. Maybe the gardener had known for a long time, and I was the only one who didn't? Too dreadful! So scary! HELP! . . . I fainted.

I awakened. Of course I wasn't a black bear. If I were, I would have eaten the gardener long ago. I wasn't a tree that could walk, either. My roots were the only part of me that could move, but they could only grow downward. Still, I felt foreboding about the gardener. Just now, he had stared at me again, hadn't he? He pretended to be bending toward the wisteria, yet he shot a glance at me. That turbid gaze seemed to be coming from my forebears. What was he seeing in me? I—a dying willow—a plant using something whose name I didn't know to give me the nourishment to survive, a monster that had fainted and then revived and was struggling at death's door: if I had to look at myself, I would surely be unable to see myself clearly. I conclude that I must look at my image through the gardener's eyes. I know that he sees a lot of things when he looks at me, but I can't figure out what. When I look at him (we plants use our bodies to see), his fixed eyes embarrass me. Out of embarrassment, I can't look at him very long, and so I have no way of knowing what I look like in his eyes. The only thing I know is: this person has seen through me all along. He's the sort of strange person who can see everything in his surroundings distinctly.

Oh, I'm so hollow! In this moment, my inner hollowness surprisingly caused me to tremble. I trembled violently; even my roots were trembling deep in the earth. What had I come in contact with? Something was down there! I couldn't be certain what it was: it was apparently something solid that didn't move, and yet it also seemed to be alive and movable. I felt that my roots were oriented. Right, they spread in the direction of that thing . . . Did I touch it? No. I hadn't contacted it, but I was very sure it was down there. When my roots exerted themselves to spread out and engendered this confidence, my hollow feeling lightened a little. But I was still trembling because of the hollowness.

The Indian azalea was still muttering, "It's really a black bear. Who can imagine it?"

I found her words exciting, and I couldn't help but say, "Hey!"

This time, my voice traveled to distant places. I noticed that the plants in the garden were listening respectfully. They were no longer astonished. They seemed to be concentrating, and my voice actually lingered a long time in midair.

When the lingering sound vanished, the plants in the garden all began whispering. They were saying "black bear." Maybe they (and the gardener, too) believed that I was the reincarnation of that savage black bear. But then why were they so admiring? The gardener brandished his hoe in my direction. Did he want to destroy me? No, he was helping me by loosening the soil! It was as if his work were saying: the invisible nutrition in the air could reach my roots through gaps in the earth.

Just then, I saw that walking plant, our garden's wisteria. The wisteria didn't walk with his own feet, for he had no feet; he clung to the gardener's back. He went wherever the gardener went. This was so exciting! A dark color — nearly black — arose on his body. His roots were swaying on the gardener's back; mud was still stuck on it. No matter how much I thought, I couldn't figure out how he had flown out of the ground and begun to cling to the gardener's back. In general, if we plants break away from the soil, the only path ahead is death. This is probably why he hadn't changed into a walking plant but instead clung to the gardener's back. He must have plotted this for a long time. Of all of us, he was the one who was hoping the most to walk, judging by what he had said in the past. Now he was fulfilling his wish, even surpassing it. He had become one with the gardener. He had become the most fortunate guy in the world. I thought that the precondition for the wisteria attaining his goal was his knowledge that the gardener would not let him lose his life.

The gardener was rushing around in the garden. The wisteria

was nervously and excitedly clinging to his back and trembling. I inwardly admired him, but I recognized that I was unlikely to achieve such high-level treatment. He was a vine; I was a tree. Only vines could cling to people. Trees had better stay in the ground and figure out another path. The gardener finally finished what he was doing and reached the place where the wisteria had been before. He took him off his back and planted him in the ground again. I heard the wisteria moan contentedly. He must be very proud of the risk he had taken. But I thought if he had known the result ahead of time, it surely didn't count as any great risk. As for me, where was my way out?

I had no way out. My way out lay in thinking of a way out. It lay in "thinking" itself. I was still thinking, wasn't I? I hadn't yet died, had I? My roots were twice as long as they were when I first came, weren't they? This was the advantage of plants that couldn't walk! If I had the same skill as the wisteria, my roots probably wouldn't run so deep. All right, I'll stay in this spot. My future is unpredictable. A greater danger is waiting ahead of me. The gardener got ready to go back. He turned to look at me and gave me a knowing smile. He was a person who didn't know how to smile; he smiled like a dead person. It was in this way that he achieved a tacit understanding with me.

Under the ground, that thing pressed against my root again.

The temperature dropped after midnight, and the wind picked up. Daisy snuggled under her quilt; to keep the cold air away, she wrapped her tiny body tightly in her bedding, her head hidden in the center of the quilt. Someone was pouring water in the kitchen — back and forth, back and forth from one container to another. The sound gave her goose bumps.

Ah, the wind! Like kids crying to come in, it kept pushing the door, causing it to creak and groan. How cold was it outside? Thick ice must be forming. Yesterday when she worked her way out of the backyard, she saw ice in the gutter. Ordinarily, the sewage looked terrible, and it stank, but when it formed ice it turned beautiful — like an icy black beauty. As Daisy was thinking of these things, the cold sharpened, and it was as if her heart were stuffed with a ball of ice.

The person in the kitchen shouted, "Daisy! Daisy!" Who was it?

He kept shouting, and Daisy kept answering. But the quilt smothered her voice. At last, Daisy jumped up. Groping in the dark, she dressed and put on a pair of boots. She intended to light an oil lamp, but the matches on the bed stand were wet, maybe because of the snowflakes that had drifted in. Daisy heard Dad and Mama sleeping soundly. When it snowed, they always slept well. Who was in the kitchen? No one. It was just the ice that had formed in the sink. It blinked at her in a sinister way. She looked outside: it was bright out there. The sky was an inspiring off-white; the wind had stopped.

She went through the kitchen and out the back door. The snow was deep, more than halfway up her boots. Each step required great effort. Not daring to go far, she stood in the backyard. Just then, bird calls came from the sky. There were five birds—the same off-white color as the sky, but a little darker. The sky was strangely light. They kept circling over her head, now higher, now lower. It was as though something had attracted them, and also as though they couldn't find a place to alight. Their sorrowful sound was something Daisy had never heard.

It was so cold that the branches on the willow trees had turned into popsicles and were resentfully flashing their fluorescence. Daisy was curious: Would she be frozen if she stayed in the back-yard a long time? She withdrew cautiously to the doorstep. A bird dropped to the earth right in front of her. Daisy bent to pick it up, but it soared away. She tried again, and this time she got hold of it. But what she grasped wasn't the bird; it was snow. She stood there holding the snow, thinking to herself, This isn't a dream. She took another look: the other four "snow birds" had stopped not far from her and were looking at her curiously. They weren't an off-white color, but a bright silver that stood out in the shadows of the wall.

"Daisy! Daisy!" That unknown voice called again from the kitchen.

Once again, she heard the chilly sound of water being poured back and forth between containers.

She glanced past the wall into the distance: a river was there.

The surface of the river water was also light, fusing with the light of the sky, and river and sky were indistinguishable. The river water was probably frozen. Now except for the voice in the kitchen calling her every so often, it was curiously quiet all around. Daisy motioned the birds away. She jumped on the stairs to frighten them, but the birds didn't respond.

Daisy didn't want to go back to the house. When her gaze stopped at the river, she recalled crossing it with her brother. The ice was so slippery that they had slid back and forth on it, playing wildly. And then her brother had made his way into an ice cave. She saw him go in and knew it wasn't an accident. At that time, it was as quiet as it was now all around. And the sky was dazzling. She remembered it all so well.

"She got up so early. This child has too much on her mind."

It was Dad speaking. Daisy's nose was already numb from cold. She went back to the kitchen. How odd: her dad wasn't in the kitchen. She heard snoring from the bedroom over there; he was still sound asleep. Who was impersonating Dad? Daisy was amused.

Mama got up and came to the kitchen to cook breakfast.

Daisy took off her boots and helped Mama start the fire. She warmed up quickly.

"Mama, last night someone was making a disturbance in the kitchen," she said.

"That's okay. Your grandpa used to live here."

As Daisy watched the flames, her heart constricted.

■

It was a snowy morning. Dad and Mama went to the river to see relatives. Daisy stayed at home, a little bored. She was also tired of looking out at the snow covering earth and sky. She embroidered for a while, and then put her embroidery away and sighed. A thought came to her: she would go and look at the tombs. She didn't like going to that kind of place. Every spring on the grave-sweeping holiday, she avoided going there with her parents. She was afraid. Now she was fourteen years old, so naturally she was no longer afraid. Still, for some reason she had never gone.

She walked through two villages and came to a third. The tombs were a kilometer and a half past the third village. This village was called Mosquito Village. The name reminded her of the mosquitoes buzzing everywhere in the summer. No one was in the village. The door to each home was closed. Not even a dog showed up. Taking a closer look, she saw a layer of snow on the flagstones in front of each house. Was this village uninhabited? Or was everyone hiding inside and not coming out? Stifled sounds came from some houses. Dogs. They were suffering terribly.

A dark-faced boy who looked like a leopard was fishing in a hollow at one end of the village. Thick ice had formed on that hollow.

"Where are you heading?" he asked fiercely as he raised his unruly eyebrows.

"I'm going to look at the tombs."

"You'll die. You'll never come back from there. You'll freeze to death."

"Blah-blah-blah. How could that be?"

"This summer, Qibao went by himself and never came out. At least three people have to go in together, so that if something happens, someone can come back to report it."

"Are there zombies out there?"

"Bah! No, not that kind of thing. You're still going, aren't you?"

His expression became earnest, as if he was afraid that Daisy would give up her plan.

And so Daisy walked into that endless expanse of white. At first she could still hear the muffled whimpers of dogs. And then all was silent.

Looking down, she saw her footsteps in the snow. Then, a little scared, she turned around and looked again. She saw that in fact she hadn't left any footprints in the snow. Daisy stood there indecisively. She wanted to go back to Mosquito Village, but Mosquito Village had disappeared and she couldn't remember how to get there. Luckily, the snow had stopped, and the sky was clean and fresh. The tombs in the distance were like packages of white steamed bread. There was no end to them! How could so many people be buried here? Did outsiders also choose this place for their graves? Daisy recalled what the boy had said: she was afraid of going in and being unable to get out. She also feared freezing to death. She thought the boy had purposely made her come here. Oh, what an evil boy!

She finally reached the tombs. All of them were exactly alike. Which one was her brother's? She stopped thinking about it. Silence was everywhere. She would like to hear a voice, but there was none.

All of a sudden, she saw a plump little animal crouching on the massive tombstone to her right. It was pale red, and its skin was so thin that it was transparent. Its legs and feet were weak, quivering as they tried to support its disproportionately large body. Its head was wrinkled, sort of like an old man's. She was attracted to this little creature and no longer felt terrified. What species of animal was this homeless little thing? A rat or a frog? Maybe it had a home in a certain tomb and it had come out for a walk and a breath of fresh air.

Daisy mustered her nerve to pet it. Its skin was warm, like satin. It was indifferent, staring at her through half-open eyes. For some reason, the expression in its eyes made Daisy think of Dad. Dad was so lonely. This summer, he had deliberately fallen asleep in the backyard, letting the mosquitoes bite him. He had even told Daisy to take the mosquito repellent away. After midnight, she heard him singing army songs.

Maybe it was a rat, but why did it have no tail? Rats were high on the list of animals she liked. She had dreamed of living in the oldest house in one end of the village. Rat holes were everywhere inside the house and outside the house. These little creatures were always busy with something. Daisy wanted to hear it make a noise, but it didn't utter any sound. It seemed afraid of the cold; it should go back into its hole.

She was a little cold. She needed to move around to warm up. As she was thinking this, she saw a road. It forked away from the tombs, leading to an open area. Daisy ran a few steps and then turned around to look at the little thing again. Then she ran into the distance, her mind all at once empty. The space between sky and earth had become very light, and Daisy narrowed her eyes. She didn't feel very good. She stopped and turned around. She wanted to run back to the tomb where the little thing was. She ran and ran, but never saw the tombs. It seemed she had lost her way at the fork of the road. Not only did she not see the tombs, but Mosquito Village had also disappeared. Daisy began to worry. Where was she? In her memory, this should be a place with many watery depressions, with some hills rising beyond them. Perhaps the watery depressions had now been frozen over, but she didn't see any hills, either. This was simply a clearing. Daisy had never seen such a large clearing; it was even larger than the cemetery she had just passed. The word *plains* was not in her vocabulary. The sky was abnormally light, and her eyes hurt. There was no way to observe places a little farther away. Just then, a wisp of smoke curled up before her.

She ran toward the smoke. It appeared to be quite close, but it was a long time before a girl's profile gradually came into focus. She was a girl much like Daisy, wearing yellow clothes and burning hell money for her ancestors. The snow had melted on the large clearing all around her. A pile of not yet burned hell money still lay on the ground.

"Hey! Hello! Can you tell me if there's a village near here?" Daisy asked.

"Are you asking if there's a cemetery? I can tell you; there isn't."

Concentrating on the fire, she didn't bother to look at Daisy.

Daisy thought, What a strong-minded person! Daisy thought that if she followed her she would come to an inhabited place, but it seemed the girl wasn't leaving any time soon. Daisy squatted down and watched the fire with her. The girl didn't appear to be happy with Daisy, and she moved to keep her distance from her. After a while, she couldn't stand it any longer and said to Daisy, "If you think you'll be able to get home today, you've miscalculated."

"Then, where's your home?"

"Hunh."

"Do you live with the little mouse?"

"How did you know? Huh?"

She was staring at Daisy in amazement.

"I saw it!" Daisy said, thrilled. "It's so cute! Take me over there, take me there, okay? What's your name?"

All of a sudden, the girl prodded the hell money with a bamboo stick, and the burning pieces of paper flew toward Daisy's face. Daisy's face hurt from the heat. She covered her face with her sleeve and retreated.

She smelled a strange odor. When she stood still and looked all around, the little girl had already run off. The hell money on the ground was scattered all over. Some of it was still burning; most of it had been extinguished. A stink began rising from the hell money. The sky was still so light that she couldn't see anything even a little way away. Daisy was puzzled: where on earth did the girl live? How could she have disappeared so quickly without a trace? Suddenly she was ashamed of her timidity. She thought, Why couldn't I also run into the snowy area as the girl did? Why should I be afraid of getting lost? Anyhow, hadn't she been lost all along? The moment she was going to run off, she saw the little animal squatting there. Was it the same one? Before she could see it clearly, it took off toward the snow. It ran fast on its thin legs, so she couldn't catch up with it. But it hadn't run far. Daisy saw it go into a ditch: there had been a wide earthen ditch here all along.

Daisy squatted beside the ditch and looked down. Besides the footprints of the little creature that had been left there just now, the snow-filled ditch unexpectedly contained human footprints. They must be the girl's. But the ditch didn't go anywhere. Glancing down from above, she saw that it was just a short ditch dug out manually. Where had the girl and the "rat" gone? The girl and "rat" were actually living somewhere in the open country! This idea was exciting. She left the ditch and strolled ahead.

She didn't know how long she walked. The light faded, and the shadows of hills appeared faintly ahead of her. Mosquito Village must be below the hills, but why did it seem as far away as the horizon? Furthermore, Daisy could not see the footprints she had left in the snow. How strange: the girl just now had left footprints. Even the "rat" had left footprints! She jumped up and down a few times, but left no impressions in the snow she stamped on. She remembered that the same thing had occurred eight years ago. Later she had forgotten the incident, not remembering it until now. That time, their family of four had walked along the river on the snowy land. They were going to Auntie's home. Daisy had looked back and had seen that she was the only one who had left no footprints in the snow. She tugged at Dad's clothing and asked about this. In a bad humor, he said, "Children shouldn't always be looking all around." At the time, she felt that this was a serious matter, and she was shaking from fright. Even after they reached Auntie's house, she continued shaking. She suspected that she was suffering from a fatal disease and that she wouldn't live much longer, and that her parents knew this but somehow they hadn't told her.

It would soon be dark. At last, she reached Mosquito Village. To her surprise, Daisy saw her father standing at the entrance to somebody's home. He was eating corn on the cob.

"Dad!!" Daisy was crying as she rushed toward him.

"You've come back—that's good, that's good," Mama said as she emerged from the house.

The three of them went home in silence. No one talked the whole way.

It was dark before they ate dinner.

"Daisy, how come I always see a butterfly on your right cheek?" Mama asked.

Daisy looked by the light of the kerosene lamp and saw a butterfly. It was black, clinging to the lamp chimney. She rubbed her cheek, and felt quite uncomfortable.

"You can't imagine," she said to Mama, "that place is truly another world."

"I probably cannot imagine. I'm old," Mama said despondently.

Daisy was exhausted and fell asleep right away. But she woke up later, perhaps because of the water noise that person made in the kitchen. "Daisy, Daisy!" he shouted at her.

Daisy was tired, and her whole body hurt, but she felt excited.

The one who had called her was the boy from Mosquito Village. He was standing outside the kitchen, his face pressed against the window. Daisy walked over and opened the door.

"Look!" He pointed at the sky.

That kind of bird was filling the sky. Two were flying low, sweeping past in front of him, their feathers brushing his face. He burst out with "Aiya!"

"Does it hurt?" Daisy asked him.

"Sure it does. Their bodies are copper, their wings iron."

"So strange. But only yesterday, they were still snowflakes. I captured one of them . . ."

"You're lying!" He said sternly, "How could you capture them? Impossible! This kind of bird comes out only on snowy days. No one can capture them."

Daisy noticed that he was standing barefoot in the snow, and she couldn't help but admire him. She motioned him into the kitchen to warm himself by the fire. He thought it over carefully before saying, "Okay."

They went into the kitchen. Daisy had just closed the door when they heard the birds bumping into the door, making *da, da, da* sounds. The door started to shake.

"See. I told you they had copper bodies and iron wings."

Daisy lit the firewood in the stove. She saw the boy's face gradually grow thinner in the firelight. Her heart thumped. She struggled hard, and said in a small mosquito-like voice, "You're a lot like my brother. Tell me about Mosquito Village."

"I can't speak of Mosquito Village things to outsiders."

Daisy sighed. She turned the flame up. She looked again: a black butterfly as large as a bat was resting in midair—that was where his face should be. And his hands were scratching at the ground, making a heap of earth scraps.

"What are you doing?" she asked him in amazement. Inwardly, she was scared.

"The thing you ran into in the cemetery—it's my friend! Now do you get it?" He shrieked, "Look at how sharp my claws are—That comes with practice!"

"Ah! Ah!" Daisy sighed lightly.

"That place belongs to us. It's always like that on snowy days. You saw that. I squat with it in the cemetery. You don't appreciate the place, so why on earth did you go there?" He made a gnawing sound with his teeth.

The fire had not gone out yet when he left. Daisy supposed he was loath to spend time with her. She stuck her head out the door and saw the silvery white sky. All was quiet in the world. Not even the willow branches murmured. They were drooping in silence.

"Daisy! Daisy!" Mama shouted as she walked in. "Who was here?"

Mama pointed with the tip of her toe at the small hole scratched out of the ground.

"Someone from Mosquito Village," Daisy said softly.

"I see. It's been so many years, and yet their descendants still haven't dropped the idea!"

"Who?"

"Those outsiders. Back then, you were still little. Your dad went to Mosquito Village for a short-term job, and got acquainted with them . . . Oh, why should I tell you this? It's all in the past. Forget what I said."

She put the pot on the stove, getting ready to steam rice.

"I'm sleepy, Mama," Daisy said.

"Of course you are. You haven't slept well since you came back from there. Go to sleep."

Daisy went back to her room and lay down, but she couldn't sleep. She was agitated, so she hurriedly dressed, put on boots, and went outside. She was in a daze, and only heard her father say from behind, "Daisy, ah, Daisy, where are you going?"

As she passed the wide-open door, she kicked over a small bench without realizing it. She walked straight out of the backyard and came to the highway. She was so sleepy, but why hadn't she been able to sleep? Later, she leaned against a large willow tree and dozed. In a dream lasting only two or three minutes, she saw a flock of silvery white birds plunge down like shadows sweeping over from midair. All of a sudden, the ground was covered with dead birds.

And then, the "rat" emerged from the heap of bodies. She awakened with a start and returned to the backyard. Mama was just saying to Dad, "It's those outsiders . . ."

"Daisy, are you okay now?" Dad asked sternly.

"I'm terribly sleepy. It's so light over there, and I couldn't sleep . . . ," she said vaguely.

"Did you get a good look, Daisy? What I saw was merely a dark blur. The moon had risen, but it didn't light up anything. What were you looking for in the house?"

"A rat. Let me rest my head on the table and take a nap."

She closed her eyes and still didn't fall asleep. She was dispirited, yet also excited. Indistinctly, she heard her mother calling her in the kitchen.

"Daisy, Daisy, it's here!"

Daisy sprang up and dashed to the kitchen.

"Where? Where?" she asked.

Mama pointed with the tip of her foot to a newly shaved-out little hole.

"It ran out quickly," Mama said dejectedly. "Just like a bullet! Snowfall is good for this kind of animal. They can sneak off in the snow in the blink of an eye, and leave no trace."

"Was it the kind with thin legs?" Daisy asked.

"Yes. They're the outsiders' pets. They eat the outsiders' corpses until only the skeletons remain."

"It's so light out . . . ," Daisy said, yawning.

"As light as a mirror!" Mama took over the topic excitedly. "Snow fell again just now. That boy from Mosquito Village circled our house many times. As he walked, from time to time he bent over and buried something in the snow. He stared at our house. I could see that he was the child of those outsiders!"

"What's wrong with the outsiders' children?"

"Why don't you believe me, Daisy? It isn't good for you."

"What's the matter with the outsiders' children?" Daisy doggedly raised the same question.

"Outsiders have no homes. They wander around all night in the wilderness."

"I see. Mama, are they like those rats?"

"You're a bright child, Daisy."

"I'm terribly sleepy."

At last, Daisy fell asleep.

■

In her dreams, many people called her. She heard them all. She wanted to answer, but couldn't make a sound. Dad called her to breakfast, Mama called her to lunch, Auntie called her to dinner, the boy from Mosquito Village called her to go fishing, Little Wan asked if she could borrow some thread for embroidery.

She ran about in the villages that she frequently dreamed of. She knew that she had never been to these villages, but the moment she fell asleep, they entered her dreams. The villages were covered by snow, and the huge weeping willow branches were swathed in ice. The sky darkened. No one was visible in the entire region. Her steps were light, too light to be real. She stopped for an instant and touched a willow branch. A thought flashed through her mind: It's going to be dark soon. The popsicle-like branches caused her to tremble, and she let go of the branch. She occupied herself for a while under the tree, scraping away at the snow until muddy earth was revealed. She made a mark, intending to return the next day.

It was the next morning when she smelled smoke and suddenly woke up. She saw Mama's face above her. Mama was smiling as she watched her.

"Yesterday, your dad and I went to that home again."

"What home?"

"The one in Mosquito Village. He told your dad that because you had discovered their secret, the villagers had all moved away. Now his family is the only one left there. How did you happen upon such a place?"

"So you and Dad have known about this place for a long time?"

"Yes. Your dad was a short-term laborer there for years. Sometimes he stayed overnight. He went there with the Mosquito villagers at night. But each time he lost his courage on the way and returned by himself. He has regretted this for years. He felt disgraced."

"Have all of them moved? Is that one family still there?"

"Now that family has also left. Naturally, the rat still lives there."

"Oh, my poor dad," Daisy sighed.

At breakfast, she didn't dare look at Dad. She ate with her head down.

When she finished and looked up, she realized Dad had already left the table.

"Your dad decided to go out by himself. Staying at home in such snowy weather makes him uneasy."

"Where did he go?"

"The place where you went," Mama said with a smile.

Daisy jumped up, rushed to her room and put on boots, and then chased after him.

Dad had reached the other end of the village. His silhouette was a tiny black dot.

"Dad! DAD!" she shouted through tears.

Dad stopped and waited for her.

"Why are you crying? Why are you crying?" he asked absent-mindedly.

"Where are you going?"

"Mosquito Village."

He shrugged his shoulders. Daisy walked in silence with him.

When they reached Mosquito Village's tall old willow tree, Dad suddenly said, "Daisy, do you still remember the road you took?"

"Road? I didn't pay any attention. I was just walking. Every-where, everything was white . . . Let me think. Oh yes—smoke! Someone was burning hell money."

"You have a good memory. It's helpful."

While they were talking, they came to a courtyard. Last time, Dad had stood at this door eating corn on the cob. But now the doors and windows were tightly closed. No one was here. The odd thing was that under the eaves were two benches. "Someone knew we would be coming," Dad said as he sat down.

"Who?" Daisy sat down, too.

"I don't know. But this is the way things always are in Mosquito Village. The moment you enter this village, you're being watched. This time, they're all gone. Even this family has left."

"But you say that someone is watching us. Who's watching now?"

Dad didn't reply. He was listening closely. Daisy pricked up her ears. But she quickly wearied of listening, because there was nothing to hear except for the monotonous sound of the wind.

Daisy stood up; she wanted to look all around. When she walked to the wall, she saw the boy. He was running south, leaping like a goat.

"Hey, hey!" Daisy shouted.

The wind broke her voice up. The boy didn't hear her. She turned around to look; her father was no longer under the eaves of the house. He was walking to the back. Daisy followed him, an ominous premonition rising in her mind. She saw a beam of white light shining on the dog shed behind the house.

The dog shed was large. Two old dogs were inside. One was missing its right ear. They snuggled up to each other, fearfully watching the two people. They were shaking.

"They're cold," Daisy said. She thought she was going to cry.

As Daisy and Dad crouched at the door of the dog shed, the wind gradually strengthened. The dog shed shook, as if it would be blown away. The whirlwind carried snowflakes with it; they struck Daisy and her father. In a second, everything was dark.

"Dad, let's get out of here! Let's go! Now!"

Just as they dodged aside, a huge pile of snow slammed onto the dog shed. The shed collapsed. The two old dogs didn't run away. Without uttering a bark, they were buried under the snow. Daisy kept asking herself, "What just happened?"

"Let's go back," Dad said.

"It's better to stay beneath the eaves, Dad. The wind is too strong. We can't see anything. Something could go wrong."

As Daisy implored him, Dad, to her surprise, started laughing.

"You worry too much. What could go wrong?"

They walked into the gale. Sometimes the snow blown by the whirlwind toppled them, and they were almost buried. Daisy and Dad did all they could to dig out of the snow and extricate themselves. They walked and stopped, walked and stopped. Daisy's face was so frozen that it was numb. She couldn't see anything. She just followed Dad. Only one thought remained in her confused brain: "That boy actually can live in the wilderness in such snowy weather . . ."

"They're outsiders!" By the time Dad said this, they were home again. "Outsiders aren't the same as us. If they want to leave, they just leave. If they want to stay, they just stay."

"Then what about the dogs?" Fear showed in Mama's eyes.

"They should be all right," Dad asserted.

Daisy remembered the expression in the eyes of the old dog that was missing an ear, and she twisted uneasily in her chair. The people had gone, but they'd left the dogs behind; they must have hearts of steel. Someone whispered to Daisy, "It's because you discovered us that we moved away . . ." She was stunned, and shifted her gaze to her dad. Dad was smoking: the smoke he exhaled formed a white mushroom cloud that covered his face.

After tidying the kitchen, Daisy went back to her bedroom. The bedroom was small, with a narrow window facing the backyard. Daisy walked to the window. She simply couldn't believe her eyes.

The boy was sitting on a pile of snow. He was naked, resting his head on one hand as if asleep. He must have been exhausted from running.

Some people were entering from the gate in the backyard: their faces were familiar. They were all squinting at the dazzling white sky. Daisy heard them enter the house with slow, heavy steps. The building creaked with each step they took. Daisy fancied that they were old elephants emerging from the forest.

Mama stood at the door and said to Daisy, "The outsiders have arrived."

## THE QUEEN

1.

People in Wang Village had a great hobby—watching the queen walk along the flagstone roads through their village. The queen was returning to her home, a deserted wilderness north of the plains. That rather large wooden house had been built when the old king was young. After years of being battered by wind and rain, the wood had darkened, but it hadn't yet rotted. It was still strong. The old king and his queen had long since died; the elders in the village could still dimly remember them. After the old king and his queen died, the Wang villagers quite naturally began calling the couple's only child Queen. No one knew how old she was—a person's age was the last thing that the villagers cared about. Their impression was that the queen wasn't yet old, nor was she young. It was best to say she was ageless. Everyone knew the queen was arrogant, for she lived alone in an old house in the wilderness, unwilling to move to the village. If she had wished to move to the village everyone would have welcomed her. She lived in the old house. Every day she went to the market to buy groceries and incidentals. She drew water with a wooden bucket from the well at the gate of her house. A mischievous boy from Wang Village called the queen a drone to her face. He was later twig-whipped fiercely by his parents, who were deeply ashamed of his ill-bred behavior. But he was only a little kid: he would learn from this lesson and grow up. The villagers thought that each person should understand the hidden meaning in the word *queen* and behave accordingly.

What did the queen think of the villagers? Hard to say. Everyone knew she was amiable and polite. She greeted people when she saw them, and she was happy to help others (this seldom happened, though, because she lacked opportunities to help). Yet when she went through the village, she never stopped to chat with the people she encountered. She apparently was always busy, and her thoughts were elsewhere. One could see this from the vague expression in her eyes. The queen had never locked her door. One day, unable to contain his curiosity, a young man slipped into her spacious living room. At the time, the queen was at the market. What happened after that? Nothing. The young man stayed in the house fewer than five minutes and then came out, his face deathly pale. The villagers said, "This is the boundary that the queen has set. How can someone simply walk into the queen's residence of his own accord?" This young man had to suffer the consequences.

The villagers certainly didn't know what the queen was thinking, much less what she thought of them, but they had been born with a strict sense of propriety. This led them to maintain a respectful distance from the queen. Perhaps this awareness arose from communication between the two sides? Or perhaps from certain age-old regulations for interpersonal relationships? The young man later told people that the queen's home was spotless. Hanging on one wall was the old king's crown. Although the furniture and utensils were old, they twinkled with an imposing radiance in the gloominess. The king's throne was on the living-room carpet. In the dining room, an enormous coal lamp sat on the long table. As soon as he entered, he felt he was suffocating. In a few short minutes, he thought he would soon faint. And so he groped his way out. "So scary. Scary," he said. Although the villagers had not burst recklessly into the queen's home, as he had, they nodded in unison upon hearing his vague narrative: in their imagination, the queen's home was just like this. The queen seemed to be hardworking—at daybreak, someone had seen her draw water from the well; someone else had seen her carrying a lantern at midnight looking for herbs in the wilderness. The villagers inferred that she must be working to maintain the tidiness of the "imperial palace," and of course she also cooked her own meals. On windy days, ash and sand blew in, so the rooms had to be swept every day. Keeping the house spotless was no easy task. Speaking of cooking, the villagers thought that the queen was probably careful about what she ate. They guessed this because she looked spirited and energetic, and because she loved to buy food. Sharp-eyed people noticed that her favorite foods were mushrooms, celery, wild boar, mustard greens, and roasted peanuts. People said admiringly, "What simple preferences!" She apparently valued the flavor as well as nutrition. Good smells always wafted from her kitchen. The villagers wanted the queen to eat well and rest well. They loved her cleaning and her skills in the kitchen. They thought these were the source of their fascination with her charm. As for the queen herself, of course she ate well every day and rested well. And she did like cleaning and cooking, but not in order to be fascinating. Then for what? This is a riddle.

As for time, the queen had two contradictory attitudes: one was extremely befuddled—she couldn't figure out which day it was. Was it Tuesday or Thursday? Was it the third day of the month or the eighth day? Sometimes she got the month wrong. The other was extremely meticulous. For example, what would she do at particular hours of the day? And for how long? How would she schedule her activities over the next seven days? How often would she go away each month? She had to abide meticulously by her own regulations. She connected her daily activities like notes in a melody, and she would say rather contentedly, "Look at me—like a fish in water." The villagers didn't care (perhaps they didn't know) about her confusion over time, but they appreciated her strictness with time. They thought this was noble. When the market was about to close, they gathered on both sides of the road. They would look at their watches and say, "The queen will arrive in eight minutes." "Still seven more minutes . . ." "Four more minutes . . . ," and so forth. This was the moment they waited for excitedly. It was a stately moment. The queen arrived and greeted the villagers. She walked like the wind and soon disappeared from their sight. She had to hurry home to peel potatoes, shuck broad beans, and light the fire to cook her meal. After eating, clearing the table, and tidying the kitchen, she had to sit down and write her daily work diary.

The "work diary" was actually simply a record of her day's activities, as well as some accounts. Writing her work diary gave the queen her greatest joy and satisfaction. Afterward, she felt relaxed and reinvigorated. Because this activity was so absorbing, the queen sometimes deliberately broke away from her writing and stood outside for a while and looked at the sky. Then she returned to her desk and continued with her record and her accounts. Once when she was looking at the sky, a little black bird fell onto her shoe, pecked at her shoelace, and flew away. In that split second, she felt overwhelmed by this great favor. As she deliberately prolonged her happiness, heaven once more generously gave her greater happiness. The contradictory thing was that her palace had no calendar; she had never bought one in the market. She had a radio; with it, she received messages from the world. This little box could tell the queen the date and the year. The queen would listen half-heartedly. After a few minutes, she would forget it all. Perhaps she had too much to fill her time, and she was too busy to pay attention to extraneous things. After writing in her diary, she had to sweep the carpet—such a pleasurable activity. Cleaning the coal lamp was enjoyable, too. Each time, she polished its glass cover until it reflected her face as clearly as a mirror. She looked into the glass cover and said softly, "I'm getting old . . ." She felt an inner joy that was incomprehensible to others. Why was she happy about growing old? Because it meant she was becoming more and more experienced and determined. It also meant that she was drawing closer and closer to her parents, the old king and queen.

People believed that the old king was originally from Wang Village. Someone even said that he used to be a knife sharpener. Later, he increased the distance between the villagers and himself by building a big house in the wilderness and calling himself king. He married a young woman from another place. Folks said that the couple went away for half a year and came back rich. But the villagers didn't know how they had done this. In fact, no one cared how they became rich. Everyone deeply venerated the old king. "He's our king." People were often near tears when they said this. Their faith was not inspired by any oracle; it came from their innermost beings. And because of this simple feeling, when the old king and his queen died in quick succession, everyone quite naturally called their daughter queen. This queen was much like her father!

Although she lacked her father's skill at sharpening kitchen knives, in her imposing manner and with her omniscient vision she proved even more a monarch than her father. A queen who kept the palace neat and tidy, who was unruffled in everything she did, who strove for self-improvement was surely worthy of the villagers' veneration. Someone noted that they revered her more than they had the old king! It was only because of this queen that this transcendental palace also carried a sense of the mundane. Anyone walking past the wooden house could tell what the queen was eating that day. The aroma of the food made the villagers hungry. They couldn't imagine what the palace would be like if the queen were not there. The queen should live in the palace forever. Was this the difference between her and the old king? The villagers didn't want to probe this question. They venerated their queen, loved their queen (of course, she was their queen!): this was enough. Hey! Just look at the queen's nimble footsteps: Wasn't it like flying?

A lad named Drum ran into the queen at night in the "desert." Drum had gone out because he had a splitting headache. The desert was made of crushed rock; no plants grew anywhere for several miles around it. Yet under the moonlight late at night it looked beautiful—a stretch of glistening silver light. Drum thumped his head desperately and walked in the desert. Suddenly he saw the queen. Dressed in white, the queen was like a floating immortal. He was at least two hundred meters away from her. On a night like this, Drum hallucinated that he had come to the moon. He forgot his headache. He wanted to catch up with the queen and talk with her. This was a rare opportunity. He picked up his pace, but for some reason he couldn't catch up with the queen. Finally, he began running, but he still trailed behind her. The queen was also running, her white skirt blowing in the wind, moving like a sail. "Hey, hey—" Drum shouted, as he ran faster and faster. But the queen ran even faster, and soon disappeared without a trace. Drum stopped and looked blankly all around. There was now only a stretch of silver light. Where could the queen have gone? Could she have dug her way into the ground? Drum finally realized that his headache was gone. He excitedly thought back to the scene just now and was reluctant to leave the gravel that glittered like diamonds. He vowed silently, I have to come back here again tomorrow night.

The next night, he had no headache; as soon as his parents fell asleep, he slipped out of the house. There was no moonlight. He walked a long time, trusting to his memory to find that desert. He stood beside the desert. It was dark all around. Rarely seen, such desolation was simply terrifying. He wasn't a coward, but he didn't want to stay here long. Without the queen, the desert was hell. The walk home was endless. Even though he walked fast, when he got home it was already light. He remembered that someone wearing a conical hat on the road had asked, "Did you have good luck?" He had hurriedly answered, "It seems so . . ." It was dark at the time, and he hadn't gotten a good look at the person. Drum didn't give up; later, he went back to the desert several times. But each time it was dark; he missed the silvery moonlight night.

He told his Uncle Mi about his experience. Uncle Mi was silent for a while and then said, "Don't go there." "Why?" Drum asked. "Because you yourself don't want to go. Besides, the queen occupies your heart, doesn't she? Drum, you must improve yourself!" Drum was grateful to Uncle Mi. Even after many years had passed, Drum still remembered that night vividly. In the daytime, he went to the desert, where he picked up some stones and brought them back.

The stones were dull, not a bit shiny. But Drum liked these stones; he rubbed them with his hands and told them what had happened that night.

After some of the elderly villagers heard about Drum's experience, they discussed it in private. But they didn't want to make their comments public. Smiling, they said to Drum, "You were lucky, Drum. That evening, the queen was hurrying to rendezvous with her parents." "How do you know?" Drum asked in amazement. "We always know a little about this kind of thing ahead of time." The elders were concerned for the queen and also happy for her. After all, she was having a reunion with her family. But to waste her strength like this at night: Would this harm her health? Early the next morning, she appeared again beside the well. These old people had heard their elders say that the old king and his queen were buried "on the other side" of the desert—a place that they themselves had chosen. But no one knew exactly where on the other side of the desert. Apart from the queen, no one had gone there. It must be remote, a place with many acacia trees. After Drum told the villagers his news, they watched the queen even more closely for the next few days. In those few days, the queen seemed even more spirited, and she played old records in the palace. These were marches. It seemed that the old king's vitality motivated the queen, and she was vigorous as she put the palace in order. In Wang Village, there was no larger or more stately place than the palace. It was the villagers' spiritual sustenance. Even shepherd children were always looking toward this place on the plains.

During that extraordinary night, the queen didn't sleep. After she returned from "the other side" of the desert, she washed her face with well water and then sat down at her desk and began writing her work diary. Her record was cryptic. For example: "three stones," "one ditch," "nursery rhymes," "sending a signal," and so forth. You could guess the meaning of some others. For example: "one kilometer in ten minutes," "five kilometers in half an hour," and so on. They probably indicated how fast she walked that day. She was very engrossed in writing her work diary. Her cheeks were rosy and her eyes shining like a teenage girl's. After she finished writing in her diary, she paced for five minutes in her room and recalled the boy named Drum. She seemed to know why he had run to the desert. She wondered, What would his future be like? Would those diamonds that disappeared shatter his life someday or might they change into a Rubik's Cube in his hands? She wasn't at all worried about him. His pursuit had made clear his determination. Then the queen turned to thinking about the reality of the palace—swallows were nesting in the eaves for the first time. This was inspiring.

2.

Ever since the young man had burst into the queen's home several years earlier and been so scared by the atmosphere that he ran out, no one had ever tried it again. Everyone felt that it would be an offense. However, something strange occurred. A little girl named Zhu Zhu went to the market with her mama. The careless mama had no idea how she lost Zhu Zhu in the crowded market. Zhu Zhu waited for a long time next to a load of potatoes, and still didn't see her mama. And so she decided to go home alone. She thought she knew the way. But the farther she walked, the less familiar the scenery was. She didn't stop until she reached a large wooden house. She thought she'd better go in and ask someone how to get to Wang Village.

She went in, but no one was there. In high spirits, Zhu Zhu climbed onto the dining room table and fiddled with the coal lamp for a long time. Then she looked around the living room. She thought the two portraits and the crown on the wall were not very attractive, and the three porcelain vases were too large. Just then, she noticed a small staircase concealed behind a large cupboard. When Zhu Zhu tiptoed up the stairs, she heard her heart palpitate. Would people think she was a thief? If they caught her, she would say she was looking for her mama. But would they believe her? She reached the second story. It was unlike the spacious first floor, which had numerous rooms. The second floor had only one room, which was open and dark. Next to the room was an almost vertical narrow staircase. Zhu Zhu entered the room and heard a woman ask, "Little girl, how did you come up here?"

"I don't remember. I'm looking for my mama . . . ," Zhu Zhu answered frantically.

"You don't make a point of remembering the way you took? That's not a good habit." The woman seemed unhappy.

"I can change, I promise. Now I do remember. I came up from the other staircase on the side. Now may I go down?"

"No. You can't go back now. Come over here."

Zhu Zhu tried taking a step ahead. She stepped on the woman's foot. Horrified, she started crying.

The woman picked Zhu Zhu up and set her on her knee. She said, "Don't cry. See how brave our Zhu Zhu is!"

"Who are you?" Zhu Zhu asked, as she wiped away her tears.

"I'm the queen. You've heard of me, haven't you?'

"Hello, Queen. How can I see your face?"

The queen was sitting on a swivel chair. She turned in another direction, and Zhu Zhu saw the Milky Way in the deep blue sky. Zhu Zhu realized that she and the queen were sitting in midair. But she still couldn't see the queen's face. The queen urged Zhu Zhu to jump down. Afraid, Zhu Zhu grabbed the queen's skirt tightly and wouldn't let go. The queen grew angry. She stood up, flinging the girl off. Zhu Zhu heard herself hit the water; she dog-paddled a little and reached the shore. Then she indistinctly heard the queen shouting, "That's the Milky Way . . ."

Zhu Zhu recognized the brook in the village, and she saw her mama running toward her. Crying and laughing, her mama held her.

"I saw the queen!" Zhu Zhu said proudly. "She hugged me, and I almost got to the Milky Way. It would have been great if I hadn't been afraid."

When they reached their home, it was crowded with many people who wanted to hear what Zhu Zhu had to say about the queen. Zhu Zhu was regretful as she said, "It would have been so great if I hadn't been afraid."

Then she started crying.

"This child—what's wrong with her?"

"The queen shocked the wits out of her."

"The queen gave her inspiration. The girl was really fortunate."

"This child was born insatiable."

For a while they made all kinds of comments. Then, losing interest, they quickly dispersed.

As soon as the crowd left, Zhu Zhu stopped crying. Looking at the window, she actually sneered.

"What are you sneering at?" Mama asked in astonishment.

"They kept asking about this. How can anyone ask others about such things? I will never speak of it. Mama, I can't tell you, either. You won't blame me, will you?"

"Of course not. I'm also sorry that I let you get lost. Still, it seems that you grew up as a result. When they said you're insatiable, I was happy. A child who isn't insatiable is boring, and so they were praising you." Mama smiled.

Zhu Zhu changed out of her wet clothing and braided her hair. She was no longer regretful. She thought to herself that she would have more opportunities, lots of them. It wasn't that hard to find the queen's home.

As for the queen's nighttime activities, people guessed all kinds of things; the villagers also took note of a variety of omens. Without exception, each person thought that the queen's activity was very important. Just think about it: a queen was running around in a place not far from the village. What's more, she was the queen of Wang Village! Although this wasn't too strange, it symbolized the villagers' innermost passion, but they weren't content with seeing something superficially—they liked to delve into it in detail. Everyone thought it was wrong to follow her deliberately, but this didn't mean that people criticized those who had the good fortune to run into her by chance. People approved of that because it was almost like destiny. The old king's palace in the wilderness was a vague concept. It was far away, and its surroundings were quite desolate. No matter how one looked at it, this was a suitable place for the queen to live. None of the Wang villagers would be so presumptuous as to call on the queen in her palace.

But one night it did happen. It was an enchanting autumn evening when Widow Zhen had just had a terrible fight with her live-in lover and then furiously walked out in the wild. She walked ahead blindly: she couldn't see the bats flying around, nor could she hear the nocturnal birds' singing, because the world suddenly vanished from her field of vision. She was pushed ahead by the power inside her body. She didn't mind being lost—maybe she wanted to be lost. Anyhow, she didn't want to go back home. Wherever she went would be fine. She wouldn't regret it even if a wolf devoured her.

In the dark, Zhen ran into a wooden wall and hurt her forehead. She nearly fainted. She thought doomsday was approaching. After a long time, she gradually regained consciousness and discovered that she was sitting on the ground. The gate creaked open.

"Did you come to see me?" a woman asked calmly.

"Yes. I'm calling on . . . ," Zhen answered obscurely.

"Then come in right now! Didn't you hear the wolves roaring?" she said sternly.

Zhen tried hard a couple of times, but was unable to stand up. The woman dragged her in. The clatter of the gate closing was earthshaking.

She couldn't see anything in the house. For some reason, Zhen felt pleased. Her insane urge to go walking disappeared. She sensed that she was sitting on a high-backed chair. The woman was sitting across from her. Zhen couldn't help saying softly, "Are you the queen?"

"It seems so." The voice was teasing.

"I really didn't come here on purpose to disturb you."

"But you did. You guessed right: I don't need a companion. But I do like to lecture others: that's my failing. It's easy to solve your problem. I'll help you solve it right now."

Zhen was stunned. She waited, wondering how the queen would do this. But after about ten minutes, the queen hadn't made any sound or motion. Another ten minutes passed, and still nothing happened. Zhen grew impatient, but she waited a while longer and finally extended her hand. She probed in the dusky space across from her, but didn't touch anything. She walked over to it; she didn't encounter any obstacle because in fact the queen wasn't there. But just now she had definitely been sitting across from her.

"Queen!" she shouted.

Her eerie voice echoed in the high, empty room. She broke out in a cold sweat. Something was tangled up with her feet, and she sat down on the floor again. She grabbed the thing with her right hand. Oh, a snake! The snake bit her, then struggled free, slipping away with a rustling sound. She sensed that the back of her right hand was swelling quickly. She might die soon.

"Queen, save me! I'm dying!" she shouted, over and over.

She shouted until she was hoarse and then she knew no one was there to save her.

She would have to save herself. Enduring the pain, she looked for the door, and found it after a while. She pushed and pushed, but the door wouldn't move. It seemed to be bolted from the outside. She was tormented by pain; she was exhausted. Even worse: fears surged up in her mind like waves; she felt that poisonous juices were spreading all through her body.

"No!" she screamed.

She had never been weak. Never in her whole life. Even so, she felt that her "No" was frail and weak, not much stronger than a mosquito's buzzing. She started kicking at the door. She thought that since she could still kick the door, she probably wouldn't die. However, she seemed to be kicking cotton each time, for there was neither sound nor resistance from the door.

"Zhen, Zhen . . . ," her lover called to her from the darkness. His voice seemed quite funny.

"Bah! Why are you here?" Zhen roared.

"I'm in your home."

Frowning, Zhen began to think. Her family couldn't have moved to the palace, could they? Could the palace have changed into her home? Just now, the queen had definitely been sitting across from her, hadn't she? Wasn't she going to help her "solve her problem" right away? What kind of problem was it? At this point, her "problem" unfolded before her. She saw an abyss. Of course she didn't want to fall into the abyss but neither did she want to leave immediately. Her injured hand seemed to remind her: she had no choice. Her hand was swollen like a dumpling.

Zhen giggled for no reason and said to the darkness, "Liuhei (this was her lover's name), turn on the lamp."

This time, she waited a long time without getting a response. Zhen sensed a numbness starting to spread out from her heart. But why wasn't she losing physical strength or consciousness? This kind of death was frightening.

Zhen began moving. Every two steps, she kicked out blindly. Then she heard bursts of sound coming one after another; perhaps she had shattered some porcelain dishes. Unable to resist her feeling of schadenfreude, she wanted to damage some more things before she died. At a minimum, she wanted to scare the despicable Liuhei. After kicking some more, she felt something was wrong—why were porcelain dishes being constantly kicked over? Was Liuhei up to some mischief? She had no sooner thought of this than she lost her enthusiasm for breaking things. Just then, she happened to feel a high-backed chair with her foot—probably the one she had sat in before. After sitting down, she heard the queen talking across from her.

"Hasn't your problem been solved?" she asked impatiently.

"Thank you, Queen. I think so. There's nothing for me to do in the palace, so I'd better go home." Her throat felt dry as she spoke.

"Go home?" the queen sneered. "How?"

"I don't know. Am I dying?"

"You have to ask yourself that."

The queen's last words were fluttering in the air. Zhen wanted to kick the door again. Time after time, she wildly kicked an imaginary gate. All at once, she fell to the floor.

"Liuhei, go to hell!" she cursed.

She heard the queen snickering, and at the same time she touched the door handle—her own home's door. Creaking, the door opened. It was light inside because it was already daytime. Everything was where she had left it. Her embroidery was on the windowsill, as if suggesting something. Someone knocked on the door: it was the village chief.

"Zhen, I heard that you drove Liuhei away. He's a good man."

"Who said this? It's nonsense. Liuhei had something urgent to do and went home."

"Oh, I see. What a relief. Zhen, I always think you're a remarkable woman."

"Get out of here. Don't you have any work to do? Did you come here just to jabber?"

Covering his mouth with one hand, the old man giggled. She pushed him out the door.

Outside, the frogs were croaking. Was it going to rain?

Recently, the queen really did come to Wang Village—and often. You could see this from some people's expressions. The village chief arose early and set out to collect manure. As soon as he went out, he ran into the young, neatly dressed oil peddler.

"You're out so early. Who will buy sesame oil at this hour?" the village chief teased.

"I came out early for people's convenience, for pleasure, or because I had a happy encounter last night. These are all possible reasons. It doesn't have to be for business," the young oil vendor said.

"Ha-ha! A happy encounter! Can you talk about it? I'd love to hear it."

"No, I can't."

"I wish you happy encounters every day!"

The village chief—this old fox—had guessed what the young oil vendor's encounter was because he had run into similar occurrences many times. He knew that the queen honored the village with her presence. Although she did so at midnight and although no one had really seen her, who else could it have been? Look at Woman Ji, who sat beside the road at twilight combing her hair. The left side of her face was reflected in the setting sun: she looked splendid and magnificent in profile! That's right: the village chief liked describing her with these words.

"Hi, Ji, the matchmaker's coming for you," the village chief said, to please her.

"Who cares? After she came, I got the magic wand that makes me pretty! Chief, take a look at me. Do I still need a matchmaker?" She approached the chief aggressively.

The village chief backtracked. He grumbled to himself, I shouldn't have crossed the line.

As he was thinking to himself, the village chief picked up pig manure and dog poop. He intended to go home. The moment he turned around, he saw the black-garbed queen standing right in the middle of the road. How had she changed into a headless queen? The village chief wanted to detour around her. He veered left, and the black-garbed headless person blocked the left side; he veered right, and she blocked the right side.

"You're really, you're really active . . . ," the village chief stammered. "We—you and I—let's dance!"

He didn't know where his courage came from. He threw the basket of manure to the roadside, and extended his rough hand to the queen. As soon as the headless queen held his hand, the village chief felt that he was spinning like a windmill. He heard himself shout, "Save me," but where could he stop? He was being continuously tossed into midair. He waved his arms in the air. Then he heard someone say, "Now I see this old guy's nature."

At that, the village chief fell down. He sat in the mud, his butt sore from the fall. The person who had just spoken asked, "Why did you stop dancing?"

The village chief asked if he had seen the queen.

"The queen?" The person stared. "I think that is Death!"

"Could be. I felt so good just now. Too bad she left."

"If she hadn't gone, could you be here? She's not interested in you. You're a lousy dancer."

The village chief picked up his basket and headed for home. He tried hard to recall his dancing just now: he didn't feel at all inferior and he was sure it had been the queen.

"I danced with the queen today," he told his wife as soon as he got home.

"My God. I saw this long ago. You've become another person," his wife said.

"The queen played the role of Death; I played the role of Death's son."

"That's so exciting," his wife said.

He held his hand out to his wife, and the two of them began twirling like a windmill. Oh, what happiness! While in midair, he thought of something and became a little worried. "The manure, manure . . . ," he kept saying. After he fell to the ground, his wife asked him what he had muttered while he was dancing.

The village chief's vision blurred, and he answered, "I left the manure outside the door. Did you and the queen talk with each other last night?"

His wife pointed outside.

The village chief pushed the door open, and saw the crown on the ground.

"It isn't appropriate, is it, to put the crown at the entrance to an ordinary family's home?" The village chief stooped and picked up the crown. He sized it up in the sunlight.

"Why isn't it? It would look good on you."

His wife smiled surreptitiously. Her expression inspired him, leading him to remember his morning encounter on the road. He realized that the queen had been pervading their lives. She wasn't a visitor; there's no way she would stay in Wang Village. Still, there was no way she would leave, either. This was so intriguing. Before the old king died, he had also pervaded their lives one time, but the Wang villagers no longer remembered this. The village chief's mother had told him, "On a night like that, the stars are dark, and the earth burns from within its crust . . ." Because no real disaster occurred, everyone adopted a wait-and-see attitude.

After the village chief put the crown into a large cabinet, the cabinet sparkled with sound. "Look! She trusts us so much!" his wife whispered to him. "After all, she's our queen!" he whispered back.

They were both a little deranged, pacing back and forth in front of the cabinet, loath to leave.

"Chief! Chief . . . ," someone shouted outside. He was around thirty.

The chief pulled a long face and went out.

"Why are you still here? You promised to leave."

"I promised to disappear from Wang Village . . . but last night . . ."

"Stop!" the village chief interrupted, "What do you want now?"

"Give me a job."

"Clean the manure out of our pigpen. Don't stop until you're stinking with sweat!"

"Sure thing!"

The village chief went inside and closed the door. His wife was staring at him, rebuking him coquettishly.

"What? He's young, but he's been a pessimist for eleven years. What a disgrace."

■

After taking a long time to make the decision, the queen really did arrive at Wang Village. She came to the long-established Wang Village, but she didn't like the villagers to recognize her and consider her one of them. She felt that would be awkward for her, lacking in style. As the queen hesitated, the unusual connections between her and the villagers took shape. Someone felt that he had a direct connection with the queen because he argued with her every day and the result of the argument would guide him in his actions. His life would be unbearably dull if he missed even a day of this kind of argument. When people asked him where he and the queen argued, he led a bunch of people into the kitchen, and, pointing at the iron pot of congee, he said, "This is she. We always argue in the kitchen." At first, everyone looked blank, and then they sort of understood. They gave him a thumbs-up and said, "You're a lucky man."

The queen knew that she had a huge group of supporters whom she would never see. They had all kinds of disabilities, but they were strongly determined. Her relationship with them was indirect. "Sometimes indirect influence is greater," she proclaimed in the palace. The moment she made this proclamation, she recalled Woman Jiao. Jiao had only one leg; she would turn eighty-five next year. She had lived alone all her life in the house next to the tofu workshop. People said that she used to be good at making tofu, but now she was old and infirm and could no longer do that. One day, when the queen was returning from the market, the throngs lining the street to welcome her included the one-legged Woman Jiao. The queen had seen her out of the corner of her eye much earlier: the old woman had stood on tiptoe in order to be seen. She wanted to get the queen's attention. The queen was greeting many people, but she didn't speak with Jiao. When she passed by the old woman, the queen glanced at her sharply and then immediately looked away. But in this lightning-quick exchange, the two women formed a long-term friendship. After this, the queen now and then heard fragmentary news of Woman Jiao from analyzing the local atmosphere. For instance, she knew that the old woman had resumed working in the tofu workshop. This gratifying news allowed the queen to see the contours of the palace in the village.

"Grandma Jiao, did you see the queen at night?" asked the little girl Binghua.

"Yes. At the time, the village sky was really bright!"

"Is the queen pretty?"

"I never got a good look at her."

Grandma Jiao had never seen the queen clearly—she had cataracts. What she had seen was a moon with many defects. Since she had cataracts, how had she been able to use her gaze to forge an exchange with the queen on the road? When Binghua asked her this, Grandma Jiao answered a little testily, "It was an out-of-body experience."

■

The young guy who had previously rushed impetuously into the queen's home was Yueyue. His situation was the same as Woman Jiao's. The queen valued his courage, and she kept nurturing him in secret. She believed that he would play a pivotal role in Wang Village in the future. Since the first time that Yueyue had taken the tragic risk and retreated from the palace with its rarefied air, the seeds of curiosity and uneasiness were sown in his heart. Thanks to his great enthusiasm and vague memory, he later made three more attempts to charge into the palace. He bungled each attempt. In his last try, he couldn't find even a trace of the palace or the queen. Some yurts appeared on the plains. No matter which yurt he entered, the people welcomed him with the same sneer. But now Yueyue was more mature than before: he no longer feared grotesque faces; he was just a little embarrassed. He saluted these people and then withdrew. The queen, hiding in a secret place, took all of this in and was very pleased.

Yueyue wondered whether his previous impression had changed and led him to a fork in the road. Or could it be that the queen's palace had disintegrated and turned into these yurts and pigpens? Either of these possibilities would make him even more curious, for after all he was a local villager. "Queen, palace . . . ," Yueyue chattered. From behind, he heard a woman's voice respond, "Yueyue, Yueyue . . ." Yueyue figured that the person responding to him must be the queen. He decided to make a fourth attempt.

He ran wildly around the desert, reaching the middle of the pebbles. The sky was gloomy; a light rain made the pebbles slippery. The pebbles looked dark and dull. Yueyue said to himself, This is the last time. He would not cower. Limping on the pebbled desert, he tried his best to proceed.

"Yueyue, are you exercising your legs?" Auntie Mao hailed him.

Yueyue looked up and saw the village trail.

"Don't run around blindly," Auntie Mao said wryly. "The thing you're looking for is in your home. Search in all the nooks and crannies."

Auntie Mao had a reputation in the village. What she said often came true.

Yueyue didn't search the hiding places in his home. Instead, he bought a few bolts of black cloth and covered all the windows in his home. Then he sat there recalling how the queen's palace looked. Each day he remembered one detail, and gradually the palace became vivid in his mind. The last two props that he remembered were a golden cane and the coal lamp. The coal lamp was placed on the long table in the palace dining room, and the golden cane was next to the door of an inner room in the palace. Yueyue carefully moved the golden cane and slowly pushed the door open. In one step, he strode outside. Across from him was his family's pigpen. The pigs were wailing in hunger. Yueyue shouted as he ran, "Queen! Queen . . ." He charged into his kitchen and began chopping vegetables for pig feed. Beads of sweat rose on his young face. This was great! He wished he could have such an adventure every day. Look, hadn't the queen hung candles from the palace on the wood-smoke-blackened wall of his kitchen? He—Yueyue—was an ordinary country boy, but the queen had kept looking after him. He started boiling the pig feed. Surprisingly, he brandished the spatula as if he were royalty.

"Yueyue, Yueyue!" a woman called softly from somewhere in the room.

Yueyue's eyes were beaming like a rainbow.

Qiu Yiping, a thirteen-year-old middle school student, was secretly in love with her thirty-five-year-old cousin with the whimsical name Xuwu. An orphan whose parents had died long ago, he was a scientist researching hot-air balloons. Qiu Yiping hadn't seen him in the past, but in the previous year Xuwu had often visited her village to test hot-air balloons and had become close to Qiu Yiping's family.

Whenever her cousin came to the village, Qiu Yiping grew so excited that she couldn't concentrate on her classes. As soon as school was out, she rushed home and went to the mountain to the east to look for her cousin. He was tall, wore glasses, was a little hunchbacked, and walked a bit sluggishly. He didn't look at all bright.

The mountain on the east was called Tomb Mountain; it was more than a thousand meters above sea level. Generally, Xuwu launched his hot-air balloons from the middle of the mountain and let them float along the contours of the mountain: they floated above Yiping's village. Everyone in the village would come out to watch this rare sight. Each time, Yiping swelled with pride.

Her cousin had stayed overnight with her family only twice— both times because it was raining hard. Ordinarily he slept in the wicker basket below the hot-air balloon, where he kept the things he needed for daily use. Day and night, Yiping yearned to soar into the sky in the hot-air balloon with her cousin, but he had never invited her to go along. He said, "It's dangerous." She didn't believe him. She thought he looked down on her and was weary of her pestering him.

On the mountain, her cousin sometimes took off his coat and wore only a sailor shirt. He curled up like a shrimp and repaired the hot-air balloon's heater. Sometimes, he did nothing, but just sat there looking at the sky. No matter what her cousin was doing, Yiping liked to be beside him; she would even like to be with him for a lifetime.

The hot-air balloon was red, the color of the sun setting at twilight. Many times, Yiping thought that her cousin looked at the hot-air balloon as though he were looking at his sweetheart. Yiping had heard her parents say that he hadn't married and that he didn't have a girlfriend, either. Could it be that the hot-air balloon was his girlfriend? When Yiping pondered this in the middle of the night, her eyes glinted in the dark, and she felt warm all over. She made up many stories about girlfriends her cousin had had in the past: she was sure he had had girlfriends in the past. She yearned to be with him at night on the mountain, viewing the moon and stars. But that was impossible, for her parents and the neighbors would all say she was shameless.

▪

It was Sunday. Qiu Yiping had gotten up early and hastily done the housework—washed and dried the clothes, prepared food for the pigs, fed the chickens, swept the courtyard, and cooked the breakfast. Then she had gulped down two stewed potatoes and slipped out of the courtyard. She started running toward Tomb Mountain, because she was afraid her family would stop her.

When she had climbed halfway up the mountain, she saw that her cousin was still asleep in the wicker basket. He had covered one side of his face with a quilt, and he looked very funny. The sound of Yiping's footsteps awakened him, and he suddenly sat up, hastily reaching out for his glasses.

"Oh, I overslept. I was really exhausted before daylight," he said, embarrassed. "You can't imagine, Yiping. I ascended to the top of the mountain and then even higher. Even higher! All of a sudden, I saw her. She was flying past like a big bird. My God!"

"Who? Who was flying—flying past like—like a big bird?" Yiping began stammering.

"You don't understand. You don't get it." Her cousin waved his hand, revealing his annoyance.

"Let's not talk about it anymore," he added.

He was wearing a blue-and-white-striped sailor shirt as he stood at one side and washed his face and brushed his teeth. He looked like a bittern. After he had cleaned up, he took some bread out of the basket and cut it into several small pieces, dipped them in catsup, and ate slowly. He offered some to Yiping, but she turned him down. She didn't want to make a pig of herself!

Seeing that her cousin's mind was elsewhere, Yiping thought he had pretty much forgotten her existence.

"Cousin, let me ride in the hot-air balloon just once! Just once!" Yiping begged.

"How could I do that?" He was immediately on his guard. "If your parents found out, they would break my neck! And what would the other villagers say? . . . Don't be silly."

"We could keep them from seeing. I could run out quietly in the middle of the night. No one would know. Didn't you say just now that when the big bird flew past, you didn't get a good look at it? If you teach me how to operate the hot-air balloon, I can take care of it and you can get a good look at the bird!"

When Yiping said this, she really had no idea how her cousin would respond, but she was desperate, so she chanced it.

Her cousin seemed touched by what she had said. He stared at her and asked, "Do you really think so? What the hell. Is this possible?"

"Sure it is! Of course! Really!" Yiping shouted.

Her cousin carefully folded the bread wrapper and put it away. He looked at the chestnut tree next to him as if he had something on his mind. Then he said very slowly: "Yiping, sit down."

Yiping sat down nervously on the rock. She was blushing.

"Do you know about Venus?" he asked.

"Yes. I've seen her at twilight." Yiping relaxed.

"She's what I saw before daylight! At that time, it was dark in all directions, but she was radiant. She seemed to be green colored. I reached out my hand and I could almost touch her, but a force pulled me away, and so I was separated from her. I really regret that. Why didn't I jump over to her then? At worst, I would have died! It was a great opportunity that not everyone can have—and I missed it. What's wrong with me? When I landed here, it was almost dawn. I suddenly felt weary of the world and fell asleep. I was completely out. Did you come to help me, Yiping?"

"Yes, I did."

"Do you think I can succeed?"

"Yes, you will," Yiping whispered. But what she thought to herself was, I hope you don't succeed. You should land with me.

Something crossed the cousin's mind. He frowned and asked Yiping, "Have people in the two nearby villages said anything about me recently?"

"Yes. Someone said that you're looking for your tomb. Is that true?"

"Ha-ha-ha-ha! Ha-ha!" Her cousin began laughing uproariously.

"Of course I fly around Tomb Mountain because I want to find a suitable burial place. This whole matter must be connected with Venus, isn't it?"

"I don't know." Yiping shook her head, and her face clouded over.

They fell silent. Both of them looked at the sky and then looked at the village below the mountain.

When they parted, they agreed that Yiping would slip away from her home at midnight and Xuwu would meet her at the foot of the mountain. When Yiping went down the mountain, her cousin shouted behind her, "Yiping, you must take an afternoon nap, because if you doze off later, we're both done for!"

"I know, cousin! I won't doze off!" Yiping answered excitedly.

She ran home and immediately picked up the bucket and went to fetch water. She went once, and then once more, until the two water containers were full. When she sat down to rest, Auntie Li dropped in.

"Is your cousin a man or a bird? He flew over my head, and I was so scared I fell down! It was too eerie, wasn't it? — a big guy flying back and forth over your head! I've lived a long time, and nothing like this has ever happened in our village before."

Yiping was entranced. She looked at Auntie Li and laughed out loud.

"What's so funny? Huh?"

When Auntie Li left, Yiping noticed that she also had a smile on her face. What on earth was Cousin up to? What did he want to communicate to the villagers?

After Yiping ate, she cleaned up the kitchen and went to bed. She planned to take a long, long nap.

She closed her eyes and counted. As she counted, she grew excited again and forgot how far she had counted. So she started again. She started over again several times to no avail. She looked at the clock. More than an hour had passed when she decided to get up and go to the field and pick beans.

As she picked beans, she looked at Tomb Mountain. One moment, it seemed that she saw a small red dot climbing to the mountain top. When she looked more carefully, she saw nothing. Probably the sun had been shining in her eyes. While Yiping was thinking about her cousin's dangerous behavior, she heard people talking behind her.

"That Xuwu — he's risking his life."

She turned around and saw that no one was there. Who had been talking?

Yiping was busy the entire afternoon with the beans, washing them and drying them. Finally she finished everything.

When the sun set, she ran out of the house and looked carefully at the sky. She looked and looked, but she didn't see Venus. There was no star at all in the sky. When she was about to enter her courtyard, Auntie Li appeared. She blocked the way and wanted her to answer a question.

"Xuwu has been staying in our village for such a long time: Does that mean he wants to marry you?"

"What nonsense!"

Very uneasy, Yiping pushed her away and dashed into her courtyard.

.

Yiping didn't go to bed until late. Before she went to bed, she opened the back door.

Every now and then she shone her flashlight on the clock. When it was almost midnight, she got dressed and sneaked out. As she stood at the courtyard gate, she looked back once. Her home looked dark blue. How could this shabby adobe home be dark blue? Ordinarily, it was a not-quite-yellow, not-quite-gray color. Was it because of the moonlight?

Yiping walked very fast, almost jogging. After a while, she reached the foot of Tomb Mountain. At night, the mountain looked very large, as though it wasn't a mountain but was the whole world. But her cousin wasn't waiting for her at the foot of the mountain. Yiping was worried and afraid: she heard her heart thumping against her chest. After waiting a while, she decided to climb the mountain. She thought maybe Cousin had forgotten what he had said and was simply waiting for her where they usually met.

As she climbed the mountain, she heard a strange bird calling several times. She was so afraid that she felt death was approaching. She said to herself, I'm not afraid to die. After she said this three times, she felt more courageous. She was proud of herself, too.

Finally, she saw her cousin sitting on a rock next to the hot-air balloon. His head was drooping; it seemed he didn't realize she had arrived. Could he have forgotten their plan?

"Cousin, let's get going!" Yiping shouted.

"Ah! You're here!" He was startled. "No need to hurry. Sit down for a while first."

Yiping sat on another rock. She was shaking all over.

"The time in the sky and the time on earth aren't the same," her cousin said slowly, one word at a time.

"Show—show me how to—to operate the balloon, okay?" Yiping said, her teeth chattering.

"I've set it on automatic. You don't have to do much. When she gets close, we have to be ready. If I do make up my mind and jump over to her, you must begin landing immediately. It's easy. All you have to do is pull the switch."

Xuwu spoke rapidly. Yiping wasn't very sure of what he had said. She blinked, and her emotions surged.

They sat in the large wicker basket, her cousin holding the joystick, and the hot-air balloon began slowly leaving the ground. Yiping was frightened and didn't dare look down. She wanted to get control of her feelings. Her cousin started talking nonstop.

"Yiping, you can't imagine the encounters I've had in the sky. People think that hot-air balloons can't fly very high, but this is just what ordinary people think. I've told you that I actually encountered Venus—and not just once, either! In that moment and that place, I assure you if someone had been helping me then, would I have flipped over onto it? What do you think? She was dark green. I sensed that she had a hairy surface. Could it be a kind of moss? I really regret that I missed the opportunity. What's wrong with me — always having 20-20 vision only in hindsight? Yiping, I know that the villagers don't appreciate what I do, and yet I really long for their understanding. These people are all my relatives. My parents grew up here; later they moved away. It was a scandal, but I bet you never heard it from your folks! And so when I came to this village last year, it was like coming back to my real family. You must think this is strange — Why do I sleep on the mountain? I don't know why; I just have to shut myself away from the villagers so that I can sleep in peace. The villagers are all my relatives — Auntie Li, Uncle Huang, Uncle Liu, your parents. They keep coming into my dreams."

Suddenly, his words were interrupted. Yiping felt acutely dizzy. She thought, The basket must be bumping against the mountain. This was the end. In a feeble voice, she shouted, "Help!"

When she opened her eyes, she realized that this wasn't the end. The hot-air balloon was descending; she could already see the rooftops in the village. Those rooftops were the dark blue color that she'd seen earlier when she ran out — unearthly but lovely.

"Cousin, we're descending. Aren't you going to pursue Venus?"

Yiping felt a little disappointed.

"I miss my relatives so much! You can't understand this feeling, for you're too young. See: Uncle Li has walked out! He's going to the outhouse; he has diarrhea. Our village is a multi-surname village, made up of refugees who came from many places. They established this village. You must know this."

Yiping didn't know anything about this. She looked hard, but she couldn't see Uncle Li. Between two houses, next to a bamboo fence, it seemed there was a shadow slipping across. But the hot-air balloon was floating too fast with the wind, and she couldn't get a good look.

"Cousin, let's go up! Why do we have to stay so close to the village? I'd like to see Venus. There's nothing to see in the village. Look, you've swerved again: we're still floating near the rooftops. What are you really looking for?"

"Me? Didn't you say the other time that I'm looking for a burial place?" Xuwu laughed out loud. "I see your papa. He got up and he's chopping firewood in the dark. He's always like this. The year I came down with cholera, he carried me on his back to the county hospital."

"Don't we have any way to ascend? I'd like to go up to a place several thousand meters high."

"That's impossible. Haven't I told you? I have only low-grade fuel. At most, my hot-air balloon can climb five hundred meters . . . And I'm also not very interested in heights. In this deathly still night, my heart is close to this village."

"Has . . . it . . . always . . . been . . . like . . . this—" Yiping asked in a lingering tone.

Glancing at her cousin, she saw him snickering. Yiping realized that there was an enormous distance between the two of them. She grew dizzy and grumbled, "Where did you come from?"

Her cousin didn't answer at first. After a while, Yiping heard his voice; it was intermittent and seemed to be coming from the ground.

"Here's Auntie Li; she's sticking her head out the window . . . Now she's walking into another room. She's thinking about me . . . She's my relative. Oh, you mustn't lean out; you'll scare her . . .

Here's some thick smoke: it's your mama cooking breakfast in the dark . . ."

Yiping couldn't see anything, because her eyes were filled with tears that had suddenly gushed up. She quietly and repeatedly asked her cousin, "Should I cry? Should I cry? . . . Should I . . ."

"Go ahead and cry, go ahead," her cousin said.

His voice was still coming from the ground. Was it possible that he was no longer beside her?

Yiping stretched her hand out to the right—she was startled when she felt nothing but air! At the same time, she heard a dull sound: the wicker basket had turned upside down on the ground, and she had rolled into the paddy field next to it.

It was already light in the east. Yiping scrambled up. She was covered in mud like a clay figurine.

Her mama stood in the field and called her, "Yiping! Yiping! What's wrong with you?!"

Yiping washed herself with water from the field and then went home. She covered her face with her hands so that her mama couldn't see her face.

"I was dreaming! I was dreaming!" she said as she walked.

"Oh, so you were dreaming. That's really dangerous." Her mother sighed.

As soon as she got home, Yiping took a shower and washed her hair. After that, she went into her bedroom and bolted the door.

Not until she sat down on her bed did she remember what had just happened. Had the hot-air balloon flown away while she was rolling into the field? When she climbed out of the paddy field, she hadn't seen the hot-air balloon. Apparently her mama hadn't seen it, either! So had her cousin flown the hot-air balloon away?

Yiping felt weak all over, but her eyes were dry; she wasn't crying. She also remembered that when she was in the basket her cousin's voice had come from the ground. He had said, "Go ahead and cry. Go ahead." So the hot-air balloon must have flown away by itself. Had her cousin jumped to the ground before she had? Yiping felt that her face was burning hot. She was so ashamed! She wished she could find a hole to hide in.

She didn't know how much time passed before she heard a voice next door in her parents' room. It was Auntie Li.

"He didn't come this morning. That's the way he is. When you make a point of waiting for him, he doesn't appear. He plays hide-and-seek with you. I can't stand his always flying over my head. It's scarier than a big horsefly!"

"He's almost finished with his experiments. I guess he'll leave soon," Mama comforted her.

"Really? But I don't want him to go. Isn't this strange? The year of the big snowstorm, he slid into the well but survived. He's really lucky."

Sighing, the two women went to the hall. Yiping wondered why they were sighing.

At twilight that evening, the sun was just setting, and Yiping was standing in the garden looking at Venus. Venus wasn't green, but chrysanthemum yellow.

"Do you see her?" Her cousin's voice—distant and feeble— came from the mountain over there.

Yiping looked down, a smile on her face. With all her might, she looked at that mountain. She seemed to faintly see a white dot swaying in the bosk. The sky darkened quickly. When she looked at the sky again, Venus had really turned green.

## TRANSLATORS' ACKNOWLEDGMENTS

The following persons at Yale University Press, as well as an anonymous reader, have gone out of their way to be helpful: Kristy Leonard; Danielle D'Orlando, with the Margellos World Republic of Letters; and Dorothea Halliday, managing editor. The talented Nancy Ovedovitz created the intriguing cover design. Susan Laity, senior manuscript editor, has brought to this undertaking everything that one could ask for: she is capable, collaborative, thorough, sensitive, and understanding. Working with her has been a pleasure. John Donatich, director of Yale University Press, has been patient and encouraging throughout. He is a leader of Can Xue's considerable cheering section, and over the years he has been consistently supportive of her and her writing. We greatly appreciate the professionalism and enthusiasm of this remarkable team for this project, and we thank them all. Finally, as always, we thank Can Xue for entrusting her incomparable works to us.

### Chinese Publication History

"Story of the Slums": part one: originally published as "Pinminku de gushi zhiyi" by *Qingnian wenxue* in China, copyright © 2006 by Can Xue; part two: originally published as "Pinminku de gushi zhier" by *Huacheng* in China, copyright © 2007 by Can Xue; part three: originally published as "Pinminku de gushi zhisan" by *Furong* in China, copyright © 2007 by Can Xue; part four: originally published as "Pinminku de gushi zhisi" by *Baihuazhou* in China, copyright © 2007 by Can Xue; part five: originally published as "Pinminku de gushi zhiwu" by *Zuojia* in China, copyright © 2007 by Can Xue.

"Our Human Neighbors": originally published as "Yuren weilin" by *Shanghai wenxue* in China, copyright © 2016 by Can Xue.

"The Old Cicada": originally published as "Laochan" by *Huacheng* in China, copyright © 2010 by Can Xue.

"The Swamp": originally published as "Zhaozedi" by *Tiannan* in China, copyright © 2013 by Can Xue.

"Sin": originally published as "Zui e" by *Hunan wenxue* in China, copyright © 1996 by Can Xue.

"Shadow People": originally published as "Yingzu" by *Shanhua* in China, copyright © 2010 by Can Xue.

"Crow Mountain": originally published as "Guiwu" by *Zuojia* in China, copyright © 2011 by Can Xue.

"Catfish Pit": originally published as "Nianyutao" by *Changjiang wenyi* in China, copyright © 2012 by Can Xue.

"Lu-er's Worries": originally published as "Lu-er de xinshi" by *Zuojia* in China, copyright © 2012 by Can Xue.

"Her Old Home": originally published as "Jiuju" by *Shanghai wenxue* in China, copyright © 2013 by Can Xue.

"I Am a Willow Tree": originally published as "Yizhu liushu de zibai" by *Renmin wenxue* in China, copyright © 2013 by Can Xue.

"The Outsiders": originally published as "Waidiren" by *Shanghai wenxue* in China, copyright © 2012 by Can Xue.

"The Queen": originally published as "Nuwang" by *Dayi wenxue* in China, copyright © 2018 by Can Xue.

### Translation Publication History

"Story of the Slums," part two: Published by *Conjunctions* (Fall 2015) in the United States, copyright © 2015 by Karen Gernant and Chen Zeping.

"Our Human Neighbors": Published by *Conjunctions* (online edition, Summer 2017) in the United States, copyright © 2017 by Karen Gernant and Chen Zeping.

"The Old Cicada": Published by *Words Without Borders* (November 2013) online, copyright © 2013 by Karen Gernant and Chen Zeping.

"The Swamp": Published by *Ninth Letter* (Fall 2015) in the United States, copyright © 2015 by Karen Gernant and Chen Zeping.

"Sin": Published by *Conjunctions* (Fall 2011) in the United States, copyright © 2011 by Karen Gernant and Chen Zeping.

#### Stories Originally Published in English Translation

CAN XUE, pseudonym of Deng Xiaohua, has written many novels, volumes of literary criticism and philosophy, and short works of fiction. *I Live in the Slums* is her tenth book to appear in English. Her novel *The Last Lover* (2014) won the Best Translated Book Award for Fiction. *Five Spice Street* (2009) was a finalist for the Neustadt Prize. *Frontier* (2017) made the 2017 "Best of" lists of National Public Radio, the *Boston Globe*, and *World Literature Today*. *Love in the New Millennium* (2018) was long-listed for the Man Booker International Prize and the Best Translated Book Award. In 2001, Can Xue moved to Beijing from Changsha, Hunan. She has recently moved to Xishuangbanna, Yunnan, where she continues writing and jogging every day.

KAREN GERNANT and CHEN ZEPING have translated four previous books by Can Xue: *Blue Light in the Sky* (2006), *Five Spice Street* (2009), *Vertical Motion* (2011), and *Frontier* (2017). Gernant, professor emerita of Chinese history at Southern Oregon University, and Chen, professor of Chinese linguistics at Fujian Normal University, Fuzhou, have been translating contemporary Chinese fiction for more than twenty years. In addition to their work with Can Xue, they have published a collection of stories by Zhang Kangkang (2011), a volume of stories by Alai (2012), and two novellas by Zhang Yihe (2017).

# THE
# TIME
# OF
# MURDER
# AT
# MAYERLING

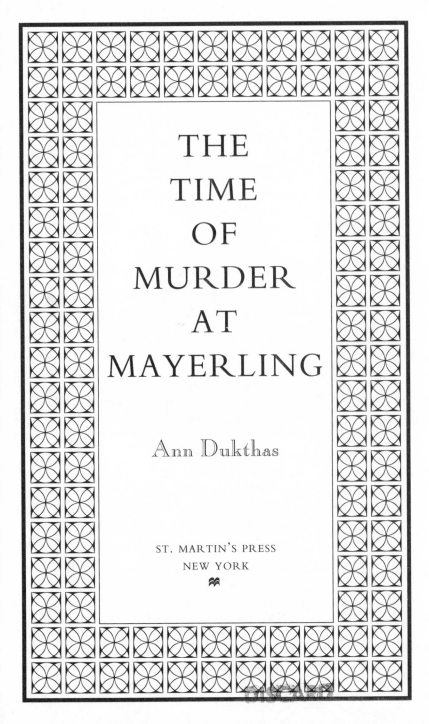

# THE
# TIME
# OF
# MURDER
# AT
# MAYERLING

Ann Dukthas

ST. MARTIN'S PRESS
NEW YORK

Library of Congress Cataloging-in-Publication Data

Dukthas, Ann.

    The time of murder at Mayerling: a Nicholas
Segalla time-travel mystery / by Anne
Dukthas.
       p.     cm.
  ISBN 0–312–14676–0
    1.   Austria—History—1867–1918—Fiction.
2. Rudolf, Crown Prince of Austria, 1858–1889.
3. Vetsera, Marie Alexandrine, Baronesse,
1871–1889.  4. Mayerling (Austria)—History—
Fiction.  I. Title.
PR6054.O37T565  1996
823'.914—dc20               96–25616

First edition: December 1996

10  9  8  7  6  5  4  3  2  1

*For Robert, Evelyn, and Gemma Bearne*

# Prologue

*Vienna—May 1994*

Ann Dukthas sat on the edge of her bed in her suite of rooms at the Hotel Imperial in Vienna. The flight from London and the taxi journey into the city centre had been pleasant and trouble-free. Ann had unpacked and dined in the restaurant below. Afterwards, as she returned to her room, a special courier had called out her name across the foyer.

"Miss Dukthas!"

She walked across. The young man had asked for some proof of identity, then handed over a thick manilla envelope. Ann now stared across at the package lying unopened on the polished tabletop. She had received, from her mysterious acquaintance, Mr. Segalla, the invitation to fly to Vienna two weeks ago. Despite constant questioning by her curious, sometimes envious friends, Ann had told them nothing about this enigmatic stranger who had entered her life. She got up and walked across to the window, half listening to the noise from the traffic below.

"Yes," she murmured. "Enigmatic." That was the best description of Mr. Segalla. She recalled his Italianate good looks, those hooded, cynical eyes and, for the umpteenth time, Ann wondered if the story he had told her was the truth. She had done her own research; after all, that was her calling. Time and again, she had come across references, be they in America, Europe, or the Far East, to a man who claimed to have never died. A figure who moved in history's shadows, though now and again he was glimpsed, or trapped, in its light. Legends flourished about him: how he was condemned by some ancient curse to wander the face of the earth; how he could never grow old, never die.

On the few occasions they had met, Segalla had refused to elaborate on such stories. He had produced evidence for his claims and would say no more. He was, however, more forthcoming on how he had survived in different places across the span of centuries.

"I have developed the skill, Ann," he had remarked once, "to live deep in the shadows. Moreover, human nature never changes. Governments and kings always need the likes of me."

Ann went and picked up the parcel Segalla had sent her. Every so often he would do this: invite her to some city, provide for her fare and accommodation, and then deliver a manuscript written, in fictional form, which revealed the truth behind some great mystery of history. She had studied the letter he had sent her before she'd left London, then done her own research about the death of Prince Rudolph and Maria Vetsera at the imperial hunting lodge of Mayerling on the thirtieth of January 1889. Never once had Dukthas, a professional historian, encountered such a mystery. It was like clutching moonbeams: they were there, but when you reached out, there was nothing. The tragedy and mystery of Mayerling had tantalised historians for the last hundred years. The death of one of Europe's most important princes seemed, at first sight, so obvious. Both Rudolph and Maria had left notes and letters proclaiming what they were going to do. Their corpses were examined by the most eminent pathologists in Europe. Nevertheless, there was something wrong, something intangible which made many historians believe that, dreadful though Rudolph's death was, it masked a greater tragedy.

Ann picked up a paper knife and slit open the envelope and gripped the package more tightly. Was this truth . . . ?

# Chapter 1

*Mayerling, Near Vienna—January 1889*

The lights of Mayerling hunting lodge glowed like beacons through the darkness. The men outside its gates pulled up their fur-covered collars against the biting wind. They thrust gloved hands into pockets and concentrated on the light rather than on the dark, sinister forest which surrounded the lodge or the wind which shook the trees like some earthbound soul not knowing where it should go. Now and again, as the wind fell, some bird would cry, sharp and raucous; the men would catch their breath, stare sheepishly at each other, stamp their feet, and quietly curse the court comptroller, who was keeping them waiting. They did not want to speak: it was too dangerous. At the end of January 1889, Vienna and its court had the air of a mausoleum, yet beneath the official mourning, rumours crackled and spread. Prince Rudolph, the emperor's son, heir to the Hapsburg Empire, and Maria Vetsera, his mistress, had been found dead at Mayerling. Was it true, people whispered, that Prince Rudolph had killed himself and, before he did, callously murdered his seventeen-year-old mistress? The court had desperately tried to stifle such rumours, yet the more it did, the worse they became. Even the Vienna newspapers, carefully controlled by the imperial police, were beginning to ask embarrassing questions. "Where was the woman's corpse?" "When would she be buried?" "Would there be a postmortem?" "Would the official papers be released?" Two of the men standing in the freezing cold would have liked answers to such questions, and soon. One of them was

3

about to protest at being kept waiting so long when the door to the lodge opened, and a figure beckoned them into the warmth.

Inside, the lodge smelt sweetly of pine logs, faint cooking smells, the whiff of a rich cigar, the good things of life. However, beneath this fragrant perfume was a sharper, acrid smell, more reminiscent of a Viennese hospital than an imperial hunting lodge. The group of men tramped down the passageway through a billiard room, where a weak fire flickered in the canopied hearth, and down a dark, bleak corridor. They stopped before a door at the end. The comptroller ripped off the purple imperial seals, inserted a key, and pushed the door open. Inside was cold and musty. The men walked gingerly forward. The comptroller cursed as he fumbled to light the lamp. When he held it up, the small lumber room was bathed in an eerie glow of light. At the far end was a table with a heap of old clothes piled high on it. One of the men gasped as he glimpsed the elegant, laced-up boot peeping out from underneath. The comptroller, sensing his companions' anxieties, walked briskly across. He put the lantern down, and removed the heap of clothes with one sweep of his arm. The men gathered round and stared at the young woman's corpse.

"She was beautiful," one of them whispered, pointing to the lustrous auburn locks which cascaded down to the young woman's slender waist. Her face was chalk white. Her eyes, so beautiful and vivacious in life, stared sightlessly up at them. The smooth evenness of her temples had been marred by the ugly bullet wound, and the blood which caked her head looked like some ghastly red cap. The physician in the group clutched the girl's hand; her fingers were very stiff.

"It's forty hours," the comptroller explained. "God rest the poor woman, but she's been dead forty hours."

The physician struggled to uncurl her fingers. He carefully plucked out the faded rose still grasped there, as well as the damp, lacy handkerchief rolled up in a ball between her fingers: Maria Vetsera's last act before she had died.

"Do you think he killed her?" One of the group asked.

"He?" The Comptroller asked. "You mean His Imperial Excellency Prince Rudolph?"

The man's eyes fell away as he mumbled an apology.

"Common rumour says differently." Alexander Baltazzi, Vetsera's swarthy-faced uncle, spoke up. "They say poor Maria shot the Prince before herself. She was only a child." He continued, his face drawn and bitter. "But she was not a member of the Imperial Family. Noblesse oblige, I am sure she will take the blame."

"So, you recognise the corpse?" The Comptroller asked sharply. "You identify it as your niece?"

"Yes," Baltazzi replied. "She is Maria Alexandra Vetsera."

"Then you must leave," the Comptroller replied. "Our good physician here will carry out a postmortem. Afterwards you can reclaim the body for burial."

Baltazzi was about to object. The Comptroller drew a small square of paper from his waistcoat pocket. He undid it slowly and showed Baltazzi the imperial seal.

"That is what His Excellency the Emperor wishes." The Comptroller whispered, "He, too, has lost a son. It is his wish, and the direct order of Prime Minister Count Taaffe, that it be so."

Baltazzi and his companions left. Outside Loschek, personal valet of the late Prince Rudolph, led them back into the billiard room. The servant, his face wet with tears, built up the fire and silently served them small glasses of cognac and rather lukewarm cups of coffee. Baltazzi would have loved to have questioned him but the Comptroller's orders had been quite explicit. If he wished his niece's body to be released for Christian burial, Baltazzi would have to follow the very strict protocol laid down by the imperial court. No questions were to be asked of any official; the autopsy was to be carried out in private, then Maria Alexandra Vetsera was to be buried as soon as possible. Loschek moved like a ghost round the room. Baltazzi lit a cigar and watched him carefully. He was certain that, even if he was not under orders, Loschek would still say nothing: he was Rudolph's creature. Baltazzi drew deep on his cigar, trying to control the fury seething within him. He, Maria's mother the Countess, and their entire family had been given sharp, rude treatment by the imperial court.

"You see, my dear chap," Prime Minister Taaffe had murmured, "the real tragedy is the death of the prince."

The prime minister had been lounging in a chair in his offices at the Hofburg. He had agreed to give Baltazzi no more than ten minutes. Most infuriatingly, Taaffe had spent most of that time indulging in the niceties of etiquette: Would Baltazzi want coffee? A cigar? Was the room warm enough? Baltazzi had almost screamed at the prime minister to come to the point. Taaffe, his saturnine face a mask of surprise, had finished lighting his cigar, blown a series of smoke rings, and then repeated himself.

"You do see, my dear chap, the real tragedy is the death of His Imperial Excellency, Prince Rudolph. Your niece"—again the long pull of the cigar, then Taaffe forced a sympathetic smile—"your niece is, how shall I say, an embarrassment."

"She's a corpse," Baltazzi tartly replied. "Last time I saw her she was a young, vivacious woman with all her life before her. Now she's dead, shot by that same Imperial Excellency, Prince Rudolph."

"No one asked her to be his lover," Taaffe replied, sitting back in his chair. "No one asked her to go to Mayerling."

"My sister, the girl's mother, came to you anxious that something might happen."

"My dear sir." Taaffe leaned on the arm of the chair, flicking the ash from his trousers. "What danger was there? Prince

Rudolph was known for, how can I say, his love of any pretty face—"

"But this was different," Baltazzi broke in.

Taaffe's face became serious. "In what way, sir? Did you know the prince was going to kill himself?"

Baltazzi drew back from the trap. Taaffe sighed loudly as if he realised Baltazzi dared go no further.

"So, what are you here for?"

"Release of my niece's corpse."

Taaffe stared up at the ceiling.

"For the love of God!" Baltazzi pleaded. "It's over a day since she was killed!"

"Took her own life," Taaffe corrected sharply. "It's over a day since Maria Alexandra Vetsera, your niece, took her own life. Whatever." Taaffe waved his hand airily. "You and one other may go to Mayerling tonight. The body will be examined and dressed for burial. By this time tomorrow the corpse of Maria Vetsera must be buried in the priory of Hieiligenkreuz."

"So soon?" Baltazzi sprang to his feet.

Taaffe rose with him. The prime minister's face was now hard. He walked over and stopped only a few inches from Baltazzi.

"You have a choice, sir. You may go to Mayerling tonight and organise the burial of your niece. Or I can send others to do it for you. The decision is yours."

Baltazzi had curtly agreed, then spun on his heel and left the prime minister's office for the long, cold journey to Mayerling. An imperial official had also come, bluntly informing Baltazzi and his companion what was to happen. Baltazzi had no choice. He sat back in the chair. He sipped the cognac, the cigar held listlessly between his fingers as his mind raced with possibilities. He tried to sift the truth from the gossip, rejecting the scandal and the lurid stories now circulating Vienna. According to the available evidence, Prince Rudolph, for God knows what reason, had, in the early hours of 30 January, formed a suicide pact with Maria, then killed her before committing suicide. Baltazzi stared, weary eyed, at Loschek standing in the shadows. But why hadn't someone heard a shot?

Baltazzi moved his feet restlessly. So many questions! So many problems! Why hadn't the imperial court kept a closer eye on Rudolph? Baltazzi sipped at his cognac. If the rumours were correct that Rudolph's mind was unbalanced, that he was suffering from the advanced stages of syphilis, why had his father not kept him in Vienna? And Maria, so vivacious, so young, so full of life? Baltazzi remembered her at the racecourses: such a constant visitor the jockeys gave her the nickname "Turf Angel." Why did she want to die? Was she so in love with her syphilitic prince?

"So many questions?"

Baltazzi turned and stared at the lugubrious face of his companion, Count Stockau, whom Maria's mother had appointed as her attorney. Baltazzi had always dismissed Stockau as a fool with his luxurious muttonchop whiskers, bloodhound eyes, and ever wet lips. In the last twenty-four hours, however, Baltazzi had changed his mind. Despite his appearance, Stockau had a sharp, cunning brain, advising Baltazzi that they should keep their mouths shut and their ears open.

"This is against all Christian decency," Baltazzi exclaimed, gesturing at the passageway leading to the chamber where Maria's body still lay. "Why the secrecy, the lack of basic courtesy?"

Stockau sighed and leaned over the padded arm of his chair.

"A Hapsburg prince has died," the lawyer whispered. He raised his hand as Baltazzi opened his mouth. "In your eyes, sir, a degenerate, a murderer and a suicide. Now, you are full of grief at Maria's death. However, what happens if Rudolph was as innocent as Maria?"

Baltazzi sat up. "What on earth do you mean?" he whispered.

Stockau scratched at the tobacco stains on his white moustache.

"There are the suicide notes," Baltazzi whispered. "They both wrote letters saying they were going to die."

"Letters can be forged," Stockau growled. "Rudolph and Maria, God rest them, were hysterical. They were in love with the idea of a romantic death. They might have constantly scribbled such notes. Remember," Stockau muttered, "remember the morning the bodies were discovered—"

"Can't we visit the room?" Baltazzi interrupted.

"No, we can't," Stockau retorted. "The prince's quarters are strictly off-limits until the official commissioner has reported to His Imperial Excellency. So"—Stockau dabbed at his lips with a handkerchief—"remember, Loschek broke the door down. Count Hoyos, Prince Rudolph's friend, viewed the corpses, then left for Vienna to inform Their Imperial Majesties that their son had been poisoned." Stockau held up a finger. "Yet now we are told, and we have seen for ourselves, that Maria was shot through the head before the prince turned the pistol on himself."

"And has Hoyos explained the difference?" Baltazzi asked.

"He claims he only took a superficial look: he noticed blood on their faces and thought that this was due to a haemorrhage. Certain poisons are known to cause that."

"That's ridiculous!" Baltazzi whispered. He peered across to where the imperial official who had accompanied them from Vienna sat half dozing in his chair before the fire. "It's ridiculous!" Baltazzi repeated. "Some people now claim the top of the prince's head was as loose as a pan lid. . . . So, what's the truth?"

Stockau leaned away. "Pilate asked the same question," he hissed. "And never got an answer. I suspect the same will happen here."

"We are ready now!"

Baltazzi whirled round. He wondered how long the comptroller had been standing there.

"The body," the comptroller stuttered, coming forward. "The corpse is dressed for burial."

Baltazzi got to his feet, threw his cigar into the fire, and went back to the room. His heart missed a beat: Maria was now laid out on the table, fully dressed in coat, boa, hat, and elegant leather boots. Her eyes were closed, her headdress covering that dreadful, bloody hole. As he looked down at her, Baltazzi thought she was asleep, and nearly stretched out his hand to shake her awake: those beautiful eyes would open, that generous mouth would break into a smile, and she would get up and tell them it was all a joke, a pretence, a bad dream. He stretched out and took her hand. Even her little gloves had been put on. It was no dream. The hand was hard, lifeless. Baltazzi breathed in deeply, fighting back tears.

"Oh God!" he prayed. "Oh Lord, what will happen?"

"She's dead," the physician intoned flatly. "Killed by a bullet through the right temple which exited above the left ear."

Baltazzi went to raise the veil. The comptroller grasped his hand. Baltazzi stared at him.

"I'm going to kiss her," he declared. "I'm going to lift her veil and kiss her on the lips. If you don't take your hand away, sir, I swear . . ."

The comptroller released him. Baltazzi lifted up the veil, so fine and gauzelike, and, bending down, kissed those lips. He caught a whiff of that perfume Maria always wore, fresh and fragrant. He couldn't stop the tears from falling. He found it hard to raise his head. Stockau's arm was round his shoulder; the old lawyer was murmuring his own condolences. Baltazzi let the veil fall and stood up.

"Where is the coffin?" he asked.

The comptroller stared blankly back.

"The coffin?" Baltazzi repeated. "If she's to be taken to the priory of Hieiligenkreuz, we need a coffin. Surely, man, you have seen to that?"

"There will be no coffin, no hearse!" the Comptroller replied sharply.

"For pity's sake!" Baltazzi exclaimed. "This is the Baroness Maria Vetsera, a young noblewoman, not some piece of meat on the butcher's slab!"

The comptroller swallowed nervously and wet his prim, dry lips.

"Orders from above," he murmured.

Baltazzi cursed foully. Stockau gripped him by the arm.

"Don't do anything rash," the old lawyer murmured. He looked at the comptroller, flanked by the official escort from Vienna. "Surely the emperor can't be so hard?"

"His Imperial Highness is not being hard," the comptroller replied. "He deeply regrets, as do I, the circumstances of this young woman's death. However, the city is rife with gossip and rumour. If a coffin is made and a hearse has to be brought, that will only take time as well as attract attention."

Baltazzi looked down at his niece's corpse.

"I thought I would see you in white," he said softly, "with a garland of roses in your hair, and we would dance on your wedding day."

Deep in his heart Baltazzi knew it was foolish to protest. This was Austria, the heart of the Hapsburg Empire; the emperor's word was law. He knew what would happen if he objected any further. Maria's corpse would simply be removed by imperial officials and buried in some God-forgotten spot. At least he could be sure where Maria would be laid to rest. The priory was consecrated soil, not some pauper's grave in the forest. Baltazzi drew in a deep breath.

"I agree," he declared. "But how?"

"There's a carriage waiting."

Baltazzi gaped in horror as the full implications sunk in.

"Oh no!" he gasped. "Oh, for the love of—!"

"I have my orders," the comptroller interjected.

Stockau gripped Baltazzi's elbow. "It's time we were gone." He helped Baltazzi lift the corpse up. Linking arms through the dead girl's, they carried her between them, as if she were a living person, down the passageway and out of the lodge into the waiting carriage. The comptroller and the imperial flunkey followed. At the end of the path, three men stepped out of the darkness. One wore a small, English-type bowler hat, and the lower half of his face was swathed by a thick, heavy scarf. He pulled this down, smoothed his moustache, took off a leather glove, and extended his hand.

"I am Joseph Kinski."

The eyes beneath the hat were glittering with cold, and the sallow face was pinched and pale, but there was a friendliness, a sympathy Baltazzi immediately sensed. He struggled to shake the man's hand.

"Herr Kinski," the Comptroller declared, "is a detective. The other two are plainclothes constables. They are both armed," he added warningly. "They will accompany you to the priory."

Baltazzi, still holding his niece's corpse, looked over his shoulder, his face twisted into a smile.

"And will you come?"

The comptroller shook his head and opened his mouth to reply.

"I know. I know," Baltazzi replied. "Orders from above. Now piss off, you vermin!"

He turned back and saw the smile in Kinski's eyes.

"I, too, am under orders," the detective declared.

Baltazzi, fighting back a sob, just nodded.

"Yes, yes, I know." He fought to keep his voice steady. "But there are orders and there are orders. Some people like them, others simply tolerate them: which are you, Kinski?"

"I am distressed," Kinski replied. "I have been briefed, sir; I am sad for you." He gestured at the dead girl still cradled between Stockau and Baltazzi. "God rest her soul." He took a step closer and looked over Baltazzi's shoulder as the comptroller and the officials slammed the door of the lodge shut. "Good, they have gone. May I? I have to . . . ," the detective stammered.

"Yes."

Kinski delicately lifted the veil and stared at the white, dead face of Maria Vetsera. He let the veil fall, stepped away, and crossed himself.

"I saw her once," he murmured. "When I was on duty at the racecourse. I saw her laughing. She was a . . ."

"She was a merry soul," Baltazzi finished the sentence.

"It's best if we go," Kinski exclaimed. "Let me help you."

Baltazzi and Stockau, still carrying the corpse, clambered into the carriage. They sat on one seat: Maria Vetsera's body was supported between her uncle and Stockau; her head lolled to one side. Kinski rapped out orders. The two constables climbed in with them and sat opposite; the doors were shut and the blinds pulled down. Baltazzi heard the shouts of the driver and the crack of the whip, and the black carriage lurched forward. He had to catch and hold steady his niece's corpse as he fought to control the fury and rage seething within him. Through a gap in the blind, Baltazzi saw the lights of the lodge disappear.

"This will be a terrible journey," Kinski spoke out of the darkness. "We are under orders not to take the main road."

Baltazzi couldn't protest: he was too exhausted, too angry. What's the use? he thought. Maria was an innocent victim, caught up in the Byzantine intrigue of the Viennese court.

Kinski stretched across, a leather-covered brandy flask in his hand. He offered it first to Stockau, who drank greedily. The old lawyer had kept silent throughout. He did not wish to say anything: every move, every minute of this terrible night would be reported back to the imperial council. Nevertheless, he was touched by Kinski's kindness.

"Thank you," he growled.

The detective offered it to Baltazzi, who made to refuse.

"Go on," the detective urged. "Believe me, sir, by the time this journey is finished, only God and brandy will help you."

Baltazzi snatched the flask and took a great gulp. He leaned back, allowing the brandy to wash his mouth and warm his throat and belly. In the end the detective was correct: Baltazzi felt as if he were caught up in some nightmare. The horses slipped, the carriage wheels rattled across the icy track as they entered the forest. The winds bending the trees made the blinds flap, buffeting the carriage as if some dark power were escorting them on this macabre journey. Now and again the carriage stopped so the driver could caulk the horses' shoes, and then they'd rumble on.

Baltazzi grew stiff and cold; as the journey progressed he became more and more aware of Maria, her body pressing into his, the faint fragrance of her perfume which even the carbolic soap used by the physician could not completely erase. Now and again her boa or hat would tickle his face. He felt that if he could only pinch himself, he'd wake up, the nightmare would be over, and Maria would be laughing and teasing as she always had. Baltazzi eased himself on the leather seat. He had promised his sister he would do everything in his power to find out the true mystery behind her daughter's death. Now he quietly regretted that vow. The emperor had issued his orders and no one would dare disobey. Yet, perhaps . . .

He leaned forward and touched Kinski's hand. The detective lifted his head, pulling down the muffler from his face and pushing back the ridiculously small bowler hat.

"You are married, Herr Kinski?"

"Yes sir." The man smiled. "Sophie and I have four children. A small house on the outskirts of Vienna." The detective rubbed his hands together. "Do you wish me to take your place? You must be cramped."

Baltazzi shook his head. "Detective, have you been in this business from the start?"

Kinski's face changed; his eyes lost their friendliness; under the walrus moustache his lips tightened.

"I am a detective inspector," he replied. "I work for Baron Krauss."

"I know the minister of police personally," Baltazzi replied sardonically. "I asked you a question, Detective Inspector."

"The facts are simple," Kinski replied. "Most regrettably, on the thirtieth January this year, His Imperial Highness Prince Rudolph, together with"—he grimaced apologetically—"together with Maria Vetsera committed suicide at the hunting lodge of Mayerling."

"How?" Baltazzi asked sharply.

"You know that, sir. You have seen the bullet wounds?"

"Where are the bullets? Where's the revolver?" Baltazzi retorted. "Why didn't anyone hear the shots? Why was it first reported in Vienna that Prince Rudolph had taken poison?"

"I don't know," Kinski replied. "Such questions do not fall within my jurisdiction."

Baltazzi sat back in his seat. "God forgive you," he murmured. "God forgive you, Kinski. Pray to God that one of your children doesn't die in mysterious circumstances." He lurched forward, almost dragging the corpse with him. "Pray God, Herr Kinski, that some flint-hearted, cold-faced detective inspector does not reply, when you ask him why your child died, that it's not in his jurisdiction."

Kinski's response was to proffer the brandy flask. Baltazzi pushed it away. He sat back, the tears streaming down his face, even as one of the constables shouted that the lights of Hieiligenkreuz Priory were now in sight.

A few days later another funeral took place in Vienna. Franz Joseph, Hapsburg emperor, God's vice-regent on earth, stood beside his son's coffin outside the sealed doors to the vaults of the Hapsburg burial place in Vienna. He tried hard to compose himself. This was it: the end of his line and dynasty. The embalmed body of Rudolph, his only son, now lay in the coffin beside him. This ornate casket, covered with a purple, gold-encrusted damask cloth, rested on the thick, padded shoulders of the pallbearers. The emperor wished he could turn and run, not only from this bleak, vaulted place, but back through time. If he could only have grasped Rudolph when he was a boy, told him things had changed, plotted and planned furiously against the terrors the future would hold. The emperor closed his eyes.

The empire he had inherited creaked and groaned under the iron hand of history: different peoples, the Czechs, the Hungarians, the Serbians, the Bosnians, all demanding their freedom and liberty from the Hapsburg crown. Beyond his far-flung, cumbersome borders the great powers, France, Germany, and Russia, watched intently for the sickness to spread. Franz Joseph was a realist. He was born to rule, and the loss of his only son and heir was not only a personal tragedy but a serious blow to the future power of the dynasty. The emperor saw himself first and foremost as a Hapsburg prince, not a father or a husband. Now he resented that: his wife was not here. Court etiquette forbade that. Yet, perhaps it was best: he could not bear the pained accusations in Elizabeth's eyes. She had come here herself the night before and wandered the vaults. She had stared where her son's coffin would lie, murmuring, "How could he? How could dear Rudolph kill himself now that spring is nearly here?"

Franz Joseph broke from his reverie as he heard a cough. He turned round as the woman, four paces behind him, dressed completely in mourning, lifted her veil and blew her nose. Franz Joseph stared disdainfully at his daughter-in-law. If he could go back in time that's something he would rectify. Stephanie! Stephanie of the Belgians! Fat faced, blond haired, frumpish and gauche. Rudolph should never have married her! Empress Elizabeth had warned him about that.

Franz Joseph glimpsed the bishops, the clergy staring at him curiously. The hostility in the emperor's eyes deepened. He would remember them, with their sanctimonious faces and pious ways: Rudolph had never liked them. The emperor had to exert all his influence with the Vatican to combat their malevolence. Rudolph may have committed suicide, but he had only done so when the balance of his mind was disturbed. Consequently, according to canon law, Rudolph's soul and corpse still deserved a full requiem mass and burial in a consecrated place. Franz Joseph breathed out noisily: well, that was his decision. He would not even contemplate the truth behind his son's death. So many possibilities! The verdict of suicide would pale beside the enormity of what really happened.

The lord chamberlain, taking Franz Joseph's sigh as a sign, briskly walked forward and rapped with his staff of office on the closed vault doors. From inside a voice asked, "Who is there?"

"His Imperial Royal Highness, the Most Serene Crown Prince Archduke Rudolph."

"We know him not," the reply came.

Again the chamberlain knocked. Again the question was asked: "Who is there?"

This time the reply was briefer: "Archduke Rudolph." But the response was the same: "We know him not."

The chamberlain knocked a third time. Once more he was asked, "Who is there?"

This time his answer was simple: "A poor sinner."

"Then he may enter, Et Lux perpetua Luceat ei."

The great iron doors swung open. The cowled Capuchin stood aside, and the chamberlain walked in. The pallbearers and the emperor followed to lay Rudolph's coffin with those of his forebears. Just before they descended the steps, when the coffin was handed over to the prior, the grand marshal of the court asked the customary question:

"Do you recognise the mortal remains of Rudolph, archduke of Austria and, in his lifetime, heir apparent to the throne?"

"Yes, I recognise him," the prior replied. "And from now on we will keep pious watch over him."

The funeral continued and Rudolph's remains were laid to rest.

After the service the emperor chose to walk in the silence of the Capuchin gardens. Swathed in his thick, heavy, fur-lined coat, his face protected by a silken black muffler, Franz Joseph stopped and stared at the frozen branches of a beech tree.

"No sign of life," he murmured. "No sign of spring."

He believed in the resurrection of the body, but for him, there would be no spring, no Rudolph, no heir apparent. He heard a sound behind him and looked round. Edward Taaffe, elegant in his black mourning dress, hat in hand, bowed stiffly.

"Your Imperial Highness, my deepest condolences."

"You never liked him in life," the emperor replied.

"Your Imperial Highness, I did not want his death."

The emperor breathed in noisily and beckoned Taaffe near. For a few seconds he studied the fat, expressionless face, podgy cheeks, and that stiff, elegant, oiled moustache. He must always remember, he thought to himself, Taaffe was not Austrian. Two hundred and fifty years ago, Taaffe's ancestors had come from Ireland to Vienna to defend the city against the Turks. He must never trust him completely.

"I am your most loyal servant," Taaffe murmured, as if he could read his emperor's thoughts.

"Then, if you are," Franz Joseph replied, "swear you will keep secret the dreadful truth about my son's death, no matter how mysterious that truth may be!"

Taaffe bowed from the waist. "Your Imperial Highness, you already have my solemn oath on that."

The emperor stroked his moustache and stared up at the crucifix which dominated the Capuchin convent.

"The Vatican will not leave us alone," he murmured. "His Holiness the Pope, not to mention that devil in scarlet, Cardinal Rampolla his chancellor, believes the Church is being mocked and fooled." He stamped his foot in a surprising gesture of annoyance. "Why don't they leave the dead alone!" he muttered.

Taaffe stared at his master expectantly. The emperor was moving to the crux of the problem. The prime minister knew there had been a flow of telegrams and secret memoranda between the imperial chancery and Pope Leo XIII at the Vatican.

"Why did the clergy hate him so?" Franz Joseph whispered.

"Your Highness, he attacked their hypocrisy. He made them feel restless in their comfortable beds." Taaffe spread his black-gloved hands. "They may not know the Scriptures but they know their canon law. A suicide should not receive Church burial, his body should not lie in consecrated ground. Why, Your Imperial Highness?" He stepped closer.

"They have sent a special emissary."

"A priest?"

"No, one of their agents, a layman: Nicholas Segalla."

Taaffe's head snapped up. "Segalla?" He ran his fingers along his lips. "I have heard that name."

"He flits here and there!" the emperor snapped. "Who he is, or what he does, is immaterial. He has got to be watched, Taaffe!"

The prime minister looked up. "Your Imperial Highness, I apologise, I was trying to place the name."

"I want him watched," the emperor repeated. "Till he leaves Vienna. He must do so today, though I suppose he will return." The emperor looked at the beech tree. "He'll be back in spring to search out the full truth and, God have mercy on me, even I do not know that!"

# Chapter 2

Nicholas Segalla, special emissary of Pope Leo XIII, sat in the small, comfortable visitors parlour at the Carmelite convent drinking tea with the widowed Crown Princess Stephanie. After the funeral obsequies, people had gone their different ways. Segalla, noticing the princess was left to her own devices, had used the good offices of the papal nuncio, Monsignor Galemberti, to introduce himself. He had kissed the tall, frumpish princess's hand, murmured his own condolences and those of the Holy Father. Stephanie, her eyes red rimmed with crying, her face even more pasty under the black mantilla lace veil, had been only too pleased at the diversion: she willingly accepted Segalla's offer of tea and biscuits in the visitors parlour. Indeed, Stephanie had been bemused, rather intrigued, by this saturnine, black-haired stranger, so courteous in his manners, so aware of all the particular courtesies. Stephanie needed these. She was used to insult: throughout the funeral ceremony she had kept her body stiff, her face impassive. Nevertheless, how she had seethed at the petty insults of the emperor and the leading courtiers. They had held her responsible for the crown prince's death. She could read it in their eyes: if only she'd not been so gauche; if only more loving; if only . . . Stephanie would have loved to have screamed the truth at them. Nevertheless, after years of marriage to Rudolph, secrecy and subtlety had become second nature to her.

Crown Princess Stephanie picked up a china teacup and smiled over the rim. Well, Herr Segalla was handsome: clean-shaven, his face darkened by the sun; his eyes sent a shiver down her spine. He reminded her of a hawk she had once held: unblinking, never missing any item. Segalla was thin lipped, at least now, his face pulled in a mask of official mourning, his jaw set. He was not a priest, she was certain of that, though he was dressed like one. A long black overcoat opened at the throat to reveal a white shirt collar with a diamond stud in the centre. She glanced to the right, where he had put down his silver-topped cane and leather gloves. Be careful, she warned herself. The emperor was correct: Segalla, for all his swarthy good looks, exquisite manners, and beautifully tailored clothes, had been sent by the Vatican to search out the truth behind her husband's death. Segalla put his cup down. He leaned across and clasped her hand gently in his: a warm, friendly touch which broke all the rules of Spanish etiquette which governed the Viennese court.

"Your Imperial Highness," he murmured gravely though his eyes were smiling. "His Holiness sends his deepest condolences, to which I add my own."

"Your journey was pleasant?" Stephanie asked, slowly drawing her hand away.

"As much as could be expected. I took the express train from Trieste. It was cold, there was snow on the rails, but a comfortable way to travel. I believe Your Highness is also a lover of trains?"

Segalla listened as Stephanie chattered about her different journeys to different parts of the Austrian Empire. He tried to recall what Cardinal Rampolla had told him about her: dull, insipid, a mere empty-headed puppet. Her own father, the king of the Belgians, hated her for her stupidity. The only person who had wanted the marriage was Rudolph himself, who saw her as the ideal submissive wife.

Segalla studied Stephanie's face. Her cheeks were pasty white like lumps of dough, the unpainted lips looked bloodless, though her eyes were large and lustrous. Segalla wondered how this woman had tolerated the different amours and the extravagant lifestyle of her dead husband. The crown princess's voice was monotonous. Once or twice Segalla had to stifle a yawn as Stephanie, grateful at last for an attentive audience, chattered about a recent visit to the island of Lacroma. She must have glimpsed the tightening of his lips—she stopped abruptly and laughed.

"I am sorry, Herr Segalla." Her face fell. "But the last few days have been terrible, terrible."

"You were able to pay your respects?" Segalla asked. "I mean, to your dead husband?"

"Eventually," The crown princess replied. She swallowed hard and gripped the cup to stop her hand trembling. "They brought Rudolph's body back to the Hofburg during the night."

"At what time did it arrive?" Segalla asked.

"I forget." Stephanie rested her elbow on the arm of the chair and rubbed the side of her head. "Yes, about two o'clock in the morning of the thirty-first. I couldn't sleep. The news had arrived the day before. I wanted to get out to Mayerling." Her hand fell away. "But they"—she spat the words out—"His Imperial Highness would not let me go. So I spent the day in my own quarters. Little Elizabeth, our daughter, had to be comforted."

Segalla nodded sympathetically.

"In the morning," Stephanie continued, "they allowed me and Elizabeth to come down. We had a wreath ready." She dabbed the tears at her eyes. "Rudolph's favourite flowers: carnations, white roses, and lilies of the valley." She stopped, head down, and pulled a handkerchief from the cuff of the sleeve of her rather ugly mourning dress.

"Your Highness," Segalla intervened. "If this is painful?"

"No, no." Stephanie sniffed, wiping her nose on the back of her hand. "Little Elizabeth brought a bouquet of white moss roses."

She picked at a loose thread in her dress. Segalla glanced at the door. It would only be a matter of time before the Austrian secret police found where he had gone. The imperial authorities had made it very clear that none of Europe's royalty, not even the German kaiser, had been invited to the funeral. Segalla's presence was only tolerated out of respect to the Holy Father: as his letter of invitation had said, Herr Segalla would have to leave Vienna and stay away from the court until the official time of mourning was finished.

"In other words," Rampolla had remarked, "you are to attend the funeral, Segalla, but be on the first train out of Vienna."

Segalla turned back to Stephanie. "Your Highness," he began, "there are many stories about how your husband died. . . ."

"He committed suicide," Stephanie interrupted sharply. "His mind was sick, his body was rotten. Herr Segalla, tell the Holy Father how grateful I am that the Vatican allowed my husband to be buried in consecrated ground with the full rites of Holy Mother Church." Stephanie sniffed. "The Holy Father was compassionate, not"—her voice rose alarmingly—"not like certain Church officials here in Austria. They immediately quoted canon law; no suicide can be given Church burial."

"Yes, yes," Segalla intervened smoothly. "But the Church also says that, if the balance of mind is disturbed, the suicide victim can hardly be held responsible for his actions."

"And that applied to Rudolph," Stephanie snapped. She shook her head slightly. "As I have said, he was sick in mind and body. These dreadful stories that he was murdered are ridiculous."

"Your Imperial Highness," Segalla asked, "you saw the wounds?"

"No, on the first occasion poor Rudolph's head was covered by a white cap of bandages. His face had been cleaned. He looked as if he were asleep. He was at peace. When I returned, after the autopsy, his corpse had been embalmed, the forehead and temples covered in wax. He had been dressed in his general's uniform." Stephanie smiled thinly. "He would have liked that."

"And the wounds?" Segalla asked.

He felt uncomfortable at his bluntness, but his masters in Rome had made it quite clear they wanted answers.

"On his right temple," Stephanie murmured. "Nothing more than a dark line, a little over an inch long." She glanced up. "The rest of his head was covered by the coffin cushions."

"Your Highness"—Segalla picked up the teapot and filled her cup—"Your Highness is to be commended for her calmness."

Stephanie shrugged. "I am not a hypocrite, Herr Segalla. My husband killed himself after he had shot his mistress, the Baroness Vetsera. And no," she hurried on, "that does not concern me. We had ceased to live as man and wife many years ago. The little Vetsera . . . " Stephanie paused and closed her eyes.

"Your Imperial Highness?" Segalla intervened.

Stephanie shook one gloved hand delicately. "No, no, you must tell the Holy Father this," she whispered. "Maria Vetsera was one of many." She laughed sourly. "There was the Russian, God knows where she is now. The courtesans of Vienna: Mitzi Caspar the actress, Countess Larisch." She looked at Segalla squarely. "In the first years of our marriage I tried, I did try my best. Rudolph used to like to go out in disguise at night, visit the drinking shops and cafés, and I would accompany him. That's where he met Bratfisch, his personal cabby. I had no real stomach for it: after the birth of our little Elizabeth, the prince went his way and I went mine." She picked up the cup and sipped carefully.

"And you hold no resentment against him?"

Stephanie laughed. "Resentment, Herr Segalla? His death had nothing to do with me: it was more the deadening ritual of the Viennese court which killed him." She leaned closer. "His father would give him no responsibility whatsoever. Rudolph was brilliant. He had plans to reform the empire, but all his father and Prime Minister Taaffe would allow him to do was play at being a soldier. Do you know he once told me that, one morning, he spent hours working on a memorandum about which polish should be used on the buttons of officers' uniforms?!"

"Life is tedious," Segalla murmured. "Your Imperial Highness knows that, yet Your Imperial Highness does not take her life."

"This Imperial Highness," Stephanie replied, tapping the bodice of her dress, "is not baited and trapped like poor Rudolph was. He was impetuous, rash." She put the cup down. "You have heard the rumours," she whispered. "Terrible fights with his father, and his health was always delicate."

"Do you think he died for love?" Segalla asked.

"Love!" Stephanie lowered her head and sniggered. "I have told you, Herr Segalla, Baroness Vetsera was one of many; she was no different from the rest." She felt beneath her cloak and took out a small reticule, snapped open the gold clasps, and brought out a square piece of paper. "Herr Segalla, read that." She pushed it into his hands.

Segalla undid the paper carefully.

"It's a copy," Stephanie declared. "Written out by the imperial police."

Segalla studied the letter carefully. On the top was a short memorandum saying the original had been deciphered by the Austrian Ministry of Foreign Affairs with the words "A hoax? Blackmail?" written beneath. Segalla read it carefully.

> *My beloved Stephanie,*
>
> *Before departing this life I must briefly explain to you my reasons for doing so. You know as well as I do how matters stand between me and you, so I will not lose any more words. But to business. It was my misfortune to have made the acquaintance of the Baroness Maria Vetsera; she is now urging and pestering me constantly to administer to you—that I have to utter it!—poison in some way or other; she is terrible, a real torture to me, but I can't do anything about it. Always and permanently she carries*

*with her a flagon which she wants to give me at every opportunity, but I always refuse her.*

*The reason why I cannot do anything against her any longer is that she feels herself to be a mother, hence probably also her great irritability. I can't go back now, come what may. I only know that Maria Vetsera will herself drink the poison; if not voluntarily, then she will be forced. I have summoned her to Mayerling; there everything will be decided.*

*My last wish, that you may one day be Empress of Austria; I hope you will fulfil it for me if at all possible; don't forget our little Elizabeth, and now a thousand good wishes and be*

> *Cordially kissed by*
> *Your*
> *Rudolph*

Segalla lowered the letter and looked up in astonishment.

"It's a forgery," Stephanie remarked, quietly plucking it out of his hand. "But it proves one of the many stories circulating in Vienna how the Vetsera woman had some sort of hold over him—"

She jumped at the knock on the door, then rose and curtseyed as the emperor stalked into the room. Segalla also rose and bowed from his waist.

"Your Imperial Highness."

The emperor approached; with one hand he helped Stephanie to her feet, then extended the other for Segalla to kiss. The emperor smiled at Stephanie, but Segalla could see he was angry.

"Madam, your carriage awaits you."

Stephanie curtseyed once more, threw a quick glance at Segalla, then swept through the door, slamming it behind her. The emperor waited, his head slightly cocked on one side.

"Herr Segalla, you are most welcome. I received His Holiness's letter of condolence; he lost no time in sending you."

Segalla bowed once more. "It was only fitting, Your Highness," he replied. "The Holy Father thought that if both Monsignor Galemberti and I were present at the funeral, it might still clacking tongues."

"And has my daughter-in-law's clacked?" Franz Joseph asked.

"Excellency, she is grieving. I could not leave Vienna without observing the courtesies."

"Ah yes, the courtesies." The emperor took a step nearer.

Segalla noticed his red-rimmed eyes were blazing with anger.

"When you return to His Holiness, Her Segalla, give him my regards and good wishes. My heartfelt thanks for his support during this grievous time. And tell his secretary of state, Cardinal Rampolla, that I have spoken the truth."

"His Holiness may come back to you on that," Segalla retorted. "He has heard many stories about your son's unfortunate death. If it was anything but suicide His Holiness would proclaim it throughout Europe."

The emperor glanced away. "It was suicide," he murmured. He spread his hands in an expansive gesture. "When the period of mourning is ended, Herr Segalla, I have already promised the Holy Father that, if he wishes to send an extraordinary envoy to sift through the facts, that will be acceptable." He straightened up, tying the top button of his coat. "And he'll probably send you, won't he, Segalla?" The emperor looked the papal envoy over from head to toe. "We'll cooperate as far as we can, but these matters are finished." He spun on his heel and walked to the door. He turned, his hand on the latch. "Herr Nicholas Segalla?"

"Yes, Your Highness?"

Franz Joseph walked back into the room. He pulled a pair of black leather gloves from his coat pocket and put them on carefully.

"You will be welcome next time," the emperor said slowly. "But I understand Monsignor Galemberti is waiting for you. He will see you off at the station."

"Your Highness is too kind."

"No, Segalla, I am not too kind, just wary." He took a step closer. "In the imperial archives there are references to another Segalla, a man of the shadows, a friend of Pope Pius VI, whom Bonaparte imprisoned. A Segalla who was busy in Paris shortly after Napoleon's defeat at Waterloo, who later visited him at St. Helena and was there when he died. A Segalla who appeared in Paris when the Bourbons were overthrown in 1830. A Segalla whom Napoleon III investigated, though the findings of the investigation were destroyed in a mysterious fire."

"Our family is an ancient one," the papal envoy replied. "Perhaps just as ancient as the Hapsburgs, or even more."

"Then, if that's the case," the emperor replied sardonically, "you should always remember the past is a mystery, and that applies to the death of my son as to anything else."

"Your Excellency, you said it was suicide?"

"There are suicides and there are suicides," Franz Joseph retorted.

Segalla wiped the sweat from the palms of his hands on his coat.

"Your Excellency, it's wrong to pry, but . . . ?"

"Yes, yes, you are right! It is!" Franz Joseph replied. "Now, sir, your coach is waiting." And, without a backward glance, the emperor walked out of the room.

Segalla picked up his black-topped hat, collected his cane, and walked slowly out into the passageway. For a while he just stood in the shadows, waiting until the rest of the court had left, then walked down towards the cavernous entrance hall. The plump, white-haired Monsignor Galemberti, the papal envoy in Vienna, was taking his farewells of Father Prior. Galemberti waved Segalla over and they walked towards the door: the Monsignor buttoned up his scarlet-lined cloak under his podgy chin and glanced sideways at his companion.

"You are not welcome here, Nicholas," he murmured.

"I gathered that," Segalla replied. "What is it, Galemberti, shame, fear? What do they have to hide?"

Galemberti led him through the doorway and out onto the steps.

"We'll go no further," Galemberti declared. "There's someone waiting for you in the carriage." He smiled impishly. "Cherchez la femme, Nicholas; it's a woman."

"Who?" Segalla asked.

"Don't worry," Galemberti joked. "It's not one of the ladies from the town wanting to bid you an affectionate farewell, though it could well be. It's Countess Marie Larisch, a friend of both the crown prince and Baroness Vetsera." Galemberti held a warning finger up and turned sideways as if the woman were actually watching him. "She's got the morals of a Borgia," he explained. "Totally without scruples, a consummate liar."

"So why does she want to talk to me?"

"God knows, but she may be able to throw some light on this shadowy business."

Galemberti undid the clasp of his cloak and played with the golden pectoral cross, stroking it carefully, lovingly, as if seeking its protection.

"At the moment," he continued, "the Hapsburg court is in shock. The emperor was fearful that the Church might not allow ecclesiastical burial for his son, but now the subterfuge will begin. Everything at Mayerling is closely guarded. The police are not allowed to investigate, the court doctors are sworn to secrecy."

"But why?" Segalla asked.

"A number of reasons," Galemberti replied. "First, it may be just shame. Shame that a Hapsburg prince shot a young woman, then killed himself. Second, their deaths could be the result of some drunken brawl: the logical end to a sordid affair. Third"—Galemberti's voice dropped to a whisper—"it might be murder; yet, even here, there are many theories. The Germans disliked the crown prince. The new kaiser and his first minister, Otto von

Bismarck, were fearful that, if Rudolph became emperor, he would take Austria away from Germany. Then there's Taaffe, Franz Joseph's favourite. He and Rudolph hated each other like cat and dog. Finally, there's the possibility that Rudolph may have been involved in some sort of treasonable activity: that his death at Mayerling was a secret execution." Galemberti buttoned up his robe again. "What you must do," he said, taking Segalla by the arm and leading him down the steps, "is relate all I have told you, and all you have seen and heard, to His Holiness in Rome. The Holy Father," Galemberti continued, "has been most magnanimous. However, he may well send you back, Nicholas, once the official period of mourning is over."

"And what use will that be?" Segalla asked, pausing halfway down the steps.

"The Church must find out," Galemberti replied. "One way or the other the Holy Father must satisfy himself." He sighed, pulled out a red-and-white spotted handkerchief, and blew his nose noisily. "Oh, the emperor will cooperate, but, believe me, Nicholas, by the time you return, the truth will be even more obscure." He cleared his throat. "Anyway, how did you find the crown princess?"

"Lonely," Segalla replied, putting his hat on. "Chattering, distracted by shock."

"No one likes her, poor woman," Galemberti said. "The Hapsburgs were never known for their intelligence. Poor Stephanie, God bless her, was, in that sense, a perfect match for our dead prince."

"What will happen to her?"

"She has the Princess Elizabeth. She will become an imperial dowager."

"And not return to Belgium?"

"I don't think they want her back," Galemberti said. "Whilst Franz Joseph insists that she stay here to look after her daughter."

Segalla tapped his walking stick against the ground.

"And you, Galemberti, with your mischievous eyes and insatiable curiosity?"

Galemberti shook his head. "I know nothing. I understand there has been a postmortem. The imperial commissioner of enquiry discovered a gun in the bedroom and certain letters but, apart from that, nothing else. Of course, rumours abound. Stories that Rudolph is still alive, that he's hiding out in the forest." He saw the blind of the carriage move. "But the countess awaits, Nicholas." He shook Segalla's hand. "When you come back," he whispered, "I'll have what I can find ready for you. Don't come into Vienna. We will meet at Mayerling itself. Oh, don't worry," Galemberti added. "By then the guards will have been withdrawn. The emperor intends to convert the lodge into a Carmelite convent. Rudolph's bedroom will become a chapel of reparation."

"For what?" Segalla asked archly.

"God knows," Galemberti replied. "That, Nicholas, is the mystery."

He opened the door, and Segalla took off his hat and climbed into the carriage seat. He pulled back the blind and nodded at Galemberti, then tapped the top of his carriage with his cane. The driver cracked his whip and pulled off. Segalla settled back and carefully removed his gloves. He was aware of the woman, dressed completely in black, sitting opposite him; he noted her lace veil and fragrant perfume; but only when the carriage had trundled through the gates of the Hapsburg mausoleum did he bow gently towards her.

"Madam, you sit there like a ghost!"

The woman lifted her veil. Segalla stared at the pretty, oval-shaped face, the white alabaster skin covered in fine powder, her carmine-painted lips, the dark kohl under the close-set, self-centred eyes. The woman took a glove off and extended her hand. Segalla kissed it lightly.

"You are the countess Marie Larisch?"

The woman nodded, her eyes intent on him. Segalla shifted in his seat uncomfortably. For some reason he took an instant dislike to her. She was pretty, even attractive, with her auburn hair peeping under the black, elegant bonnet. The mouth was smiling, her hand soft and warm, but she had the look of a vixen. A woman born for trouble.

"You asked to see me," he said sharply.

"Yes I did." Her voice was low and throaty. The woman smiled but her eyes never changed. "I am a good friend of Monsignor Galemberti."

"Does he know that?"

Her smile faded.

"You are also a friend of the dead prince," Segalla continued, easing himself in the corner. "And of Baroness Maria Vetsera. Madam," Segalla insisted, "I have not much time. So, what you have to say, say quickly."

"I was her friend," Larisch replied. "And yes, Herr Segalla, you have not got much time. However, I have bribed the driver to take us by a circuitous route to the station. I was one of the last persons to see them alive," she continued.

"Who, the prince?"

"Well, no," the woman stammered. "Baroness Maria. You see, Herr Segalla, she and the prince had an assignation. They died on the thirtieth January but they had been lovers for some time."

"And?" Segalla asked.

"Maria was under the strict supervision of her mother and her uncles, the Baltazzis," Larisch explained. "They totally disapproved of her relationship with the prince. They did not want to see Maria become the plaything of the Hapsburgs."

"Ah," Segalla muttered. "In which case, Countess, you supported them in this noble cause?"

"No." Larisch leaned forward. "I did the opposite, Herr Segalla. Maria was desperate to see her prince. It was I who arranged for her to leave her family home on the morning of the twenty-eighth. I took her down to a jeweller's in the centre of Vienna thinking that she was to meet the prince for a brief talk. I—" She stammered. "I went inside, but when I returned, the Baroness Maria had left by another carriage. I then raised the alarm. I went to see the police, President Krauss, even Prime Minister Taaffe. I finally went to Maria's home." She leaned back. "The Vetseras were beside themselves. I couldn't tell them where their daughter had gone."

"And the authorities?" Segalla asked.

Larisch spread her hands. "They said it was none of my business and certainly none of theirs."

"Did Maria take a bag?" Segalla asked. "Possessions? As if she intended to stay away for some time?"

"Not that I could see," Larisch replied.

"Did she give any indication," Segalla asked, "that she and her lover were intent on a suicide pact?"

Larisch closed her eyes and shook her head.

"God be my witness, Herr Segalla, no! Never once did she even intimate about the coming tragedy. I honestly thought that all she wanted was to spend a few hours with the prince, perhaps in some house or hotel on the outskirts of Vienna."

"And you were prepared to do that?" Segalla asked. "Allow Prince Rudolph to commit adultery. Act as a procuress, bring a young noblewoman to him?"

Larisch sat back as if she had been slapped, her lips thin and bloodless.

"Herr Segalla, that was not my business. They were already lovers."

"As you and the prince once were?" Segalla asked sharply.

Larisch looked away, tears in her eyes.

"Yes," she murmured. "For a short while."

"So, why did you do this?" Segalla asked remorselessly.

Larisch ran a gloved finger round her lips.

"The prince," she began, closing her eyes. "The Prince was strange. Rudolph had his moods. He hated his father and was unhappy in his marriage. He flitted like a butterfly from flower to flower. Maria Vetsera was besotted with him. Yes, I brought them together. I agreed to help her meet the prince on that fateful day. Because"—her head came up, her lower lip quivering—"because I am in debt, Herr Segalla. Both Maria and the prince gave me money to help them."

"And so why do you come to me?"

Larisch cleared her throat. "On the morning of the twenty-eighth," she replied flatly, "I collected Maria from her house and, as I have said, we drove to Vienna. She then disappeared. Now the finger of suspicion pointed to me." She drew herself up. "I am the daughter of Duke Ludvig of Bavaria. I am a kinswoman of the emperor's. In a few weeks, Herr Segalla, my role in this matter will become public knowledge. The emperor has already forbidden me entree to any of the royal palaces. Within the week, I will be banned from Vienna itself. When you return to Rome, Herr Segalla, tell His Holiness that I had no part, no knowledge of what was to happen."

"I could do that," Segalla replied. "But, as you have found out, Countess, everything in life has a price!"

Larisch gazed unblinkingly back.

"I'd like to know what you know," Segalla said. "What you think, what you suspect. Do that," he continued ruthlessly, "and His Holiness will know of your cooperation in this matter."

Larisch's lips moved as if she were talking to herself.

"We shall soon be at the station," Segalla reminded her.

The countess looked away. "Rudolph was unbalanced," she began slowly. "He often talked of suicide. There again, whether he would go through with it is another matter!"

"And Maria?"

Larisch shook her head. "She was frightened of death. Two weeks before the tragedy, she went to some fortune-teller, one of those fairground charlatans, who warned her to be careful."

"And Maria's reaction?" Segalla asked.

"Sheer terror!"

"So why the suicide at Mayerling?"

"I have heard the stories," the countess replied. "I can't accept them. Rudolph could be dissolute. He liked his wine and he liked his drugs, particularly morphine. He liked to portray himself in tragic roles. He loved intrigue and clandestine meetings, but he didn't love Vetsera enough to die for her."

Segalla hid his surprise.

"Oh, don't be shocked," Larisch replied tartly. "A few days before Rudolph left for Mayerling, he spent the night with a former mistress, Mitzi Caspar. There were others whom he favoured."

Segalla leaned back. Why, he wondered, would a prince commit suicide with a woman he didn't really love? Whom he could discard as easily as he would a torn coat or a pair of boots? To all appearances the deaths at Mayerling were the result of a suicide pact: but was that the truth?

"What do you think happened?" he asked.

The countess shook her head. "I don't really know, Herr Segalla. If I had had an inkling of what was going to happen, I would have gone to Mayerling myself. But"—her eyes held Segalla's—"I do not think it was suicide. Something else happened. Something which Maria or Rudolph never told me."

Segalla caught the note of jealousy in her voice and realised how this woman, so accustomed to using others, had now been used herself and left to face the consequences. Larisch leaned over.

"Think, Herr Segalla," she hissed, "of little Maria turning her head for the prince to put a bullet through and then Rudolph, full of drink and morphine, lifting a revolver to his head: that did not, could not, have happened." She sat back as the coach stopped.

Segalla opened the door and got out of the carriage.

"I shall remember you in Rome, Countess Larisch."

The woman forced a smile and slammed the carriage door shut. Segalla walked into the railway station, puzzled by what Larisch had told him, totally unaware of the sandy-haired, military-looking young man who followed him down to the platform and stayed until Segalla's train had left the station.

# Chapter 3

T wo months later Detective Inspector Joseph Kinski was totally surprised when he met the papal emissary at Vienna's main railway station. Segalla noticed this and laughed as he shook the detective's hand.

"What did you expect?" he teased, his dark eyes full of merriment. "A mouldy monk? Or some doddering old man?"

Kinski, on that rare occasion, blushed, shuffled his feet, and tried to explain. He looked over his shoulder at Sergeant Brunner, then laughed.

"Signor Segalla." He grasped the man's hand again. "I'll be honest, I didn't know what to expect." He beckoned Brunner forward to pick up Segalla's case and small valise.

Segalla shook his head. "I'm young and I'm fit," he remarked, then pulled back the cuff of his coat: the valise was chained to his wrist.

Kinski shrugged. "Do you want some coffee, some chocolate?" he asked.

Segalla pointed to the buffet car on the train. "I've eaten and drunk enough to last me until the Second Coming." He smiled secretly at what he had said, picked up his case, and followed Kinski and Brunner out of the station.

Once he had settled into the small cab, his case in the luggage rack at the back, his valise placed on the seat beside him, Segalla produced his letters of attestation. Kinski pretended to study these carefully but secretly watched his visitor. He had been surprised. Segalla must, he reckoned, be about his age, mid-thirties. He had the look of an Italian: swarthy faced, the hair carefully oiled and groomed; slightly hooked nose, clean-shaven face, thin lips, and firm chin. Kinski was fascinated by the eyes.

"Watch the eyes!" he constantly advised Brunner, his stolid, faithful sergeant. "The eyes and the upper lip. If a man is lying, you'll see a shift in the eyes, a bead of sweat on his upper lip." Brunner had listened to his advice carefully, and then, as usual, totally ignored it. Kinski himself now began to doubt the wisdom of it. Segalla's eyes were strange, full of gentle mockery, yet suddenly became hard, even cruel, as if Segalla had seen things, suffered deeply, and trusted no one.

The carriage rattled over the great cobblestones of the strasser. The carriage swayed slightly; the horses' clopping hooves became lulling. Kinski looked up furtively. Segalla's eyes drooped, his head went back, he began to sleep. The detective breathed out deeply—his visitor was a man like any other! He made to put the letter of attestation into his inside pocket, then jumped as Segalla's hand went out, his eyes still closed.

"Joseph, I will need that back." Segalla stirred and opened his eyes. "Vienna crawls with spies and—"

"And plainclothes policemen!" Kinski snapped as he handed the documents back.

Segalla grinned. "Out of your own mouth." He quoted from the Bible. "The dixisti."

The detective, regretting his temper, offered his ever ready brandy flask.

"Signor, I am sorry; you will sample?"

"Not at the moment, but I thank you, Joseph; and, by the way, no 'Signor'—I am not Italian."

Kinski replaced the stopper in the flask. Segalla noticed the "J.K." elegantly carved on the silver top and the way the detective caressed it.

"Your flask was a gift?" he asked.

"Yes, yes, it is. Last Christmas my children, they saved their pennies: a present to their dear papa."

"A lot of pennies," Segalla remarked.

Kinski looked up: he was going to say "Signor" but Segalla lifted a finger.

"Either Segalla or Nicholas," he remarked quietly. "You were going to say?"

"I have four children," Kinski confessed with an embarrassed smile.

"Then you are four times blessed," Nicholas replied.

He pulled back the blinds and stared across the elegant boulevard.

"We are going to your hotel," Kinski offered. "I thought you might wish to wash, eat, and perhaps take a rest after your journey."

Segalla let the blind fall. "No," he answered. "I wish to begin now. Time is precious." He smiled. "Well, that's what Cardinal Rampolla said to me. Let us first visit Hieiligenkreuz. I think the Baroness Maria, God rest her, is the key to this mystery."

Kinski nodded, turned, pulled back a flap, and shouted an order to Brunner. The carriage suddenly swerved, the horse breaking into a canter. Segalla closed his eyes again. Kinski took the brandy flask out and cradled it in his hands. He'd kissed Sophie and his four children good-bye that morning. His lips still felt sticky from the jam which always seemed to cover their faces whenever he left them after breakfast. He tightened his lips. He'd see little of them whilst Segalla was in Vienna. Baron Krauss, president of police, and Prime Minister Taaffe had made their orders most explicit: Be courteous; be attentive. Observe the protocols but don't cooperate. And, where possible, obstruct.

"Is that wise?" Kinski had asked.

"Detective Inspector Kinski." Baron Krauss had stretched across the table, his thickset face almost hidden by his beard, moustache, and luxuriant lamb chop side-whiskers. "Kinski, you are one of the best policemen we have," Krauss growled. "You have a large family. You must be sure this Segalla leaves Vienna no wiser than he arrives. If you succeed there will be no block to your promotion or advancement, either in Vienna or anywhere in the emperor's domain. Segalla is a papal snooper. Their Imperial Highnesses were deeply offended by Cardinal Rampolla's attitude to the sad death of their only son and heir."

"Who is this Segalla?" Kinski had asked.

"As we have said," Taaffe snapped. "A snooper, a spy!"

Kinski had glanced quickly at the prime minister sitting, legs crossed, one hand elegantly covering the lower half of his face. He'd glimpsed something there. Fear? Trepidation?

Kinski had accepted his orders and immediately gone to his friend at the police archives. Old Johann had been as welcoming as ever until Kinski had mentioned Segalla's name.

"Do you know anything about him, Johann?"

"Oh, no, no!" the archivist had stuttered, and then he had almost pushed the detective out of the door.

Kinski did his own research but he failed to discover anything except that both Krauss and Taaffe feared this papal emissary. Kinski sighed noisily. He'd been handed a poisoned chalice. God knew what would happen. Sophie, of course, had been delighted: her petite, heart-shaped face, those eyes which he loved to distraction, had filled with delight.

"Oh Joseph!" She'd flung her arms around his neck, pressing her small, slight body against him. "This is advancement, what you always wanted."

Kinski had smiled and nodded, basking in her approval, hiding his own anxieties. However, he knew he couldn't deceive her for long. This morning at breakfast he had caught her glance, the furrow in her brow, and the false gaiety in her eyes. Kinski sighed and then pulled back the blinds. Brunner, an excellent cabman, was making great progress. They were already at the outskirts of the city. Kinski wished he had gone to mass that morning, or at least spent five minutes in front of the statue of St. Antony of Padua, his patron saint. He wanted this investigation to go well—and quickly. Segalla must get back on the train to Rome, having studied everything and learnt nothing. Kinski opened his eyes. Segalla was studying him, a lazy smile on his face.

"You do not want me here, do you, Detective Inspector?"

"A blunt question deserves a blunt answer. No, I do not. Prince Rudolph is dead, cold in his grave; the same is true of Maria Vetsera."

"Quieta non movere."

"Pardon?"

"Let sleeping dogs lie," Segalla translated. "But His Holiness needs to be assured."

"Of what?"

"Of the truth."

"That," Kinski remarked dryly, looking away, "is a great rarity."

"Which is why," Segalla replied, "I must search for it."

Kinski studied the emissary from head to toe: the tight, white collar with a small golden medal covering the top button; the black frogged coat with the lamb's wool trimming; the smart, almost military-looking grey trousers; galoshes and shining shoes. Segalla wore little jewellery. Kinski suspected he had a fob watch in the waistcoat but nothing else except the curious-looking ring on the fourth finger of his left hand.

"It's a chancery seal," Segalla explained, catching his glance. "Used by medieval clerks." He held it up.

"Are you a wealthy man, Herr Segalla? Do you collect antiques?"

Segalla's smile was dazzling, the laughter bubbling inside him.

"I am wealthy in ways you are not, Detective Inspector. Yet, in the end, you have more than I. Yes, yes." He dropped his hand. "I have a fine collection of antiques but not here, a small villa outside Rome. Have you ever been there?"

The conversation became more desultory. Segalla peeped through the blinds again. They were now in the countryside, the horses moving swiftly. He breathed in the fresh fragrance of spring.

"You have been seconded from other duties?" Segalla asked abruptly.

Kinski shrugged. "Yes. A murder, and a very clever one at that." He straightened up. "But the hangman can wait."

He pulled up the blinds and poked his head through the window. Hieiligenkreuz was in sight. Kinski recalled that dreadful journey when he had brought Maria Vetsera's body for burial. He had arrived at the Cistercian priory in the dead of a wintry night, but even now, on a spring morning, the grey, forbidding stone looked no more welcoming. The carriage stopped in front of the main gates. Segalla and Kinski got down. Brunner, pleased at the progress he had made, pulled out a heavy clay pipe, lit it, and sat back, blowing great puffs of smoke into the air.

"We'll be some time," Kinski remarked.

Brunner, without taking the pipe from his mouth, just nodded.

"The horses will need attention."

"I'll let them cool for a while." Brunner didn't even bother to take the pipe out of his mouth.

Kinski winked at Segalla and, going up, pulled on the bell rope. They heard the patter of sandaled feet. A grille high in the door swung open and a face peered out. Kinski spoke quickly in German, the key was turned, bolts were pulled back, and they were led into the priory grounds. The lay brother smiled and left them to their own devices. Kinski took Segalla round the greystone priory buildings, through the gardens where cowled monks hoed and dug at the soil; they passed the church, the smell of incense still heavy on the air, and into the quiet, overgrown cemetery.

Kinski led Segalla along the rough-beaten track and stopped

before a mound of earth covered with dried, rotting camellias. The inscription on the smooth grey headstone was simple. "Maria Vetsera, Born 19 March 1871: Died 30 January 1889."

Segalla knelt down and studied the inscription carefully.

"Who brings the camellias?" he asked.

"Maria's mother and sister," Kinski replied. "They come every month."

"Why?" Segalla abruptly asked.

"I suppose because they miss her."

"No, no," the papal emissary apologised. "Why was she buried so quickly? Why wasn't she taken to a hospital for a proper post-mortem? Why was it so important that she had to be hurried to her grave at the dead of night?" Segalla got up, brushing the dirt and grass from his coat. "I know, I know, you were only acting on orders from above." He stared across at a cypress tree. "How many times have I heard that?" he murmured. "And how many more times yet?"

"Don't condemn me!" Kinski snapped. "I'm a policeman, Herr Segalla. I had nothing to do with her death. It is easy for you to come trotting over the Alps and pass judgement."

Segalla read the biblical quotation on the headstone: "Man Cometh Forth Like a Flower and Is Cut Down." He took off his black gloves and grasped Kinski's arm.

"We are all creatures of the dark, Joseph. We do our best under the circumstances in which we find ourselves. I am sorry. I deeply apologise. I did not mean to be judgemental. You are not just a policeman, you are a very good one. A man of integrity. I don't think you liked what happened any more than I do."

Kinski grinned and shook his hand.

"Now"—Segalla linked his arm through the detective's, and they walked back towards the church—"tell me, most erudite of policemen, according to the little I know, Prince Rudolph met Maria Vetsera outside Mayerling on the twenty-eighth January. Were they under police surveillance?"

Kinski was sharp enough not to be flattered by Segalla's ear-lier words, but, there again, he could see no difficulty in telling the truth this time.

"Yes, Herr Segalla, they were, at least on the thirtieth. My colleague, Edward Bayer, was stationed in the woods near Mayerling. However, he may have arrived after the deaths had occurred."

"But surely," Segalla persisted, staring up at the tympanum of Christ in glory above the chapel door. "Rumour says that Prince Rudolph was not of sound mind, volatile; he should have been watched. . . ."

"Herr Segalla," Kinski retorted, "I do my job. I look after and love my family. I very rarely read the newspapers; certainly not the scandal and gossip of the court. Yet," he hurried on, "now and again, I am attached to duties at court. I saw and met the Prince on a number of occasions. He did not strike me as a man intent on suicide."

"And the lady Vetsera?"

"I was often on duty on the race course." Kinski smiled and gestured at Segalla to walk into the entrance of the church away from the cold breeze. They sat on a small bench just inside the porch. "They called her the 'Turf Angel.'" Kinski continued. "Her uncle owned race horses. She was well known to the Jockey Club. Baroness Vetsera was pretty, vivacious. She liked wine and the company of men. Romantic, a little stupid but def-initely in love with life."

"Not a young woman to take her life lightly? Did you see her corpse?" Segalla asked. He watched the detective's grey eyes carefully: he knew Kinski was going to lie though he did not want to.

"Yes, yes." Kinski glanced away. "Her corpse was removed at night, wedged between the only two mourners allowed. It was dressed in the clothes she wore when she came to Mayerling. Be-fore we left the lodge, a doctor pointed out the bullet holes. One single shot, through the right temple, exiting above her left ear. Death must have been instantaneous."

"So, I go back to my first question," Segalla said. "Why bury her so quickly unless there was something to hide?"

"Read the autopsy report," Kinski retorted.

Segalla pulled a face. He'd been closeted for hours with Cardinal Rampolla: the hawk-faced cardinal had been quite blunt in his directive.

"Don't expect to be shown anything, Segalla," he had rasped. "And, if you are, believe only half of what you read."

Segalla rose, left the church, and walked back along the pebble-covered path. He paused, closed his eyes, breathing in the country air. He'd been in Rome for a decade now, deeply attracted to the saintly Leo XIII. Segalla had sworn a personal oath of loyalty and service to the pontiff. He admired the way Leo was trying to steer the Church through the growing clamour and clangour of the industrialised world. Yet his time was running short: Rampolla was growing suspicious. The Vatican secret police were searching amongst the archives and that sinister Cardinal, the "éminence grise" behind the papal throne, was already hinting at this and that. How a man called Segalla had been of great assistance to Pius VI when he had been captured by Napoleon. How, in the archives of the Jesuit college in Rome, were reports of a Segalla acting on behalf of that order in England during the 16th and 17th centuries. And how was it such a family had such an allegiance to the Church? Of course no man could live forever! Rampolla was growing increasingly suspicious. Now and again, Segalla would catch Rampolla's black pebble eyes studying him intently. Segalla sighed. Yes, it was time to move on. Perhaps travel back to London to his house just off Ludgate or that quiet, isolated farm in the Yorkshire Dales? The world was changing. Perhaps the time had come. . . .

"Herr Segalla?"

The papal envoy turned and smiled apologetically.

"I'm sorry. I was thinking of something else."

"Perhaps you should rest," Kinski offered. "Your suite of rooms at the 'Imperial' are ready."

"Oh no." Segalla gripped his small valise more tightly.

Kinski noticed how it was still chained to his wrist.

"I'd like to visit Mayerling. I'm meeting someone there."

Kinski's mouth gaped in surprise. He coughed to cover his confusion even as he cursed himself. He had totally underestimated Segalla. Baron Krauss said if the papal envoy wanted to visit Mayerling, he had no objection but Kinski was to keep his superiors informed. Segalla must have arranged this before he arrived in Vienna. Kinski took his brandy flask out. He gulped quickly to hide his confusion.

"Then, if it's Mayerling"—he was sure Segalla was quietly laughing at him—"Mayerling it is!"

They left the priory. Brunner was still sitting on the cab smoking his clay pipe, head nodding. Kinski marvelled at how this fat, squat sergeant of his could sleep in the strangest of places. He took his pipe out of his mouth as Kinski approached.

"Is it back to the city?" He growled.

"No, Mayerling." Kinski raised his eyes heavenwards.

The sergeant took his pipe out of his mouth and grinned.

"If he continues like this," Brunner whispered, "there'll be no more little Kinskis. Your wife will hardly see you."

"Keep your thoughts to yourself," Kinski taunted back. He waited until Segalla got into the coach. "Are we being followed?"

Brunner put his pipe back in his mouth.

"Don't be bloody stupid!" He growled through clenched teeth. "Not unless Baron Krauss has trained the pigeons. He'll not do it that way, sir." He continued. "But, I wager that someone watched us as we left and they'll be waiting at every gate when we return." Brunner wiped his watery eyes. "And I'd bet my pipe to your brandy flask there'll be someone waiting for us at Mayerling."

"That," Kinski murmured as he opened the door, "is not a wager I intend to accept."

He got into the carriage and threw himself on the seat and sat back. Brunner cracked his whip and took the coach back on to the main Baden road.

"Detective Kinski, I apologise." Segalla was no longer teasing. "But, let's be honest, you're not here to assist me: you are here to watch me?"

Kinski's face remained impassive.

"And undoubtedly," Segalla continued, "knowing Baron Krauss as I do, he'll have others watching you and some more watching them. Like you, I have a job to do: orders from above. I am a guest in Vienna but I am no man's puppet. All I intend to do is meet people who prefer to talk without a police spy at the keyhole."

"I am no police spy," Kinski retorted.

Segalla grinned. "No, you are not, Joseph, and that's going to make my work all the more interesting. Now, is there any brandy left in that flask of yours?"

They reached Mayerling late in the afternoon. As the coach swung off the Baden road into the Schwechatbach Valley, Kinski tapped on the ceiling of the coach and told Brunner to stop.

"What time are you expecting your visitor?"

"Oh." Segalla undid his cloak and glanced at his gold fob watch. "Not for another hour and a half, what the English would call teatime."

Kinski shrugged. "You might as well see the hunting lodge in daylight," he offered. "It's a beautiful view!"

He and his visitor got out and stared down the valley at the elegant whitewashed buildings dominated by a church spire which lay on either side of the road before it rose to the brow of a wood-covered hill.

"On the left"—Kinski pointed—"is the home farm. It was all once owned by the priory we have just left. However, two years ago Prince Rudolph bought, then refurbished it as a country retreat."

"And the hunting lodge lies to the right?" Segalla asked.

"Yes, the church is that of St. Lawrence. The lodge buildings form a horseshoe around it. Very elegant, I have heard, with cabinets, billiard rooms, guest rooms, a rifle room, and a skittle alley. Everything a man needs," Kinski concluded, "just before he blows his brains out."

"You have no sympathy for the dead prince?" Segalla asked.

The detective shrugged. "Why should a man who has an empire at his feet, a faithful wife, a daughter, everything he wants, kill himself? Do you go to church, Herr Segalla?" Kinski smiled his apology. "Remember Christ's words: 'What does it profit a man if he gains the whole world yet suffers the loss of his immortal soul?' "

"If he committed suicide?" Segalla remarked quietly. He turned back to the coach. "And there you have it, Joseph; why should a man commit suicide?"

They settled back inside; Brunner closed the door and climbed back into the seat, and the coach rattled on.

"Come on, Joseph." Segalla leaned forward. "It's not treason to speculate. You say you do not read the newspapers, but you are a shrewd man, you listen to the gossip. Who'd want Prince Rudolph dead? The emperor?" Segalla shook his head. "To lose his heir and only son? What real enemies did Rudolph have?" Segalla continued remorselessly. "Who'd hate him so much they'd want him dead?"

"I have heard," Kinski replied, "that the kaiser feared the day Rudolph would ascend the imperial throne lest he take Austria and its empire away from German influence. Rudolph, in turn, deeply resented our defeat by the Prussians at Sadowa."

"The kaiser?" Segalla asked. "Surely not. If his hand were found in this, there would be war. He'd be humiliated, a pariah in European circles. Who else?"

Joseph shrugged. "My wife, Sophie, is of Hungarian descent. We've heard rumours from Budapest that Hungary wanted its own sovereign and independence."

"And Rudolph supported that?"

"According to those who know," Kinski replied. "Prince Rudolph believed the Hapsburg Empire could not remain as it is. We have lost our territories in northern Italy. We face protests in Prague, in Budapest, and in the Balkans. Rudolph argued that we should let these go and reconstitute Austria as a sovereign state."

"And who would oppose that? His father?"

Kinski nodded.

"And who else? I mean, here in Austria?"

Kinski smiled. "I'm a detective, not a politician, Herr Segalla."

"Call me Nicholas."

"Whatever." Kinski continued. "You must ask yourself, Nicholas, who could carry out such a murder?" He held up his fingers. "Who had the means for such a bloody act? Who could cover it up later?"

"And what do you think?" Segalla asked quietly.

Kinski didn't know why he replied: perhaps he wanted to show this enigmatic, sardonic man that he, too, wasn't a puppet pulled by strings.

"After I attended the burial of Maria Vetsera," he declared, "I'll be honest, I went back to Vienna and made my own enquiries. The order to remove her body so quickly in the dead of night did not come from the emperor or the imperial court but from Edward Taaffe, the prime minister."

Segalla sighed and leaned back; what Kinski said hardly differed from what Rampolla had told him in Rome.

# Chapter 4

The woman travelling under the name of Julia Weiner stared through the window in the first-class carriage of the Vienna-to-Berlin express. She felt very comfortable: she sat against the padded upholstery, being served coffee in thin white china cups with a small glass of schnapps after a meal of roast duck and fresh vegetables. She smoothed down the new coat she'd bought. She was glad she was leaving Austria: her velvet reticule contained enough money to start a new life. She would change her name again perhaps? Buy a pastry shop and marry some handsome young man? She closed her eyes and breathed in, smiling to herself, then jumped as the carriage door was flung open. The stranger who entered was dressed in a broad-lapeled jacket, belted at the waist; thick serge trousers; and tightly laced, polished ankle boots. He had the luxuriant moustache and whiskers of a cavalry officer. He smiled lazily across at the woman. She simpered back.

"You are travelling to Berlin?" he asked, sitting down.

"Well, not really," she replied. "A small town outside; I hope to stay the night there, then travel on."

She had resolved on that, as soon as she had left Vienna; she'd be careful. But the stranger looked safe, certainly not like a policeman. His eyes were light blue, and she always liked that; he had auburn hair and a blunt, forthright face. She'd met someone else like that; Julia closed her eyes quickly to remove the memory.

"Madam is unwell?"

She opened her eyes. It was good to be flattered. No more "Take this" or "Take that." She simpered back and straightened the bonnet on her head.

"Just a thought from the past."

"Ah, yes. The past." The young man took his cigar case from inside his jacket, picked one out, and lit it. "It's strange," the man declared, settling back into his seat.

He paused as the waiter opened the door. Before Julia could object, her companion had ordered a bottle of champagne, a bucket of ice, and two crystal glasses. The roll of notes which he drew from his pocket was as thick as a pack of playing cards. He dealt these out with all the lackadaisical care and charm of a professional spendthrift.

"Champagne?" Julia's eyes sparkled. She pulled her arm back and so lifted her coat and dress to display the white flounce of frilly petticoats beneath.

"It's strange," the young man continued. "Here you are talking about the past and here am I travelling to the same small town as you." He blew circles of cigar smoke into the air. "I have been lucky," he murmured. "My uncle bequeathed a most generous legacy." He smiled. "And now I intend a short tour, Germany, France, even England."

"By yourself?" Julia asked.

"So far." The young man smiled back.

The waiter returned with the champagne. Julia noticed it was Veuve Clicquot. She'd seen that served at the grandest tables. Nevertheless, she hid her surprise. She didn't want this young man to get the wrong impression. She was a lady, not some tart to be picked up at any man's whim. He dismissed the waiter, pulled the bottle dripping with the ice from its silver bucket, and filled the two glasses.

They toasted each other and sipped, letting the fragrance wash their mouths. He smacked his lips appreciatively but then frowned.

"I really shouldn't have done that," he apologised. "I can find another carriage. It's just . . ."

"No, no stay, at least until you've finished the glass."

They finished that and Julia held out hers for more. The young man filled it, chattering about how he had been a hussar officer in one of the line regiments.

"There's no future in the army," he added darkly. "Now Prince Rudolph has gone."

"Did you know him?" Julia squirmed on the seat.

The young man caught the glimpse of black stockings above gold-laced boots.

"Oh, I met him on a number of occasions," the young man replied. "From afar. I was a mere lieutenant." He laughed sharply. "And yourself?"

"Once or twice in the crowds, as he left the Hofburg or journeyed around Vienna."

"Ah well." The man raised his glass. "May he rest in peace."

Kati Polzer, now calling herself Julia, joined in the toast. They finished the bottle and he ordered another. By the time they had reached the station in the small, sleepy town of Freidenhof, Julia was feeling a little giddy, giggling and chattering, yet she had a good head and it would take a few more glasses of champagne before she fell asleep. The young man was attentive. Outside the lonely station, she admired the masterful way he hired a cab, tipped the porter, and placed her cases carefully in the back. The driver cracked his whip and they fairly bowled along the main road. It was only a short journey past the houses and closed shops. Darkness was already falling, and the gas lamps glowed eerily in the mist swirling down from the fields high above the town.

Julia found herself still giggling and, now and again, the motion of the carriage threw her against her companion. He was most gallant, steadying her and saying he was looking forward to a good meal at the restaurant.

"Oh yes." He winked at her. "The hotel is famous for that."

A short while later the cab stopped. Porters ran up, their aprons emblazoned with the hotel's insignia, the Prussian eagle. The young man helped Julia up the steps and into the foyer. She looked round and sighed with pleasure. This was what she wanted: soft carpets underneath gleaming oaken furniture. Tastefully decorated walls, electric lamps, men hurrying hither and thither at her every whim whilst this gallant young officer attended to all the details. He used great discretion, booking a room on the first floor for Julia and a separate one for himself on the floor above. They went to their rooms. For a while Julia lay on the four-poster bed before washing her hands and face, applying makeup delicately to remove any ravages of the journey, painting her lips bright red, flicking her earlobes and watching the cheap stones shimmer in the light from the mirror. She made sure her reticule was carefully hidden—after all, a lady never paid for her meal—and went downstairs to the restaurant. Her companion, whom she now knew as Ernst, already had a table booked, and the evening was the pleasantest Julia had experienced for many a year. Afterwards, as Ernst ordered brandy and a cigar for himself, Julia, eyelashes fluttering, raised a hand delicately to her lips to stifle a yawn as she had seen the great ladies do and said she must retire. Ernst half rose from his chair and watched as Julia, slightly swaying, went up the stairs, throwing coy glances over her shoulder at him.

She was half-undressed, in her choker, bodice, and flounced petticoats, when the expected soft knock came on her door. She opened this. Ernst was leaning there, two brandy glasses in his hand. She stepped back and invited him in. The brandy was forgotten in passionate kisses and embraces as he removed the rest of her clothes. They fell on the bed, Julia crying out at the rough way he took her. Afterwards she lay stretching like a cat.

"Come." Ernst was leaning above her. "Let me at least take your choker off."

She half lifted her head from the pillows. The garrote string was round her throat before she even realised, pulling tight. Julia kicked and struggled, but within a minute, she was dead. Her former lover didn't even spare her a second glance. He dressed quickly, thoroughly searched the room, and found her reticule. He then went out into the passageway, locked the door, and slipped the key into his breast pocket. Downstairs he collected his cloak. He didn't bother about his luggage. What was the use of suitcases full of old newspapers? "Ernst" walked back swiftly through the night and, looking at his fob watch, smiled grimly. He had done everything on time. Within the hour he had caught the midnight express back into Vienna without anyone the wiser.

Segalla, much to Kinski's annoyance, had made himself very much at home in the hunting lodge. They had arrived through the southern gate into the courtyard, its gardens laid out in the French style. The keeper, Wodicka, who proudly introduced himself as chief huntsman, said he was also acting caretaker. Friendly and grizzle-faced, Wodicka was much impressed by Segalla and even more so by the silver coins the papal emissary slipped into his callused hand. With Kinski trailing behind, Wodicka, rattling a huge ring of keys, showed Segalla the church of St. Lawrence and then around the gardens with their lawns, fishponds, rifle range, skittle alley, and gorgeously decorated baroque tea pavilion at the far end. Segalla declared himself impressed by the whitewashed buildings, their roofs covered with light grey wooden shingles. Wodicka then led them up the pebble paths and into what he still termed "Prince Rudolph's suite." He offered to take Segalla upstairs, but the envoy shook his head, smiling over his shoulder at the dour-faced Kinski.

"The prince's suite was entirely on this floor?" he asked.

"Oh yes, sir."

Wodicka led them through the dark-panelled billiard room

with its beautiful green-baize-covered table and polished, heavy furniture: the rows of cues along it were stood to attention like a line of soldiers. Then they walked through the guest rooms which flanked either side of the building: small, comfortable quarters with four-poster beds, rugs, tables, chairs, and large cupboards. They went across a vestibule and Wodicka showed them the prince's quarters. On the left was the entrée room.

"This is where poor Loschek stayed." Wodicka pulled a face. "The emperor told him to keep an eye on his son!"

Then they went into the prince's bedroom, to the right of this across the passageway. Segalla noticed the wooden panelling in the door had been replaced.

"Of course," Wodicka explained. "Count Hoyos and Prince Coburg had to shatter it so as to unlock the door."

Segalla stared round the stone-vaulted bedroom: he examined the furniture and carpets and walked across to study the great bed; small tables stood on either side of it.

"The bodies were found here?"

"Of course they were."

Segalla smiled to himself but didn't turn round. He'd caught the change in Wodicka's tone and knew Kinski was warning the huntsman to keep his mouth shut. Segalla went on and opened the door to a snug bathroom, and they walked through that into a small recess where a spiral staircase led up to the floor above.

"The morning the prince was found," he asked, coming out of the bathroom, "all these doors were locked?"

Wodicka was now standing behind Kinski.

"That's right," the detective confirmed. "The door to the bedroom, as well as the door beyond leading to the spiral staircase, were both locked from the inside."

"And the windows?"

"Closed and shuttered, man!" Kinski snapped. "For heaven's sake, it was the dead of winter!" He turned to Wodicka. "It looks as if we are going to stay here. Perhaps you could light fires in two of the guest rooms?" He turned back to Segalla. "We are going to stay, are we not?"

"I am afraid so," Segalla replied. "It will be dark soon and my guests should arrive. A night journey back to Vienna will be too long and arduous."

Kinski cursed quietly even while he forced a smile. His superiors would be furious with him for allowing himself to be tricked so easily by this mysterious envoy. But what could he do? Kinski glanced around and suppressed a shiver. The shadows were growing longer, and, though he had little imagination, this bedroom—well, he had told Frau Kinski many a time that corpses never bothered him; but this was different. Perhaps it was because the heir to the Hapsburg throne had been killed here. Or was it just his strange visitor, standing so silently, staring down at the bed.

"Were the bullets removed?" Segalla asked without turning.

"I believe so!"

"How many?" Segalla asked.

"Two, I suppose."

Segalla looked around. He knew that tomorrow every obstacle would be placed in his path if he wanted to come back here; nevertheless he could see nothing amiss.

"The emperor has ruled," Kinski declared, "that the hunting lodge is to be closed and converted into a Carmelite convent. I believe this will become a chapel of reparation."

"I don't think God wants reparation." Segalla walked towards Kinski. "He wants justice."

"Even if he's a Hapsburg," Kinski replied without thinking.

Wodicka returned to say two guest rooms had been made up. Kinski sardonically ushered Segalla down the passageway into one of the prepared chambers. A pine-log fire now burnt merrily in the hearth.

"Wodicka will bring coffee. Anything else?"

"Some rolls, butter, a little jam."

Segalla undid his coat, took out a silver key, and unlocked the valise chained to his wrist. He sat down on the edge of the bed.

"My visitor will be here shortly," he announced.

In the event he was wrong. Darkness had fallen when Kinski, desperately eager to see whom Segalla was meeting, heard the noise of a carriage in the courtyard. He hurried out to stand in the doorway. A huge portly figure came swaying towards him. Kinski would have cursed with every filthy word he knew: the one man he had been told to watch Segalla's meeting! Instead he smiled, bowed, and shook the podgy hand of Monsignor Galemberti, papal ambassador in Vienna.

"Is Segalla waiting?"

Despite his great girth and white, moonlike face, broad jaw, and heavy jowls, the monsignor had a soft voice.

"He's waiting for you, Your Grace."

"In which case he shouldn't wait any longer, should he?" Galemberti took off his black, broad-brimmed hat and undid his great cape lined with red piping. "Austrian roads are terrible." Galemberti grinned puckishly. "Almost as bad as Italy's." He threw the coat and hat at Kinski whilst clutching the black brief-case even tighter in his hand. "I'll see Segalla by myself." He brought out one great paw of a hand and laid it on Kinski's shoulder. "You are a policeman?"

"Yes, Your Grace. Detective Inspector Kinski."

Galemberti pushed his face closer. "And a good Catholic?"

"Of course, Your Grace."

"In which case you will not listen at doors or keyholes, will you?"

"I never do, Your Grace!"

"Good, then keep it that way!"

The monsignor allowed himself to be escorted along the corridor. As soon as Kinski closed the door behind him, Galemberti put his small valise down and embraced Segalla. Galemberti stood back, his eyes twinkling with devilment.

"You caught them on the hop, Nicholas!"

"Not for long, Your Grace."

"Oh, stop that rubbish," Galemberti replied. "Luigi." He eased himself into a chair. Segalla sat opposite on the other side of the fireplace. "I don't want anything to eat or drink." Galemberti warned as Segalla stretched for the small handbell: "Well, not until we have finished." He opened the valise and handed across a thin file. "I have spent a lot of money," he declared. "That's all I could find. Study them at your leisure. However"— he leaned back, stretching himself, one hand held out towards the fire—"Cardinal Rampolla told me to brief you on this matter. So where do I begin?"

Galemberti paused, chewing the corner of his lip. The monsignor believed that his bluff, jovial exterior put people at their ease, made them more manageable; he didn't think this applied to the man sitting opposite, fingering his gold cuff links in the double-cuffed shirt. Segalla, in turn, was careful: Galemberti was an astute diplomat who had proved his colours in the recent conflict over whether Prince Rudolph should have a church burial. He had achieved the miraculous feat of upsetting nobody. As Cardinal Rampolla had caustically remarked, that was almost cause for instant beatification.

"Prince Rudolph," Galemberti began, "was the only son and heir of Emperor Franz Joseph and his wife, Elizabeth. You'll meet them; they are both cold fish. Franz Joseph, despite his public face and demeanour, spends more time with an actress than he does with his wife. She, in turn, loves nothing more than the giddy tour of European courts. Rudolph was a delicate child. Born in 1858, barely thirty-one by the time he died. He was given certain posts in the empire, particularly in the army. He was liberal by outlook. He believed Austria should stay away from Germany and always pressed his father to implement radical political and military reforms."

"Was he listened to?" Segalla asked.

"Hardly ever. A few days before the Mayerling disaster," Galemberti continued, "rumour has it that Franz Joseph and Rudolph had a very bitter row. God knows about what. According to my spies, and you must remember I am only repeating the tittle-tattle of the court, the emperor accused Rudolph of conspiring with Hungary to set up an independent, constitutional monarch."

"With Rudolph wearing the crown?"

"Exactly," Galemberti replied. "But it's only gossip."

"And his wife?"

"Rudolph married Stephanie of Belgium in 1881. His mother was always opposed to the marriage; at the time, Rudolph thought it was a perfect match."

"And was she?"

"God forgive me, Nicholas, but you've met her. Many call her frumpish, not very bright, gauche, lacking as much in the social graces as she does in physical beauty. They had one daughter, Elizabeth."

"And Rudolph's mental state?"

"Ah!" Galemberti clasped his thickset fingers. "Now we come to the rub, the crux of the matter. According to the autopsy, and it's in the papers I've given you, the physician claimed to have found changes in the brain which could account for the balance of his mind being disturbed." He looked squarely at Segalla. "However, first, we have no real proof they found that. Second, even if there were lesions or other damage, we have no proof they would affect his behaviour. There's no doubt that Rudolph could be dramatic, slightly hysterical: he talked of suicide, but talking and doing it are two different matters. We know he was ill. He had rheumatism, and what the physicians termed 'catarrh of the bladder.' "

"But you know more?"

Galemberti nodded, then abruptly got up and walked towards the door. He opened it, looked down the deserted passageway, closed the door, and returned to his chair.

"I bought information from the court pharmacist. According to this, Rudolph, at least two years before his death, was taking sodium salicylate as well as zinc sulfate."

"These are medicines used to cure venereal disease," Segalla added. "Specifically, gonorrhea. If that disease had reached his brain . . . ?"

"If he had that disease," Galemberti confirmed, "his behaviour would have been bizarre, but, again, there's no real proof."

"And Maria Vetsera?"

"A butterfly," Galemberti replied. "Bright, vivacious, and flirtatious. She may have been in rivalry with her mother, the Countess Helene. A few years ago, Maria's mother also flirted with Rudolph but with very little success."

"So the daughter succeeded where the mother failed?"

"So it seems."

"And the prince's moral life?"

"He was accustomed to taking mistresses. Two are well known. Countess Larisch." Galemberti wagged a finger. "You've met her. She's now treated by the court as a pariah: she's a consummate liar who changes her story as much as a ship tacks sail in a blustery wind."

"And the second?"

"Mitzi Caspar. A different sort of person altogether. Intelligent, prudent, loyal, and reserved. In the months since Rudolph's death, she has never tried to enter the limelight but keeps herself to herself."

"Was Vetsera the sort of person to commit suicide?" Nicholas asked. He picked up a poker and jabbed the burning logs, which snapped in a burst of sparks.

"No," Galemberti replied. "No, she was not. She was romantic, passionate, a little stupid, a young woman swept off her feet by the attentions of the crown prince. Shakespeare's phrase, 'More sinned against than sinning,' applies to Maria Vetsera."

Galemberti was about to continue, but Segalla, stretching over, rang the small bell. A few minutes later Wodicka appeared. Segalla realised he must have been waiting nearby. He studied the man carefully: Wodicka was no spy but simply desperate to ensure that all went well. He promised to bring sandwiches and a pot of hot coffee. Whilst they waited for him to return, Segalla did not bother to close the door. Instead, warning Galemberti with his eyes, Segalla simply chattered about Rome and the papal court, who'd received preferment and who had not. Once Wodicka had brought and served the coffee, Segalla closed the door behind him.

"Before I left Rome," he began, "Cardinal Rampolla told me the gist of the problem. To all intents and purposes, the Holy Father accepted Emperor Franz Joseph's assurance that his son and Maria Vetsera committed suicide whilst the balance of their minds was disturbed. He ignored all the rumours, including those from your good self. Nevertheless"—Segalla stared into his coffee cup—"the Holy Father is still alarmed. Franz Joseph now has no heir apparent. Prince Rudolph's daughter is only a child. The emperor has been reigning for forty years, which have seen the great empires round him grow stronger whilst the Hapsburgs grow weaker. I do not wish to teach you history, Monsignor Galemberti, but the Hapsburg Empire is also known as the Holy Roman Empire. It covers a vast, unwieldy area of central Europe, most of it Catholic. Czechoslovakia, parts of Poland, Hungary, and Austria. To the north lies a stronger Germany, and Otto von Bismarck's relationship with the papacy is not a cordial one. To put it bluntly, the Holy Father is worried. If Franz Joseph dies, his empire will disintegrate. What will happen then? Will Prussia swallow it up as it did the other German states? Or will central Europe be plunged into a terrible war as the empire tears itself apart?"

"So the Holy Father—," Galemberti began.

"The Holy Father is very worried," Segalla intervened. "Was Prince Rudolph's death an unfortunate accident? Or are there darker forces at work here?"

Galemberti put down his cup. "And what do you want from me?" he asked harshly.

"A description of the events surrounding Prince Rudolph's death. The Vatican bankers have been pouring money into your coffers, my dear Monsignor."

Galemberti shrugged to show that if Segalla was threatening him, he was not worried.

"Surely," he murmured. "Rampolla in Rome told you this?"

"A little."

"Then"—Galemberti leaned back—"let me begin from the beginning. According to what I have learnt, Rudolph left his rooms at the Hofburg Palace on the morning of twenty-eighth January. He told someone: 'Expect me tomorrow afternoon. I shall be back by five o'clock. I shall dine together with Their Imperial Highnesses.' He then went to say good-bye to Stephanie, his wife. He also told her that he would be back in Vienna on the following day, when his father, the emperor, had arranged a formal dinner party."

'So Rudolph definitely intended to stay at Mayerling only one night?'

"That's what he said," Galemberti replied. "It was an excellent way of fobbing off Stephanie. Now he left at about eleven-fifty. At the same time Maria Vetsera also left Vienna by a different route."

"And no one was concerned?"

"Well, that's where the lies begin. According to police reports, Larisch seemed to fear something might happen, as did Vetsera's mother, the Countess Helene. They both went to see, at different times, both the president of police and Count Taaffe, the prime minister. Yet Rudolph's movements were not regarded as extraordinary. An inspector was later sent to keep an eye on Mayerling, but apart from that, nothing."

"Did the prince intend to stay at Mayerling alone?"

"No. Two of Rudolph's close friends, hunting partners, Count Hoyos and Prince Coburg, were also there. Apparently Rudolph and Maria Vetsera arrived at Mayerling late in the afternoon on the twenty-eighth. Hoyos and Coburg arrived at about ten past eight the following morning. Both were looking forward to a day's shooting. As they approached the lodge, they saw all the blinds were drawn and the gates closed, as if no one was in residence."

"But the prince's servants were there?"

"Oh yes. His valet, Loschek, his favourite cabdriver, Bratfisch, and a cook—a young woman called Kati. They have all made statements to the police." Galemberti nodded towards the doors. "Of course, Wodicka, the chief huntsman, and other grooms and servitors of the stable were present." Galemberti sipped from his coffee cup. "Hoyos and Coburg were shown into the billiard room. A few minutes later the crown prince appeared, still in his dressing gown. Breakfast was served and the crown prince ate with gusto. He talked about how icy the roads were on his journey from Vienna. Because of this he'd caught a cold. So he excused himself from the day's hunt."

"And the prince's demeanour?" Segalla asked.

"He was cheerful and ate heartily enough."

"And Maria Vetsera?"

"Nothing," Galemberti replied.

Segalla sat up in the chair. "What do you mean? The woman was with him. Didn't she have her own quarters?"

Galemberti shook his head. "No. Apparently she stayed in the prince's room. Count Hoyos did not even know she was there until Loschek told him the following day, just before they broke the door down."

Segalla scratched his chin. "So the only real proof we have that

Maria Vetsera was there that Monday or Tuesday is what Hoyos found on the morning of the thirtieth?"

"Precisely."

"Continue," Segalla said.

"We don't know what happened at Mayerling during the twenty-ninth, except the prince must have stayed in his quarters. Coburg returned from his hunt early in the afternoon. He'd been invited to the emperor's dinner party at the Hofburg. Before leaving, he had tea with the crown prince, who was again in high spirits. Rudolph remarked that he had something to tell Coburg but seemed a little embarrassed. In the end, he told him nothing except to convey his regrets to the emperor that he was unable to attend the dinner party. Coburg then left Mayerling, took a cab to Baden, and caught the train to Vienna. Later in the afternoon telegrams arrived at Mayerling informing Rudolph that the Hungarian Defence Bill had been passed despite intense opposition."

Galemberti paused as a hooting owl broke the dark silence outside. The churchman shivered and smiled apologetically.

"In Italy," he remarked quietly, "they say an owl's hoot means a ghost walks."

"And Hoyos?" Segalla asked sharply.

"He came back from hunting later in the day. The prince had already sent a telegram to his wife apologising for not appearing at the emperor's dinner party because he had a heavy cold. Anyway," Galemberti hurried on, "Hoyos arrived for dinner with the prince at seven o'clock." Galemberti rested his elbows on the arms of the chair and steepled his fingers. "Again Hoyos was the only guest. Maria Vetsera made no appearance. The conversation was about the hunting skill of certain dogs."

"And the cook?"

"He also talked about Kati the cook, whose dishes"— Galemberti closed his eyes and smiled slightly—"included soup, pâté de foie gras, roast beef, venison, and sweets; the crown prince ate with considerable appetite. He also drank a modest amount of wine. According to Hoyos, Rudolph had a streaming cold but he was cordial, calm, and charming. After that Hoyos retired." Galemberti tapped his foot against the file he had brought. "In there I have a copy of a last letter from Maria Vetsera. She ends with the phrase 'Bratfisch whistled wonderfully.' "

"What does that mean?" Segalla asked.

Galemberti shrugged. "The cabman is, apparently, a very good singer and could whistle sweetly. So it means that Rudolph and Maria must have been entertained in their quarters. Apart from that, Loschek said the crown prince instructed him: 'You must not let anyone into my room, even if it is the emperor.' Then he retired."

"Loschek occupied the room next to his master's? Did he hear anything?"

"Nothing except Rudolph and Maria talking in very serious tones for most of the night, though he could not make out what was said."

"He heard them talk?" Segalla asked. "But not the sound of gunshots?"

"Ah." Galemberti raised his hand. "Let us have some more coffee. Now we come to the hub of the mystery."

# Chapter 5

"T he next morning," the monsignor continued, "at about six-thirty, according to Loschek, Prince Rudolph came into the anteroom, dressed in his morning coat. He instructed his valet to call him again at seven-thirty: Bratfisch was to be ready with his carriage. He then went back to his bedroom, whistling to himself. At seven-thirty Loschek tried to rouse his master. He was unable to do so. He also discovered both the bedroom door as well as the door leading to the spiral staircase—you've seen the room?"

Segalla nodded. "Yes I have."

"All of them were locked. Loschek peered through the keyhole; the keys were in the lock on the other side. The valet panicked. He hurried across to get Hoyos, who came and knocked as well. On getting no reply, Hoyos gave the order to break the door down. Only then was Hoyos informed that Prince Rudolph was not alone but had the Baroness Maria Vetsera with him."

"Was Hoyos surprised?" Segalla asked.

"According to all the information I have seen and people I have talked to, yes. As all this was happening, Prince Coburg arrived back from Vienna to rejoin the prince's party. He agreed the doors should be forced. First the one to the anteroom and then the door to the bedroom were forced. Loschek smashed through a panel and unlocked the door by putting his hand through and turning the keys."

"Stop," Segalla said. "Loschek was there with Hoyos and Coburg?"

"Correct."

"And who went into the bedroom?"

"Loschek. He came back and said, according to Hoyos, that Rudolph was lying bent over the bed, a large pool of blood around him. He said death had presumably been caused by poisoning: toxics such as potassium cyanide are known to produce haemorrhages."

"But no firearm?" Segalla asked. "Loschek goes into the bedchamber, his master has shot himself and his mistress, but he doesn't smell the cordite, he sees no revolver?"

"Oh, it becomes stranger still," Galemberti replied. "The reasonable thing was for Hoyos and Coburg to view the bodies. According to German intelligence they did, but in fairness to both, we must remember the heir to the Hapsburg imperial throne had been found dead. In such circumstances people are concerned: they want no blame attached to them. Hoyos especially—he had been Rudolph's guest at Mayerling. The finger of suspicion must point to him: I suspect he compromised. He probably walked into the bedroom, took a quick look, then decided to leave."

"What happened then?"

"Hoyos immediately believed he should tell the emperor. Bratfisch took him down by carriage to the Baden railway station, but before he left, he arranged for a telegram to be sent to the imperial physician, Weiderhofer, summoning the good doctor to Mayerling. Apparently Hoyos reached the Hofburg in Vienna with his news, spoke to several high-ranking courtiers, and eventually the emperor was informed."

Segalla leaned forward. "What exactly was he told?"

"That the prince and Maria Vetsera had committed suicide by taking poison."

"No mention was made of gunshots?"

"None whatsoever. Indeed, in their first communication, the

authorities tried to cover this up by saying the prince had died of a stroke or heart attack. A commission of court officials was dispatched to Mayerling to search for any documents and to enclose the body in a coffin. By the time they arrived, Physician Weiderhofer and Prince Coburg had been very busy. The revolver had been found, along with certain letters and a looking glass which Rudolph apparently used to shoot himself. Maria Vetsera was hardly changed by death. She held a rose in her hand and a small handkerchief which showed that she had cried a little."

"These letters?" Segalla asked.

Galemberti tapped his valise. "They are all in there, fragments, copies of what I have seen."

"And the story about Rudolph's suicide being due to poison?"

"Well, it wasn't until Weiderhofer returned to Vienna that the truth was told. According to witnesses, Franz Joseph's grief knew no bounds. He fell to the floor and writhed in pain." Galemberti shrugged. "The next day a postmortem was carried out and the battle with the Church authorities began over whether a suicide could be buried in consecrated ground."

Segalla got up and stretched. "And what do you think, Monsignor?"

"Do you know anything about Katherine Fieldman?"

Segalla shook his head.

"She's a Dominican nun," Galemberti continued, "who founded an orphanage in Alsace. She prophesied Rudolph's death."

Segalla pulled a face.

"Oh no, this was before witnesses, three years ago. According to Katherine, she was in Vienna during the Corpus Christi procession and caught a glimpse of Prince Rudolph. A short while later she had the following vision:

" 'I saw the crown prince sleeping, entangled in a thin net, hanging dangerously over the edge of a precipice. Then my vision changed to another direction. I saw the prince in a pavilion with many windows right in the middle of a thick wood. He was lying lifeless on the bed, his whole body covered with blood.' "

"This is ridiculous!" Segalla snapped.

Galemberti opened his eyes. "Is it, Nicholas? You are a Catholic. People have visions. Two years ago in a letter to a Viennese noblewoman, Maria Theresa, the visionary warned that,

" 'If the crown prince persists in his foolish passions, he will die a violent death.' "

Galemberti sipped from his coffee.

"Now a month ago," he continued, "the Emperor, through Archduchess Maria, asked Sister Katherine to come to Vienna for an audience. Katherine was no actress. She wrote back that she had no need to travel to Vienna, she would only be the object of many confusing questions which she had no desire to answer. However, the visionary did add,

" 'Tell the emperor that his son did not commit suicide. He was murdered. It would be easy enough for the imperial court to find the guilty person if it wanted to do so.' "

"And you believe this visionary?" Segalla asked.

"I have heard rumours." Galemberti replied. "Rumours that the wounds were not as we think: how the bullet which killed the Prince did not pass from the right to the left but from the left, behind the ear, and upwards. In addition, the Vetsera woman had a bullet hole in the crown of her head."

"So, someone came into the room and shot them?" Segalla asked. "And what was Loschek doing when all this happened?"

Galemberti smiled. "To answer your question with another question, what was Loschek doing even if the Prince did commit suicide?"

"A mystery on both counts," Segalla replied. "Here we have a young man and woman killed by bullets to the head. However, no shots were heard. Although again"—Segalla pointed to the bed—"a blanket could have been used to silence the sound, whilst the walls of the hunting lodge are quite thick, two to three feet in places."

Galemberti took a dossier from the valise and laid it on the table.

"Yet all this still doesn't solve the problem," Segalla continued, "of why Hoyos first thought that the prince and Vetsera had been poisoned."

"Read the documents with care; they might help," Galemberti replied. "Two commissions were sent to Mayerling. The first was to look for the prince's will—there's a copy of that in the folder. The second was to establish the cause of death."

"Was the pistol found?" Segalla asked.

"The autopsy refers to bullet wounds, but no, there is no mention either of the calibre of bullet or the type of gun which was used. Now," the monsignor continued, "Rudolph is supposed to have slept with at least two pistols beneath his pillow. It must have been one of these."

Segalla rose and walked towards the window.

"Let us say, my dear Monsignor, that it wasn't suicide. The problem still remains: How did an assassin get into the room, bearing in mind the doors were locked on the inside, shoot the prince and Vetsera—who, surprisingly, never resisted—then leave with no one hearing a thing?"

"I don't know," Galemberti replied, staring into the darkness. "But I have heard all sorts of gossip. One view is that the authorities in Vienna, whether the emperor or Count Taaffe, did not trust Rudolph. There was a rumour the young prince saw himself as a newly crowned king of Hungary."

"And?" Segalla asked.

"And," Galemberti replied, "accordingly, our young prince was kept under constant watch." He rose and joined Segalla at the window. "So, what happens if Rudolph was a traitor to both his father and the Hapsburg Empire? The state regarded him with deep suspicion and decided to act. Maria Vetsera's mother was very upset when her daughter disappeared on the twenty-eighth January, but the authorities showed no concern about Rudolph."

"You mean they were already having him watched?"

"Precisely," Galemberti replied. "But not by policemen. In the Austrian army, there's a unit called the Roll Commando: they are a crack corps of sharpshooters, a special force used to carry out, how can I put it, highly delicate matters of state. There are rumours that a unit of these Roll Commandos was in the woods round Mayerling." Galemberti shrugged. "What if the order was given? Rudolph is a traitor, he has to die before he causes civil war in the empire. Members of this commando corp forced a window—there's no evidence of what state they were in, open, loose, or broken—shot the prince and his young mistress, and then disappeared."

"Is that possible?" Segalla snapped, shaking his head in disbelief. "According to the evidence we have received, Franz Joseph was distraught at his son's death. I cannot believe, whatever Rudolph had done, that Franz Joseph would condone the murder of his only son and heir. Of course, others may have taken matters into their own hands. However, anybody who acted without Franz Joseph's authority would incur his imperial wrath. Such a person would have been summarily dismissed from office, not to mention arrested on charges of high treason and murder."

Galemberti sighed, and they returned to their chairs.

"Ah, well," he declared. "It's one rumour amongst many. And here's another." Galemberti picked at the tassels on the arm of the chair. "It's about Maria Vetsera. According to the autopsy, and again I am quoting rumour, she died at about two o'clock in the morning."

"Which means," Segalla replied, "that Rudolph must have sat beside her corpse for four to five hours before taking his own life. However, Loschek heard them talking well into the night, but not the revolver shot which killed her. I find that hard to believe."

"As you would," Galemberti added sharply, "that Vetsera was pregnant?"

"But if Rudolph had gonorrhea, he'd be impotent."

Galemberti shrugged. "Well if he was, perhaps Maria Vetsera changed that." He walked to the door and then turned. "I have told you all I know, Segalla; the rest is up to you. I'll give you some advice. Don't try to talk to any of the court officials: they are all under oaths of secrecy. They certainly won't tell you the truth, and if they have to speak, they will try and distract you with lies."

"And the others?" Segalla asked. "The principal witnesses, Hoyos, Coburg, Loschek, and Bratfisch?"

"Try your best, but, there again, you will find truth a rare commodity in Vienna. Tell me"—Galemberti took a step back into the room—"before he died, Rudolph is supposed to have telegraphed the Holy Father in Rome about a letter he'd sent?"

"I have heard the same," Segalla replied. "But, according to Rampolla, the Holy Father was unwilling to talk about the matter, and Prince Rudolph's letter was returned unopened."

"Then I wish you well, Nicholas."

"You'll not stay?"

Galemberti grinned. "Neither of us should be here, least of all me. You have an excuse, I don't. So I'll wait till you've studied those papers and be gone." And, opening the door, the corpulent monsignor slipped like a shadow down the passageway.

Hardly a minute passed before there was a knock on the door. When Segalla opened it Kinski and Wodicka stood there.

"You are staying the night, aren't you?" the detective asked brusquely.

Segalla tapped him on the shoulder. "My apologies to you, your wife, and your superiors, but yes I am, Joseph. I would be very grateful for whatever can be served up from the kitchen. . . ."

Wodicka bowed and hurried off. Kinski kept peering over Segalla's shoulder.

"Don't be curious, Joseph." Segalla smiled. "But tell me, do you carry a revolver?"

Kinski nodded. "A small bulldog. Seven-millimetre bore; it holds six rounds."

"May I borrow it?" Segalla asked. Then he laughed. "Don't worry, Joseph, there's no woman hidden here and I will not do myself any harm."

Kinski left and Segalla waited in the passageway till the detective returned. The revolver he handed over was small and squat.

"It's well oiled," Kinski declared.

Segalla weighed it in his hand, the barrel turned away from them.

"I'll give it back to you tomorrow morning," he promised.

Kinski made to protest.

"I'm not going to shoot anyone," Segalla replied. "I swear that. Prince Rudolph shot himself; I want to study bullets, how fast it takes to load, the grip, the trigger mechanism."

"But did he use that type?"

"Something like it," Segalla lied. "I promise, I will do no harm to myself or anyone else."

Kinski shrugged and left. Segalla walked back into the guest room. He closed the door and pulled the curtains across. He put Galemberti's dossier on the table but didn't open it until Wodicka had returned with some bread, butter, a dish of cold pheasant, and a small carafe of white wine. He placed these carefully on the table. Segalla hid his smile at the fellow's contrived slowness, his eyes constantly gazing here and there, apparently instructed by Kinski to find out what he could.

Once he had left, Segalla locked the door. He ate a little of the pheasant and bread, sipped at the wine, and then, turning his chair to the fire, opened the dossier Galemberti had left. There were two files. The first contained about thirty sheets of paper, all marked "Private and Confidential," bearing the papal notary's seal. The top piece was an extract from the postmortem carried out by the imperial surgeons at the Hofburg Palace in Vienna on 31 January 1889. A brief note from Galemberti declared that the postmortem document itself was now lost and this was only "the medical opinion published in the official State newspaper on 2 February 1889." Segalla looked up: the oil lamps Wodicka had lit were dim, so he lit a three-branched candelabra, brought it closer, and studied the medical opinion carefully.

"Firstly," the document began,

> His Imperial Royal Highness died as a result of a shattering of his skull and the interior part of the brain.
> 2) This shattering was produced by a shot fired against the right temple at close range.
> 3) A bullet fired from a medium-calibre revolver would produce the injury described.
> 4) The projectile was not found since it left the head by the exit wound which lay above the left ear.

Galemberti had inserted in brackets beside this: "Bullet later found."

> 5) There can be no doubt that His Imperial and Royal Highness himself fired the shot and that death was instantaneous.
> 6) The premature fusion of the coronal features, the clear flattening of the cerebral convolutions, and the distention of the ventricles are pathological findings which, experience shows, are usually accompanied by abnormal mental conditions.

Again Galemberti had inserted in brackets beside this: "This is not necessarily so. The damage could have been caused by the bullet. I understand from other medical men that such abnormalities can temporarily occur. His Royal Highness the Prince was suffering from a severe cold."

Segalla looked at the signatures of the physicians at the end of the "medical opinion."

"I'd love to question those," he murmured, yet realised this would be useless. If there was any conspiracy they would be carefully watched whilst he stayed in Vienna. Moreover, if they were telling lies, they were now part of the deceit.

Segalla took out his own fountain pen, putting down the gold-edged top as he once again studied the document. He doubted if the postmortem report, on which this "medical opinion" was based, still existed. Even so, the memorandum clearly showed there was something to hide. He started to write down his own criticisms.

"Point 1: Why does it say, 'Firstly, the Crown Prince died'? What is meant by 'Firstly'?" Segalla stopped writing, collecting his thoughts before continuing. "Were the physicians simply enumerating their points; if so, why not just use a number as they did later on? A person can only die once. Were the doctors implying something else killed Rudolph?" Segalla tightened his lips: "If so, what? And why the bullet wounds? Was there more than one cause of death? And had the physicians simply described the most obvious?" Segalla stared up at a painting on the wall which showed one of the great boulevards of Vienna, full of smartly dressed characters and prancing horses.

Why, Segalla reflected, did Hoyos take the news to Vienna that Rudolph had been poisoned and only later was the true cause of death published? He continued writing:

"Was the prince poisoned, then shot afterwards? And why did the doctors talk about a medium-calibre revolver? Weren't they shown the gun found near the prince? There must have been one there. What type of gun had it been? How many shots had been fired? Why hadn't they searched more thoroughly for the bullets? Galemberti had remarked that they had found one. Where was that, as well as the bullet which had killed Vetsera?"

Segalla put his pen down. Perhaps he should not write so much: even though his valise was chained to his wrist, it could still be stolen. He picked up the piece of paper, tossed it into the fire, and, leaning back in his chair, watched it turn to ash. He got up, went over, and opened his case. He searched amongst the change of clothes until his hand gripped the small leather case. Segalla took this out carefully, feeling a twinge of guilt at the deception he was planning. He undid the clasps, took out an Italian infantry officer's revolver, and weighed it carefully in his hands. Rudolph might have used something like this: nine-millimetre bore, twenty-three centimetres long and fourteen centimetres high. It had a small trigger, hammer, and a revolving drum holding six rounds. Segalla placed the gun quietly on the bed. Two years ago in Rome he had been attacked by footpads and used his revolver. He remembered the struggle in that stinking alleyway. The knife drawn back, his assailant's face grimacing in hatred. Segalla had managed to free his hand, draw the revolver, and shoot the man through the head which had shattered like a pumpkin. Now, according to what he knew, the top of the prince's scalp had been damaged, but the cranium had not been shattered, whilst Vetsera's head simply bore bullet holes.

Segalla sat down in his chair. The "medical opinion" was not worth the paper it was written on: it posed as many questions as it tried to answer. A clumsy device by some court official eager to get across the point that Rudolph's mind had been disturbed because of psychological factors. Accordingly he had committed suicide whilst his mind had been unbalanced, so the Church authorities could not refuse ecclesiastical burial. Segalla sifted amongst the other manuscripts that Galemberti had left. He picked up a brown manilla envelope with the word "Photographs" scrawled on it. There were two: both showed the crown prince's corpse. In the first, the top of his head was covered in a bandage. The second picture, however, showed the crown prince lying in state at the Hofburg after the autopsy had taken place. The head was now unbandaged, the wound to the right temple being nothing more than a long, dark scar. Segalla held the pictures up to the light. Neither photograph was a source of interesting evidence. However, the second did show how the court morticians, probably using wax and paste, had worked hard to restore the prince's shattered temple. These explained why the photographs had been taken in the first place: more propaganda to demonstrate that Rudolph had taken his life and there was nothing to hide.

The next document was a protocol dated 31 January 1889 and gave a description of the wounds to Maria Vetsera. Segalla underlined the relevant passage. "In the left frontal lobe is a ragged area of loss of skin, five centimetres long and three centimetres wide: in the neighbourhood of which the hair is singed. This, therefore, is the entry point of the bullet. This runs through the brain, ending two centimetres above the outer ear, forming a narrow, sharp-edged perforation. The bones around the exit and entry points are splintered. Likewise the top of the skull. Otherwise no other injury is observable. The injury was absolutely lethal and death must have been instantaneous."

Segalla put this down. "If the hair was singed," he murmured, "that means the gun must have been held very close to her head. If a revolver like mine had been used, even of less calibre, more shattering would have occurred." Segalla drummed his fingers on the table. What were they trying to hide? Why was Vetsera's body buried so quickly?

He recalled the information he had been given in Rome: Vetsera being found on the bed, a rose between her fingers, a small, damp handkerchief clutched between her left fingers, which meant she couldn't have fired the shot. Segalla returned to the dossier. Most of the documents were newspaper reports published before the secret police had impounded them. Segalla dismissed most of these: they either gave lurid accounts or simply repeated the changing court story. How the prince had been poisoned or died of a stroke and, finally, what they thought was the truth, that he had shot himself. At last he turned to a buff-coloured envelope which bore Galemberti's personal seal. Segalla tore this open and took out the sheaf of documents, which was prefaced by a short note from his informant.

"My dear Segalla, this is what I could find of the letters left by the crown prince and Baroness Vetsera. They are fair copies of what I could learn. They are arranged in order for you to study."

The first was to the crown prince's trusted friend Szogyeny. "Dear Szogyeny," it began.

> *I must die. That is the only way of at least leaving this world like a gentleman. Be so good as to open my desk here in Vienna in the Turkish Room where we so often sat together in happier days, and treat the papers as set out in my last will herewith enclosed. With warmest regards and with all good wishes for yourself and for our adored Hungarian fatherland.*
>
> > *I am yours ever,*
> > *Rudolph.*

There was a codicil to the letter asking that certain monies be handed over to his former mistress Mitzi Caspar, whilst "All letters from the other Countess Larisch and the little Vetsera are to be destroyed at once."

Segalla held this letter between his hands. It bore no date. Why did Rudolph say, "I must die"? As if, on the whole, he preferred not to? Moreover, this had not been written at Mayerling. The phrase "here in Vienna" meant that the letter must have been written before 28 January, when the prince left for the hunting lodge.

The second letter was to his wife, Stephanie. Segalla studied Galemberti's note at the top of the copy: "Undated and not handed to his wife until 31 January."

*Dear Stephanie,*
*You are rid of my presence and plague: be happy in your own way.*
*Be good to the poor, little girl who is the only thing that remains*
*of me. Give my last regards to all friends. I am going calmly to*
*my death which alone can save my good name.*

*Embracing you most warmly,*
*your loving Rudolph.*

Segalla underlined the last phrase before the salutation.

"Why," he muttered, "could only death save the prince's good name? In what respect and why?"

The prince's final letter also bore a memorandum from the inquisitive Galemberti, saying it had been found in a desk drawer at Mayerling. It was addressed to no one and its staccato language made it difficult to follow. The letter went on as follows:

*Mayerling, 30 January 1889: Parting!*
*Time is running short! I conclude:*

*The Emperor will not abdicate in the foreseeable future. He is*
*heading for decline. Eternal waiting with continuous injuring*
*plights and repeated serious conflicts unbearable! Aspirations with*
*regard to the family magnifique but dangerous! Be watchful! No*
*understanding anywhere but crushing matrimonial relations. The*
*young Baroness chooses the same way because of hopelessness of*
*her love for me. Expiation!*

*Rudolph.*

Segalla pushed this letter into the centre of the table and carefully grouped around it the other missives he had read.

"What have we got here?" he murmured. "A prince who believes he has to die but does not want to. A prince who finds nothing to live for." He tapped the last letter. "But this, my dear Segalla, is curious. This letter shows the prince different in both tone and tenor. It is difficult to understand, hysterical, written in a hurry and addressed to no one."

Segalla got up and walked to the window. He pulled back a curtain and stared out into the darkness. Most suicides, he reflected, are consistent. Rudolph is not. He writes letters, planning his suicide even whilst he is in Vienna. These are cool and analytic, almost as if he were being forced to commit a dreadful act. He tells no one he is going to die. Indeed, if his telegrams to Stephanie can be believed and his conversation with Count Hoyos did take place, the prince was calm, probably planning to go on a hunt or at least return to Vienna; yet suddenly he writes this strange final note just before he kills himself and his mistress.

Segalla returned to the table and opened the second file. According to Galemberti's introductory memorandum, a sealed letter from Prince Rudolph to Maria's mother was found at Mayerling and handed over to the emperor. He sent it to Vetsera's mother through her lawyer, Count Stockau, to open it in his presence. When it was, these letters from Maria Vetsera were found. Segalla now studied Galemberti's copies of these. The first was short.

> *Dear Mother,*
> *Forgive me for what I have done; I could not resist love. In agreeing with him I wish to be buried by his side. I am happier in death than in life.*
>
> > *Your Maria.*

To her sister, Hannah, she had written:

> *We are both going blissfully into the uncertainty of the beyond. Think of me now and again. Be happy and marry only for love.*

*I could not do so and, as I could not resist love, I am going with him.*

> *Your Maria.*

*P.S. Do not cry for me. I am crossing over peacefully. It is wonderful out here. Once again farewell.*

Finally to her brother, Franz, Vetsera had written,

*Farewell, I shall watch over you from the other world because I love you very much.*

> *Your faithful sister.*

Segalla sifted amongst the other documents on the table: copies of the prince's will which told him nothing. Finally, an artist's impression of what Loschek must have seen when he had broken the panel leading to the crown prince's bedroom: a mirror on the far wall, a chest of drawers, a large bed, two corpses lying there. The prince on the far right, Vetsera on the left. According to Galemberti, this had been hastily drawn by a reporter who had forced his way in and caught a glimpse before the bodies were removed. Segalla studied this, then scooped up all the documents and put them back in their file. He refilled his cup and sat down, sipping carefully. He heard a footfall in the passage outside. He grasped Kinski's revolver, holding it down by his side. He relaxed at the tap on the door.

"Pax vobiscum," the voice whispered.

Segalla rose and unlocked the door, and Galemberti swept into the room.

"I have spent my time walking round this godforsaken place." The monsignor threw his coat over the back of a chair. "It would not be difficult to imagine Rudolph and Vetsera's ghosts walk here. Well." He wheezed as he lowered himself into a chair. "What did you think of the documents?"

"With all due respect, Your Eminence," Segalla replied, "they tell me very little. The autopsies do not reveal the full truth, whilst the letters are only copies. If banknotes can be forged, so can letters." Segalla pushed out his feet. "Yet all the evidence points to Rudolph killing his mistress, then killing himself. The letters do at least show that both decided on that. No other cause of death has been put forward. The prince was highly strung. Vetsera was very young. . . ."

"And yet?" Galemberti asked.

"That's the weakness." Segalla scratched his chin. "It's almost as if, my dear Galemberti, the government is desperate to prove that it was suicide and nothing else. Otherwise, why don't they produce the full documented postmortem? Why can't these letters be studied in the original? There were court commissions sent here, yes?"

Galemberti nodded.

"Why can't their findings be made public? And, above all,"— Segalla tapped the documents—"Rudolph was a crown prince, the heir to the Hapsburg throne. What was so terrible about his life that he had to commit murder, then take his own?"

"So where will you start?" Galemberti asked. "The emperor's orders are quite explicit. You cannot look at official documents, and no one working at the court would even dream of telling the truth."

The monsignor's eyes widened as Segalla stood up, Kinski's revolver in his hand, and walked towards the window. Segalla opened this and, before the monsignor could stop him, fired twice into the night.

# Chapter 6

In Annagasse Street, in the Seventeenth District of Vienna, known as Hernels, Bratfisch the cabby man left his little house, as he always did at the same late hour. He made his way dolefully down to the small café which stood opposite Woolners stables. Those he passed glanced sly-eyed at him. Two old women busily gossiping on the steps drew back into the shadow of their houses. Once he had passed, they put their heads together.

"Oh yes," one of them breathed, fearful that the cold evening breeze might waft her words down to the stubby-legged cabby man. "A different man," she declared, "since his master died at Mayerling: reticent as a monk he is."

"He was such a good whistler," the other one replied. "And he could sing like a nightingale."

She stared at the cabby's retreating back. She felt like adding that Bratfisch was clothed in mourning black. However, Bratfisch had always dressed like that: a regular sight in his small bowler hat perched on top of his thin, horsey face, he'd go swaggering down to collect his cab and trot off to serve his imperial master. Now there was no whip in his hand, no swagger to his gait. Dour as a mourner, Bratfisch walked, shoulders stooped, head down, eyes on the pavement. As usual, he would go into the small café, where he would meet Loschek, his comrade, former gun loader and personal valet to the dead prince.

Three times a week, ever since the tragedy at Mayerling, Bratfisch and Loschek would meet at the same time, at the same table, and order the same large French cups of coffee, croissants, butter, and jam. They hardly exchanged a word of greeting. They refused to talk until the proprietor, who would have given his left arm to know what they were whispering about, had moved well away. Oh, people had tried—journalists, the curious—but they all received the same reception: blank stares and, if they persisted, a growled threat from Bratfisch that, if the intruder wanted answers, he could arrange an interview with Police President Krauss.

This evening, to begin with at least, was no different. Loschek was already sitting at the table. It was his turn to pay, so the coffee and bread had already been ordered with the greasy-aproned proprietor standing at a respectful distance. Bratfisch sat down; Loschek looked up and nodded. For a while they ate and drank silently. Then Bratfisch took out cigars, offered one to Loschek, matches were struck, and they became almost hidden behind a thick haze of smoke. When this cleared, as usual, they had their heads together whispering. The proprietor sighed and turned away. He glanced through the half-open kitchen door, deciding he could spend his time better watching young Ursula bend over the kitchen sink hoping, as he always did, that the steam would become too much for her and she would begin to unloose the buttons on her generous bodice. The door opened and the proprietor whirled round. Usually, Bratfisch and Loschek were the only customers at this late hour. Moreover, the newcomer was no local workman. He had blond hair, a luxuriant bristling moustache, a lean, sardonic face, and cold blue eyes. A soldier, the proprietor thought; the type of young man Ursula would be only too willing to lift her petticoats for. The stranger walked across.

"Coffee!" His voice was clipped. "Coffee with cream! Make sure it's fresh!" The man smiled and threw his greatcoat over his other arm. "A small glass of cognac." He looked at the tray of confectionery on the counter. "And one of your pastries."

The proprietor waved him to a table. The young man shook his head.

"No, I'll be sitting with my friends over there."

He walked across and, without being invited, picked up a chair and sat down next to Bratfisch. He leaned his elbows on the table and smiled dazzlingly at his "friends."

"Piss off!" Bratfisch growled.

The man undid his grey hunting jacket. The cabby glimpsed the holster pushed into the inside pocket. The stranger stifled a yawn.

"I've been travelling," he said. He took out a cigar, plucked Bratfisch's from his hand, and lit his own.

"Go away," Loschek asked. "Please."

"No, I won't."

The stranger handed the cigar back. He cocked his head to one side and looked searchingly at Loschek, studying his craggy face, large nose, deep-set eyes, and luxuriant muttonchop whiskers. The stranger pulled on his cigar. He was about to speak but paused as the proprietor served his coffee, cognac, and pastry. The stranger handed him a fistful of notes.

"Go away," he ordered. "Lock the door to the café. My friends and I don't want to be disturbed."

He picked up a small jug of cream and poured it slowly into the cup. Bratfisch turned, one fist raised.

"Don't do that," the stranger said. "I am not a policeman. I am not a journalist but I am very dangerous."

Bratfisch's hand fell away. The young man sipped at the coffee.

"You can call me Ernst." He smiled. "And think of me as your friend."

The two former servants of the crown prince shuffled their feet. Loschek glanced quickly at Bratfisch and winked.

"Be careful," the former valet was saying. "This man is different."

Ernst looked over his shoulder and watched the proprietor pull the bolts across.

"Now"—Ernst leaned back—"we have a lot in common. All three of us know what really happened at Mayerling."

"It was suicide," Loschek broke in.

"Tell me, Loschek," Ernst replied. "If I put a gun in your hand and pointed it at your head and made you pull the trigger." He kept his voice low. "Would that be suicide or would it be murder? Or"—Ernst pulled on his cigar, warming to his task—"what happens if I put poison in your coffee? No, no, what happens if Bratfisch put poison in your coffee and then, when you were dead, I came and put a bullet through your head? Who is the murderer? Or, let me see: what happens if you were supposed to guard someone and you didn't? You were lax in your duties and that person was murdered? Who'd really bear the guilt?" Ernst picked up the small glass of cognac and swallowed it in one gulp, smacking his lips noisily. "Or, what happens if I murdered Bratfisch here but then made it look, Loschek, my dear, as if you were the guilty party?" He grinned at both men. "Murder and suicide are identical twins! You can't tell one from the other, can you?"

"If you know so much," Bratfisch retorted, "why not go and see the police? Or, better still . . ." He scraped back his chair.

"Oh, you can do that," Ernst replied, drawing on the cigar and blowing the smoke full in Bratfisch's face. "But I might not be here when they arrive. Or, then again"—he picked up the pastry and snatched a mouthful—"perhaps I will be. I might tell them a story. I'll present myself as a loyal subject of the emperor, very curious about certain loose threads in that terrible business at Mayerling." He smiled. "The police are just as curious as everyone else."

"What loose threads?" Loschek snapped.

"Oh, the same loose threads you come here every morning to talk about," Ernst replied. "Let me see; here we have our brave crown prince putting a bullet in his young, plump mistress, then one through his stupid noddle, but no one in the hunting lodge hears it?" Ernst's fingers flew to his lips in mock curiosity. "And surely I have forgotten something? Where were the brave Loschek and Bratfisch when all this was happening?"

"We were at our posts," Loschek retorted.

"Were you?" the stranger replied. "Would Kati the cook swear to that? I mean, if she were here?"

"The prince used a blanket to muffle the noise of the shot," Loschek replied quickly. "The walls of the hunting lodge are very thick." The valet leaned forward, trying to hide his fear under a show of defiance. "Go and ask Kati where I was. In my room all night."

"Yes, no wonder the press would love to ask you that." Ernst drew his brows together. "I mean, here is our noble prince writing letters, discussing suicide pacts with his beloved and you, in the room next door, knew nothing of it."

"Even if I did," Loschek replied defiantly, "it's a long ride back to Vienna."

Ernst smiled dazzlingly. "A telegram's much quicker!"

"We have told our stories," Bratfisch declared sourly. "We knew nothing of the prince's death. Oh, he talked about it often, but people who discuss suicide very rarely do it."

Ernst looked at him, round-eyed. "And the first you knew about it was when that fat-bellied Hoyos smashed open the door?"

"He didn't do that," Loschek replied. "I did."

"Yes, yes, so you did." Ernst chewed the corner of his lip.

"You are a journalist," Bratfisch declared, turning back to the table and sipping at his coffee. "You know nothing!"

"I know you made mistakes," Ernst replied softly. "The station-master at Baden told me about Hoyos's mistake, Herr Bratfisch!"

Bratfisch's hand tightened round his cup.

"And no one has bothered to speak to Wodicka?" Ernst continued ruthlessly. "You made a dreadful mistake with him just before you drove Hoyos off to the station!"

Bratfisch began to tremble so much that he put his cup down. Loschek just sat, his mouth open, his face all drained of colour.

"Good." Ernst tapped his cigar. "Now I have your attention."

"What do you want?" Loschek spluttered. "We have no money."

"Oh, I don't want your money," Ernst replied crossly. "What I want is you to think. A man's arrived in Vienna, his name is Nicholas Segalla. He's from the Vatican. Dark-faced, sharp-eyed, he's no man's fool. The emperor controls the police and his empire. The Great Powers like Germany and France have to keep their suspicions to themselves. However, that old fool in the Vatican is a different matter. He has a yearning for the truth. For all I know he may even feel slightly guilty about Rudolph's death. Oh yes"—he fluttered his eyelids—"you can see how much I know. Now Segalla," Ernst continued, "might ask you questions."

"And what do you suggest?"

"What do I suggest?" Ernst smiled. "Now, the real reason for my visit. All three of us know what happened at Mayerling. The truth, the real truth." He pulled on his cigar. "Kati the cook also knew the truth," he continued. "She did a little plundering of her own." He shrugged. "We let that go, but leaving Vienna?" He grinned at their shocked faces. "Oh, yes, she's left for good. Don't worry about her, that's what I've come to tell you: don't worry. Keep your mouths shut and stay where we can see you and all will be well."

"What happened to Kati?" Loschek asked.

"Just think about what I have said," Ernst retorted, "and all will be well. Just that." He stubbed out his cigar, drained his coffee cup, and got to his feet. "It's all so beautifully complex," he murmured. "Everyone's guilty."

Bratfisch also rose. "Where are you from?" he asked. "The emperor?"

"Yes, you could say that," Ernst replied. "And, then again, perhaps you couldn't."

"Were you out at Mayerling?" Bratfisch asked. "When our master . . ."

"Why on earth should I be there?" The stranger stepped back in mock anger. He tapped Bratfisch on the chest. "What on earth are you implying, my dear chap? How was I to know our poor prince was going to commit suicide?"

And, spinning on his heels, the stranger walked to the door. He pulled back the bolts and walked out into the night.

Segalla stood at the entrance to the dead prince's bedroom in the hunting lodge at Mayerling. He deliberately closed his mind to the confusion and chaos he'd caused the night before. Even Galemberti had protested before sweeping out, muttering under his breath. Kinski had fairly danced with rage, but Segalla really didn't care. He had studied once again everything Galemberti had left and reached the conclusion that what the papal nuncio had provided posed more questions than answers. He had slept for a while and was determined to be here, standing in the very spot Hoyos had on the morning Crown Prince Rudolph had been found dead. The windows were shuttered, the curtains pulled. Segalla had lit the candles, taken up his position again, and then blown them out before studying the bedroom carefully. Despite the rising sun, the room was very dark.

"Well, well, well!" Segalla took two or three more paces into the bedroom. "I have learnt two things. . . ."

"And I have learnt you're a dangerous man."

Segalla whirled round.

"My dear Joseph."

"You shouldn't be here!" Kinski retorted.

"I know," Segalla apologised, coming back and closing the door behind him. "But I told Wodicka I had your authority to have it opened." He saw the anger flare in the detective's eyes. "Don't blame him, blame me."

"I do." Kinski took a step nearer, his usually cheery face now tight in anger.

"Now, Joseph!"

"Don't Joseph me!" Kinski said. "You know and I know that I have to report to my superiors everything that has happened. They will not be pleased. Last night, firing a pistol twice in the dead of night!" He put his hand out. "I want mine back."

Segalla took it from his pocket and handed it over.

"I fired the pistol, Joseph. You came running." He saw the detective's face relax. "Now, if you want to tell your superiors about how two gunshots in the dead of night can be heard on the other side of the lodge by you and Wodicka, not to mention Sergeant Brunner, then that's your business. Now I suspect you have a very low opinion of Baron Krauss's intelligence, but even he will realise what I have established: if you had heard the gunshots, why weren't they heard when Prince Rudolph killed himself?"

"There was no one about," Kinski replied; then he could have bitten his tongue out.

"Exactly!" Segalla replied. "And there wasn't last night either."

"And this?" Kinski pointed to the bedroom door.

"Well, Joseph, the door to the prince's bedroom was forced round about eight o'clock on the morning of January thirtieth, yes?"

Kinski nodded.

"And, being the dead of winter, there'd be very poor light?"

"Agreed."

"Don't forget, if the prince and his mistress had been left alone for some time, the lamps and candles would have burnt out. Consequently," Segalla continued, "the room would be in complete darkness: Loschek hurries across to the bed and glimpses blood. He thinks the prince has taken poison and haemorrhaged. He hurries out and tells Count Hoyos, who probably is reluctant to come into the room. Our good nobleman glimpses the death scene and hurries off to Baden." He paused as he glimpsed the cynicism in Kinski's eyes. "What's the matter, Detective?" he asked brusquely.

"Oh, I take what you say about Count Hoyos." The policeman smiled. "But I must admit your rash action in shooting a revolver twice in the air in the dead of night has made me think. It sounded like a thunderclap." He jabbed a finger at the bed. "But a pillow could have deadened the sound of the fatal gunshots."

Segalla opened his mouth to reply but then decided not to. "You came looking for me, Joseph?" he asked.

"We have just received a telegram," Kinski replied. "The line between here and Vienna is still connected." Kinski pulled a face. "Police President Krauss is not pleased. He expected to see you at the Hotel Imperial, or at least his spies did."

"And?" Segalla asked.

Kinski heaved a sigh. "I telephoned Krauss last night. I told him where you are. He's furious. He says you are to return immediately. The emperor wishes to see you at noon in his summer palace at the Schonborn."

"Where's the telegram?" Segalla asked.

"It's waiting with your breakfast on the table in the billiard room."

"Then you'd best get it," Segalla replied. "Don't you know the diplomatic protocol? That telegram should be brought immediately to me."

"Breakfast is waiting," Kinski answered.

"And so am I," Segalla replied.

Kinski strode off. Segalla waited until the detective was gone; then, putting his hand into his greatcoat pocket, he felt for his revolver pouch and hurried back into the darkened bedroom. He seized a bolster and ripped a blanket from the bed. He padded these together and, in quick succession, fired two bullets. The shots still rang in a long echo as Kinski came charging back into the room.

"For the love of heaven!" the detective roared, his face red with fury.

He advanced threateningly on Segalla, who stood at the other side of the bed, slipping his revolver back into the pouch, impervious to the goose feathers and pieces of fabric floating about. If Kinski knew anything about diplomatic protocol, he forgot it now. He dashed round the bed and seized Segalla by the lapels of his coat. His usually gentle eyes were now blazing with fury, his lips curled in anger.

"You bastard!" he hissed through clenched teeth. "You arrogant bastard!"

"Are you going to hit me?" Segalla asked quietly. "If you strike my face, the emperor might notice the bruise. So I suggest a blow to the chest or stomach."

"It doesn't matter." Kinski let go and pushed him away and stood, chest heaving, hands clenched. "Do you wish me sacked?" he bellowed. "You will get back into your first-class carriage and travel back to Rome whilst Joseph Kinski explains to his wife and children that his career is in tatters. You haven't been twenty-four hours in the country and you have done more damage to my reputation than a career full of mistakes!"

Segalla sat down at the foot of the bed.

"I am sorry," he apologised. "Truly I am. You are a good detective, Kinski. Before I left Rome, Cardinal Rampolla told me that you were waiting for me, the best policeman in Vienna. A good Catholic, a good family man, who has grasped the collar of more malefactors than the best in Scotland Yard or the Surete in Paris." He held a hand up. "He told me how, in Vienna, if a case proves impossible, then they call on Kinski. You can't be bought or sold. You take no bribes. You belong to no secret societies. You adore your wife and children." He smiled thinly. "Can't you see, that's why they put you with me? You won't take my gold or silver. You won't be fooled by promises of promotion or possibly a letter of congratulation from the Holy Father."

"Why did you take my revolver when you had your own?"

"I wanted to establish certain facts. I fired yours out of the window in the dead of night. You heard it. If I'd used my own, you would have demanded I hand it over. I then used my own, during the day, and tried to silence the sound." Segalla spread his hands. "I'm sorry for the deceit."

Kinski ran his finger round the collar of his shirt, shaking his head.

"And when I see the emperor," Segalla continued, "I shall protest bitterly about your presence. How you have impeded my every step. How I could have learnt much more from my trip to Mayerling if you had not been present."

Kinski sat down on the bed beside him.

"I am sorry I grabbed you." He smiled weakly. "You say I can't be bought but now you are flattering me."

"No, I am telling the truth," Segalla retorted. "You have a task to do and so have I. Don't forget that the emperor and his ministers have been waiting for me. They'll have everything tied up in neat little bows. All paths blocked. People will be unavailable for questioning. Documents that are too sensitive to be produced will be lost." He grasped Kinski's hand and squeezed it. "What would you do if our positions were reversed?"

Kinski nodded. Segalla looked round the bedroom.

"I wager if I came here again there'd be a regiment of guards and a multitude of imperial flunkeys watching my every step. I'll never get the opportunity again."

"And now you've proved," Kinski retorted, "that even with the use of a heavy bolster and a thick blanket, the sound of a gunshot cannot be silenced." He stared round at the mess on the bed. "Wodicka will be furious," he added.

"Now he can be bought," Segalla replied.

He opened his coat and drew out a heavy brown wallet. Kinski hid his surprise at the thickness of the sheaf of notes wedged there.

"I was supplied with money," Segalla explained, "before I left Rome. And I can draw on any bank in Vienna." He took out a sheaf of notes and thrust them into Kinski's hand. "Give that to Wodicka." Segalla stood up. "And I think I have spent enough time here. We can break our fast on the journey to Vienna." He caught Kinski staring at him curiously. "What's the matter, man?"

"The phrase." Kinski got to his feet. "To break your fast? It's antiquated. It's as if you are a monk or a priest."

"Perhaps I am. Perhaps I was." Segalla put his wallet away. "But tell the good Sergeant Brunner we should be out of Mayerling"—he drew his watch out of his pocket—"well, within a quarter of an hour."

They made their abrupt farewells and left, Brunner driving the horses at a fast trot. For a while Segalla slept whilst Kinski made notes in his small leather pocket book. When the carriage began to slow down, Segalla woke. He pulled back the blinds and looked out. The countryside was beginning to disappear: it was now dotted with small villages and farms.

"We should stop for a while," he remarked. He tapped his stomach. "Something for the inner man. Yes, Joseph?"

Kinski turned, pulled back the flap, and shouted instructions to Brunner to stop at the next hotel. A few minutes later they did, and took coffee and biscuits in the small, deserted lounge. Brunner slurped his cup quickly and, grunting, stretched over and refilled it. Then, sitting back, he lit his pipe and began to puff slowly on it. Kinski grinned and pointed to him.

"I have always said he could be a fire-eater. It's that foul pipe he smokes."

Brunner took it out of his mouth, blowing perfect circles of tobacco smoke.

"Do you think," he asked squarely, "all this running round the countryside will achieve anything? Do you really hope to catch an assassin this way?"

"Why do you think the crown prince was murdered?" Segalla asked quietly.

Kinski glowered at his subordinate. Brunner, unperturbed, drew on his pipe and blew some more smoke rings.

"I'm assigned to this case as well," he said crossly. "I'm driving the bloody carriage."

Kinski grinned at Brunner's usual bluntness. "My sergeant has a theory on everything," he added wearily.

"And, unlike my inspector," Brunner answered tartly, "I couldn't give a damn about my superiors in Vienna."

Kinski pulled a face and picked up his coffee cup. Segalla watched them with interest. Superficially there were tensions between these two, yet Brunner apparently respected Kinski, who, in turn, tolerated his sergeant's directness.

"I just think it's strange," Brunner continued, "that our crown prince, the heir apparent to the imperial throne, is allowed to go wandering outside the city in the dead of winter with only a valet and a cabby driver to look after him."

"Which means," Segalla remarked, "that secretly they did watch him, I mean the authorities in Vienna."

"That's where my sergeant is mistaken," Kinski interrupted. "The crown prince's great hobby was hunting. He invited two of his old friends, the prince of Coburg and Count Hoyos, to Mayerling. What's more important is that the court did not learn, until too late, that Maria Vetsera was accompanying him."

"That's a load of bloody nonsense!" Brunner interrupted. "Mother Vetsera was looking for her daughter on the very day she disappeared from Vienna. Every policeman in the city knows that."

Segalla put his cup down. "I've heard the same. However, just because a Prince takes his mistress on a hunting trip, that doesn't mean they're both contemplating suicide."

"No, it doesn't," Brunner retorted. "But study the newspapers, Herr Segalla, and the court circulars, they're now full of reports of how ill the Prince was. How he mentioned suicide on many occasions. If that was the case, surely Rudolph should have been watched?"

"But it would appear," Segalla replied, "that the Prince left many indications that he would return to Vienna."

"Aye he did." Brunner sucked on his pipe. "But they can't have it both ways. If they thought he was ill, why did they let him go or not supervise him better? And, if he wasn't ill . . . ?"

"Why should a healthy man commit suicide?" Segalla finished quietly.

"It was love," Kinski interrupted. "He and Vetsera were deeply in love."

"Aye and so am I," Brunner replied. "There's a young girl in the sweet shop I go to every morning to buy tobacco. I love her deeply and I think she likes me. But, whatever happens, I am not going to commit suicide over her."

"But you are only a sergeant," Kinski teased.

"Aye," Brunner replied. "And Prince Rudolph, God bless him, was all high and mighty. What I can't understand is that here is a man who's supposed to commit suicide with his mistress for love. Correct?"

Segalla nodded smilingly. Brunner jabbed the stem of his pipe towards him.

"But if this Prince loved Vetsera so much, why did he spend a night with a former mistress only two days before he left for Mayerling?"

Segalla sipped from his coffee cup and shook his head. Sergeant

Brunner was stating what he already knew, but after his visit to Mayerling, Segalla could now see how complex the mystery was. If Rudolph was suicidal, he should have been watched. If he wasn't, why commit suicide? If he was so in love with Vetsera to forge a suicide pact, why return to former mistresses? If he shot himself, why weren't others alerted by the noise? If he was murdered, how was it done so silently, without anyone being suspected, never mind apprehended?

He glanced up. Brunner was grinning at him.

"Welcome to the maze, Herr Segalla! Clever, yes?" Brunner tapped his pipe bowl on the ashtray. "Too clever by half," the sergeant growled. "That's why I think it's murder."

# Chapter 7

B runner's carriage sped up through the avenue of trees towards the main entrance of the Schonborn Palace. Segalla
glimpsed slender obelisks which some previous emperor had
decorated the grounds with. Now and again they'd pass lonely
enclosures decorated with marble statues or ornate fountains,
whilst here and there, glinting across the park, the greenhouses
and conservatories, for which the palace was famous, caught and
reflected the afternoon sun. The carriage stopped in front of the
main doorway, a huge, intricately carved portico.

"You'd best go in yourself," Kinski remarked dryly. "Policemen always use the back entrance."

Segalla winked at him and got out, handing his hat and cane
to a periwigged flunkey; he followed another, as resplendent as
a turkey-cock in his stiff brocaded jacket and powdered wig, up
into the palace, along corridors decorated in the rich baroque
style. Every inch of wall was covered in paintings and tapestries:
each niche was filled with statues or heavy vases full of dry, stiff-
ened flowers. The atmosphere in the palace was oppressive; the
steel tips of Segalla's boots echoed like a drumbeat whilst the
flunkey seemed to glide ahead of him like a ghost. Segalla noticed the man wore soft leather pumps. Now and again they
passed servants or even soldiers on guard; these, too, wore soft
footwear. Segalla recalled the Empress Elizabeth suffered from violent headaches and could not abide any strident noise. They
went up a broad, sweeping staircase, its marble steps covered in

thick Turkish carpet, then down a well-lit passageway. Here the servant left him and a court chamberlain, stiff as a statue, led him through adjoining rooms towards the imperial presence.

Segalla pinched himself against the air of unreality as he experienced the oppressiveness for which the Viennese court was so notorious: rooms silent as the grave; servants who moved in the shadows, ruled by a rigid code of etiquette; sentries wearing ornate costumes which would have been out-of-date a hundred years earlier; above all, the stuffy court protocol where, at each door, one official was replaced by an even more exotic one until the chamberlains, who led Segalla into the imperial presence, were dressed like the field marshals of some Ruritanian army, their different coloured jackets covered with medals.

The imperial salon was a welcome relief. A fire burnt in the hearth and the windows were flung open. The emperor and empress, who knew of his arrival, sat together on a couch, hands clasped. They reminded Segalla of puppets, mannequins acting out a part, loving husband and doting wife, though the confidential reports from the Vatican told him differently. Franz Joseph, for all his stiff sobriety and public virtue, enjoyed the favours of an actress. Empress Elizabeth, her dark beauty now fading, spent most of her time in a meaningless pursuit of pleasure: travelling hither and thither across the empire, absorbed in horses, her one and only real interest. As the chamberlains closed the door behind him, Segalla sank to one knee before the couch. He first kissed the emperor's hand, then that of Empress Elizabeth; both were cold. Neither stirred, and Segalla wondered whether they'd keep him kneeling. And if they chose to do so, he'd have little choice: it would not be the first time the Hapsburg court had kept some unwanted envoy on his knees. He heard a match strike and glanced up quickly. Franz Joseph was busily lighting a thick Cuban cigar. The empress, as doll-like as ever, was staring fixedly at him.

"Oh, for goodness' sake!" Franz Joseph suddenly stirred. He

blew out the match and unloosened the buttons of his jacket. "For goodness' sake, Segalla, sit down!" He indicated a chair opposite.

Segalla bowed and did so. The empress smiled as if that were what she wanted as well, but Segalla was not fooled. The emperor had acted as if he were being absentminded. In reality he had made Segalla kneel longer than usual, just to remind the papal envoy that he was not too welcome in Vienna. Franz Joseph picked up a small bell on the table beside him and rang it. The door opened and servants entered, carrying trays.

"You'll have some tea, Segalla? Good, good, good!"

Franz Joseph drew on his cigar and watched as the servants filled china cups, placing them delicately on tables; these were followed by small, exquisitely gilt-edged plates bearing the same pattern, and then silver forks, napkins, and delicious-looking pastries.

"Come, come, eat." The emperor took his plate and, cutting up a piece of cake with his fork, popped it into his mouth.

Elizabeth, like some doll, did likewise, her hands trembling slightly. Now and again she'd tut under her breath as a crumb fell onto her black brocade dress. The servants left.

"You had a good journey?" The emperor dabbed his mouth with a napkin, put the plate back on the table, and returned to his cigar.

"Yes, Your Highness."

"You should have come here first." Franz Joseph smiled through the billowing smoke. "You have an excellent suite of rooms at the Hotel Imperial?"

"I thought it best if I visited Mayerling, Your Highness."

Empress Elizabeth's head went down as if the very mention of the hunting lodge brought back memories.

"Why are you here?" the emperor asked bluntly.

"His Holiness is disturbed," Segalla answered. "Your son died in mysterious circumstances. Your Highness may remember how the Holy Father allowed a Church burial—"

"Yes, yes, yes!" the emperor interrupted. "I know all that. My gratitude to Rome is a matter of public record. Why do you have to come back?"

Segalla decided to end this verbal fencing once and for all.

"I have seen telegram number eight thirty-five," he declared.

Some of the ebullience left Franz Joseph's eyes.

Segalla continued remorselessly. "Your Highness may recall telegram number eight thirty-five, in which you promised the pope how, in the fullness of time"—Segalla used a scriptural phrase—"His Holiness would know the truth about what happened at Mayerling on January thirtieth this year."

Franz Joseph flicked the cigar ash, not caring that it fell on the carpet, but simply rubbing it in with the toe of his boot.

"Oh yes, I remember. I met you on the day of my son's funeral, Segalla. I have told you and the Holy Father the truth. My son, whilst the balance of his mind was disturbed, killed the Vetsera woman and then took his own life."

"And you'll let me see the documentary evidence?"

Franz Joseph shrugged. "Impossible. Most of it has been destroyed." He leaned forward. "You must have expected that reply."

"Why was it destroyed, Your Highness?"

"To curb those who would like to poke about in matters which do not concern them," the empress whispered.

Elizabeth now sat with her hands in her lap, her beautiful, jet black hair covered by a veil.

"You must have expected such a reply." The empress repeated her husband's words carefully as she raised her ivory white face.

Segalla steeled himself against the agony in those beautiful eyes.

"The Vatican," Segalla replied slowly, "is not poking about, Your Excellencies, for the sake of causing pain." He bowed to the emperor. "May I be blunt?"

"I wish to God you were."

"You do not want me here," Segalla replied. "Let us, for the sake of argument, accept that what you have told me about your son's death is the truth. Nevertheless, it was a dreadful act: we have a Hapsburg prince, heir to the imperial throne, who shoots a seventeen-year-old girl and then kills himself. The less the world knows about that the better: suicide and murder are best hidden."

Empress Elizabeth's shoulders began to shake, and she put her face in her hands. Franz Joseph, however, did not even bother to glance in her direction. Instead he watched Segalla, his icy, protuberant blue eyes never flinching.

"I speak the truth," Segalla declared. "But I apologise for the pain I cause. You may call it blunt to the point of coarseness. Nevertheless, Your Highness, what happens if you are wrong? What happens if others caused your son's death?" He paused as Franz Joseph drew deeply on his cigar. "What happens," Segalla asked, "if forces outside, or even within, the empire conspired to destroy your son?"

"I would take the appropriate action," Franz Joseph declared.

"Would you?" Segalla replied. "Would you really? What could you do? Aren't you curious about the anomalies in the published story?" He held up his hand. "If your son's mind was so disturbed, why was he allowed to go to Mayerling by himself? Secondly"—Segalla let his hand drop—"yes, I have been to Mayerling: I have seen the prince's quarters. Here we have a young man fire a revolver in the middle of the night or just before dawn, yet no one heard it? Thirdly, why did Count Hoyos report to you that your son had been poisoned? Why are there rumours," Segalla continued ruthlessly, "that a special unit of the Roll Commandos was in the forest near Mayerling? Why were the police not called in to investigate? Why weren't the findings published? Why were the records destroyed? Why are those"— Segalla chose to ignore Empress Elizabeth's sobs—"who attended your son's corpse sworn to secrecy?" Segalla let his hand drop. "Why this secrecy? Why all this obfuscation?"

"I don't know." The Empress Elizabeth's head came up.

Segalla was shocked at the change in her expression: her face seemed to have aged in minutes. A muscle high in her cheek was twitching, and her hands, clasped tightly together, came up and down on her lap.

"I don't know! I don't know! I don't know!" she exclaimed.

Franz Joseph stared at his wife; his hands went out as if to embrace her, but then fell back. He glanced quickly at Segalla, and in that look, Segalla realised the truth.

"You don't really want to know, do you?" he whispered. "Your Excellency is telling me the truth, or at least some of it. You don't really know the full truth and I suspect you really don't want to know!"

Segalla was sure the emperor was going to agree with him.

"Your Excellency," he insisted. "You must open your eyes and your mind to the real dangers present here. If your son was murdered by some group or individual, either here in the empire or elsewhere, then your throne, not to mention its relationship with the Holy See, is in grave jeopardy." Segalla remembered his hushed conversations with Cardinal Rampolla. "You now have no heir." Segalla's voice had dropped almost to a whisper. "What would happen, Your Excellency, if some accident, God forbid, happened to you?"

"There are other princes," Franz Joseph interrupted quietly, though he didn't raise his head.

"There is no heir," Segalla repeated remorselessly. "At a time when your empire needs one. To the north and east are two great empires: the kaiser looks hungrily towards those Germans who, he believes, should be part of a 'Gross Deutschland' whilst the czar sees himself as the protector of those Slavs in Serbia and Bosnia. If Germany moved to secure its so-called rights, Russia would move as well. And if Russia moves, France is sworn, through numerous treaties, to aid and protect it."

"And if France moves?" The emperor was now looking at him. "Great Britain acts as well."

"Yes, Your Excellency. As the Hapsburg Empire unravels, the Great Powers will not stand and idly watch."

Franz Joseph leaned back in his chair. "And does the Holy Father really concern himself with the affairs of this world?"

"The Holy Father," Segalla replied, "believes that all of Europe is sliding towards a war. He is no prophet with some divine insight. Thirty-three years ago your armies were defeated at Sadowa. Austria still smarts at this Prussian victory. Twenty-eight years ago the Prussians bombarded Paris: France remembers and demands the return of Alsace-Lorraine from the kaiser."

"And, of course, Britain," the emperor added slyly, "is fearful of the growing German navy and the kaiser's dream of a great empire in Africa."

Segalla paused. For the first time he felt unsure. The emperor caught his mood. He smiled and, getting up, walked round the back of the couch to a table. He fumbled with some keys, opened a drawer, and took out a manilla envelope. He dropped this into Segalla's lap and went and sat by his wife.

"You may open it, Herr Segalla." He smiled thinly. "True, Austria is not as strong or powerful as it once was. True, we are overawed by a great Germany and a Russia which masses its troops constantly on our borders." He spread his hands. "True, we are the most faithful son of the Holy Father, but we, too, have our friends in high places. Your master, Cardinal Rampolla, has perhaps not told you everything. The Vatican has other reasons for prying into what happened at Mayerling."

Segalla opened the envelope and took out the sheet of paper inside. He studied this carefully. Written in English, under the heading "Most Confidential and Secret," was a copy of a tele-gram sent personally by the British prime minister, the earl of Salisbury, to Cardinal Rampolla at the Vatican. The British prime minister gave a short but caustic analysis of the growing rivalry between the Great Powers that was very similar to the discussion he had just had with Franz Joseph. However, in the final paragraph, the British prime minister had written:

> We ask his holiness to use what powers he can to establish the true facts behind the death of the Imperial Prince Rudolph at Mayerling in January 1889:
> 1. Was Prince Rudolph murdered?
> 2. If so, was it the work of outside forces?
> 3. Or was it the work of some group or person at the Imperial court who wished to destabilise the Austrian Empire?

Salisbury concluded, "In the interests of peace it was essential that these questions be addressed and answers sought. H.M. Government would be most grateful for any help the Vatican could provide in this matter."

Segalla hid his smile. Now, at least he felt the circle was complete. He had speculated on why the papacy was so absorbed with Rudolph's death. He understood Leo XIII's fears, but now he could detect Rampolla's hand. The Catholic Church in England was coming out of the catacombs; by sending Segalla to Vienna, the Vatican was cooperating with the British government, and might win concessions not only for Catholics in England but also in Ireland, on the verge of civil war.

"Poor Rudolph," the emperor murmured. "He seems to be more important in death than he was in life."

Segalla handed the paper back.

"You knew all that, of course?" Franz Joseph asked ironically.

"Of course," Segalla lied. "Your Excellency," he continued,

"I know my questions must pain you, but the sooner I have the answers, the quicker I will leave Vienna."

Franz Joseph spread his hands. "What I can I will tell you: my son and I were estranged."

"Over what?"

"Over matters of policy. Rudolph was young and liberal. He disliked the papacy. He thought I was authoritarian, that our army was weak. He did not like our close alliance with Germany."

"Did he conspire against you?" Segalla asked.

Franz Joseph flicked the ash from his cigar, then placed his hand over his wife's.

"Nonsense," he retorted. "Oh, I have heard the stories about how my son was supposed to be conspiring to make himself king of Hungary, an independent sovereign ruler." He made a rude sound with his lips. "Pipe dreams! Not even Rudolph was that stupid!"

"How stupid was he?" Segalla asked quietly.

"Oh, he meddled. Very friendly with a Jew," the emperor added disdainfully. "A newspaper editor, Szeps. He encouraged Rudolph to think of himself as the people's prince." His eyes became softer. "Rudolph hasn't seen the riots in the streets, the piles of bodies left to rot when the radicals have had their day."

Segalla sipped from his cup.

"Was he a happy man?"

"Who is happy?" Franz Joseph retorted.

"Rudolph was very young," Segalla answered. "A prince with literally the world at his feet, yet he committed suicide. A man who once told his sister Valerie, 'If I could live to be a hundred, I would still be distraught at the idea of death.' "

"We are all like that," the Empress Elizabeth replied sharply.

She had withdrawn her hands from her husband's and was now tightly clutching the front of her dress.

"Then why did he change?" Segalla asked.

"He was ill," the emperor replied quickly. "He had different infections, a severe fall from his horse. The doctors will tell you that, when they did the postmortem, his brain was damaged. He was of unsound mind. His head was turned by the attentions of the little Vetsera, not to mention the drink and the morphine."

"But did you have him watched? Your Excellency, the Austrian secret service is famous. . . ."

Franz Joseph stubbed out his cigar on one of the fine china plates.

"Rudolph was eccentric. I'll answer your questions bluntly: yes, he was watched. We knew he was going to Mayerling. There was a small squad of the Roll Commandos in the woods nearby, but they stayed there. They reported nothing amiss. What we didn't know was that the Vetsera woman was with him."

"But with all due respect, Your Excellency," Segalla replied, "Maria's mother told that to Baron Krauss, the police president, as well as to Count Taaffe, your prime minister."

"They didn't think it was important," the emperor snapped.

"Did your son's moods change?"

"He was given to fits and tantrums," Franz Joseph replied. "Sometimes he drank, a little unwisely."

"But nothing remarkable?"

"No, nothing remarkable!"

"Your Excellency, if I may . . . ?" Segalla paused.

"Ask!" the emperor snapped.

"There are rumours that you and your son had a violent quarrel only a few days before he took his own life."

"That's a lie. I do not wish to discuss it any further."

"And when did the prince plan to go to Mayerling?"

"He left on the twenty-eighth," Franz Joseph replied. "But, from what we can gather, he invited Count Hoyos eight days beforehand, when they were both at the imperial hunting reserve at Orth on the Danube."

"And this was well known in the court?"

"Oh yes."

"And you saw no danger in it?"

"Why should I? Rudolph loved his hunting. Mayerling was his favourite lodge."

"Yet, Your Highness, on the twenty-ninth, you hosted an imperial dinner party for the German ambassador?"

"I thought Rudolph would return," Franz Joseph replied. "But he claimed to have a cold. He was with Loschek and Bratfisch, not to mention Count Hoyos and Prince Coburg. I could see no need to worry."

"And did Count Hoyos ever explain why he brought the wrong message to Vienna?"

Franz Joseph sighed. "Yes, that did intrigue me. Count Hoyos is a good friend of the family, a close confidant of Rudolph." The emperor smiled bleakly. "Segalla, you have been to Mayerling and used your wits. Hoyos did not go fully into the room, it was dark. Loschek reported that the prince was dead, lying in a pool of his own blood. He drew that conclusion and then he left. Hoyos wasn't a doctor."

"And what happened to the items in the room?" Segalla asked.

"They don't concern me. They were burnt, destroyed. Otherwise there would have been a black market in grisly relics."

Franz Joseph stood up. Segalla did likewise.

"Herr Segalla"—Franz Joseph gently brushed some ash from the lapel of his jacket—"this is becoming quite ridiculous. The questions you are now asking are totally irrelevant."

"If I had the relevant documents, Your Excellency."

"You cannot!" The emperor almost shouted, red spots of anger high in his pale face. "Herr Segalla, there is a protocol to these matters!"

Segalla bowed and apologised.

"Someone else wishes to see you." The Empress Elizabeth spoke up. She stepped by her husband and came so close, Segalla could see the red flecks in her eyes and how thickly covered with paste her face was.

"You have an invitation, Herr Segalla. The Princess Stephanie wishes to see you before you leave, and we have graciously granted that request." Her body became stiff with anger, her lips one thin, bloodless line. "In the end, Herr Segalla, my son was destroyed by his unhappy pursuit of women. I blame Vetsera for turning his mind to morbid fantasies. Vetsera, Larisch, and Caspar!" The words were spat out like bullets. "But, above all, his good wife, so prim and proper, so judgemental—and coming from the family she does!"

Segalla just stared back. He'd heard the stories about Stephanie's father, Prince Leopold of Belgium: a notorious womaniser, he'd even been refused an audience by Queen Victoria. His own wife had left him until the Catholic Church had ordered her to return as a matter of Christian duty.

"Tush, tush now!" Franz Joseph took a step forward, placing a hand gently on his wife's shoulder. "There's no need for this. Stephanie is heartbroken, as we all are."

The emperor picked up the bell and rang it. The door opened and two chamberlains came into the room.

"Take Herr Segalla," the emperor ordered, "to Crown Princess Stephanie's apartments." He extended a hand for Segalla to kiss. "Before you leave for Rome, Herr Segalla, you will have a chance to, er"—the emperor paused—"to ask all your questions. But, in the meantime . . ." He let his words hang in the air.

"One final matter." Segalla drew himself up. "Joseph Kinski, the detective. Is he really necessary?"

"Yes!"

"He is a thoroughgoing nuisance!" Segalla snapped. "He hinders and obstructs. My visit to Mayerling was innocuous, yet I was hustled—"

"Kinski is there for your protection," Franz Joseph interrupted. "To guarantee your safety. If he goes, so must you."

Segalla took his cue, kissed the proffered hand, and followed the chamberlains out into the corridor.

He was led along the corridor up a flight of stairs and into a room where Crown Princess Stephanie, still dressed in black, sat at a table reading a book. She smiled and rose as Segalla entered. He kissed her hand, then she grasped his elbow and steered him to one corner of a couch whilst she sat down opposite him.

"I heard you were coming," she exclaimed, clapping her hands in pleasure. "And we have so few visitors."

Her face was plumper, smoother than the last time they'd met. Stephanie was more serene, clothed in widow's weeds; she seemed to have come to terms with both her loss and her lack of status. For a few moments they exchanged pleasantries, Segalla conveying His Holiness's good wishes and politely receiving hers in return.

"Madam." Segalla shifted on the couch to face her more directly. "Your father-in-law said you wished to see me."

"Yes, yes, I do." Stephanie splayed out her fingers and studied the rings before glancing up quickly. "I know why you are here, Herr Segalla." She smiled slyly. "I listen at doors, I confess." She shrugged quickly, a rather ugly gesture coming from this dumpy woman. "I also have so much money, a generous pension but little to spend it on except servants. Ah well, you believe," she continued in a rush, "that my husband, Prince Rudolph, did not commit suicide?"

"And you?" Segalla asked tactfully.

"I have been wondering too." Stephanie straightened up, her back rigid, hands on her hips. She looked away towards the window, blinking furiously. "What I say, Herr Segalla," she said without turning her head, "is in confidence."

"Of course, Madam."

"I can understand the confusion"—Stephanie looked at him

directly—"about Count Hoyos bringing the wrong version back to Vienna. However, I have heard that when the shutters were opened, my husband's bedroom was in great disarray: items smashed, pieces of furniture overturned."

Segalla hid his surprise. "And from where did you learn that, Madam?"

"Just gossip."

"And who do you think was responsible?"

Stephanie licked her lips and looked at him from under her brows.

"If you read the press reports, Herr Segalla, you'll find that, according to the accepted story, on the afternoon before my husband was found dead, the only people in the hunting lodge were Loschek his valet, Bratfisch the cabby driver, and Kati the cook. You agree?"

Segalla nodded.

"Prince Coburg had already left for Vienna whilst Count Hoyos was out shooting. Now, according to what I have heard, Alexander Baltazzi visited Mayerling on the afternoon of the twenty-ninth and there was a furious argument."

"Do you know about what?"

"Oh, about the Vetsera woman. Baltazzi wanted to take her home." She shrugged. "That's all I know."

"Did you know Maria Vetsera very well?"

Stephanie drew her head back primly. "Oh, of course not! She was a pretty little thing but, there again, Herr Segalla, one amongst a crowd. Rudolph had so many amours: the poor girl, like the rest, probably thought she was the only one." Stephanie chewed her lip. "After all, in the first years of our marriage, I thought the same."

"So Prince Rudolph did not love her so much as to commit suicide?"

"My husband, Herr Segalla, loved no one but himself. He was absorbed with his own ambitions and dreams, constantly meddling in matters of state. At one time the great liberal, on the other an Austrian general issuing papers about army reforms."

"Would you say his mind was disturbed?"

Stephanie paused. "He had violent mood changes. There were rumours that he once insisted, or tried to be present, when a fellow officer made love to his wife. On another occasion, when out riding, he jumped his horse across a funeral hearse."

"But these are rumours, Madam, surely?"

"I used to think they were," Stephanie snapped back. "But last year, just after Easter, I and my husband went on a cruise in the Adriatic on board the man-of-war the *Greif*. I discovered Rudolph was taking more morphine than was good for him." Princess Stephanie paused to collect her thoughts. "That part of the Adriatic is rather treacherous, studded with small islands and rocky shoals. Anyway, the *Greif* struck a reef and the captain decided that perhaps it was best if the guests were sent to the nearest island. I was in my state room. There was no danger of sinking as the sea was quite calm, but the ship was leaking. Rudolph was in the restaurant. I went down there." She paused and swallowed hard. "He couldn't walk. He couldn't even stand up. He had to be trussed up like a parcel and lowered into the boat." She sat up, breathing noisily through her nose. "I am sorry, Herr Segalla; you must think I am bitter. Yes, I am. I am bitter that Rudolph's selfishness deprived me of a husband and his little daughter of a father. They say that suicide results from utter desperation or complete selfishness; I think Rudolph's was due to the latter."

"So you believe your husband did commit suicide?"

"Perhaps." Stephanie leaned back in the chair, fingering the gold cross round her throat. "Perhaps he did." She blinked back her tears. "I'm being wistful, pretending that Rudolph still loved me too much to leave me like that."

"So, Baltazzi's visit?"

"Oh," Stephanie murmured, head lowered. "It may have

been a factor. Rudolph would have become even more hysterical, his mind turned to dark thoughts."

"Madam." Segalla stretched across and touched her hand. "The very nobility of your grief"—he hoped the flattery was not too obvious—"has impressed all. You understand the Holy Father's anxiety over this matter?"

Stephanie nodded.

"Have you seen any of the documents?" Segalla asked slowly. "Anything which may confirm or dispute the public findings?"

"Yes, there was one. Some chatter I heard. It was about the Vetsera woman. I heard it from a chambermaid who knew one of the doctors who attended her autopsy." Stephanie flailed her hands. "According to him, the Vetsera woman had been dead for hours, long before Rudolph killed himself."

She stood up, and Segalla did likewise.

"Think of that, Herr Segalla. My husband shot that young lady, perhaps hours before he took his own life." She wetted her lips. "How decadent can you get?" She glanced at Segalla. "Please ensure the Holy Father knows that, for it is a matter the imperial court will not publish."

# Chapter 8

Segalla sat at his desk in his plush suite in the Hotel Imperial, sipping at the brandy and soda he had ordered from the restaurant. He had left the Schonborn just before dusk: a valet had informed him that His Imperial Majesty would be contacting him shortly so would Herr Segalla return to his hotel and stay there? Segalla smiled as he recognised the hidden threat. The now taciturn Kinski had personally escorted him into the foyer of the hotel, saying it was best if Segalla stayed there until he was collected the following morning. The papal envoy sipped at the brandy, relishing the warmth in his mouth and at the back of his throat. The Hapsburg Authorities had certainly been hospitable. The Hotel Imperial was the best in Vienna. The roast beef he had eaten for dinner had been exquisite, the manager and the Maitre d'Hote fussing about him. After his meal, Segalla tried to test the waters. He'd collected his hat and cane and had walked towards the main entrance but a plainclothes policeman had blocked his way: a huge, thickset mountain of a man with a rubicund face, bristling moustache, and watery blue eyes.

"It's best if you go up to your room, sir," he said softly. "Inspector Kinski would like that."

Segalla had bowed mockingly and returned to his room. He had unpacked his own case and made sure his personal valise was safely stowed away in the small safe on the other side of the room. Now Segalla tried to make sense of what he had learnt. He would have liked to have gone to sleep but so much had happened. He put the brandy glass down and leaned back in the chair.

"What do we have here?" he murmured. "Prince Rudolph goes to Mayerling with his mistress. He kills her then puts a bullet in his own brain. No one hears the shots. Hoyos, one of the witnesses who broke in, then travels immediately to Vienna with the wrong cause of death." Segalla paused: that's it, he thought, the only real inconsistencies I have found. "Why didn't anyone hear the gunshot and why did Hoyos say the Prince had been poisoned?"

He jumped at a knock on the door.

"Come in!" he shouted.

The door opened and a valet, dressed in the livery of the hotel, padded softly across the carpet. Segalla studied him carefully: the servant was young with striking light-blue eyes and a military-styled moustache.

"Is there anything you require, sir?"

"How long have you been working here?" Segalla asked abruptly.

Light-blue eyes blinked momentarily. "Oh, for a few months, sir."

"And you enjoy your work?"

"Oh yes, sir."

Segalla took a note out of his pocket and pressed it into the man's hand.

"Perhaps another cognac later?"

The man smiled, bowed, and walked out, closing the door quietly behind him.

"And, if you are a hotel worker," Segalla muttered to himself. "I am the Holy Father."

He must remember he was surrounded by spies, the authorities would keep a very close eye on him. He studied the pad on his desk. He wasn't going to be given any official documents and, now Franz Joseph knew about his visit to Mayerling, his every step would be dogged. He got up, walked to the window, pulled back the curtain, and stared down. The street below was quiet, a light rain had begun to fall, keeping the crowds away; the only sound was the clatter of horses' hooves and carriage wheels. Segalla walked back to his desk, picked up his pen, and began to write.

1) If Rudolph was murdered, surely the Imperial Authorities would hunt down the assassin, *unless* [he underscored the word] the assassin was so powerful such a hunt would only create a crisis which might threaten the very throne. However, that seemed unlikely. If the assassin was Austrian, surely Franz Joseph would show no mercy? Yet, if he was from abroad, the Emperor would regard his son's murder as an act of war.

2) If it was suicide, however, certain anomalies still existed. Why? Rudolph was not besotted with Vetsera and why were there inconsistencies about the sound of gunfire? Hoyos' inaccurate story? What were the Imperial Authorities trying to hide?

Segalla threw his pen down in disgust.

"Perhaps he did commit suicide," he muttered. "After all, Rudolph was an adulterer, a murderer, drunk on alcohol and morphine. Is that what Franz Joseph was trying to conceal?"

He heard a knock on the door, strode across and opened it. The man outside immediately brushed by him into the room.

"What the . . . ?"

"Close the door!" The stranger retorted. "For pity's sake, man, don't worry, I'm no police spy!"

Segalla's visitor was old, well past his sixtieth year, with a shock of white hair, but his face was youthful, his eyes bright. He was well but soberly dressed, his moustache and beard closely clipped. He was short and squat, broad of shoulder, giving the impression of incredible strength. He walked across, took off his coat, threw it over the back of a chair and sat down.

"Please, you have the wrong room, sir?"

"Don't be stupid. You are Nicholas Segalla, papal envoy. My name is Maurice Szeps."

"Ah yes," Segalla replied. "Close friend of Prince Rudolph, as well as editor of a Viennese newspaper." Segalla sat down in his own chair. "You shouldn't be here, sir."

"Well, I am now," Szeps growled. "I gave my police spy the slip. A member of my synagogue, who looks very similar to me, is now leading two hapless policemen one hell of a dance all over Vienna.' He smiled in a display of fine, white teeth. "Now, Herr Segalla, you can throw me out or call for the porter but you'd be the poorer. And, no, I don't want a drink, I simply want to tell you what I know."

"Which is?"

"The truth."

"I believe Pilate asked the same question."

"He was a Roman," Szeps teased back. "And, if he had waited for an answer, the good Jew would have given him it."

Segalla smiled and extended his hand. "Herr Szeps, you are most welcome. You'd best tell me what you know before my valet, who is also a police spy, comes back to see if I want more brandy."

"Prince Rudolph did not commit suicide," Szeps began bluntly. "Oh, he liked the Vetsera girl, she was fresh and nubile. She made him feel virile. She was passionate, a merry little soul who was deeply in love with life and liked nothing more than a dance or a visit to the race course. Oh, to be sure," Szeps took off his gloves and tossed them to the floor. "Like so many of our wealthy Viennese, she had fanciful notions about death, as did Prince Rudolph. However, talking about death and committing murder and suicide are two different things."

"But there are the letters," Segalla insisted. "The letters found at Mayerling from both Rudolph and Vetsera."

"Oh, for the love of God, man!" Szeps retorted. "It is easy to forge a note. There are people in Vienna who would give you passports for every country in Europe, not to mention a pocketful of their currencies!"

"What proof do you have?" Segalla asked.

"First," Szeps ticked off his fingers. "Rudolph definitely decided to return to Vienna from Mayerling. He wanted his pleasures. He was sulking away from his family."

"About what?"

Szeps shook his head. "I don't know but he did have the most furious row with his father."

"About what?"

"Again I don't know. Now Rudolph may have written letters saying he was going to die. God knows the man was hysterical enough. However, whilst he was at Mayerling, he sent a number of telegrams saying that he intended to return to Vienna on the thirty-first. I also know that he made similar arrangements to send Mary Vetsera back by a separate route."

"And there is documentary evidence of this?"

"Oh yes. The telegrams exist."

"And no one has questioned them?"

"No."

"And what else?" Segalla asked.

"Secondly," Szeps continued. "A member of my faith, a carpenter called Frederick Wolfe, owns a shop at Allend near Mayerling. He and his elder brother Aoilus were occasionally called to the hunting lodge to polish the parquet floor, apparently this was done early in the morning. On the day Rudolph was found dead, about four o'clock in the morning, the Wolfe brothers tried to enter the lodge, but Rudolph's valet, Loschek, stopped them and sent them home. A fortnight later Frederick and his brother were summoned back. They were ordered to clean the floors, including the prince's bedroom. The chamber was dirty, but one thing Wolfe remembers were large stains of dried blood or mucus on the floor."

"But that's hardly surprising," Segalla intervened. "If the prince shot himself and his mistress, the bedclothes would be soaked in blood, and some of this would drip onto the floor."

"True," Szeps replied. "But Wolfe claimed the bloodstains were in a different part of the room, well away from the bed." Szeps leaned forward, eyes bright with excitement. "But what is important about Wolfe's testimony is that, according to all the newspaper reports, the prince was found dead shortly after eight o'clock. However, four hours earlier, we have the hunting lodge sealed off and the people being turned away."

"So, you are saying that the prince's corpse was found much earlier?"

"Of course."

Segalla shook his head. "It doesn't make sense. If the prince's corpse was found earlier, Count Hoyos must have known, and someone would have left for Vienna."

"How do you know they didn't?" Szeps replied. "There are telegraph facilities at Mayerling as well as in the nearby village of Allend."

"So Hoyos, Loschek, and the others," Segalla retorted, stretching out his legs, "quite happily sat with the prince's corpse for a number of hours?"

Szeps shrugged. "I know it sounds ridiculous," he muttered.

"It's too much to base on the testimony of a workman," Segalla replied. "Moreover, if the corpse was found earlier, why didn't Hoyos just tell the truth as soon as he reached Vienna?"

Szeps smiled. "Ah, that is the mystery. You see, from what I can gather, Hoyos approached certain courtiers, who decided it was best to tell the empress first and she would tell her husband. Apparently, about the same time, Maria's mother came to the palace seeking the whereabouts of her daughter. The empress gave Vetsera tragic news. She fell to the floor at the empress's feet and exclaimed: 'My unfortunate child. What has she done?' The empress was most cold and left her lying on the floor with the words: 'Remember now, tell people that Rudolph died of heart failure.' "

Szeps stretched out his hands. "Can't you see what's happening? The news was changing all the time."

Szeps dug deep into his pocket and handed over a sheet of newspaper. It contained an official report that "Archduke Prince Rudolph died suddenly of heart failure between 7 and 8 o'clock at his hunting lodge at Mayerling." Szeps then handed Segalla a second newspaper, the *New Free Press*. This time the report read:

> It is still not possible to obtain authentic information of the cause or the nature of the tragedy. We understand the news of the death was known about 8 o'clock. It was reported that the prince was found dead in bed at Mayerling with a firearm near his body. It was originally believed that he died of heart failure, but a report we have just received and which we are unable to verify confirms that the crown prince died as the result of a firearm wound.

Szeps then handed over the official Austrian newspapers for the evening of the thirtieth and the morning of the thirty-first. This time the story had gone back to Rudolph dying of a stroke or heart failure.

"See!" Szeps cried triumphantly. "Here we have the heir to the Austrian throne die in tragic circumstances. On the one hand we have a witness, Count Hoyos, saying he was poisoned. The empress immediately claimed it was due to heart failure and this version is repeated in newspapers on the thirtieth and even the thirty-first. Yet, already, on the day the body was found, one newspaper hints at the truth."

Segalla handed the newspapers back. "Wait a minute."

He got up and went across to open the safe, keeping his back to Szeps. He took out his own valise, opened it, and went through the files. He grunted his satisfaction as he read the official telegram sent to Rome on 30 January at 5:25 P.M.

"The deeply distressing news has just arrived that His Imperial Highness Prince Rudolph has died suddenly." Segalla's eyes ran along the translation and stopped at the sentence "The cause of death is believed to have been heart failure."

He handed this to Szeps.

"Here is a telegram, dispatched from Vienna some six and a half hours after Hoyos arrived at the Hofburg, and still they are trying to peddle the story that Prince Rudolph had died of heart failure." Segalla sat down. "But why?" he asked. "The authorities must have known that the truth would eventually come out. So why tell newspapers and the papacy a lie?"

"And others," Szeps interrupted. "Similar telegrams were sent to Germany, London, and France. All claim the prince died of a *coup de sang,* a heart attack or stroke."

"Who would be responsible for this?" Segalla asked. "The police?"

"No," Szeps shook his head. "Count Edward Taaffe, the prime minister."

Segalla picked up his cognac glass and rolled it between his hands. "Why?" he repeated. "Taaffe knew the truth would soon be out. People would demand to see the corpse. There had to be an autopsy. Not even Taaffe and his secret service could keep such a matter hidden for long." He glanced at Szeps. "Do you have any ideas?"

"They panicked," the news editor replied. "I believe they panicked and didn't know what to do. Something strange had happened at Mayerling and they were buying time."

"The Vatican thought it was just a bureaucratic muddle; why should it be deliberate?"

"I don't know."

"But if they were buying time," Segalla asked, "why didn't they stick to Hoyos's story that Rudolph had taken an overdose or poisoned himself? Why all the secrecy?"

"I can't answer that either," Szeps replied. "True, they did eventually publish an autopsy report which poses as many questions as it answers; that, too, makes me suspicious. As does the unseemly haste in burying Maria Vetsera's body." Szeps dug into the inside pocket of his coat. "But that's not the real reason I came to see you, Herr Segalla. You talk of great secrecy. Was the prince's death such a great secret? Did you know that, according to a report"—he brought out a thick envelope—"Rudolph's death may have been known and discussed even before it occurred?" He tossed the envelope into Segalla's lap. "When I have gone, study that!" He folded his hands and sat like some jovial gnome on the chair. "It makes interesting reading."

"Why shouldn't I read it now?"

"Because time is short and I have no solution to the mystery it poses."

"You were close to the prince?"

Szeps nodded.

"He was not suicidal?"

Szeps shook his head. "Not at all."

"Tell me," Segalla asked, "the prince had different women?"

"Oh, yes, he found Stephanie rather boring."

"And Maria Vetsera was not special?"

"In his cups once," Szeps replied slowly, "he confided that Maria was good in bed. Made him feel potent."

"Even though the prince was suffering from gonorrhea?" Segalla saw the surprise on Szeps's face. "Oh, yes, I have heard of that."

"For a while the prince was impotent," Szeps replied. "And, yes, Maria may have cured that."

"And when he went to his women?" Segalla asked. "Was he watched by the secret police?"

"Yes, I would think so. From afar. Which carriage he took, which hotel he visited. Rudolph really didn't care. And who could complain? Franz Joseph has his own mistress."

"So why the great secrecy," Segalla asked, "when he and Maria Vetsera went to Mayerling?"

"I don't think there was," Szeps replied. "The authorities really couldn't have cared about it. However, Maria's mother and uncles, the Baltazzis, knew that if her liaison with the prince became public knowledge, she would be ruined in Vienna's high circles. That explains Maria's subterfuge and her relatives' desperation."

Segalla tapped the brown envelope. "So, you prefer me to study this when you have gone?"

Szeps nodded and rose to his feet. "I am beginning to feel sorry for those police spies." He grinned. "And I have stayed longer than I should have done."

"Sit down, please!" Segalla said.

Szeps looked as if he were going to refuse, but then sighed and, unbuttoning his cloak, sat down just as there was a knock on the door. Segalla strode across quickly and opened it. The hotel valet had returned with a glass of cognac on a silver tray.

"I thought you might need this, sir."

Segalla kept the door as closed as possible. He quickly signed the man's notepad.

"Is there anything else you need, sir?" The valet tried to peer round him.

"No thank you. I have papers to study. I'll need nothing else."

He closed the door, placing his finger to his lips.

"You have a police spy following you; so do I," Segalla whispered. "He'll probably be waiting for you at the foot of the stairs."

"In which case I'll leave by the servants' entrance," Szeps responded. "So, what do you want?"

"It would appear," Segalla replied, "that the imperial authorities are going to be as uncooperative with me as they can without giving insult. No documents will be produced, whilst I doubt if the witnesses will be able to speak freely—Hoyos, Coburg, or the servants Loschek and Bratfisch."

"So?"

"What about other servants? Rudolph apparently ate a meal. There would definitely be a cook."

"Yes, Kati Polzer," Szeps replied. "Bratfisch sometimes cooked, but Kati was skilled, and where Rudolph went, so did Kati."

"If you find her address, would you just leave it in an envelope at the desk?"

"I can find it," Szeps promised. "Is there anything else?"

"Yes. Was Rudolph a good marksman?"

"He was a huntsman."

"Do you think he could take a revolver and place it against a young woman's head?" Segalla asked. "Kill her, then kill himself?"

"No, I don't." Szeps got to his feet. "In many ways Rudolph was a child. There was no hardness in him."

"When he drank?" Segalla asked.

Szeps shrugged and buttoned up his coat. "Rudolph was not an alcoholic," he replied. "But he loved his wine. When he drank, he drank deeply. He also carried a hip flask of brandy and was not above taking morphine for pleasure as well as to hide the pain he sometimes felt."

"Did he carry his own pistol?"

"Oh yes."

"So," Segalla replied, "according to what we know, Rudolph drank with Hoyos until nine o'clock. He then went back into his room to join Maria Vetsera. They drank and talked to the early hours before carrying out their suicide pact. However, the room would go dark, and I can't imagine Rudolph, drunk, slightly drugged, delivering an expert shot to his mistress and then killing himself. And even if he did, one question still remains unanswered: Why didn't anyone else hear the shots?"

"They claim he used a pillow or blankets to deaden the sound," Szeps replied. The news editor put on his gloves, then stopped. "But of course," he murmured, "Rudolph, probably drugged on alcohol and morphine, taking such elaborate precautions to deaden the sound. He would fumble it."

"And why should he do it in the first place?" Segalla asked. "What would he care if others heard the shots? By the time anyone reached the room, he and Vetsera would be long past caring."

Szeps walked across to the window and pulled back the curtain. He stared out into the wet night.

"If I follow your meaning," he said without turning round, "you imply that Rudolph and Maria were executed. And, if they were, by whom? And I'll tell you this, Herr Segalla, Loschek, Hoyos, and Bratfisch have all acted strangely over this matter. Yet, they were fanatically loyal to Rudolph. They would never have hurt him."

"So someone else entered the room?" Segalla replied.

"But how?" Szeps asked, turning round. "The doors had all been locked from the inside. The windows were closed and shuttered. Let's say, for sake of argument, some skilled assassin did break into the room. Don't forget, he had to kill two people. Either way, they would have resisted, screamed—some form of struggle would have taken place. Rudolph and Maria would not have given up their lives gladly. Loschek and Bratfisch would certainly have acted. They would not let their master's assassin escape so easily."

"Aye." Segalla sighed. "And the shots would have been heard. The whole of Mayerling would have been roused."

"Moreover," Szeps added, "let's say Rudolph and Maria were murdered; why should Franz Joseph protect the assassin? It would certainly clear Rudolph's name. No accusation of murder or suicide levelled against him, just a romantic prince and his young love brutally murdered in their beds. Franz Joseph may have had his difficulties with Rudolph, but he would never let an assassin escape. The entire empire would have been turned upside down in the consequent hunt."

"And these difficulties between father and son?" Segalla asked.

"Oh, I have heard the stories," Szeps replied, walking to the door. "But Rudolph never told me anything. I met Rudolph two days before he left for Mayerling. I went to his quarters in the Hofburg. He was more excited than usual. He had drunk deeply. His face was flushed. I asked him what was wrong. The prince just shook his head and said he couldn't tell me."

"Did you press him?"

"Yes I did. Rudolph was walking up and down, rubbing his hands together. One minute he seemed happy, the next downcast. I tried to calm him. We talked about ordinary, mundane affairs, news from Germany, the crisis in Paris. Just before I left, the prince, who was not a religious man, asked me to pray to whatever God I chose that what he planned would come about. I asked him what. He shook his head and ushered me to the door." Szeps breathed in quickly. "And that's the last I saw of him." He pulled up the collar of his coat. "After the funeral, I made enquiries. I always thought this great secret would surface, but I could discover nothing."

He extended his hand for Segalla to shake.

"I'll do what I can, Herr Segalla, to help you. The little I know, you now know. I tell you this: Prince Rudolph may have been murdered, but by whom, how, and why is a mystery." Szeps shook Segalla's hand, opened the door, and slipped into the passageway.

Segalla locked the door behind him and, going back, picked up the brown manilla envelope, slit it open, and shook the contents onto the bed. The first was a copy of a telegram sent from

Rome by Revertera, the Austrian ambassador to Prime Minister Taaffe: "Among the many rumours," it began,

> Connected with the terrible events at Mayerling, one matter has come to my knowledge which I believe I cannot conceal from you. On the 29th, or possibly 30th January 1889 about one o'clock in the afternoon a Benedictine priest Don Gregoro de Grote, a missionary from the East Indies, left Port Said for Brindisi aboard the steamship *Paramatta*. From Brindisi Don Gregoro travelled via Naples to Rome. Upon his arrival, he related the following to the prior of the Dominican Church of St. Ambrosius. Don Gregoro claims to have been informed by a passenger on the *Paramatta* that the Crown Prince Rudolph of Austria had died by his own hand. Upon landing at Brindisi, the missionary found the baleful news confirmed. However, upon comparison with the dates, he was unable to understand and by what means, his unknown travel companion could have learnt either before, or immediately afterward, the deed was committed.
>
> Don Gregoro is at present staying in Rome. I have given him instructions to have him brought to me immediately. Meanwhile I am having enquiries made through our consular office: if the above ship made the said voyage between 29th and 31st January as well as to obtain a list of passengers. I shall return to you on this matter.

Segalla sat thunderstruck and reread the paper again. A small visiting card fell from the other papers and he picked it up. On one side it carried Szeps's name, on the other a scrawled message:

"I assure you these telegrams are genuine. They are copied virtually word for word by one of our faith who works in the cipher office in Rome. I paid dearly for them. Please destroy this card."

Segalla did so, tearing the pieces up even as he thought about what he had read. He tossed the shreds into a wastepaper basket and picked up the second piece of paper. It was dated from Rome 26 February 1889.

"Father Gregoro," it began,

> placed himself at my disposal. What he has told me offers no explanation for the incident described in my most humble report earlier this month. According to the missionary, a passenger who boarded the ship on 29 January came down from the first-class deck to his. [The missionary held a second-class ticket.] The stranger strolled over to him and a conversation ensued. The Benedictine, who is Belgian but speaks French very well, heard from the stranger's lips the observation that Crown Prince Rudolph of Austria had died by suicide.
>
> It is astonishing that Father Gregoro made no attempt to follow up what, at first sight, is a very incredible report. He himself says he had a feeling of being very unwell and, being in a somewhat hazardous state, was glad to let the matter drop. He encountered the stranger again before docking at Brindisi. Only afterwards, when the terrible event was confirmed, had he been startled that someone could have been informed about it beforehand.
>
> As to the passenger's name, Father Gregoro claims to have discovered this by accident. On a case used by him he claims to have read "Comte de Montreux." The passenger impressed him as a man of about 40. From Brindisi the comte continued his journey in a Pullman sleeping car. Where to, Father Gregoro was unable to answer.

Segalla put this down and picked up a third piece of paper, written in the journalist's hand. The message was simple and stark:

*I have made careful enquiries. The* Paramatta *could not have learnt this from another ship at sea. I have checked with friends in France, Austria, and Germany. No family known as the de Montreux are known to exist. Who this person was or where he came from is a mystery. How he learnt about the prince's death on the thirtieth or, more surprising, even on the twenty-ninth, is shrouded in mystery. Please keep these documents secret.*

*Szeps.*

For a while Segalla sat and reread both documents. When he had finished he put them carefully into his own attaché case and placed this back in the safe. For a short time Segalla just lay on the bed, bemused by what he had read. He was sure Szeps was telling the truth, yet how could the news of Prince Rudolph's death be known in the Mediterranean, even Port Said, before it even happened? Was this evidence of a deeper conspiracy? And why couldn't this mysterious comte de Montreux be traced? Was de Montreux the assassin? Or, perhaps, the mover behind the prince's death? But, if that was the case, what was he doing in Egypt when the Prince died? And if he hired assassins, professional killers, surely he'd be closer to the scene than hundreds of miles away? And above all, if he was involved in some deep, subtle conspiracy, why reveal his hand, perhaps at the latest, the thirtieth of January? Segalla made a mental note that neither telegram clearly delineated whether it was twenty-ninth or thirtieth when the conversation with Don Gregoro took place. Why tell a Benedictine monk? Or had he mistaken Don Gregoro for someone else?

Segalla turned over to one side and stared at the window's reflections of light from the street below. If there was a conspiracy, he hadn't even an inkling of who was behind it, who was involved, or what they hoped to gain by the prince's death.

"Think, Segalla!" he muttered to himself. "Try and put yourself in de Montreaux's place. You know there is a plot. You know Prince Rudolph is going to die by his own hand." Segalla opened his eyes. That was another mystery! Here was a stranger on a ship in the Mediterranean who not only knew about the death of the prince, as it happened in a lonely hunting lodge, but gave a more truthful version than even the newspapers in Vienna—by his own hand! Segalla closed his eyes and visualised himself on that ship: a conspirator who knew an important prince was about to die. He does not discuss it with his fellow passengers in the first-class section but, instead, seeks out a lonely, tired, seasick missionary whom he'd spotted walking on the deck below. Why would this mysterious de Montreux go down and tell him? Segalla sat up. "Of course!" he whispered. "De Montreux couldn't control his excitement. He was testing the water. He approached a simple priest to discover if the tragedy had occurred and was known." Segalla sat, face in hands. If the story of the *Paramatta* was true, he reasoned, there could only be one conclusion: Prince Rudolph had been murdered at Mayerling by someone here in Vienna who had communicated with his fellow conspirator, the mysterious comte de Montreux.

# Chapter 9

Segalla found it difficult to sleep. He tossed and turned, drifting in and out of nightmares. Memories of his past: dark, rain-swept nights; horsemen, cloaked and cowled, pounding along trackways; lonely castle halls lit by the flames of dancing torches; dangers pressing in from every side. The secret dagger thrust: bloody, sweaty sword fights in the narrow, dark streets of London or Paris. Segalla's terrible loneliness, as he drifted here and there, keeping to the shadows, selling his services to the rich and powerful of the world. Sometimes a priest, a courtier, a soldier, always wary that someone might disclose his secret and hold him captive.

When he awoke, covered in sweat, Segalla was pleased by the daylight, the noisy cheering trundling of the trams, movements outside in the passageway, and the faint, fragrant smell of cooking breakfast. He got up, washed, and shaved. A chambermaid brought him coffee, orange juice, croissants, and butter and jam. Segalla ate and felt better. The memory of the nightmares receded. After he had finished eating, he sat at the desk and began to list the questions which confronted him.

1. Did Prince Rudolph commit suicide? Probably not. He was sick in mind and body, addicted to alcohol and morphine, sexually promiscuous, but more hysterical than suicidal. He was involved with young Vetsera but, if rumour could be believed, not infatuated with her. Apparently he intended

to leave Mayerling on the thirty-first, planning to meet people in February. Maria Vetsera was also going to be dispatched back to her family. She, too, although melodramatic and romantic, was not the stuff of which suicides are made.

2. Why the secrecy which cloaked Rudolph and Maria Vetsera's departure from Vienna to Mayerling? Probably because (Segalla's pen raced across the page) Vetsera's kinfolk were looking for her. Perhaps Rudolph only intended what many a rich young man planned: a love tryst so he could wallow in romance and melodrama before returning to the harsh, cold world of the Viennese court?

3. If Rudolph was murdered, by whom?
   Segalla simply underlined the question mark.

4. If it was murder? How? According to all the evidence, both Rudolph and Maria Vetsera received bullets through the brain. But how could this happen? Did the assassin catch them asleep, drugged with alcohol and morphine? Yet, if so, how did the person get through locked doors and windows and leave just as mysteriously? Why didn't Loschek, Bratfisch, or Hoyos hear something? Why wasn't the shot heard by other servants or even the huntsmen at Mayerling? And, if one or more assassin entered the bedroom, how could they be so confident that Rudolph and Maria Vetsera would prove to be such easy victims? Surely there would be some resistance? Some scream or shout for help? And, if it was murder, why was it so essential to remove the Hapsburg Prince and his mistress in such a manner? After all, the assassin was risking capture, even death himself. Surely it would have been easier if their murders had been carried out on a street or boulevard?

5. If it was murder, why didn't the Austrian authorities launch the most thorough manhunt, unless of course it was someone very powerful? But surely Franz Joseph would not want his own son killed? Even the powerful Prime Minister,

Taafee, would not carry out such a deed unless he had the emperor's full approval?

6. Why the secrecy? Why wasn't the gun produced? The bullets, the description of the room? And all the other evidence so cleverly and so quickly suppressed? Rudolph's corpse had been brought out and put on public display, carefully prepared, allowed to lie in state before formal burial. Yet why was Vetsera's body so quickly hurried to the grave? Shamelessly hustled out, put in a carriage, and buried before questions were asked?

7. If it was murder, and the *Paramatta* story was true, then there was evidence of a widespread conspiracy. But who could arrange this and then be so confident that the actual assassin would not confess?

8. Why didn't Hoyos tell the truth? He'd gone to Vienna and told the emperor that his son had been poisoned, yet, even if it was dark in the prince's bedroom, Hoyos must have seen the gun? And the empress's reaction? Her words to Vetsera's mother insisting that the story be that Rudolph died of heart failure? Why did Prime Minister Taaffe peddle a similar story to the press? Surely a telegram to Mayerling would have established the facts?

Segalla put the pen down, rose, stretched, and poured himself another coffee. For a while he stared out into the bustling streets below. A flower girl, with a blue shawl over her shoulders and a leather apron round her slim waist, stood on the pavement opposite the hotel selling small bouquets and nosegays, her face peeping shyly from beneath a spotted head scarf. A dark-faced policeman in his ornate helmet walked up and down and began to flirt with her. The crowds swept by them: sober-faced men going to their offices; mothers with children, all trying to steer away from the large puddles forming in the gutter. The jingle of the carriages, the rumble of their wheels. Segalla went back to

his desk. He picked up his pen and wrote down a new heading:
"POSSIBILITIES."

    A. If Rudolph was murdered was it for personal reasons? Per-
       haps a quarrel had taken place at the hunting lodge? Per-
       haps someone else had come, Vetsera's uncle? Furious words
       spilling into violence? Pistols being drawn?

Segalla studied what he had written.
"Nonsense," he whispered. "Franz Joseph would have shown
no mercy. The same is true of a quarrel between Hoyos and
Prince Rudolph. Any attempt to cover up such a quarrel
would soon be foiled."

    B. A political murder by people outside the Empire? Rudolph
       disliked Germany but would the new Kaiser stoop to such
       action?

Again Segalla shook his head.

    C. If Rudolph had been shot by a group within the Empire,
       they would have had to obtain the co-operation, even ap-
       proval, of the Emperor and his first minister. What cir-
       cumstances would bring that about?

Segalla tapped the pen against the side of his face.
"Possibly," he murmured, leaning back in the chair. "Rudolph
might have committed some crime which would mean his own
trial and disgrace, but what? Did he kill the Vetsera woman
much earlier? Is that why no one saw her at Mayerling? Rudolph
and Maria are said to have arrived at Mayerling on the evening
of the twenty-eighth. Coburg and Hoyos arrived on the morning of the twenty-ninth. The Prince had breakfast with them
alone. No one saw Maria Vetsera. On the evening of the twenty-

ninth, Prince Rudolph supped with Hoyos. Once again there's no mention of Maria Vetsera, either by implication or anyone seeing her."

Segalla put his pen down and got up, trying to curb his own excitement. "Was it both suicide and murder?" he whispered.

Could that be the explanation? Had there been a lovers' quarrel? Perhaps Rudolph had told Maria that this was the end of their relationship? She may have argued back, even threatened blackmail? Rudolph took out his gun and shot her. He left the body in the bed chamber whilst he plotted, acting as if nothing had happened. Did Rudolph then take his own life when he realised that there was no way out for him? Or had he confided in someone and been given a choice, either face trial or do the gentlemanly thing? Had someone been sent from Vienna to ensure he did? Is that what Hoyos and the imperial authorities were trying to cover up? They didn't mean to lie, they were just buying time. Segalla sipped absentmindedly at the cup. And those letters which had been found? Did Rudolph write his whilst those of Maria Vetsera were forged and later put there? Segalla sat down. This would, at least, make sense or explain the mystery. The imperial authorities were determined not to depict Rudolph as a murderer who had shot a young woman, left her corpse in a bedroom, perhaps for almost two days, before taking his own life or being forced to take it.

"Is that why Maria Vetsera's body was buried in such haste?" Segalla asked himself. "A speedy postmortem which would not reveal that she may have been dead for days?"

Segalla turned the paper over when there was a knock on the door. "Come in!" he shouted.

Kinski and Brunner walked into the room. The sergeant had his pipe clamped firmly between his jaws, looking as serene as ever, but Kinski's face was white with fury. Segalla ushered them to seats. His offer of coffee or breakfast was curtly refused. Brunner would have accepted. Kinski, cradling his hat in his lap, glared over the shoulder of his sergeant, who raised his eyes heavenwards.

"You are out of sorts, Inspector?" Segalla asked, putting on his jacket.

"Yes, I'm bloody well out of sorts!" Kinski growled. "I've just spent the best part of an hour standing in Baron Krauss's office. The police president was not amused by your trip to Mayerling."

"I will take responsibility for that," Segalla replied.

"Oh, that's very good of you!" Kinski snapped back. "With all due respect, Your Holiness, you'll piss off back to Rome and leave me and my career in tatters, not to mention Sergeant Brunner's."

"Don't worry about me," the sergeant quipped. "I've never given a bugger about Krauss and I am not going to start now."

Segalla turned back to the writing desk. He picked up a sheet of hotel notepaper and began to carefully write. He then signed, folded it, and placed it in an envelope, addressing it to Baron Krauss. He handed this to Sergeant Brunner, plucking a banknote from his wallet.

"Sergeant, be a gentleman and a scholar. Go down to the lobby and give this to one of the bellboys. It is to be delivered to the police president as a matter of urgency."

Brunner, puffing on his pipe like a locomotive, took the letter and waddled out of the room.

"What have you written?" Kinski asked.

"A letter of protest," Segalla replied. "Saying that I have never in all my life been attended by someone such as you, Inspector Kinski." He grinned. "I have described you, once again, as a thoroughgoing nuisance who impeded my enquiries at Mayerling and has kept me a virtual prisoner in this hotel. I have informed Krauss that your presence has curtailed my enquiries. Finally, I intend to lodge a formal protest to the highest authority."

Now Kinski smiled. He relaxed and took the brandy flask out of his pocket. He toasted Segalla, then took a quick nip.

"The best way to start the day," he murmured. "I'd love to see Krauss's face when he opens that envelope. Well, Herr Segalla, I have news for you. Today is Friday. His Most Imperial Excellency the emperor has graciously agreed to set up a secret consistory to answer your questions. This will sit in the Blue Room at the Hofburg Palace at ten o'clock on Monday morning. You are summoned to attend. I shall escort you there."

"And whom will I meet?"

"Prince Coburg, Count Hoyos, the valet Loschek, the cabby Bratfisch, Doctor Weiderhofer, who performed the autopsy, and Herr Henry Slatin, who was secretary to the commission set up to investigate the Mayerling business. The consistory will be chaired by the prime minister, Count Edward Taaffe, Baron Krauss, the police president, being in attendance. If they wish to call other people, they will be summoned. You will have the right to question them. You have no authority to ask for any document and none will be shown you. You will then be given three days to reflect on what is said. Next Friday, at the same time, the consistory will sit again to elucidate or clarify any matter. On Saturday morning I am to personally put you on the express train for Milan. If you do not leave on that train, I am to arrest you." Kinski sighed and mopped his brow. "Until Monday morning you are confined to the city of Vienna. You may make visits to people you think will help you, but you cannot approach anyone without my permission." Kinski smiled grimly.

Segalla sat playing with the ring on his finger. He glanced up and caught the sympathy in Kinski's eyes.

"What else have they said about me?" he asked.

"That you are strange," Kinski replied. "That you are to be watched closely. A friend who works in the secret archives claims they are going back through the records looking for anyone bearing your name."

Segalla smiled to hide a chill of fear. It was one thing he had dreaded coming to Vienna. The Hapsburgs had ruled for almost seven hundred years: bureaucratic, they had built up a vast museum of records going back centuries. He would be glad to leave Austria within the week. True, such records also existed in Rome, but there he was safer. The Vatican state was only a small island, difficult to enter but easy to leave.

"Aren't you curious yourself, Kinski?" Segalla teasingly asked. "Wouldn't you like to go through the secret archives and find out what really happened at Mayerling? I know"—Segalla held his hand up—"you are only a policeman doing his duty. I have heard that excuse so many times."

He paused as Brunner entered the room, carrying an envelope, which he handed to Segalla. Segalla recognised Szeps's handwriting and opened it quickly. The scrap of paper inside bore Kati's address: she apparently had rooms at 14 Villenstrasse near St. Stephen's Church in Old Vienna. Segalla put the note carefully into his waistcoat pocket. He got to his feet.

"Gentlemen, it's time I saw more of this old city."

"And we would be delighted to accompany you." Kinski got to his feet. "Brunner's cab is below."

Segalla put his coat on and, taking the attaché case, returned it to the safe. He took one last look round the room, tossed the door key to Brunner, and went out into the passageway. The blond-haired, military-styled valet was outside. Segalla smiled at him and, with Kinski and Brunner hurrying behind, went along the passageway and down the stairs.

"Is he one of yours?" Segalla asked over his shoulder. "The valet we have just passed?"

Kinski shrugged.

"Oh, come," Segalla teased. "If he's a hotel valet, I'm the king of Siam."

Kinski ran the brim of his hat between his fingers.

"God be my witness, Herr Segalla, I don't recognise him. He could be one of the secrets." He caught the look of puzzlement in Segalla's eyes. "Secret services."

"And whom do they work for?"

"Directly for Taaffe, the prime minister." Kinski gestured with his hat at the busy lobby below. "Where are you going, Herr Segalla?"

"To number fourteen Villenstrasse. I wish to interview a woman called Kati Polzer."

"And she is . . . ?"

"A cook. She apparently worked for Prince Rudolph and may have been at Mayerling when he was killed."

"When he was killed!" Kinski came closer. "Are you saying, Herr Segalla, that our noble prince was murdered?"

"No, I didn't say that. All I am implying"—Segalla tapped the detective on the chest—"is that there are suicides and there are suicides."

He turned round and continued down the stairs, through the busy lobby, and out into the street. Brunner's cab was hitched to a lamppost. They climbed in, Kinski pulling down the blinds. Brunner got into the driving seat and the carriage pulled away. Progress was slow. Segalla could hear Brunner's muttered curses as they stopped and started. Now and again Segalla would pull back the corner of the blind and look out on the busy street scenes: it being Friday morning, the thoroughfares were thronged. Trams and horses pulled carriages filling the streets; the good citizens of Vienna were busy shopping before the week-end began. Segalla realised that the feast of Easter was still being celebrated: in his briefing at the Vatican, Rampolla had explained how, on weekends, the Viennese loved nothing more than to relax in the great city parks or go out into the countryside. Everyone seemed to be in frenetic preparation for this. Segalla sat back and absorbed the feel of the city: the murmur of the crowds, the clang of the trams, the fragrant aroma of coffee and baked bread from the many cafés and restaurants which lined the streets.

At last the carriage left the more elegant parts of Vienna: the streets became not so clean, the houses on either side dingy, the paint peeling. There were no elegant ladies or well-dressed men but ragamuffin children, old men and women sitting on battered stools in front of their houses smoking pipes. They gossiped, glancing narrow-eyed at Brunner's fine horse and elegant carriage. For most of the journey Kinski was quiet, but at last his curiosity got the better of him. He leaned over and tapped Segalla on the hand.

"What can a cook tell you?"

"My dear Inspector," Segalla replied. "When some wealthy burgher of Vienna is murdered, I'd wager a bottle of schnapps to a bottle of French cognac that, whilst you question the family, your good sergeant here drinks coffee in the kitchen listening to the tittle-tattle. I am not forbidden to speak to Kati, am I?"

Kinski shook his head, but Segalla could see he was worried.

"In which case," Segalla replied, sitting back, "I might have a great deal to learn."

At last the carriage stopped. Brunner got down and opened the door.

"Fourteen Villenstrasse," he declared.

Segalla got out and stared up at the five-storeyed house. It looked more like a prison than a dwelling place: grey ragstone walls, shuttered windows, the front door hung slightly askew, most of its black paint peeling off. Kinski pushed this open and they went along a damp passageway which reeked of boiled cabbage. Cats sprawled on the damp stairs, and in a corner two pale-faced children crouched, playing marbles. They watched, round-eyed, as these three well-dressed men climbed the stairs. An old woman making her way carefully down informed them, "Yes, this is number fourteen, but Fraulein Polzer lives on the fourth storey." They continued their climb, the stairs so steep Brunner had to take his pipe out of his mouth so he could climb and cough more easily.

At last they reached Polzer's apartment. A tattered card in the metal holder bore her name in faded ink. Kinski hammered on the door. There was no answer. He tried the handle and pushed, but the flimsy door was locked.

"It appears . . ." Kinski was about to tease Segalla but then thought better of it.

He sighed, stood back, and kicked with all his might. The door flung open on its hinges and they entered the shabby apartment. Brunner opened the shutters across the flyblown casement, allowing light and air, for the room smelt sour. It was nothing much: a shabby parlour with a few sticks of furniture, a kitchen, a bedroom—a cubicle really—with a narrow iron bedstead, a small cupboard and table.

For a while they searched, opening the wooden closet, pulling out drawers.

"Kati Polzer's left for good!" Brunner announced. "You can tell the signs. All her jewellery and dresses are gone, but she has left a few odd items to make people think she's going to return."

"Isn't there anything of interest?" Segalla asked.

Brunner shrugged, and they returned to their searches. At last Brunner came out of the bedroom, a piece of paper clutched triumphantly in his hand.

"It's a receipt," he exclaimed. He handed this to Segalla, who studied it curiously.

"What's Veloures?" he asked, reading the name.

"One of the more elegant clothiers in Vienna," Kinski replied, plucking it from Segalla's fingers. "According to this, Fraulein Polzer bought a rather expensive cloak for over two hundred guilders." He stared at Segalla. "Now, where would a cook find the money to buy that?"

"What are you doing here?"

A young man stood in the doorway, thin as a beanpole, his face long and white under a shock of black hair. His face was unshaven, his clothes ill fitting, probably secondhand. He carried a violin case under his arm.

"What are you doing?" He advanced threateningly into the room.

"Now, now." Brunner stepped forward to block his path and pulled out his warrant card.

The man blinked and drew back, his gaze becoming furtive. "The police—what has happened? Has Kati been found?"

"Found?" Kinski asked. "What do you mean?"

The young man put his music case down.

"I live on the floor above. I am a musician at the academy." He shrugged, rocking from foot to foot. "Kati and I, well, we had an understanding."

"Come in, come in." Segalla waved him forward and gestured to the chair.

The young man was about to refuse but Brunner grasped him by the arm and pulled him across.

"What's your name?" Segalla began.

"Peter," the young man replied. "Peter Trabuer."

"Well, Peter Trabuer, you have heard what happened at Mayerling?"

The young man put his violin case down on the floor and shrugged. "One fewer pampered prince!"

"You are a republican?" Kinski asked from where he stood behind Segalla.

"I am a Czech," Trabuer replied. "I believe each nation should have its own sovereignty. The Hapsburgs are an anachronism."

"Did Kati believe that?" Segalla asked.

Trabuer laughed. "Kati believed in nothing except her belly, her pleasures, and, above all, money."

"Did she talk about what happened at Mayerling?"

"No, no, she kept very quiet. She said all was chaos and confusion and that she had left the imperial service. She talked of leaving Vienna." Trabuer pulled a face. "At first I accepted that. Then she began to act as if she had suddenly come into an inheritance." He waved round the room. "There's nothing here.

She gave me money, a twenty-guilder note, and then shopping began. First, little things, good cheeses, a bottle of wine, gâteaux from the best cafés; then the clothes, new boots, coats, dresses, even some jewellery."

"And she never explained her newly found wealth?"

"Never once. And then, about three to four days ago, she disappeared. I didn't see or hear her leave, but one of the children downstairs saw her climb into a cab, and that was it."

"Has she written to you?" Segalla asked, now curious at this strange turn of events.

Trabuer shook his head. "Kati wasn't the one to write. Once she was out of the door, she would have forgotten me."

"Did she meet anyone?" Segalla asked.

"No, not at all. Except . . . Yes, in the evening before Kati left, I came back from the academy. On the stairs outside I met a man, quite well dressed in the military style, with light blond hair and very pale blue eyes. He didn't stop me but I got the impression he had been to Kati's room when she was out. I never got the chance to tell Kati." He picked up his violin case. "And that's all I know. Now I must leave. I have to be on time."

Segalla let him go. He stood for a while listening to Trabuer's footsteps fading on the stairs. The description he had given resembled that of the spy acting as a valet in the hotel. Segalla glanced once more round the apartment.

"There's nothing here."

"Why is Kati so important?" Kinski asked as they went down the stairs.

"I don't know," Segalla replied. "I think she is, but she has gone. Any questions I had for her will remain unanswered."

"We can circulate her description," Kinski offered.

Segalla remembered the pale blue eyes of the hotel valet.

"I doubt, Herr Kinski," he replied, "if Kati Polzer is anywhere in the empire. Indeed," he added softly, "if she is anywhere at all."

They were out on the street, Brunner going round to feed his horse a sugar lump, when the first shot rang out, sending Kinski's hat flying off his head. The detective stood in amazement, staring down the deserted street until Segalla dragged him behind the carriage. Brunner, not surprisingly, was already there, pipe out of his mouth, a fat, squat revolver in his hand.

"You are quicker than I thought, Brunner," Segalla observed dryly.

"I fought at Sadowa." Brunner hawked and spat. "There's nothing like a Prussian sniper to make you move quickly."

Kinski had now recovered his wits and drawn his own revolver.

"The bastard!" he muttered, peering gingerly round the carriage. "I just hope the horse doesn't get skittish."

"It won't," Brunner replied. "It's an old cavalry mount. It would take the crack of the Second Coming to make it move any faster than it does!"

"Is the sniper still there?" Kinski asked.

Segalla stuck his head out from behind the carriage and back again. He was just in time, for a second shot rang out, the bullet smacking into a battered lamppost farther down the street.

"He's still there," Segalla replied. "And, my dear Detective, it may be of some comfort to you that whoever is firing wants me, not you."

"Well, we can't stay here forever," Kinski muttered. "Who could it be?"

Segalla had his own suspicions, but he decided to keep quiet.

"It could be Trabuer," Brunner observed. "He knew we were coming out."

"Nonsense!" Kinski said, examining his hat. "Did you see how he had to peer, screw up his eyes? He would not be able to find the trigger, never mind aim a gun!"

"Where are the shots coming from?" Segalla asked.

"From the top of the street," Kinski replied, peering round

the cab. "There's some sort of disused fountain or drinking trough. Our would-be assassin is lurking there."

Edging round, Kinski carefully took aim and fired. A few seconds later Brunner stepped out and fired his revolver. Segalla stared up at the windows of the houses along the streets: the gunfire was already drawing attention.

"It could be one of the gangs," Brunner observed. "They don't like to see police in this quarter."

"No, no," Segalla insisted. "It's me he's after!"

"Ah well," Brunner sighed; unbuttoning his coat, he drew out a huge whistle and began to blow with all his might. As he did, Kinski once again fired down the street, cursing under his breath as people began to come out of alleyways and doorways.

"Keep blowing that bloody whistle, Sergeant!"

Brunner did so, his face turning a beetroot red.

"Just pray, Herr Segalla," he said between blasts. "If the bastard at the top of the street doesn't get us, some of the villains round here might join in just for the fun of it!"

Segalla could only agree: ragged, fierce-looking men were now appearing in the doorways. He glimpsed one carrying a musket. They were not bothered by the secret assassin but gazed enviously at the well-groomed horse and smart carriage. Brunner sighed with relief.

"Can't you hear it?"

Segalla strained his ears and heard the faint blasts of police whistles. Brunner once more blew a blast and, from behind, they heard the sound of running feet. A group of helmeted policemen, guns at the ready, came out of an alleyway and raced towards them. The men in the doorway disappeared. Segalla stepped out from behind a carriage and realised he was safe. The assassin had fled.

Kinski gave the policemen orders to escort them. Brunner climbed up into the driver's seat whilst Segalla and Kinski got inside. With the two policemen walking on either side, they left

Villenstrasse, their escort not leaving them until they were out of Old Vienna. For most of the journey Kinski simply sat and raged, still disputing that this was some assassin, and loudly cursed, "Certain denizens of Vienna's underworld."

Once they were back in the hotel Segalla told Kinski and Brunner to be his guests in the bar. Brunner, smacking his lips, headed off like an arrow. Kinski stared at Segalla.

"And where are you going, sir?"

"Up to my room. Don't worry, I won't leave the hotel without you. I need to think."

Kinski reluctantly agreed. Segalla went across to the lobby desk.

"Please send to me," he asked the smug-looking clerk, "the valet who serves my room. I have a special task for him."

"Oh, he's not here at the moment, sir."

"Oh, I am sure he isn't," Segalla replied dryly. "But I'll wait for him."

# Chapter 10

Segalla must have sat for an hour before he heard a gentle knock on the door. He opened it; the valet, dressed in his white shirt and hotel waistcoat, stood expectantly.

"You wanted me, sir?"

"Yes, I do. Could you please bring coffee and a croissant?"

The man agreed and hurried off. A few minutes later he returned bearing a silver tray with coffee and croissants. He put this down on the table, refusing to meet Segalla's eye.

"Oh, don't be in such a hurry!" Segalla declared.

The man turned, the colour draining from his face as he looked at the gun Segalla was pointing at him.

"Sir, is this some joke?"

"Sit down," Segalla remarked, waving him to a chair on the other side of the table. "Of course, you can run, but I'd put a bullet in your leg, and that would be embarrassing for you and the hotel, not to mention your masters."

Segalla gently cocked back the hammer of the revolver, and the valet hurried to sit down. Segalla eased the hammer back carefully.

"Good!" he murmured. "Now, what is your name?"

"Theodore Ernst."

"Well, that's what you call yourself," Segalla said. "Please help yourself to some coffee."

"I don't want any. We are not supposed to drink whilst we work."

"Drink!" Segalla ordered.

The valet poured himself a cup. He looked up quickly.

"Don't do anything rash," Segalla murmured. "Like throwing the cup or plate at me. Now, Theodore"—Segalla watched the man sip the coffee—"you didn't put anything in that? Good! Don't look surprised. You are no more an employee of this hotel than I am. You are a member of the Viennese secret service working on the orders of Count Taaffe."

Segalla studied the man's moustache, beard, and carefully pared nails, and the callus on his right index finger.

"Once, Theodore, you were a soldier, but you resigned your commission to carry out a task for the prime minister. You visited Kati Polzer, Prince Rudolph's cook at Mayerling. You also followed us there this morning. Were you acting on orders?" Segalla asked. The man's hand shook slightly as he lifted the cup to his lips.

"What precisely were your orders?" Segalla asked. "I am sure you were not going to kill the papal emissary to Vienna."

"This is nonsense!" the man spluttered.

"Oh, no, it's the truth," Segalla interrupted. "You followed us to Villenstrasse and fired a few shots to frighten me and make me think twice about wandering the streets of Vienna asking embarrassing questions. Now, that doesn't worry me. It might Inspector Kinski and Sergeant Brunner—they don't like being shot at. I am also sure they don't feel too kindhearted to the secret service in general. I could call them up and they could join our little party." He waved the pistol. "Or, then again, I could just shoot you and claim you attacked me. The manager will come up, all hot and bothered. He'll explain you only joined the hotel, what, yesterday or the day before? Then Kinski and Brunner will search your little room and find your gun still reeking of cordite. You did take a walk through Vienna, didn't you? So, what's it going to be, eh? Truth or lies?" Again he cocked back the hammer.

"I am a member of the secret service," Theodore hastily replied, putting the cup down. "I am the emperor's loyal servant, special aide to the prime minister. Now, sir, please lower the pistol."

"And Kati Polzer?"

The man licked his lips, smoothing the corner of his moustache with one finger.

"Kati," Segalla insisted. "Where is she?"

"She's dead."

"You killed her?"

The man nodded.

"Why, because of what happened at Mayerling?"

Again the nod.

"Are you going to tell me?" Segalla deliberately let his hand shake.

"She was a thief," the agent replied. "When Prince Rudolph died, in the chaos which followed, Kati stole some money."

"From the prince's bedroom?"

"No, apparently some money was left in the billiard room. A wallet stuffed with notes. It went missing."

"And that's why she died?" Segalla asked, staring in disbelief. "Nothing else?"

"All those who were at Mayerling," the agent replied, "were carefully examined and interrogated about what happened there. They were under strict orders not to leave Vienna without permission from the police."

"What did happen at Mayerling?" Segalla eased back the hammer of his pistol and Theodore visibly relaxed. "Were you there?"

The agent lifted his hands. "I take an oath on the Bible, sir, that neither I nor any of my colleagues were at Mayerling when the prince died."

"Not even outside in the woods keeping an eye on our errant prince?"

"It only became a crisis," Theodore replied, "after the event. Once Count Hoyos returned to Vienna, Prime Minister Taaffe sent myself and nine other agents to Mayerling."

"So, ten secret service agents are dispatched to the hunting lodge!" Segalla exclaimed. "What were your orders?" His thumb hovered over the hammer of the pistol.

"To watch and keep the press away."

"And what did you find there?"

"Chaos," Theodore replied.

"Continue."

"By the time we arrived, Prince Coburg had sealed off the bedroom. No one was allowed in. Doctor Weiderhofer was also there. A short while later the imperial commission arrived; our task was simply security."

"Were you the leader of these agents?"

Theodore smiled sourly. "No, no. I am only a small piece in the grand design."

"And afterwards?"

"I was given a simple task: to ensure Kati, Loschek, and Bratfisch kept their mouths shut and did not leave Vienna." Theodore sipped from his cup. "Three days ago I received fresh orders. I was told a papal emissary was about to arrive. I was given strict instructions that, when told to, I was to keep an eye on you. Do whatever I had to to dissuade you from wandering around Vienna asking your questions."

Segalla grinned and lowered the pistol. "So, your masters must have been furious when I didn't come straight here from the station?"

"Yes, sir, they were, but I wasn't here."

"Oh, of course not," Segalla said dryly. "You were chasing poor Kati."

"She was an enemy of the state," Theodore replied flatly. "She was a liar and a thief: she had stolen the property of her dead master and ignored the instructions given to her. Oh, she could have kept the money, that didn't offend the powers that be. However, if she left the empire, what guarantee would the authorities here have that, when the money ran out, she would not concoct some fantastic story about what had happened at Mayerling and sell it to some Prussian newspaper?"

"Of course. And the Germans would love that, wouldn't they? What kind of stories could Kati sell?"

Theodore shrugged. "I leave it to your imagination. Stories about orgies at the hunting lodge, scandal."

"And, of course, that would be a lie?"

Theodore stared enigmatically back.

"And what do you think happened at Mayerling?" Segalla asked.

"Prince Rudolph was a degenerate!" the agent spat out. "He played at being a soldier. He did not realise his glorious destiny and that of the empire."

Segalla watched the man's light blue eyes and realised he was listening to a fanatic.

"He was drunk and he was maudlin," the agent continued remorselessly. "Involved in his petty little dramas. In such a mood he probably took his own life. You agree?"

"Perhaps." Segalla placed the revolver on the table. "Anyway, I want you out of this hotel within the hour. I do not want to see you again. I couldn't give a damn what you tell your superiors. Nor do I want you replaced."

The agent got up and swaggered towards the door.

"Wait!"

The agent turned.

"I have met so many like you," Segalla said. "No morality, no sense of justice. Your God is the state and your religion is the orders it issues. I do not want to see you again, and believe me sir, I will know if you return!"

The valet opened the door and closed it with a slam behind him.

Segalla picked up the revolver and, taking the bullets out of his pocket, reloaded it, relieved that the secret agent had not decided to test matters. He put this into the drawer of the table and reflected on what he had learnt. Theodore had probably been telling the truth, or at least what he thought was the truth. What he had found significant was that here was Taaffe sending his best secret agents to Mayerling as soon as he heard about the tragedy. Men sent to close all gaps, to limit the damage and watch the servants. At the same time, however, there seemed to be no trace of any involvement by Taaffe in Rudolph's actual death. So the conundrum remained: If Prince Rudolph was murdered, and the Austrian authorities had nothing to do with it, then why had not a manhunt been launched? Why had there been no attempt made to catch the killer?

Segalla decided to stretch his legs, so he put on his jacket, locked his room, and walked down to where Kinski and Brunner were drinking coffee in one of the lounges. He informed them that he would not be leaving the hotel that day, then returned to his room, where he began to puzzle over the questions he had listed. Now and again he would lie on the bed or go for a short walk round the hotel, but, try as he might, he could make no sense of what had happened at Mayerling. He was convinced it was murder, but how, why, and by whom remained a mystery.

On Sunday Segalla attended mass in a small baroque church just near the hotel, then took a stroll in the park with Kinski and Brunner. The two policemen were plainly disgruntled and gazed enviously at the families sitting out on the grass, tablecloths spread out, enjoying the first picnics of the year on a warm spring day.

At length Segalla grew tired of their morosely answering his questions about Viennese life with grunts and monosyllables, so he returned to his hotel, telling the detectives that he would be spending the day in his room. Segalla read the daily papers, enquired if any telegrams had come from Rome, revised what he had learnt about Rudolph's murders, and decided on an early night.

The next morning at nine o'clock, he met Kinski and Brunner for a quiet breakfast in the hotel restaurant before taking a cab to the Hofburg Palace. Brunner was still speculating on who had fired at them, but Segalla could see Kinski was clearly suspicious about it being some casual assault.

"It was almost as if someone wished to frighten us," the inspector remarked. "I mean, if a man lies in wait with a gun and intends to shoot, he'd be determined to at least wound, if not kill."

Segalla pulled back the blinds as the cab rattled through the gates of the palace and up the broad thoroughfare to the main door.

"You are a good policeman, Kinski," he remarked quietly. "A man of integrity." He stared across, ignoring the man's blushes. "If they had assigned you to investigate the prince's death, the truth would be out and I would not be needed here in Vienna."

Before Kinski could make a reply, the carriage stopped. Footmen in imperial livery opened the door and brought a stepping stool to help them out. A chamberlain, dressed like a peacock, a silver peruke perched on his head like a crown, led them up to the main door and into the splendid entrance hall of the Hofburg Palace. Segalla gazed appreciatively at the priceless paintings and Gobelin tapestries hanging on the walls; most of them depicted the history of Vienna, particularly its struggles against the Turks.

"His Excellency the emperor is waiting for you," the chamberlain announced, "in the Blue Room off the Rittersalle."

He led them up the staircase. Because of his starched clothes, the chamberlain moved slowly. At the top, Segalla turned left, going towards the marble hall with its gleaming white walls. The chamberlain coughed apologetically.

"Herr Segalla, I apologise for my slowness. I did not realise you had been here before."

Segalla could have kicked himself. Kinski was looking at him curiously. How could they know that he had been here and sat and marvelled at the glories of Mozart? That he had watched courtiers from another age, when the Hapsburgs were at the height of their power, sweep through the marble hall into the Rittersalle with its twenty-four Corinthian pillars of yellow marble, brilliant chandeliers, and exquisite mosaics?

"I have studied the plans of the palace," Segalla muttered. "In my eagerness . . ." He bowed and waved the chamberlain forward.

The chamberlain led them on, through the great Rittersalle, where the emperors held their great state occasions and down a passageway, turning right into the Blue Room. This was a long, exquisite chamber which derived its name from the blue-and-gold wallpaper, a large marble fireplace of the same hue, and thick woollen carpets dyed a deep azure. A long banqueting table ran down the centre of the room. At the top sat the emperor, wearing a simple black frock jacket, a white cravat round his neck, cream-coloured trousers, and black shiny shoes. He rose as Segalla came in and came forward for the papal envoy to kiss his hand. Formal salutations were given and received. The chamberlain withdrew. Kinski and Brunner stood by the door whilst Taaffe, dressed rather flamboyantly, a silver-coloured waistcoat straining round his waist, smiled jovially and made the introductions.

Baron Krauss, the police president, was there: tall, thickset, square headed; he looked strange with the hair on both sides of his head closely shaven. Krauss stood and walked like a British grenadier. He had popping, staring eyes, a luxuriant moustache, and muttonchop whiskers. Prince Coburg, dressed in black, was tall, thin, and rather austere, with deep furrows scoring the yellowing skin of his face. He forced a smile but his eyes were hard and calculating: he clearly resented being present. Count Hoyos, balding, fat, cheery faced, with quivering jowls and a double chin, at least pretended to be welcoming. The emperor retook his seat; Taaffe sat on his right, Krauss on his left; then, on either side of the table, sat Hoyos and Coburg. Segalla sat at the far end. The emperor was cold, not very welcoming: he hardly said a word, but coughed and whispered to Taaffe. The prime minister, on the other hand, became most relaxed: he slouched in his chair, playing with his fob watch or the golden cuff links in his silk cuffs.

"You have enjoyed your stay at the Hotel Imperial?" the emperor began.

"It's a place which grows on you," Segalla replied, glancing quickly at Taaffe. "The service seems to get better day by day."

Taaffe just grinned, hiding his smile behind his hand. The emperor glanced suspiciously at him and coughed. He joined his hands together as if in prayer and leaned against the table.

"I think it's best," he began, "if we arrange matters as we have. First, may I say that you are welcome in Vienna, Herr Segalla." He pulled a face. "Well, at least as the envoy of the Holy Father. At the same time, I must point out that my son's death is a domestic matter. However, we understand the Holy Father's concern. Accordingly, Herr Segalla, you have our permission to question those who were present at Mayerling the day he died. We should finish that business today. We will then reconvene on Friday, after you have had an opportunity to reflect on what has been said. You may ask further questions. After that, the matter is closed for good." He drummed his fingers on the table. "The matter is closed for good," he repeated. "No minutes will be kept of this meeting, neither by you nor by us."

"Your Imperial Excellency," Segalla replied quickly, "I thank you for your generosity in this matter. I have experienced your hospitality," he added dryly. "I will report as much to the Holy Father in Rome."

Taaffe took his hand away from his mouth as if to speak. Segalla was sure he was going to make some reference to the attack on him in Villenstrasse, but then he apparently thought better of it. Segalla realised that, if any protest was made, the imperial authorities would simply dismiss it, not so much as an attack upon Segalla, but as a most regrettable assault upon two of its officers in a rather seedy part of Vienna, a place Segalla shouldn't have been in the first place. Segalla loosened the buttons on his coat.

"It would be best," Baron Krauss declared, "if Herr Segalla confined himself to questions. Count Hoyos's statement and that of Prince Coburg are well known and have been reported in the press." He stared fixedly at Segalla.

"I agree," the papal envoy replied. "And it's those reports I wish to discuss. Count Hoyos, you were present with Prince Rudolph on the evening of the twenty-ninth?"

"Yes." Hoyos forced a smile. "My account is well known. I arrived there with Prince Coburg in the morning. We had breakfast with the prince, then we both went hunting. Coburg returned to the hunting lodge in the early afternoon."

"And the prince was well?" Segalla asked.

"We chatted for a while," Coburg snapped, not bothering to look at Segalla. "He had a cold and asked me to convey his deep regrets to his father, the emperor, that he was unable to attend the family dinner that night. I then took a carriage to Baden station and boarded the train to Vienna."

"In the hunting lodge," Segalla continued, "who was actually present, near the prince's quarters?"

"Myself," Hoyos replied. "Though I was about five hundred yards away. Bratfisch and Loschek were closer."

"You met the prince at seven o'clock?" Segalla asked.

"Yes, we had dinner in the billiard room, which lasted for about two hours. The prince talked about this or that, hunting matters. He said he had a cold and retired. I went to my own quarters."

"So," Segalla asked, "you had no inkling either that the prince intended to commit suicide or that Maria Vetsera was with him?"

"None," both Coburg and Hoyos chorused together.

Segalla looked at Taaffe. "And is it not true, Count Taaffe, that the prince intended to return to Vienna on the thirty-first? He actually sent a telegram to a member of your cabinet in which he said he looked forward to a meeting?"

"Correct," Taaffe replied airily.

"And Count Hoyos, is it not true that he had planned a hunt for the thirtieth?"

"Yes, that is so."

"So, here we have a prince," Segalla summarised, "who leaves Vienna to be with his mistress at a hunting lodge. True, he has a bad cold: he excuses himself from the hunt, but he seems in good spirits. He enjoys a hearty breakfast with Coburg and Hoyos on the morning of the twenty-ninth. He eats and drinks well at dinner on the same day. He plans to leave on the thirty-first, but all this ends in suicide."

His words created a pool of silence. Some of the forced jollity drained from Hoyos's face. Segalla drummed his fingers on the tabletop, deliberately allowing the sound to echo through the room.

"Now, Count Hoyos, you retired shortly after your dinner with the prince?"

"Yes."

"He gave no indication whatsoever of the impending tragedy?"

"None; he was mellow, claimed he was suffering from a cold."

"Was he?"

"Yes, but not as bad as some I have seen him suffer from."

"I am sorry to repeat myself," Segalla apologised, "but you heard or saw nothing of the Vetsera woman?"

"As I have said, nothing whatsoever!"

"And, from the time you left the prince until the following morning, you neither saw nor heard anything unremarkable at the lodge?"

"Nothing." Hoyos's lower lip jutted forward. "I rose next morning and prepared for a day's hunt. It was then that Loschek, the prince's personal valet, came across all agitated. According to him, Rudolph, apparently in good spirits, had come out of his room dressed in a smoking jacket or dressing gown, I forget which, and said he wished to be summoned again at seven-thirty."

"Can I interrupt there?" Segalla took a pen out of his inside pocket and played with it, unscrewing the top. Somehow, the movement relaxed him; he was aware of how the emperor and his ministers were watching him intently.

"Here again," Segalla remarked, "we have a conundrum. You say Rudolph was in high spirits?"

"Yes, he was whistling."

"Well, by then he must have decided to commit suicide, agreed?"

"Agreed."

"So, why tell Loschek to rouse him in an hour and a quarter?"

"I don't know."

"Do continue."

"I was leaving my apartment when Loschek came over," Hoyos declared. "It must have been about eight-fifteen. Loschek said he had been knocking on the prince's door for some time but was unable to get an answer. I went across with him. Only then did Loschek tell me that Maria Vetsera was present. I didn't know what to do. If we broke the doors down, and nothing was amiss, we would look foolish. By that time Prince Coburg had arrived."

"At what time was that?" Segalla asked.

"About eight-thirty," Prince Coburg answered. "I arrived at Baden at about eight o'clock and a cab took me at a swift trot to

Mayerling, arriving there at eight-thirty. I went to the billiard room and was told something was wrong. I advised Josef here"—he indicated Hoyos—"the door should be broken down. Loschek brought an axe, smashed in the panelling, and turned the key."

"So the doors to the prince's apartment had been locked from the inside and the keys left there?"

"Definitely."

"Were there any lights in the room?"

"None whatsoever. It was dark. That"—Hoyos was fairly gabbling now—"that's how I made the mistake on how the prince had died."

"But this doesn't make sense," Segalla replied swiftly. "If Prince Rudolph had risen early, let's say six o'clock, surely he would have opened the curtains and the shutters? Lit the lamps?"

Hoyos swallowed hard, his eyes flickering to where Taaffe was sitting.

"A good question," the prime minister drawled. "And I wondered about that. But, can't you see, Segalla, my dear, if the prince wished to commit suicide, he would prefer the darkness? The solitude, the tranquillity?"

"And the gun?" Segalla turned back to Hoyos. "Did you go into the room?"

"Just a little way. I admit I was horrified. I was in shock," Hoyos spluttered. "The prince was sitting on the bed, head forward, hands hanging down. On the other side, I glimpsed the body of a woman laid out carefully. I didn't see any blood on her. You must remember the Vetsera woman was killed by one shot. She had thick, black hair, which covered the wound."

"And the prince?"

"I saw some blood on his face. I thought he had haemorrhaged. Certain poisons cause that." Hoyos shrugged. "Whatever, they were dead. I left and got Bratfisch to drive me to Baden station. I thought I should take the news myself to the emperor rather than send a telegram. When I reached Vienna," Hoyos continued hurriedly, "I approached certain court officials. They advised me that the empress should be told first; she later told His Excellency."

"So the story you brought," Segalla said, "was that Prince Rudolph had committed suicide by poison?"

"Yes."

"Then why," Segalla asked, "for that entire day, and even part of the following day, the thirty-first"—he looked directly at Taaffe—"did certain newspapers report that the prince had died of heart failure?"

"It was confusion," Taaffe replied languidly. "Herr Segalla, it is easy for you to sit in judgement on us—"

"I am not doing that."

"No, no, of course you are not. But you must appreciate the situation: the death of the heir to the Austrian throne was a great shock. The important thing was that he was dead. We were un-sure of the facts. The heart-failure story, I admit, was a smoke screen until we got full possession of the facts."

"But you had these," Segalla insisted. "You could have telegraphed Mayerling. Coburg was here. I believe Dr. Weider-hofer, the court physician, had also arrived?"

"He came about noon," Coburg replied abruptly.

"And how long would it take a skilled physician to determine that a man has not died of poisoning or heart failure, but of a gunshot wound to the head?"

Taaffe shrugged. "We saw that as a matter of little conse-quence. Don't forget, my dear Segalla, I am not saying we did not know the facts." He emphasized his words for effect. "In-deed, as the prince had been shot, we then had to ensure it was suicide and not some dreadful act of murder. Moreover, we were already thinking of the future. Prince Rudolph was not liked by the clergy. I immediately anticipated the problems this would cause in securing ecclesiastical burial." He spread his hands. "I know the truth was not told immediately, but we do have our rights in the matter. It is up to the emperor to decide whether that truth should be told."

He smiled across at Segalla, who quietly conceded that what Taaffe had said made sense. The prince had died: there would be confusion, anxiety, fear. He glanced at Coburg.

"And what happened at Mayerling?"

"After Hoyos had left," Prince Coburg replied, "I studied the scene more carefully. Rudolph had blood smears from his mouth and nose, as did the Vetsera woman. The gunshot also caused what I later learnt was an implosion, a shattering of the brain. I decided to wait: Dr. Weiderhofer was on his way."

"How did you know that?"

"Before I left, I told Loschek to telegraph for him," Hoyos countered.

"Anyway," Coburg brusquely returned to his story, "I noticed the prince's right hand hanging down beside the bed. A revolver lay on the floor. Beside the prince was a small table with a mirror on it and a glass of brandy. I sniffed it—there was no poison."

"And the revolver?" Segalla asked.

"An army version, squat and thick; Rudolph often carried such a revolver."

"Did you pick it up?"

"Yes I did. I checked the chambers. There were two bullets missing. I placed it on the table and looked round the room. It was then that I noticed the letters."

"Did you open them?"

"Of course not. I did not touch anything, well, apart from the revolver."

"What was the situation at Mayerling?"

"Confusion. Servants came in. People from the stables were milling about. I became concerned: there were precious objects, money lying around. I didn't think it was seemly for grooms to gawk at their dead prince. I cleared the room and waited until Dr. Weiderhofer arrived." Coburg shrugged. "Once he did, round about noon, I handed matters over to him."

The emperor, who had been sitting like a statue, suddenly coughed and dabbed at his moustache with a handkerchief. "Herr Segalla," he declared slowly, "I am convinced that Prince Coburg has told the truth, both to me and to yourself."

Segalla stared down at the purple blotting paper placed on the desk before him. So everything that had been said made sense. He glanced up and caught Prince Coburg's eyes: he glimpsed the mockery, and that told him everything; it might make sense, but it was not the truth!

# Chapter 11

L et's stretch our legs," Franz Joseph declared. He gestured at Baron Krauss. "Tell the servants coffee will be served."

For a while the meeting broke up. The doors were opened. Kinski and Brunner took the tray from the servants and put it on the table. Segalla caught Kinski's eye: the detective winked sympathetically at him. Franz Joseph lit a cigar, and others followed. No one approached Segalla: he was left sipping his coffee whilst the emperor and the rest gathered at the far end of the room, clustered together, whispering softly. Segalla could see by their faces how pleased they were at the way things were proceeding. Never once did Krauss or Taaffe indicate they knew their agent had been sent packing or display any embarrassment at the attack on him in Villenstrasse. Just before the meeting reconvened, Taaffe wandered over, one hand in the pocket of his waistcoat, the other holding his cigar. He leaned against the table.

"In a week you'll be back in Rome. You must miss the heat, the sun. Vienna can be so cold."

"I am used to it," Segalla replied.

"Yes, yes, I wager you are." The prime minister pulled up a chair and sat down and let the ash fall onto the table. "Your name rings a bell," the prime minister continued, smiling falsely. "I am always interested in family history. Mine hail from Ireland. My ancestors came to Vienna to fight against the Turks."

"Everyone comes to Vienna," Segalla quipped back, "sooner or later."

"I am sure they do," Taaffe replied. "Ah well." He leaned across Segalla and stubbed out his cigar in the ashtray.

"Your Excellency," he called out. "We should reconvene!"

Franz Joseph agreed. They retook their seats. The emperor gestured at Segalla to continue.

"Count Hoyos," Segalla began. "You arrived in Vienna at about . . . ?"

"Eleven-thirty," the count replied.

"We've been through this already," Taaffe interrupted. "Herr Segalla"—he sat up in his chair, clasping his hand on the table before him—"Count Hoyos performed a very sad duty, as did Prince Coburg. We have explained why false reports of the prince's death were circulated."

"The question I was going to ask," Segalla persisted, "is a simple one: was the news of the prince's death a complete surprise?"

"Of course," Taaffe scoffed. "A terrible shock!"

"But what I fail to comprehend," Segalla added smoothly, "is we now know the prince committed suicide. The Holy Father granted permission for Church burial because Prince Rudolph was not of sound mind when he committed the act." He pointed at Taaffe. "And this is the heart of the mystery. Why should a prince, with so much before him, who had already planned to leave Mayerling—he even sent telegrams saying as much to one of your ministers, Count Taaffe—why should he abruptly kill his mistress and then himself?"

"We don't know," Taaffe retorted. "You failed to mention one variable in your question. We are uncertain about the influence of the Vetsera woman on him."

"Are you saying that Prince Rudolph was infatuated with her?" Segalla asked.

"Possibly."

"Yet there's no indication that she wanted to die. Indeed," Segalla continued, "I understand the prince was still meeting other ladies with whom he had a relationship, only days before he left for Mayerling. Moreover, if Rudolph was infatuated with this young woman, why weren't both of them kept under closer surveillance?" He gestured at Police President Krauss. "On the twenty-eighth of January, when Maria Vetsera fled to Mayerling, her mother came and pleaded with you that Maria had gone away with the prince and she was concerned for both of them. However, you sent no agents down there, even when the prince failed to return to Vienna on the evening of the twenty-ninth for a family dinner?"

"We failed to respond"—Krauss paused, breathing noisily through his nose—"because we are talking after the event, Herr Segalla, not before. True, Prince Rudolph met his ladylove. But"—he spread his thick, stubby fingers—"we failed to understand the true relationship between the two. We also seriously underestimated her influence on him."

"Yet her mother was disturbed, alarmed?"

"That should be seen in context," Baron Krauss snapped back. "The Vetseras are social climbers. Countess Vetsera was not concerned about the prince's safety or that of her daughter but about her family's reputation. They wanted her to marry someone of repute at the court. Once it was public knowledge that Maria was Rudolph's mistress, she was, how would you put it, 'spoiled goods'? That's why the Vetseras wanted her back."

"Yet the question remains," Segalla persisted. "What happened at Mayerling to turn the thoughts of both these young people to suicide?"

"The prince was highly strung," Taaffe intervened. "He was known to drink heavily. Rudolph was also reliant on morphine and other drugs. Maria Vetsera may also have shared, how can I put it, these weaknesses?"

"So you are saying"—Segalla glanced quickly at the emperor, who sat, fingers to his mouth, staring down the table—"you are saying that the real cause of this tragedy is that the prince and Maria Vetsera were dependent on alcohol and other drugs?"

"It would seem so," Taaffe answered.

Segalla decided to push matters a little further.

"Yes," he declared slowly. "That would make sense." He tapped his fingers on the table. "Of course, if the prince and his mistress were addicted to morphine . . ."

"Precisely," Taaffe replied.

"And that can be established?" Segalla asked.

"Of course," Taaffe repeated. "I am more than prepared to show you the dispensary book."

"You must also remember," Krauss intervened, "that on the twenty-ninth we had no reason to believe the prince was in danger." He waved his hand airily. "His close friend Count Hoyos was in attendance. Prince Rudolph sent a telegram to his wife saying he was suffering from a cold, whilst the record will prove that, on the morning of the thirtieth, I sent Police Inspector Edward Bayer to Mayerling to ensure all was well. Bayer travelled on the same train as Prince Coburg. We had no reason to believe anything dreadful was going to happen."

Segalla turned to Franz Joseph. "And the rumours of a violent quarrel between Your Excellency and your son the crown prince?"

"Complete nonsense!" the emperor snapped. He placed his cigar in the ashtray. "Herr Segalla, we are spending a day on this matter. Do you have anything further to ask? If not, the cabby Bratfisch and the valet Loschek are waiting, not to mention others."

Segalla shrugged. "For the time being I have no further questions."

"In which case"—Taaffe pushed back his chair—"I shall bring our guests in."

Segalla watched him walk down the room and wondered why a prime minister should go to fetch a cabby and a valet. Taaffe was gone some time, and by the time he had returned, the silence had grown oppressive. The two individuals who accompanied Taaffe were clearly nervous. Both men were burly, thick-set, dressed in their best apparel. They refused to meet Segalla's eyes as they took their seats farther down the table. Segalla hid his smile. Taaffe was clever: to question the new arrivals, he would have to turn his back slightly, which meant he would not be able to see the emperor or his ministers. Consequently, these could gaze as balefully as they wanted at these two court under-lings. Both men introduced themselves. Loschek then spoke first, describing the prince's arrival at Mayerling, corroborating every detail provided by Coburg and Hoyos about the events of 29 January. Segalla heard him out.

"So you, Master Bratfisch, brought the woman to Mayerling?"

"Yes." The cabby scratched his close-cut hair and smoothed his moustache. "I often did that." He pulled a face. "We knew Vetsera's mother would prevent her coming, hence the secrecy."

"And on the morning of the thirtieth?" Segalla asked. "You had your carriage ready?"

"Yes, that was the prince's orders. I was to take Maria back to Vienna."

"And the prince would stay?"

"Yes. That's why Prince Coburg was returning for another day's hunt."

"So you and Loschek knew Maria Vetsera was in the hunting lodge?"

"Yes," they chorused.

"She never left there?"

"No," Loschek replied.

He blinked nervously, not so steady either in his manner or his voice as Bratfisch. The valet kept glancing up the table, as if seeking the approval of his superiors.

"So what did she do?" Segalla asked, choosing to ignore Taaffe's quiet snigger.

"She stayed with the prince. They talked."

"About what?"

"Whenever I entered the room, they would always stop talking, whilst from outside, I could only hear the murmur of their voices."

"And were they in good spirits?"

"They were sad, deeply engrossed in themselves. The prince was very restless."

"Did they drink? You see," Segalla added quickly, "Count Hoyos says that when he left the prince on the evening of the twenty-ninth, His Excellency was lucid and clear."

"He drank deeply later," Loschek replied. "He also had pains in his stomach and took morphine which he brought from Vienna."

"Did he share this with Maria Vetsera?"

"Perhaps," Loschek replied. "However, on the evening of the twenty-ninth both were, how can I say, a little the worse for wear. That's why," he added in a gabble, "some glasses were knocked over in the room, which gave rise to the rumours of a struggle."

"Did you clear it up?" Segalla asked.

"I did what I could," Loschek replied. "But the prince told me that he wanted to be alone with Maria. I was told to return to my own quarters. Prince Rudolph ordered that he was not to be disturbed, even by the emperor himself."

"And that was it?"

"Yes."

"There was no hint, or talk, of suicide?"

"None whatsoever, but they were slightly maudlin, lost in their own world."

Segalla turned to Bratfisch. "But that's not true, is it?"

Loschek started. "What do you mean?"

"Well, according to one of Maria Vetsera's farewell letters, she added a postscript; 'Bratfisch whistled beautifully.' "

"How did you see those letters?" Taaffe's voice was harsh; the prime minister was no longer slouching in his chair but was sitting up, almost leaning over the table.

"Surely that's neither here nor there," Segalla replied. "Loschek claimed he left Prince Rudolph alone with Maria. Yet it would appear that some form of entertainment took place."

"Oh, that was nothing," Bratfisch spoke up. "No wonder I overlooked it. Often, at night, the prince would ask me to sing or whistle, particularly the latter. He claimed I had a gift. I did so, that evening, for a short while."

"So they were happy?" Segalla asked.

"Oh yes."

"So not in the mood for suicide?"

"Of course not."

Bratfisch looked nervously up the table: neither the emperor nor his companions would like such a reply. Yet, if Bratfisch had said yes, neither he nor Loschek would be able to explain their master's sudden and fatal change of mood.

"Tell us, Loschek," Taaffe intervened silkily, "tell us what else happened that night."

"After Bratfisch had entertained them," Loschek hastily replied, "Prince Rudolph told me not to disturb them. I left but could hear them murmuring. They talked long into the night."

"Long into the night?" Segalla queried. "So"—he steepled his fingers, resting his elbows on the table—"Count Hoyos says he left the prince at nine o'clock. Prince Rudolph returned to his own chamber, where his ladylove was waiting. I suppose Maria Vetsera was fed from the kitchen?"

"Yes. I brought her a tray myself," Loschek replied.

"And we know Bratfisch entertained them for a short while." Segalla lowered his hands. "So, Loschek, what time do you think the prince asked you to leave?"

"It must have been some time between eleven and twelve."

"And they continued to talk long into the night? How long?"

"Oh, I went to bed at about two o'clock in the morning," Loschek replied.

"And they were still talking?"

"Yes."

Segalla decided to keep his own counsel on the information he had received about the floor polisher, Wolfe.

"Do you think," he asked slowly, "that the prince and Maria Vetsera both took alcohol and drugs?"

"It's possible," Loschek replied. "The prince had stomach trouble. He drank more than he should have done. I myself advised him to be careful with the morphine."

Segalla nodded understandingly. "And the events that night?" he asked. "Do continue."

Loschek pulled a face. "I slept for a few hours, very deeply."

"And when you woke up?"

"It was about a quarter to six. I went to the prince's bedroom but could hear nothing."

"And then what?"

"I was in the antechamber doing a few tasks, clearing up, when the prince came out. He was in his dressing gown. . . ."

"And how was he?"

"It was about quarter past six in the morning." Loschek now looked confidently at Segalla, as if he had reached a part of the history he knew by rote. "He looked tired but he was whistling under his breath. He told me to tell Bratfisch to have the cab ready by eight, and that I was to go away but return at seven-thirty. I think," Loschek added slowly, "he just wanted me out of the way."

"You mean, by then the prince had decided to commit suicide?"

"Yes, yes, I do."

"Do you think Maria Vetsera was dead by then?" Segalla asked.

"I don't know," Loschek replied. "I really don't, sir. All I do know is that I returned at seven-thirty. I couldn't get any answer: the doors were all locked—that was strange—the prince very rarely did that. At first, I was not too concerned: I thought he might be sleeping deeply. However, I came again." His voice dropped to a whisper. "It was about eight-ten. I could get no reply, so I went to find Count Hoyos. He was later joined by Prince Coburg: the rest you know."

"We've been through that," Taaffe agreed.

"Yes, but there are certain details I would like clarified," Segalla protested. He turned back to the valet. "You broke the door down?"

"Yes, with an axe: I smashed the panelling. I put my hand through and turned the key."

"And the room was in darkness?"

"The candles were doused. The shutters over the window had been pulled close and the curtains drawn."

"What exactly did you see?"

"The prince was seated on the left side of the bed as I looked at it, head forward. Maria Vetsera lay to his right. There was a flower in her hand. At first I didn't see the blood on her but I saw some on the lower half of my master's face. I never saw the gun, not till later, because his hand was down the side of the bed and the revolver lay on the floor."

"So you thought he had been poisoned?"

"Yes, I did. I hurried back to where Prince Coburg and Count Hoyos were standing just inside the room. They were shocked. I told them the prince had been poisoned—that was my mistake."

"And then what happened?"

"Count Hoyos sent me here to telegraph Vienna, to ask Dr. Weiderhofer to come immediately. Then he left. For a time everything was confusion. Some of the servants came in, all goggle-eyed, staring about. Prince Coburg"—the valet smiled at the cadaverous-faced nobleman—"imposed order. He ordered them all out and closed the door."

"And you, Bratfisch?" Segalla turned to the cabby man.

"I was in my carriage. Everything was ready. Count Hoyos came hurrying out with his coat over his arm. He told me, well, he ordered me to take him straight to Baden railway station. I knew something terrible had happened. I pestered him with questions." He smiled apologetically up the table. "But he didn't answer. He just told me to wait there until Dr. Weiderhofer came from Vienna."

Segalla stared down at these two servants. Like actors, he thought, delivering well-rehearsed lines. Surely Bratfisch would have known what was wrong. He would have hurried in to see his dead master. And why didn't Loschek take more careful note of the dead prince? Seize his wrist, feel for a pulse, and then see the gun?

"Do you have any more questions for these men?" Taaffe asked. He pulled his fob watch from the pocket of his waistcoat. "Time is drawing on," he remarked. "We are all, Herr Segalla, very busy people, and there are other witnesses to be called."

"Then you'd best call them," Segalla retorted.

"Shouldn't we break for lunch?" the emperor asked. "A light repast, a glass of wine?"

"If Your Excellency wishes," Count Taaffe replied, sitting up in his chair. "But, then again, since Dr. Weiderhofer and Herr Henry Slatin have been waiting for some time, it should not take long to finish these matters."

The emperor agreed. Bratfisch and Loschek hurriedly left. The few minutes' silence was broken by the arrival of Dr. Weiderhofer, short, fat, balding, with a pince-nez perched on the end of his plump nose. Count Henry Slatin, whom Taaffe introduced as secretary to the imperial commission at Mayerling, was young, tall, and slender, with a narrow, aristocratic face—a man full of his own worth and importance. Slatin bowed ceremoniously towards the emperor, then sat down, elegantly picking up the folds of his grey frock coat, whilst Weiderhofer fussed through his papers. Slatin smiled at Hoyos, Coburg, Krauss, and Taaffe; he threw a contemptuous look at Segalla.

"Dr. Weiderhofer," Taaffe began. "Count Henry Slatin. Both of you visited Mayerling on the thirtieth of January. Dr. Weiderhofer, you examined the prince's corpse. Count Slatin, you were secretary to the commission set up to investigate the tragic circumstances surrounding Prince Rudolph's death. Herr Segalla here is from Rome. The Holy Father wishes to be satisfied on the true nature of the prince's death." He sat back in his chair, wound his watch up, then waved airily at Segalla.

"Dr. Weiderhofer"—Segalla decided to be as blunt as everyone else in the room—"you arrived at Mayerling at what time?"

"About noon."

"What did you find?"

"Prince Coburg and Loschek were guarding the prince's bedroom." The doctor spoke quickly. "I was ushered in."

"And how did you find the chamber?"

"The two doors had been forced. Loschek told me why."

"And inside?"

"The room was very dark although the day had brightened. I immediately drew the curtains, opened the shutters, and unlocked one of the windows. The air was stale; I thought it best."

"There was no sign of any forced entry? I mean, through the windows?"

"No, of course not."

"What else did you find in the room?"

"There was broken glass on the floor. Some bloodstains on the carpet."

"And the corpses?"

"Prince Rudolph lay on the left of the bed, body slightly slumped, head forward. The top of his head"—Weiderhofer tapped his own balding pate—"had also been ruptured."

"Why was that?" Segalla asked.

Weiderhofer turned in his chair, using his fingers to demonstrate.

"Prince Rudolph had apparently shot himself just above the right temple. The exit wound was above the left ear. He would have died instantly, but the force of the explosion shattered the top half of his cranium."

"And the young woman?"

"She was lying down on the bed. There was a dry trickle of blood running from her mouth down to her dress: her head wound was similar to that of the prince. She, too, must have died immediately."

"And the revolver?"

"I found it on the table where Prince Coburg had put it. It was a general army revolver; two of the chambers were empty."

"What happened to the bullets and the gun?" Segalla asked.

Weiderhofer waved his stubby fingers as if that did not concern him. "I was there for medical reasons," he replied primly, taking off his pince-nez and staring owlishly at Segalla. "It is not my duty to pass judgement on what else happened."

"So, what did?" Segalla asked.

Weiderhofer shrugged. "Well, on the table there was also a mirror and a brandy glass. There was a little brandy left. I smelt it and dabbed some on my tongue."

"And?"

"It was nothing but brandy."

"And the mirror?"

"I think the prince had used it to position the revolver. I have heard that happened before in suicides."

"And how long had they been dead?" Segalla asked.

"About five to six hours; I believe Maria Vetsera had been dead a little longer."

"How much longer?"

Weiderhofer seemed a little flustered: his eyes flickered to the top of the table.

"I don't know. Perhaps an hour?"

Segalla leaned back and stared up at the ceiling. If anything proved he was being told a pack of lies, that did. The earliest the prince could have shot himself was six-thirty. If Maria Vetsera had been shot an hour earlier, surely Loschek would have heard. Moreover, would the prince have been so cold and callous as to go out whistling after murdering a woman he was supposed to have loved?

"I know what you are thinking." Taaffe now sat sideways on his chair, one arm over the back. "Why weren't the shots heard? The walls of the hunting lodge are thick; Loschek was elsewhere."

"Maria Vetsera," Segalla said sharply. "If she was killed before six-fifteen, surely someone would have heard the shot?"

"You must appreciate," Henry Slatin, sitting ever so prim and proper, spoke up. "You must appreciate, Herr Segalla, that the prince must have used blankets and cushions to deaden the shot."

"Did he now?" Segalla replied. "But none of the witnesses talked of a pillow near the prince's head."

Slatin smiled maliciously. "I didn't say that. He used the pillow for Vetsera. You see," Slatin continued, "I suspect that the prince, God rest him, killed Maria Vetsera and then himself."

"Yes, that makes me wonder," Segalla retorted. "Why all this silence on the part of the prince?"

"So no one could stop him," Slatin replied quickly.

"That is true," Weiderhofer intervened. "In my experience, Herr Segalla, people who commit suicide usually do so quietly."

"You examined both bodies?" Segalla asked.

"Oh yes."

"And there were no other marks on the corpses?"

"None whatsoever. Why should there be?"

Segalla turned back to the emperor. "Your Excellency, what happened to the blankets from the prince's bed?"

"They were brought back to Vienna and burnt. I did not want them on sale in the marketplace as curios for those who like to pry and pore over such matters."

"And the revolver?"

"The same thing happened."

"And the two bullets? Count Slatin, you were secretary to the commission who visited Mayerling?"

"We found them," Slatin replied. "Each in the woodwork behind the bed, which would be in accord with their trajectory."

You are a liar, Segalla thought. Why destroy a gun? What is it, he fumed inwardly, you are all trying to hide?

"What else did you find in the room, Count Slatin?" he asked.

"Nothing, except some of the prince's personal possessions; nothing remarkable."

"And the letters?" Segalla asked.

"They were on a dresser."

"So," Segalla continued, "you found nothing in that room which would suggest that Prince Rudolph and his mistress were killed by another hand?"

"Nothing," they both chorused together. "Nothing at all."

"Do you have any more questions for them?" Taaffe asked softly.

Segalla kept his face impassive, hiding his deep irritation.

"No, Prime Minister, I do not."

Taaffe flicked his fingers. Weiderhofer and Slatin pushed back their chairs, bowed towards the emperor, and quietly left the room.

"Well." Taaffe beamed beatifically. "Herr Segalla, we are finished . . . ?"

"There is one question." Segalla scratched his chin. He'd just listened to a tissue of lies. No one had satisfactorily explained why a young man and woman, who had never betrayed any hint of suicide, should have taken their lives so abruptly. Surely, if someone like Loschek had thought his royal master was intent on committing suicide, he would have intervened? Telegraphed Vienna or taken more decisive action?

"We are waiting," Taaffe declared.

"I am sorry," Segalla apologised. "But so far, Prime Minister, I have not found, apart from the possible influence of morphine and alcohol, any reason why Prince Rudolph should have committed suicide. Nothing appears to have happened at Mayerling to make him take such extreme measures. However, I have heard that on the morning before he left Vienna he was very anxious, perhaps waiting for a telegram?" He glanced at Franz Joseph. "Your Excellency, do you know what might have been in that telegram?"

"No," the emperor replied. "We do not. Perhaps it was a message from his lover? However, no trace of it remains."

"Are we finished?" Taaffe repeated.

"You did say," Segalla asked, "that I would be able to examine the dispensary book about the prince taking morphine?"

Taaffe nodded. "That will be brought to you before you leave."

The Prime Minister stood up and walked down the table to face Segalla more squarely. He alone, of all the men in the room, including the emperor, appeared to be the master of events. Franz Joseph, the police president, Count Hoyos, and Prince Coburg sat as if carved out of stone.

"You have listened to the evidence—" Taaffe declared.

"It is a pity I cannot see any document," Segalla interrupted.

"Herr Segalla!" The emperor abruptly rose.

Segalla, so frustrated at the lies he had been told, remained seated, ignoring the gasps of Coburg.

"Herr Segalla, we shall leave this matter now," Franz Joseph declared. "On Friday, at ten o'clock, we shall reconvene to answer any further questions. Do you have anything to say?"

Segalla pointed down the room to where Kinski and Brunner stood on guard at the door.

"I would like their removal," he declared. "I am the accredited envoy of the Holy Father. They are a nuisance and an obstacle!"

"Impossible." Taaffe smiled back. "My dear Segalla, they are there for your protection. After all," he added meaningfully, "we cannot allow anything to happen to you during your short stay in Vienna."

And, spinning on his heel, Taaffe followed the emperor and the rest out of the room.

Segalla sat and waited.

"Well, well, my dear Kinski"—he leaned back in the chair—"you can tell your grandchildren that you knew of a murder and did nothing about it."

# Chapter 12

Segalla waited for at least half an hour before the prescription book of the Vienna court pharmacy was brought down for his inspection. A servant handed it to Kinski, whispering instructions. The detective laid it before Segalla.

"Thank you," Kinski murmured. "For what you said."

Segalla grinned. "It's the least I could do, dear Kinski, so, when I am safe and sound back in Rome, who knows, it may be Chief Inspector Kinski, and you can go on to greater things." He opened the calfskin-bound tome. "However, for the moment, let us look at Prince Rudolph's prescriptions."

Segalla leafed through the carefully written pages. Most of the prescriptions were standard, many of them herbal, for the different minor ailments of the emperor and his court. Nevertheless, from 1886 onwards, Prince Rudolph's name appeared more often, and the medicines became more potent: natrium salicylicum, morphia in cocoa butter, zinc sulfate, coprea balsam. The doses of morphine became stronger and more frequent. The morphine entries had been underlined as if to attract his attention. Segalla sat back in the chair and stared across at the painting of a long-dead Hapsburg.

If these entries are correct, he reflected, by January 1889 Prince Rudolph would have almost been an addict. If he drank copious amounts of alcohol and mixed it with the morphine, such a concoction would cloud any judgement and lead to radical character changes. Was this the solution? Was Prince Rudolph an addict who, under the influence of morphia and alcohol, shot his mistress, then himself? Was all the rest merely a charade to hide all this? How could the emperor advertise to the world that his son was a drug addict, an alcoholic who capped his degeneracy by murder and suicide? Segalla ran his finger round his lips. Rudolph's enemies here in Vienna, not to mention his opponents in Germany, would love such a scandal. Segalla returned to the prescription book: he turned one sheet, thinner than the rest, where Widow Crown Princess Stephanie's prescriptions were listed for November and December 1888. Segalla did not understand most of the medicines listed there, which were probably for gynaecological complaints. He closed the book, sighed, and pushed it away.

"Are you going to leave, sir?" Kinski came across, looking suitably inscrutable. "Count Taaffe says if you find it useful, you may visit Mayerling again."

"Yes, yes, of course," Segalla replied absentmindedly. "We should leave."

They left the Blue Room, Kinski handing the prescription book back to a waiting valet. They made their way quietly along the corridors and down the stairways out to the waiting cab. Once inside, Segalla closed his eyes, preferring to concentrate on what had happened, but Kinski stretched across and thrust a piece of paper into his hand.

"I think you should read that, sir!"

Segalla opened it, pulling back the blind for better light. It was the report of Edward Bayer, the police inspector, dated Vienna, 31 January 1889.

"Acting upon superior orders," it began,

*I left Vienna for Baden by way of Southern Railway on the thirtieth of this month at six o'clock in the morning. I travelled on the same train as His Excellency, Prince Coburg, who alighted at Baden and thereupon drove straight to Mayerling by cab. I fol-*

*lowed in a second cab and we arrived there towards 8:30 A.M.*
*Prince Coburg drove straight up to the hunting lodge and I im-*
*mediately made my enquiries. Barely fifteen minutes passed when*
*I saw the cabby Bratfisch driving Count Hoyos to Baden in a great*
*hurry.*

Segalla skimmed the rest and came to the penultimate paragraph.

*Towards twelve o'clock, on the same road from Mayerling to*
*Baden, I encountered the cabby Bratfisch driving along in a great*
*hurry with Professor Weiderhofer.*

Bayer then described other people arriving at Mayerling.
Segalla studied Bayer's last paragraph.

*According to enquiries I have made, the hunting lodge is said*
*to have been exceptionally brightly lit during the night twenty-ninth*
*to thirtieth: an entertainment is said to have taken place there. Dur-*
*ing that same night Count Hoyos and the cabby Bratfisch were*
*guests of the crown prince at the Mayerling hunting lodge.*
                                    *Signed Edward Bayer, Inspector.*

"Have you read it?" Kinski asked. "Do you remember what
has been written there? It's a copy. I did it myself." Kinski held
his hand out. "Sir, I need it back."

"Thank you," Segalla murmured, and handed it over. He
pulled back the blind and stared out at the traffic. "You heard
what was said in the Blue Room?"

"Yes!"

Segalla let the blind fall. "It was a pack of lies," Segalla murmured. "According to Hoyos and Loschek, Prince Coburg was
there some time. However, according to Bayer, Coburg didn't
arrive until eight-thirty, and barely five minutes later, according

to Bayer, Hoyos was in Bratfisch's cab, racing towards Baden railway station. Now, Kinski, if Coburg arrived just before eight-thirty, he spends at least three minutes getting to the prince's quarters, yes?"

Kinski nodded.

"And, let us say for the sake of argument, Hoyos spends two minutes getting his cloak and hat before going out and getting into the cab. That means Coburg and Hoyos were together little more than a few minutes. However, according to the testimony we heard this morning, there were long deliberations about what was to be done, the breaking down of doors, the discovery of the prince's corpse, etcetera, etcetera." Segalla smiled. "Someone is lying."

"And there's more," Kinski added. "Bayer is a good policeman, scrupulous in every detail."

"What is it?" Segalla asked.

"Think, my dear Segalla," Kinski replied, imitating Taaffe. "I have served you a dish and you must eat it." He tore up the paper he had given Segalla and carefully put all the pieces into his coat pocket.

Segalla closed his eyes. He thought of Coburg's cab hurrying along the Baden road towards Mayerling. Of course . . . He opened his eyes.

"Isn't it strange that Prince Coburg, who attended a formal dinner the night before, left Vienna so early?"

"He had to be there for a hunt," the detective replied.

"Well, we can always ask Wodicka the chief huntsman what time it was scheduled for. If, indeed, a hunt was planned."

"And what else?" Kinski asked.

"Well, it's remarkable," Segalla replied, "that Mayerling is a sprawling hunting lodge, yet Coburg immediately goes to the prince's quarters. He does not go to his own room. He does not look for Hoyos but almost rushes in, as if he knows something has happened." Segalla paused, trying to curb the tingling excitement in his stomach. "So," he muttered, "let's forget all this nonsense about the breaking down of the prince's doors. Hoyos only leaves when Coburg arrives, doesn't he? It's almost as if Hoyos was waiting, as if he couldn't leave Mayerling until someone responsible had arrived."

"And," Kinski whispered, "Loschek's story about everyone being in bed doesn't seem to ring true. Bayer talks of lights being on."

"Yes, he does."

A faint suspicion stirred in Segalla's mind. So far none of what he had been told made sense. Moreover, there was something he had learnt in the Blue Room which was out of place, a phrase, a word, but he couldn't recall it. In addition, two important questions still remained unanswered. Why did the prince commit suicide? And why was a false story allowed to circulate in Vienna?

"You heard our dear Count Taaffe," Segalla remarked. "I do have permission to visit Mayerling again."

Kinski put his face in his hands and groaned.

"And, on the way," Segalla said, "we'll stop at Baden station. I want to discover how much of Hoyos's tale is true."

Brunner, with Kinski's orders shouted through the gap, urged his horse to a trot and they swept out of Vienna. Segalla dozed for a while. When he awoke, Kinski was fast asleep, snoring like a baby, and he remained so until they reached Baden railway station. As it was early Monday evening, the station was fairly deserted. Kinski, rather short-tempered after being abruptly aroused from a warm, comfortable sleep, harshly demanded the stationmaster. That officer hurried up, a self-important man with a face like a duck's, with broad, protruding lips, stuck-out ears, and wide, staring eyes. He was dressed ever so precisely in the regulation uniform. Segalla had to hide his smile at the way he marched along, swinging his arms, a large clipboard in his hand. Once Kinski made the introductions, the stationmaster became even more rigid. He bowed from the waist, assuring Herr Segalla that he would do all he could to assist. Segalla invited him out of the station into the pebble-dashed yard where the cabs waited. Kinski and Brunner walked away: he and the stationmaster sat on a bench under a large painted sign advertising the merits of a certain cordial.

"Do you remember the day Prince Rudolph was found dead at Mayerling?" Segalla began.

"Oh, yes," the stationmaster replied. "It was all confusion and chaos. People coming and going."

"Do you remember Prince Coburg?"

"Of course. He arrived on the six o'clock from Vienna. The train was a little late." The stationmaster shook his head in disapproval.

"How was he?" Segalla asked.

"Quiet, precise. He almost jumped from the train and went straight through the ticket barrier to a waiting cab."

"And Count Hoyos?"

"I remember him well. The cab came galloping into this yard. Count Hoyos demanded the time of the next train for Vienna. I replied that the next one was an express and would not be stopping at Baden." The stationmaster lowered his voice. "Then Count Hoyos took me into my office. He said the train, be it express or not, had to stop. He brought urgent news for the emperor in Vienna: his son, Prince Rudolph, had been shot. Of course, I was aghast." The stationmaster gabbled on. "So I arranged for the express to stop and he left." He shook his head. "After that, well, the station became a bustle of activity, with people coming and going. Later that day, in the evening, Prince Rudolph's corpse was brought here for Vienna."

"But you made a mistake, surely, sir?" Segalla asked. "Count Hoyos didn't tell you the prince had been shot but had been poisoned?"

"Oh, no," the fellow replied. "Count Hoyos told me Prince Rudolph had been shot. I have proof of that. You see, sir, this railway is owned and financed by the House of Rothschild. Anything I learn which may be of use to the house, in their role as bankers, I tell them. I telegraphed Baron Rothschild immediately: Prince Rudolph had been shot."

Segalla stared across to where Kinski and Brunner stood by the cab.

"Well, well, well," he whispered.

"Is there anything wrong, sir?"

"No, Stationmaster, there isn't."

Segalla shook the fellow's hand and walked over to the detective.

"What have you discovered?" Kinski asked.

Segalla winked at him and climbed into the cab. Kinski followed. Brunner cracked the whip, and they left the station and took the Mayerling road.

"Most peculiar," Segalla remarked. He tapped the toe of the detective's boot with his own. "Can I trust you, Kinski?"

"Yes, you can," the detective replied wearily. "I have shown you Bayer's report. What further proof do you need? Though I am prepared to offer it."

"Such as?"

"I was the detective," Kinski replied, "responsible for transporting Maria Vetsera's body from Mayerling to the priory of Hieiligenkreuz. Now, when the grave was being dug, I decided to inspect the corpse."

"And?"

"There were discolouration marks on the feet and legs which showed that Maria Vetsera had been dead for some time. I know"—Kinski shook his head—"you are going to tell me that she had. However, what you don't know, Herr Segalla, is that I've since made my own enquiries. On the thirtieth, when her corpse was removed from the prince's bedroom, similar discolouration was found."

Segalla clenched his fist. "So, Loschek's story about Vetsera being dead only a couple of hours before her corpse and that of the prince were discovered was a lie? What do you think, Inspector?"

Kinski looked away.

"I suspect," Segalla continued, "that everything Hoyos and Loschek told me is a lie. I don't think Prince Rudolph was seen at six-fifteen dressed in his bathrobe and whistling. I'm also beginning to wonder whether Count Hoyos even dined with Prince Rudolph on the evening of the twenty-ninth!"

Kinski muttered he could not answer that. Segalla sat back, the carriage picking up speed as it turned a corner onto the Mayerling road.

They found the hunting lodge deserted. Kinski and Brunner had to go about shouting until a harassed-looking Wodicka appeared from an outhouse.

"What is it?" he bawled back. He walked over and smiled as Segalla took coins from his pocket, jingling them noisily in his hand.

"More questions, Herr Segalla?"

"Yes, Wodicka, more questions, or rather, just one. You remember surely how, on the morning the prince was found dead, you were getting the hounds ready for a hunt?"

"Yes, yes, I remember that," Wodicka replied. "I was down at the kennels. Bratfisch had his cab harnessed, he was sitting in the seat. He told me that I was wasting my time, the prince was dead."

"And what time was that?"

"Oh, it must have been after eight and the prince's corpse had been found."

"You are sure?"

The smile faded from Wodicka's face. "Oh, Lord save us!" he whispered, looking up at the sky. "No, it wasn't!"

"What do you mean?"

"Well, it's some months ago now. It's dark in January; when

you are a huntsman you don't go by the clock, Herr Segalla; the dogs have to be ready before dawn. I saw Bratfisch's cab silhouetted against the lights of the lodge. I asked him what he was waiting for. He snapped back that it was none of my business. Moreover, I was wasting my time, there would be no hunt as Prince Rudolph was dead."

Wodicka looked over Segalla's shoulder at the two detectives standing near the entrance to the yard. He stepped closer.

"Do you know, sir, it's something I've always wondered about." He swallowed hard. "I keep telling myself it was after eight"—Wodicka glanced greedily at the silver coins in Segalla's hands—"due to all the confusion. But, if the truth be known, it must have been about seven o'clock in the morning."

"Don't tell anyone else," Segalla warned, handing the coins over. "At least for a while."

He rejoined the detectives. They left Mayerling and travelled in silence back to Vienna. Darkness had fallen by the time Segalla entered the foyer of the Imperial. Kinski and Brunner were loudly complaining about being hungry. Segalla told them to look after themselves and returned to his own room.

He passed a chambermaid in the corridor and asked where the valet was who had served him the night before. She smiled flirtatiously, plucking at her skirts as she steadied the small bonnet on her head. She said that he had left, and wasn't Herr Segalla pleased with the chamber? He flirted back, slipped a coin into her hand, and then went along to his room. He unlocked the valise from his wrist, put it in the safe, took off his jacket, and stood by the window watching the night traffic, sipping carefully at the whisky he had poured.

"What have we got here?" he murmured.

He undid the button of his waistcoat. One thing was certain. However Rudolph had been killed, he had been dead long before the time published by the authorities. Everything pointed to that: the floor polisher Wolfe's assertion that he was turned away at four in the morning; Bratfisch's casual remark to Wodicka; Coburg's unseemly haste in returning to Mayerling, and Hoyos leaving only a few minutes afterwards to take the news to Vienna. Bayer's report confirmed all this.

Segalla sipped from the whisky. But what else could he prove? Hoyos certainly hadn't taken the story of poison back to Vienna. He'd told the stationmaster at Baden that the prince had been shot, so why hadn't the correct story been circulated in the capital instead of being changed to heart failure? So, what time did the prince and Maria Vetsera die? And why had the authorities in Vienna acted so clumsily? "Perhaps they had panicked?" he whispered to himself. "That's it, they panicked."

He went and sat on the edge of the bed. Or was it panic? Or were they just buying time? But why?

There was a knock on the door; Kinski asked him if he wished to come down for dinner. Segalla, rather sleepy after the whisky, replied that he would eat in his own room, and the detective walked away. Segalla lay down on the bed, his hands behind his head, staring up at the delicately carved ceiling. The imperial authorities certainly had something to hide, he reasoned: Bratfisch and Loschek were frightened, whilst the cook, Kati, had been executed, not only for plundering the dead prince's possessions, but for trying to escape from Vienna. It was almost as if the imperial authorities had decided on a certain story and were determined to adhere to it. He heard another knock on the door.

"I don't want any dinner," he called out sharply.

He looked towards the door and noticed an envelope pushed underneath. He got off the bed and picked it up: on the back was written one word: "Szeps." Inside was a news cutting from one of those broadsheets which liked to peddle the tittle-tattle of the court. The article was about a reception held in the ballroom on the first floor of the German embassy in the Third District of Vienna on Sunday, 27 January, to honour the birthday of the German emperor, Wilhelm II. The cream of Vienna society was invited. Two items had been underlined: how the prince had gone up to his father, the emperor, to make his official greetings, but the emperor, so the gossips said, had turned away, leaving the prince furious. Further down the scandal sheet another item was underlined: how the baroness Maria Vetsera, in a pale blue ball gown with yellow appliqué, had not made the prescribed curtseys as the crown princess walked down the line. Instead the "Vetsera Woman" had remained standing upright, giving Her Imperial Highness an arrogant stare until Vetsera's distraught mother pulled her down with a jerk.

Segalla studied the yellowing piece of paper again. Szeps was apparently passing information. But what? Relations between the emperor and his son were not as cordial as they should have been, whilst clashes between wives and mistresses were commonplace.

Segalla sat down at his desk, trying to place the information Szeps had given him into context. Three matters still concerned him. First, what was the telegram Rudolph had been waiting for before he left for Mayerling? Second, why did Maria Vetsera go to a jewellers, where she changed cabs for her mysterious flight to Mayerling? And third, why was Baroness Vetsera so distraught over her daughter's actions? Was it just mere snobbery, or was it something else? After all, young Maria Vetsera was used to mixing in high society: racecourses were not really suitable for a young lady, but Maria had visited them so often the Jockey Club had given her the nickname of "Turf Angel."

Segalla went across to the safe and took papers out of his valise. He studied these for a while, yet the only firm conclusion he could reach was that Rudolph and Maria had died much earlier than anyone said. Segalla sat back in the chair and went over the events of the day. What was it he had seen in the Blue Room which had been so disturbing? No, it wasn't an expression or something that had been said. He picked up a piece of his own paper and remembered.

"The pharmacy book!" he exclaimed.

Segalla recalled the entries there and became so excited he had to pace up and down the room as he realised the implications of what he had read. He followed this line of thought and recalled Prince Rudolph waiting for that telegram. No one knew where this was supposed to be coming from. Was Rudolph's impatience linked to something else, and did the pharmacy book give the clue? Why had its entries been changed? What was the connection between these and the telegram which Prince Rudolph had been waiting for on the morning he left Mayerling? But who was supposed to send it? Segalla recalled the Vatican's anxiety in this matter and quietly cursed as he remembered the sly, swarthy face of Cardinal Rampolla.

Segalla was hungry, but he decided to wait whilst he took out his cipher book and, using a secret code known only to him and the Holy Father, wrote out a most urgent telegram begging for information. He then went into the small bathroom, made himself presentable, and went down to the foyer. At the reception desk he handed over his telegram, telling them that it was to be sent now, whilst any reply should immediately be brought to him. He realised the reception would be under instructions to take a copy of the telegram and dispatch it to Count Taaffe, but he didn't care. The cipher was most secret and it might take years for the Viennese secret service to decode it. He then went into the ornately decorated, well-lit restaurant. Kinski and Brunner were nowhere to be seen. Segalla was relieved: he sat down and ordered some soup, trout, and vegetables. As he ate, Segalla wondered what reply he would receive from Rome. He just hoped the Holy Father would not play the Jesuit with him but would tell the truth. Segalla finished his meal and was about to return to his room when Kinski and Brunner, looking as if they had eaten and drunk well, bowled into the restaurant and ambled towards him. Both men were smiling.

"We are going for a walk, Herr Segalla," Kinski offered expansively, tapping his stomach. "Would you like to join us?"

"Yes, yes, I would like to accompany you. Could you take me to a pharmacy?"

"Why?" Kinski asked, buttoning his overcoat. "Are you unwell, Herr Segalla?"

"No, no, there are some questions I would like to ask," Segalla replied.

Segalla collected his own coat from his room and, with the two detectives walking on either side of him, left the hotel. The night had turned cold and a slight drizzle was falling. Brunner offered his umbrella, but Segalla refused.

"We won't walk far," Kinski said.

They turned a corner.

"The pharmacy is down here," the detective explained. "It doesn't close till midnight."

Once they had reached the shop, Segalla turned to his companions.

"If you could wait outside?" he asked.

Kinski pulled a face but agreed. They watched as Segalla entered the shop: he had a few words with the assistant, who brought the pharmacist out. Kinski would have loved to have known what they were talking about; then he saw the papal envoy pass across a small roll of banknotes. The pharmacist looked at the door and Kinski knew that the man would never tell him the truth. Segalla talked for a while, and the pharmacist answered quite excitedly, now and again taking a book down from the shelf and opening it to show Segalla. After about a quarter of an hour, Segalla pronounced himself satisfied, shook the pharmacist's hand, and joined his companions outside.

"Don't you trust us?" Kinski grumbled as they walked back to the hotel.

"My dear Kinski." Segalla stopped and put a hand on the detective's shoulder. "If there is anyone in Vienna I trust it would be you, but you can guess what is happening. I don't think I am far from the truth, and that might be very dangerous for you."

They returned to their hotel, Segalla going immediately up to his room. The pharmacist had been a wealth of knowledge, telling him in great detail the effects of different poisons. Segalla would have worked on, but he realised it would be futile to draw any conclusions until he had received a reply from the Vatican: he called it a day, undressed, slipped into bed, and fell into a fitful sleep.

He was awakened about five in the morning by a loud knocking on his door. The bright-eyed bellboy apologised for disturbing him, but "Herr Segalla had asked that a reply to his telegram be brought to him immediately and would Herr Segalla like some coffee?"

Segalla smiled at the maid, standing behind the bellboy, carrying a tray with a steaming pot, cup, and saucer. He told the maid to bring the tray into the room and gave each of them a coin. They left quickly, closing the door behind them. Segalla wrapped a blanket around him, for the room had grown cold. He lit one of the lamps, poured himself a cup of coffee, then slit open the envelope. The telegram inside read innocuously enough, peppered by the words "Sanctus Pater," "Holy Father": a sign that the telegram came from the pope himself and was to be trusted. Segalla unlocked the safe, took out his cipher book, and began to translate.

At first the decoded words meant little: a short apology which explained that certain matters were to be kept secret only to His Holiness. However, now that Segalla needed this information to establish the truth, it was being handed over in trust. Segalla must use it wisely. Segalla continued with his deciphering. He sipped greedily at the coffee and became fully immersed in the message as it began to decode. At last it ended. Segalla knew his conclusions were right. Prince Rudolph had not committed suicide at Mayerling: he had been murdered, and the killing had been twisted to make it look like suicide. He recalled the words of the mystic mentioned by Galemberti: how the prince had been murdered and the imperial authorities could find the assassin if they cared to. Segalla threw his pen down in triumph—he was sure he had the truth! The telegram from Rome gave information only the pope would know. Leo XIII had probably thought it was irrelevant to Segalla's investigation, but it was, in fact, the cornerstone. Segalla stared across at the framed print of Franz Joseph which hung on the far wall.

"I know the truth," he whispered. "And I know why you didn't care to!"

# Chapter 13

For the next few days Segalla kept to his room. Now and again he would go down to the restaurant or for a short walk in the small garden at the rear of the hotel. Kinski and Brunner were intrigued, but Segalla kept his comments to them as noncommittal as possible. He hid his amusement at how often Kinski found excuses to come to his room. The detective always gazed longingly at the pad Segalla was covering in his cursive, elegant script.

"What are you writing, Herr Segalla?" he eventually asked.

"My dear Joseph." Segalla smiled back. "Do you really expect me to tell you?"

"Yes, I do," Kinski retorted. "I thought we were friends, as well as colleagues, Herr Segalla."

"Friendship can be a dangerous thing," Segalla replied, and returned to his writing.

On Friday morning, just after dawn, Kinski and Brunner escorted Segalla back to the Blue Room at the Hofburg Palace. They stayed, cooling their heels for an hour in an antechamber, where liveried servants offered them coffee and biscuits until a pompous chamberlain came in. He snapped his fingers and they followed him into the Blue Room: Franz Joseph sat at the top of the table; Prime Minister Taaffe and Police President Krauss sat on either side of him, whilst farther down the table were Coburg and Hoyos. The air was thick with the smell of fragrant coffee and cigar smoke. Kinski and Brunner were ordered to stay by the door. Segalla took his seat at the foot of the table.

"Well, my dear Segalla?" Taaffe pulled at the cuffs of his jacket. "Time is short: today is Friday and you must be out of Vienna by tomorrow. So, what questions do you have?"

"I have none."

Segalla kept his face impassive, but he quietly enjoyed the consternation caused by his reply. Taaffe's jaw dropped. Franz Joseph leaned forward. Hoyos blinked like some owl caught in the light. Behind him, Kinski gave a loud sigh.

"I beg your pardon." Taaffe took his pince-nez out of his waistcoat pocket and put it on as if he couldn't believe Segalla was the same person they had met earlier in the week.

"I have no questions," Segalla repeated.

"And so what will you report to the Holy Father in Rome?" Franz Joseph asked.

"Your Excellency, I think that's obvious: His Royal Highness Prince Rudolph was deeply upset over his own health and future prospects. I believe he went to Mayerling to seek consolation in the arms of Maria Vetsera. Perhaps he drank too deeply, took a little too much morphine? Anyway, a suicide pact was formed, and then both he and Maria killed themselves." He glimpsed the disbelief in Taaffe's face. "The imperial authorities did not reveal the full facts because they were frightened that Prince Rudolph's death might have been dismissed as an act of debauchery. May I add, Your Excellency, that attempts by certain people to cover up the truth were rather clumsy. Such clumsiness," he added meaningfully, "caused more mystery than the deaths themselves."

Taaffe was about to protest, but Franz Joseph held his hand up.

"Herr Segalla, you are an accredited envoy. Do we have your solemn oath that this is what you will report to the Holy Father?"

"You have my solemn oath," Segalla echoed the words. "That's what I have said this morning, and only what I have said will be the report I deliver to His Holiness, Pope Leo." Segalla took his fob watch out and began to wind it slowly. "Your Imperial Excellency, I must repeat that my investigation shows that Prince Rudolph committed suicide whilst the balance of his mind was disturbed. The Holy Father's actions in this matter have, therefore, been vindicated: His Holiness will make his feelings known to those members of the Austrian hierarchy who thought otherwise."

Segalla put his watch away. Despite appearances, he could tell that, if he hadn't been present, the group at the bottom of the table would have stood and cheered to the rafters. Taaffe was still watching him curiously, but Franz Joseph was rubbing his hands. Krauss was leaning back, twirling his moustache. Hoyos and Coburg were smiling at each other.

"There won't be an unofficial report, will there?" Taaffe asked.

"There will be no unofficial report," Segalla retorted. "I will talk to no one but His Holiness. I am more than prepared to say as much to the reporters who will be waiting for me at the station before I leave. However," Segalla continued, "Your Imperial Highness, I must lodge a formal protest on two matters. First, I would like to protest once again at the interference in my investigations, albeit professional and discreet, of the two police officers behind me. Second, I must object vehemently to the way I, Nicholas Segalla, papal envoy, am being hustled out of Vienna. I would like to rest and relax. I would like to make proper farewells to people and to present, once again, the Holy Father's condolences to Her Royal Highness Princess Stephanie."

Taaffe leaned over and whispered to Franz Joseph. The emperor nodded and rose to his feet.

"The detectives you talk about, Herr Segalla, are only doing their duty. They are meant to protect you until you board the train for Rome. However"—Franz Joseph became more expansive—"now that your business is finished, Herr Segalla—it is finished, is it not?"

Segalla nodded.

"You have our authority to stay in Vienna until Monday morning. I would like to take this opportunity, Herr Segalla, to thank you for your interest in this matter and to present my most gracious compliments to the Holy Father. Herr Segalla, these matters are concluded."

The emperor sat down, waving his hand, a gesture that Segalla could leave.

A few minutes later, escorted by a grinning Brunner and Kinski, Segalla climbed into their carriage outside the Hofburg. Kinski shouted orders for Brunner to drive them straight to the Hotel Imperial.

"Herr Segalla," Kinski said with a smile as he sat back against the cushions, "I thank you for what you said: I mean about our interference. Police President Krauss will be very pleased. However." Kinski took his brandy flask out. He offered this to Segalla, who shook his head. "However," Kinski repeated, "I have never heard such a tissue of lies in my life. If that was the truth, then I am the bishop of Spoleto."

Segalla smiled.

"I thought you were pursuing the truth," Kinski continued. "But, in the last resort, Herr Segalla, I suppose you're like everyone else. You bend lest you break."

"The Chinese have a proverb," Segalla replied. " 'If you must bend, then bend very low.' Always remember, Joseph, that just because you bend to this breeze or that, it doesn't mean you can't straighten up afterwards. Now, when we get back to the Hotel Imperial, enjoy yourself. Make sure Brunner drinks long and hard, then come and see me, when darkness has fallen. If you wish, I'll tell you the truth."

On his return to the hotel room, Segalla began packing, finishing his report and writing a few letters, courtesy notes to Galemberti, Szeps, and others he had met in Vienna, including the empress Elizabeth. He had tea brought to him in the afternoon and later dined by himself. Long after dark, just as the clock in the hall chimed eleven, Segalla heard a tap on the door, and Kinski slipped into the room.

"Brunner's sleeping like a babe," he declared. "He's as pleased as anything that Krauss will be promoting him on Monday afternoon and not assigning him to special duties in some lonely town on the Russian border."

"Do you want to know the truth?" Segalla abruptly asked from where he sat in the shadows of the room. "Are you sure you want to know the truth, Joseph? Because, once you do, you can never tell anyone what you learn tonight."

"Yes, I do." Kinski pulled a chair up opposite him. "I want to know because the truth is important. I also think you want me to know."

Segalla opened the drawer of his desk and took out a sheaf of papers.

"Then, Joseph Kinski, pour yourself a whisky, go and sit under the lamp, and read that." Segalla took a pack of playing cards out of his pocket. "And, if anyone comes looking for you, well, we are simply whiling the time away playing cards."

Kinski did as he was told. Segalla locked the door. He rearranged the table and placed the cards on it as if some game were in progress. He then poured himself a whisky, filling the glass with soda, and stood, looking out of the window at the nightlife below. He regretted what had happened this morning. He wanted to make Franz Joseph face the truth, but what good would that achieve? He might never have been allowed to leave Vienna: Kinski and Brunner would have been ruthlessly punished, and, once again, the truth would have been brutally suppressed. He heard the detective catch his breath.

"Read on, Joseph," Segalla called out over his shoulder. "There's more to come yet."

Kinski did so. Now and again he'd put the papers down, take

a deep gulp from his whisky glass, and then continue reading.

"Herr Segalla, I have finished," Kinski eventually called out. He handed the papers back: the detective's face was pallid. "You do not say what really happened," he said. "You simply list questions, and these alone do not tell the truth!"

Segalla pulled his chair up. "I'll summarise my report, Joseph. I'll speak softly and, if you interrupt, I beg you to do likewise." Segalla sipped at his whisky.

"Prime Minister Taaffe is still suspicious," he began. "He must know all my questions still stand." Segalla ticked the points off on his fingers. "First, Prince Rudolph definitely intended to return to Vienna. He sent telegrams, both before he left the city as well as from Mayerling, admitting as much. So, why did he commit suicide? Second, why didn't anyone hear any gunshots? Third, why did Bratfisch tell Wodicka, at least an hour and a half before the prince's bedchamber was allegedly forced, that there would be no hunting that day because Prince Rudolph was dead? Fourth, why wasn't there a proper postmortem on both corpses? Fifth, why wasn't there a proper ballistic report? Where's the gun? Where are the bullets? Sixth, isn't it strange that Coburg returned to Mayerling at the very moment Count Hoyos was knocking on the prince's door? And why did Coburg go there immediately? If he was so keen to start hunting, surely he'd go and change first? You don't go unannounced to the prince's quarters so early in the morning. Seventh, when they broke the door down, why didn't they see the gun? After all, there's nothing more obvious than a bullet through the brain. Eighth, why did Hoyos lie? He brought the news to Vienna that Prince Rudolph had been poisoned, but he told the stationmaster at Baden that Rudolph had been shot. Ninth, why did the authorities in Vienna keep issuing strange stories about heart failure or a stroke? Moreover, talking of coincidences, isn't it strange that, when the empress was given the news of her son's death,

Maria Vetsera's mother happened to be present? So why should the empress bother to see the likes of Countess Vetsera, the mother of her son's alleged mistress?" He paused.

"Now, my dear Kinski, this is where we begin to pose other questions. Why did Maria Vetsera go to a jewellers in Vienna on her way to Mayerling? Why did the emperor return, unopened, his son's letters to Maria Vetsera's mother? Surely he would have been intrigued, ripped open the envelopes to see if they could throw any light on his son's mysterious suicide? And then, of course, there's the *Paramatta* mystery. How was Prince Rudolph's death known, at least on the very day it occurred, by someone on a steamship leaving Egypt?" Segalla sipped from his whisky. "And, above all, what was in the telegram Prince Rudolph was waiting for before he left for Mayerling? Why was it so important? What was the cause of his argument with the emperor? And why did Rudolph tell Szeps that he hoped that what he planned would come about?"

Segalla rose and unlocked the door. He looked outside: the passageway was empty. He closed it and refilled his glass and Kinski's before continuing.

"So, where does the truth lie? I'll tell you this, Joseph. The mystery of Mayerling lies in the accepted story: I don't believe a word of it. I think Rudolph and Maria Vetsera died some time in the early hours of January thirtieth, probably between one and two o'clock in the morning."

"How?" Kinski asked.

"Oh, not by gunshot," Segalla replied. "They were poisoned. Somehow or other they were given a powerful potion, perhaps in the morphine which Rudolph shared with his mistress. Whatever, their death throes must have been terrible. Loschek and Bratfisch rushed in: the force of the poison may have caused Rudolph and Vetsera to haemorrhage. In desperation the servants called Hoyos, who immediately telegraphed Vienna. Now we know the emperor held a formal dinner banquet on the evening of the twenty-ninth: that went on uninterrupted, which makes me place the deaths after midnight. It is here," Segalla continued, "that the plot to obfuscate the deaths began to unfold. Orders were telegraphed from Vienna: the prince's room was cleaned up, which explains why the floor polisher Wolfe and his brother saw the lodge bright with lights as well as why they were turned away. The two corpses were also cleaned and put on the bed."

"But the gunshots?" Kinski asked.

"Oh," Segalla replied slowly. "The authorities in Vienna ordered those shots to be fired. Now, whether they sent a secret agent down to do it or whether Hoyos, Bratfisch, and Loschek carried out the deed, I don't know."

"But why?" Kinski asked.

"Because the authorities already knew a terrible murder had taken place and questions would be asked; I'll come to that later. Gunshots, with the revolver lying by, are easier to explain away as self-inflicted. Nevertheless, the authorities were taking no chances. Neither that revolver nor its bullets have ever been produced."

"But would the emperor order a bullet to be fired into his dead son's head?"

"I think so," Segalla replied. "Or at least Taaffe would. He'd do anything to defend the government from blame." Segalla held a hand up. "I'll explain that in due course. However, let us go back to the early hours of the thirtieth of January. The prince and Vetsera are dead. Loschek finds them. Hoyos immediately telegraphs Vienna: 'The prince has been murdered.' But they don't know by whom. Anyone could take the blame, so it's made to look like suicide. This explains away no one hearing the gunshots. The prince's alleged movements at six-fifteen in the morning, and Loschek and Hoyos knocking on the door between seven-fifty and eight-fifteen; that was a charade: they were biding their time. Coburg, fully briefed on the situation, was hurrying from Vienna. He had to arrive at Mayerling before Hoyos could leave with the news."

"Which explains," Kinski interrupted, "why Bratfisch had his cab and horse ready, allegedly for the prince or Maria Vetsera to leave for Vienna. Bratfisch was really waiting to take Hoyos to the station."

"As soon as Coburg arrives," Segalla continued, "Hoyos leaves. He travels to Baden. He's agitated. On the one hand he's peddling the story about the prince being poisoned, but then he tells the stationmaster Rudolph's been shot. This proves Hoyos did see the bullet wound, but he's so agitated, he can't be consistent. In Vienna, preparations are already moving ahead. The empress has arranged for Countess Vetsera to be present when the news is broken, and here, the obfuscation really begins."

"But why?" Kinski asked.

"Detective, when you investigate a murder, what poses the greatest difficulties in resolving it?"

"Confusion," Kinski grudgingly replied. "Yes, confusion: trying to establish how the victim died, what he was doing, and, above all, the motive and whereabouts of the possible killer."

"The same applies here," Segalla replied. "Taaffe deliberately allowed confusion to reign. This gave the imperial authorities time to continue their cover-up, arrange matters as they thought fit."

"And the letters?" Kinski asked.

"As I mentioned in my report, I have only seen copies. These can be quickly forged. Coburg could have brought them, or Dr. Weiderhofer. Don't forget, Kinski, the authorities were given a considerable amount of time to prepare their case. Rudolph died at two a.m. on the thirtieth of January, but it wasn't until the beginning of February that any precise details were leaked to the public. The letters posed no problem: they are very short. Rudolph's desks at the Hofburg were ransacked, letters copied and dispatched to Mayerling. Everything in the prince's room there was firmly under imperial control from the moment the bodies were found."

"So the authorities had Rudolph murdered?"

"No, I don't think so," Segalla replied. "But that's the brilliance of this crime. You see, Kinski, Rudolph's death could be laid at a number of doors. He was disliked by his own father, who resented his interference and ambitions. He was disliked by Taaffe and the government. Now, let's say the truth had been published: that Rudolph and his young mistress had been found poisoned at Mayerling; the first question which would be asked was, who had access to the prince? Well?"

Kinski shrugged. "There's the emperor, Count Taaffe, his mother, his wife, not to mention Hoyos, Coburg, Loschek, and Bratfisch."

"Precisely," Segalla replied. "And think of the other questions, my dear Joseph. What poison was used? How was it administered? If the truth were known, the Hapsburgs would not only have lost their heir apparent but would have become immersed in a scandal which would have rocked the throne. Consequently, it was in everyone's interests to cover up the crime before fingers were pointed. Of course, that left a scandal of a Catholic prince committing suicide, but, on reflection, Franz Joseph and Taaffe preferred to deal with that rather than face the whispered accusations of being involved in Rudolph's death."

"I accept what you say." Kinski rubbed his face. "It fits in with the little I know: the discolouration of Vetsera's corpse; the speed with which she was buried; even the secrecy surrounding the postmortem carried out on Prince Rudolph. Any reference to when they died or the condition of their bodies was carefully omitted."

"I think there was more than that," Segalla added. "I believe little Maria was pregnant."

"What?"

"In fact, I am positive of it!"

"Do you know what poison was used?" Kinski asked.

"I think the assassin was very clever: not in the food or the wine—that would have been dangerous. Oh, by the way, I suspect Kati the cook was murdered, not just because she pillaged the dead prince's goods or tried to leave Vienna, but because she might also have suspected the truth."

"But Loschek and Bratfisch, not to mention Weiderhofer and Slatin, also knew it."

Segalla put his glass down on the table. "Weiderhofer and Slatin might suspect, but they would follow orders. And what could Loschek and Bratfisch do? They would be Taaffe's most willing accomplices. After all, if Rudolph and Maria were poisoned, Bratfisch and Loschek could easily be depicted as the probable assassins. It would not be the first time in history that servants had poisoned their master."

"And the name of the murderer?"

"As the good book says, Joseph: 'Out of their own mouths the truth shall come.' "

Kinski got to his feet. "I will know before you leave Vienna?"

"If God is good, Joseph, and he is, yes, you will."

"You must trust me?"

"Yes, Joseph, I do. Someone in this city should be told the truth."

"And what about your solemn vow to the emperor?" Kinski asked.

"My official report to Pope Leo," Segalla replied, "will be that Prince Rudolph shot himself whilst the balance of his mind was disturbed. Then I shall ask the Holy Father to hear my confession and I will tell him the truth."

Kinski shook his head and moved to the door.

"The cunning of the dove, eh, Herr Segalla? And what His Holiness learns under the seal of confession he can reveal to no one. But what about me?"

"What can you do, Joseph? However, knowing the truth is important: soon, you'll know it all."

Kinski bade him good night. Segalla picked up the report and tore it up into small pieces. He took it into the bathroom and placed the pieces in the sink, allowing the water to turn it to a soggy, wet mess, which he then put in the wastepaper bin.

The following day different people came to visit. Segalla treated them courteously but made sure they did not tarry long. Amongst the visitors were Krauss, Galemberti, and Szeps. Segalla refused to commit himself, even to the newspaper editor, who looked at him sadly.

"So you have made little headway, Segalla?" he asked.

"Elizabeth of England had a phrase, Herr Szeps, about her possible involvement in conspiracies against her sister: 'Much suspected, nothing proved.' I am afraid that will be my verdict on what happened at Mayerling."

Later on, about five o'clock in the afternoon, Crown Princess Stephanie, a black lace veil covering her face, also came to the hotel. Kinski escorted her to Segalla's room. He was about to leave and join the princess's maid sitting in a chair farther down the passageway, but Segalla told him to stay. Princess Stephanie, the veil now lifted from her face, looked archly at Segalla.

"Is that wise?" she remarked, and sniffed as if Kinski exuded some bad smell.

"For both our protection, madam." Segalla waved her to the cushion-backed chair and sat down opposite. "Inspector Kinski will guard the door, just in case we are disturbed."

Stephanie's white, podgy face creased into a smile. Segalla watched those light blue eyes. He glimpsed the cunning and marvelled at how superb an actress this woman was. Who would suspect poor Stephanie? Pathetic, bumbling Stephanie?

She leaned forward, grasping her reticule. "I heard the news," Stephanie murmured, though her eyes were watchful. "How you accept the published story of my poor husband's death?"

"Tu dixisti!" Segalla retorted.

"I beg your pardon!"

"You have said it, madam—the 'accepted' story. However, we both know the truth. Your husband was murdered, madam, and no one knows that better than you."

Stephanie's face hardened, her eyes wide. She opened her mouth to reply but bit her lip.

"You may go if you wish," Segalla said. "But then again, madam, you must be curious."

"I am curious," Stephanie replied. "I am curious, Herr Segalla, why you should so abruptly deliver such a farrago of lies."

"Oh, they're not lies," Segalla murmured. "They're the truth. You see, madam, Rudolph married you. He did so against the wishes of his parents and those of the rest of his family. They never really accepted you, just as your father never really accepted you."

He looked for some reaction, but there was none.

"You, however," Segalla continued, "were married to the heir of the Hapsburg throne, and, deep down, you didn't care a damn about what anyone else thought or said. You played the frump and people left you alone! Poor Stephanie, whatever did Prince Rudolph see in her? Actually, madam, they did you a great disservice."

Segalla glanced at Kinski, but the detective was just gaping, openmouthed, at what he was hearing.

"I repeat, madam, they did you a great disservice. Never judge a book by its cover, and that certainly applies to Stephanie of the Belgians. Your husband never realised just how shrewd and intelligent his wife really was. Indeed, he was the stupid, feckless one, full of self-pity, acting out his role as a paper general. He lost himself in his dissolute practices, drinking, morphine, and a string of mistresses."

"I will not disagree with that, Herr Segalla."

"Oh, you bore it well," he replied. "In a sense, madam, I feel a terrible compassion for you. You conceived a child. You were prepared to put up with Prince Rudolph's idiosyncrasies, but Vetsera changed all that."

Stephanie blinked, but Segalla caught the hatred blazing in her eyes.

"Now Prince Rudolph," Segalla continued, "because he consorted with whores, contracted syphilis, and he gave this to you. Another cross to bear, eh, madam, along with his drunkenness, addiction, and growing impotence? You turned a blind eye to people like Countess Larisch and Mitzi Caspar. But, as I said, Vetsera was different. You knew that, didn't you? She made your husband potent and he made her pregnant. Yet worse was to come. He telegraphed the Holy Father, raising a matter he had discussed with you and his father in private."

Princess Stephanie, her head now resting on the back of the chair, stared up at the ceiling.

"Your husband wanted his marriage annulled. The Holy Father never replied: before he could, Rudolph had died at Mayerling, still waiting for a telegram from Rome. The emperor, however, was furious, and a very bitter private row took place between him and Rudolph."

Stephanie did not even move her head. She simply narrowed her eyes as if something of interest had caught her attention.

"You are listening, madam?"

"Oh, I am listening," she whispered. "When I saw you at Rudolph's funeral, Herr Segalla, amidst those pompous, arrogant, overdressed peacocks: 'There, there,' says I"—she glanced at Segalla and smiled—" 'Now there goes a man who has to be watched.' "

"Oh, and you did, madam, so cleverly. Acting the role you've always played: poor, not so bright Stephanie, fumbling her way through the complex etiquette of the Viennese court."

Stephanie laughed girlishly, her face suddenly coming to life, eyes dancing with glee.

"You would have made a great empress," Segalla declared. "This empire needs a Stephanie."

"Now, now, Herr Segalla, you flatter." Stephanie blinked coyly at him. She seemed to have totally forgotten the detectives standing behind her.

"Oh, I don't flatter. I can imagine your rage, madam. Made barren by this prince who is now going to toss you aside for a young girl of seventeen who is so full of herself, she refuses to curtsey to you at an official reception. Nevertheless, all the time you were laughing. After all, madam, you do have a lover, don't you?"

Stephanie's face suddenly went rigid, eyes hard, the corner of her lip curled as if Segalla had smacked her across the face.

"You have a lover, madam," Segalla continued remorselessly. "I don't even know his name, his station, his nationality. All I do know is that you told him your plan. You were going to kill your husband. He decided to be as far away as possible. I think he went to Egypt. He left there on the *Paramatta* just before your husband died: he called himself the comte de Montreux."

"How do you know that?" Stephanie gasped, her fingers to her lips.

"It doesn't really matter, does it?" Segalla replied. "You were the assassin. Now, your husband had announced he was going to Mayerling weeks before he did. You knew about his desire for an annulment, about Vetsera's pregnancy, and you laid your plans. Seething with rage, you may have even suspected that Prince Rudolph might arrange an accident for you. He was certainly resolute in his scheme as regards the little Vetsera. Do you know, she even visited a jewellers on her way to Mayerling? I am sure the owner of the shop is too frightened to ever tell the truth, but I suspect she bought a ring. Only God knows if the prince even married her. In Rudolph's eyes his marriage to you was null and void."

"So much speculation, Herr Segalla?"

"You chose the poison," he answered. "I know Rudolph was poisoned. I doubt if it was the food or the drink: the prince carried his own morphine, and it's easy to replace one potion with another. A calculated guess: he would never use it until he arrived at Mayerling; then, of course, he'd share it with his mistress."

"And this supposed lover of mine?" Stephanie asked archly.

"As I've said, I don't know who he is, but he made sure he was many miles away at the time of the murder. He knew the prince was going to Mayerling. You'd inform him, which explains the incident on the *Paramatta,* the ship he travelled on from Port Said to Brindisi. He wanted to know if your plot had been carried through and decided to test the water by asking some solitary, seasick missionary. Your lover was not too sure when it would happen. I suspect, whatever the potion, your husband and Maria Vetsera took it either before, or just after, midnight on the twenty-ninth and thirtieth of January. They both died in horrible convulsions, probably haemorrhaging through mouth and nose, falling to the floor, staining the woodwork. A pharmacist has informed me that a number of poisons might do this. Anyway, the noise of their deaths would have brought Loschek and Bratfisch running and sent Hoyos scampering for the telegraph to Vienna."

"A ridiculous story," Stephanie snapped.

"No more ridiculous than the forged letter you showed me in which the writer, probably yourself, claimed that Rudolph and Vetsera were plotting to poison you. I wonder"—Segalla played with the chain of his fob watch—"if that's how you convinced your lover that you had to strike first before Rudolph struck at you. You played me like a fish," Segalla continued. "Feeding me stories of how Vetsera was one amongst many. Of course, that was a lie. Rudolph had written to the Holy Father; he told the emperor that he wanted an annulment, how he would make Vetsera his wife and their child heir apparent to the Hapsburg throne. And what would happen to poor, frumpish Stephanie then?"

"A child?" Stephanie snorted. "What proof do you have of that?"

"Very little," Segalla replied. "Except that it lent urgency to Rudolph's plans and explains why Maria's corpse was not given a proper postmortem."

For the first time ever, Stephanie began to fidget as if uneasy.

"And, before you ask, madam, I have all the proof I need of your guilt. I have examined the pharmacy prescription book: there's a sheet of paper, flimsier than the rest, containing prescriptions for the widow crown princess Stephanie, dated November/December 1888; but, as we both know, madam, you weren't a widow until the end of January 1889. After the deaths at Mayerling, you arranged, or did it yourself, to paste that new sheet in with unimportant prescriptions to conceal others that, perhaps, might provoke interest. Poisons perhaps? Or medicine for your own syphilis and gonorrhea? You did it hurriedly and made that mistake."

Stephanie was now breathing quickly, her chest rising and falling.

"But they wrote letters," she stammered.

"Oh yes, those letters," Segalla retorted. "Do you know what I find curious, madam? That no one has ever found the originals. Secondly, here we have a prince dashing off to Mayerling, supposedly to commit suicide, yet he leaves in his desk at Vienna letters telling everyone what he would do. That was risky, wasn't it? Particularly the way Rudolph was watched. Did you put them there?"

"And the gunshot wounds?"

"Ah." Segalla smiled. "That's what makes you such a brilliant assassin, madam. You hoped for one of two things. First, either Rudolph and Vetsera's deaths would be dismissed as suicides. Or, secondly, if murder was suspected, who was the guilty party? Who would suspect poor Stephanie? The finger of accusation could be pointed at Taaffe, Hoyos, Loschek, Bratfisch, the Baltazzis, even the emperor himself. But how could they suspect poor Stephanie, miles away in Vienna, secretly hoping that her plan would come to fruition? It's like a chess game where everyone watches the one piece, the prince. So who would bother about Stephanie?"

"The gunshots?" Stephanie repeated.

"Ah yes, madam, the real brilliance of your plot: you see, Rudolph's death handed a poisoned chalice to the Viennese court. Suicide by poisoning was a little too difficult to defend, so the emperor or Taaffe, with the connivance of others at Mayerling, had those shots fired. How you must have laughed! Concealed your silent glee because Stephanie the pawn had become the master chess player."

"Surely the emperor would suspect?" Stephanie retorted.

"I don't think he does," Segalla replied. "He's too arrogant. He probably blames some other faction in his court, but never his dim-witted daughter-in-law."

"And the prescription book?" Stephanie asked, smoothing the creases of her black dress.

"Oh, I am sure you could explain that away. After all, not even the emperor wants to sully his own son's name any further by revealing that Rudolph also gave his poor, innocent wife syphilis or gonorrhea."

Stephanie lowered her head, her shoulders shaking. Segalla thought she was crying.

"Madam?"

Stephanie lifted her head: the tears on her cheeks were those of merriment as she fought to control the laughter deep in her throat.

"Herr Segalla, you are clever. However, if I were you, I would leave Vienna and never come back." She shook her reticule, making the coins inside clink. "I told you once that I had plenty of money and nothing to spend it on. There are those in the archives who can be bought; these, perhaps, could trace a Segalla here and there. Count Taaffe might become intrigued, even more so than he is now, and you might never leave Vienna."

"I thought you'd play that card." Segalla pointed at Kinski. "That's why the detective inspector is present. He'll ensure I leave Vienna and, if I don't, he knows a newspaper editor called Szeps who will be very interested in my story."

Stephanie looked sideways at the policeman.

"But when I have gone," Segalla continued, "every so often I shall dip into what happens here in Vienna. I expect to hear how Inspector Kinski's career proceeds from strength to strength."

Stephanie raised her eyebrows archly. "Is that all, Herr Segalla?" She got to her feet.

"Yes, that's all, madam, except good wishes for your wedding day."

Stephanie stopped beside Kinski. She smoothed down the lapel of his collar.

"I like you, Joseph Kinski," she murmured. "If I have nothing to fear from you, you have nothing to fear from me." And opening the door, the widow crown princess Stephanie swept out, then slammed it behind her.

Kinski came and sat down, loosening his collar.

"I can't believe it," he gasped. "But what you say is the truth. No confession"—he jabbed a thumb over his shoulder—"but that murdering bitch has fooled everyone."

"A very powerful lady," Segalla replied. "I tried to ensure that she learnt as little as possible, especially about the ordinary people who provided me with the clues: Bayer, Wolfe, Wodicka, the pharmacist, and the stationmaster." Segalla paused. "I did the same to the emperor and Taaffe: they must never know about these clues, or Kati Polzer will not be the last to die." He pointed to the door. "Thank God, Franz Joseph thinks Stephanie is dim-witted: the emperor was openly furious at his son's determination to secure an annulment, but he hasn't realised how that, more than Rudolph's deep love for Vetsera, brought murder to Mayerling."

"What did Stephanie mean about your name being in the archives?"

"Nothing." Segalla got to his feet. "You have heard enough, Joseph Kinski? It's not a cliché when I say that, in these matters, knowledge can be a dangerous thing."

"Why didn't you question others?" Kinski asked, getting up. "The Baltazzis, Mitzi Caspar?"

"What could they tell me, Joseph? No one suspects the real truth. They'd start ranting on about Taaffe or the emperor." He came across the room and shook the detective's hand. "I'll see you tomorrow, Joseph. But don't ever breathe a word of what you have heard today."

The next morning Segalla boarded the ten o'clock train for Trieste. He told the few reporters waiting at the station that he had nothing to add to the official story of Prince Rudolph's death and that he would report as much to the Holy Father.

Baron Krauss came to see him off but didn't linger long, and it was Joseph Kinski who took Segalla gently by the elbow and steered him to the door of the waiting carriage. He gently pushed Segalla up the steps. Segalla didn't even bother to acknowledge the detective's presence, but slammed the door behind him. Only as the train began to pull out of the station did he catch Kinski's attention and wink. The detective stared solemnly back through the window, and then, rubbing at his eyes, turned away.

Segalla sat back in the seat. His hand brushed the pockets of his greatcoat; concerned, he dug deeper into the pocket and pulled out the brandy flask. He sat staring at it, rubbing gently at the initials "J.K." Segalla smiled sadly and pulled off the stopper.

"To Joseph Kinski!" he toasted softly. "Ad multos annos."

# Conclusion

*Vienna—May 1994*

Ann Dukthas sat in the tearoom of the Hotel Imperial. Nicholas Segalla sat opposite her. On the table between them stood a battered leather brandy flask bearing the initials "J.K." Ann studied Segalla's secretive, sallow face, his perfectly groomed hair: he was dressed exquisitely in a dark blue silk tie and brilliant white shirt; his waistcoat and suit were of pure wool.

"You look well, Nicholas." She patted the manuscript on her lap. "But is this the truth?"

"It's the truth," Segalla replied. "Every document, every newspaper cutting, every statement about Mayerling can be traced elsewhere." Segalla looked round the now empty tearoom. "And as for proof. Years later, when the convent at Mayerling was opened, Franz Joseph is supposed to have declared: 'The truth is far worse than any of the versions.' Prince Philip of Coburg told his wife, 'It is terrible but I cannot, I must not, say anything except that they are both dead.' Hoyos told Archduke Johann Salvatore of Tuscany: 'Do not ask for details. It is too frightful. I have given the emperor my word that I shall not say a word about what I have seen.' "

"But Wodicka's revelation? The mistake Hoyos made at Baden, not to mention the accounts of the Wolfe brothers?"

"Oh, they can be traced," Segalla replied. "But most modern investigations dismiss them as irrelevant. What I do know"—he straightened in the chair and put down his teacup—"is that the emperor did, years later, trying to establish a secret consistory to find out exactly what happened. However, these secret papers on the Mayerling mystery have disappeared. On the seventh of March 1965 Edward Taaffe, grandson of the prime minister, wrote to the historian Dr. Judtmann: 'It is entirely correct what my father publicly stated before me, that the circumstances of the Mayerling affair were far more frightful than can be imagined.' "

Segalla pointed to the manuscript on Ann's lap. "You can see why they were frightened."

"And Stephanie?"

"Oh, she lived on, continuing to fool people. She wrote her memoirs. You should read them, Ann. Of course, she makes no mention of me. Instead, Stephanie casts herself in the role of prophetess, hinting that only she realised how Rudolph was heading for disaster. She later married a Hungarian count and spent the rather unhappy rest of her life at Oroszvoc Castle in western Hungary until her death in 1945." Segalla smiled. "Years later I established that the nobleman she married, Count Elemer, was in Egypt when Prince Rudolph died so mysteriously at Mayerling."

"And the pharmacy prescription book?"

"It is still there to be examined. A historian, Paul Christoph, has recently written a monograph on the mysterious entry and different type of page for November/December 1888, but few historians see it as significant."

"And Franz Joseph and the others?"

"The emperor saw the collapse of the Hapsburg Empire during the turmoil of the First World War. Empress Elizabeth was killed by an Italian terrorist. Hoyos, Coburg, Taaffe, and Krauss went the way of all flesh."

"And Brunner? Kinski?"

"Oh, Sergeant Brunner married that girl from the sweetshop. Joseph survived two world wars. When the Russians pulled out of Austria, I visited him again. Sophie was dead, he was a very old man, but when I walked into his granddaughter's living room, Kinski recognised me immediately. He was one of the few people who knew my secret. I brought his flask back, but Kinski refused:

" 'Keep it,' he declared. 'I made my own enquiries, Herr Segalla! I know who you are and I always prayed that you would return.' "

Segalla lifted his cup, sighed, and sipped from it, lost in his own thoughts.

"You can check the archives," he declared. "Though the newspaper cuttings don't tell you much."

"Even though the reporters did get into Mayerling?" Ann asked.

"Oh yes, but in Hapsburg Austria the authorities were more concerned about what a journalist wrote than what he discovered."

"Only one thing concerns me."

"Yes?"

"The *Paramatta* mystery," Ann continued. "Why should Stephanie's accomplice make such a foolish mistake?"

"As you can see from the manuscript," Segalla replied, "I wondered about that at the time. I think there are two reasons. First, Stephanie's accomplice was secretly so excited, so tense about what was happening, he had to find out if the crown princess's plot had been successful. A lonely, seasick missionary, intelligent enough to listen to the news but too lonely to be of any danger, was the perfect choice. My second reason"—Segalla pointed to a clock standing on a mantelpiece—"perhaps he'd become confused, lost any sense of time. A hundred years ago people were not so precise about crossing time lines." He lowered his head. "Time lines," he repeated. "Now, all have crossed the final line between time and eternity. Some are no loss, but Kinski . . ." Segalla raised his eyes and blinked away the tears. "Have you been to Mayerling, Ann?"

She shook her head. Segalla held out his hand.

"Then come, let me take you there. Not by a car or train. I've hired a carriage and horses. I want to go the same way I did with Kinski, and on the journey, I will toast his memory in the finest brandy!"